# THE OCEAN IN THE SKY

*Tandemstar: The Outcast Cycle, Book Three*

GENE DOUCETTE

Copyright © 2021 by Gene Doucette

All rights reserved.

No part of this book may be reproduced in any form or by any electronic or mechanical means, including information storage and retrieval systems, without written permission from the author, except for the use of brief quotations in a book review.

Cover art by Jeff Brown at Jeff Brown Graphics

Map design by Cat Scully

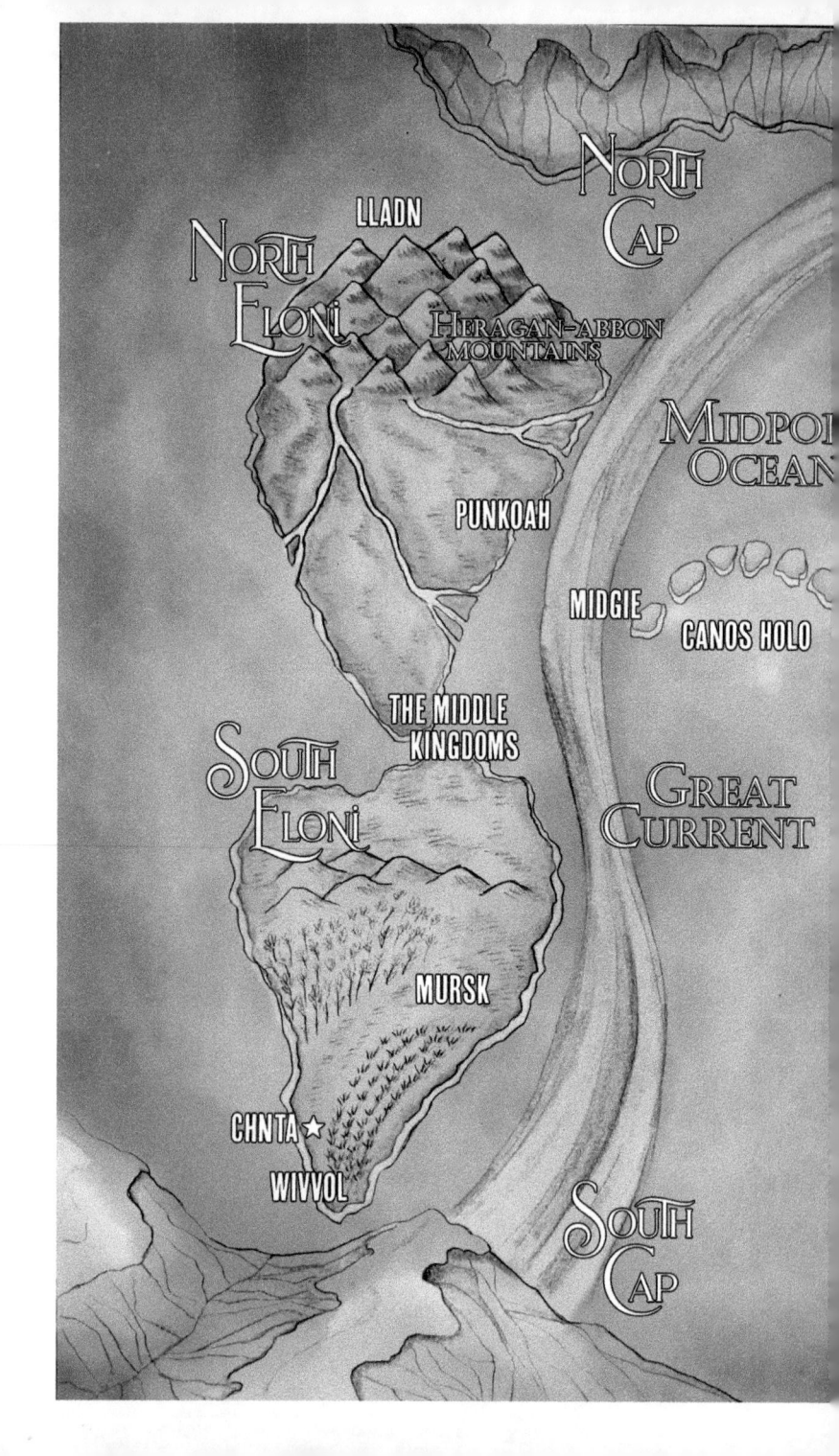

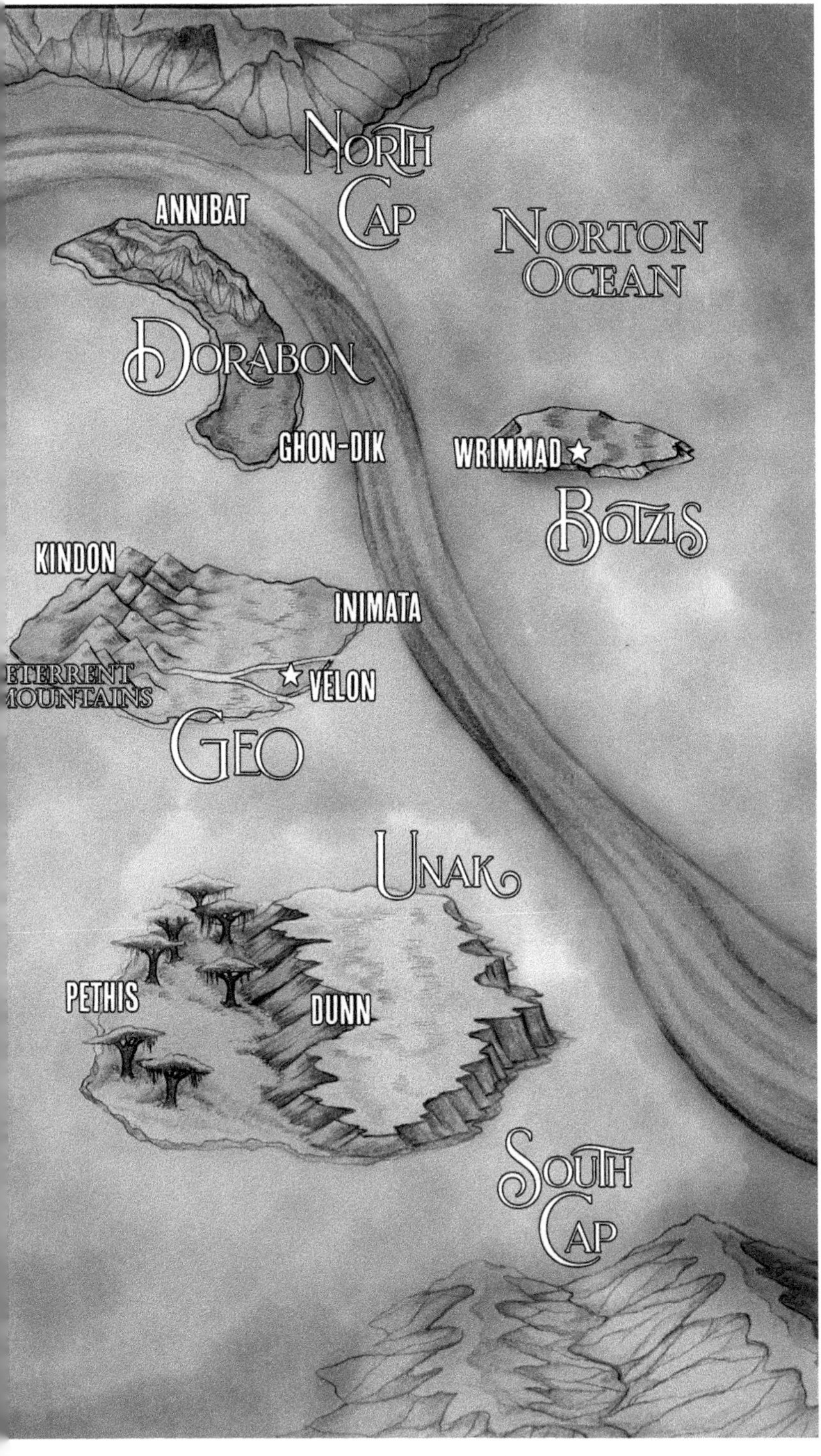

North Cap
Annibat
Norton Ocean
Dorabon
Ghon-Dik
Wrimmad
Botzis
Kindon
Inimata
Deterrent Mountains
Velon
Geo
Unak
Pethis
Dunn
South Cap

# PART I

Captain of the Vessel

## Chapter One

Growing up in the orphanage, the islands of Canos-Holo were always spoken of with reverence, at least among the other children. It was a "paradise", with big beaches, perpetually temperate weather, beautiful people and so on.

The young Makk Stidgeon didn't even know what a beach *was* at first, and could count on one hand the number of things he'd seen in his life to that point which would qualify as beautiful, so when told about the beaches he imagined a blue sky on a sunny day. Thus, for about five years his mental image of Canos-Holo was that of islands floating in the clouds.

Canos-Holo continued to fill the slot of "ideal vacation destination" in Makk's mind even after he'd gotten clarification on what a beach actually looked like, yet every time the place came up in conversation he thought first of clouds.

Not that he didn't get to see any clouds on this trip. They took a commercial flight on a wingplane to get to Canos-Holo (over Elicasta's objections) and even though it was just a quick hop over the Deterrent Mountains to reach Aggo—the largest island in the chain—they did spend some time traveling through clouds. But when they did it, he didn't have Canos-Holo on his mind at all; he was thinking back to the *last* time he'd gone over the Deterrents, as a soldier on his way to fight the Kindonese.

Elicasta wanted to take a null-grav vessel. There were null-gravity cruise ships that left Pulson Harbor once a week, skimmed along the southern edge of Geo and curled up to Canos-Holo, where they spent a day at each of the seven major islands before turning back again. Had they *actually* been vacationing, this probably would have been the way to go, but since they weren't—since they were trying to get to the islands before Viselle Daska disappeared again—there was some need for haste, and the cruise ships weren't known for their speed on the high seas; it would take them a week to reach Canos-Holo by ship, whereas the wingplane over the continent took less than one day.

Makk also wasn't a big fan of null-grav travel, but thought he might be okay with it if they were hovering just above the water, rather than going up and down.

As soon as they touched down in Aggo (which was the only one in the chain with an airport) and secured lodging in one of the many available resort hotels, Makk began making inquiries as to where one might go to hire a boat. This wasn't because *he* wanted to hire a boat—although he didn't tell anyone that—but because he wanted to visit the part of the island where the people who did such a thing for-hire might congregate.

Makk was doing this based on a couple of assumptions. They happened to know that Viselle had quite recently been at rest in the middle of the Midpoint Ocean southwest of Canos-Holo. Unless she was a *very* good swimmer, she had to have been on the deck of a boat at that time. He was looking for the person who piloted the ship that took her out there. Maybe, if he was extremely lucky, Viselle was still around.

He wasn't expecting this to work out because that wasn't the kind of luck he usually had. But it was a start.

It wouldn't be this hard if the tech that gave them Viselle's location at that one point in time *continued* to give it to them, but for some reason that wasn't possible. (Elicasta understood why, but every time she explained it to Makk the explanation made his head hurt.)

While he was busy trying to find the boat that took Viselle out to the middle of the ocean, Elicasta tried to enjoy doing actual vacation things while simultaneously undergoing some manner of withdrawal.

She'd decided to go dark, which in Veeser terms meant not streaming anything new. She had a large file of evergreen vids, about half of which had been streamed previously, to keep her subscribers...well, not *happy*, but not disappearing in massive numbers, until she worked out what she wanted to do.

Short-term, it was evident that she'd begun putting her own wellbeing ahead of her stream's health. That meant not letting Calcut Linus know she and Makk were currently in Canos-Holo, which would be impossible if she started streaming from the islands. Long-term? Unclear. Makk pointed out that Calcut was perfectly capable of evading capture for the rest of his life, while she couldn't stay in hiding for the rest of *her* life. She told him to shut up.

So, she did vacation-like things. She went swimming at the beach and she drank drinks that were too sweet and came with small umbrellas. She still wore her rig while doing most of this because she said she felt naked without it, and besides it was waterproof. Makk considered challenging her to go a day without keeping tabs on the news streams—or whatever she considered valid streaming news sources—but he was pretty positive not only would she be unable to do this, she would resent him for suggesting it. Also, he needed her to keep using the rig to check in on the tech Ba-Ugna Kev gave them, in case Viselle popped up on it again.

They had only discussed the potential scope of Kev's tool a few times since their abrupt departure from Velon—could they use it, for instance, to hunt down Calcut? —mostly because at that time there was a sense that they were on the cusp of catching up with Viselle, after which they'd have some proper answers.

Two weeks later, they still hadn't discussed their options if they *failed* to find her. Not that they were done searching but they were quickly running out of places to look.

∾

They only spent four days on Aggo, which was long enough to rule out the boats for rent on the entire island. The problem was that none of them went out as far as the coordinates Makk provided them with, so the odds of Viselle employing one from there was pretty low.

Aggo was the third in the chain of seven (going from right to left) so there were three other islands closer to the coordinates to try out.

The next island down—Lopa-Oah—was more of the same. They spent another four days there, which was twice as long as they needed to because 'Casta insisted they do a *little* vacationing for at least one night that turned into two. (Makk underestimated the potency of those too-sweet drinks with the tiny umbrellas, and found himself unable to ambulate properly the following day.)

"I think your problem is that your idea of a vacation *is* hunting down a fugitive," Elicasta said at one point, while he sat on their veranda and drank water in small doses.

"You're not wrong," he said, "but I don't understand why you think that's a problem."

"It's not *my* idea of a vacation," she said.

"But we're not really vacationing. This is still a fugitive hunt."

"An unsanctioned fugitive hunt you haven't told your boss about, with no backup or local pollie engagement. What are you even going to do when we catch up to her?"

"Dunno yet," he said. "I'll figure it out when it happens."

"If we find her at all."

"Yes."

He had a *lot* of questions for Viselle, and about three-quarters of them were questions he didn't want someone other than Elicasta privy to, which was all the reason he needed not to involve local law enforcement.

As for not looping in Captain Llotho...Elicasta was working under the impression that Makk was currently taking sanctioned vacation time, but the truth was that he didn't tell Llotho where he was going or *that* he was going. Makk was technically absent without leave.

In terms of his career, this was not an excellent strategy. But with the maelstrom that was about to touch down on the department following the streamed murder of Ba-Ugna Kev, Makk was pretty positive he would have been pinned down in Velon for weeks otherwise.

After Lopa-Oah, they headed to T'Patto, which was the least impressive. The hotel was basically a dive bar with beds. But, the charter boats there *would* take them to the coordinates, so they spent a day aboard one such boat and went out to the geolocation.

Unsurprisingly, there wasn't anything there.

"You expecting an island city maybe," the captain said, referring to one of the half-dozen floating cities known to roam the planet's oceans. "You won' find 'em in these waters."

"Don't know *what* I expected," Makk told him, "but it's just water."

"I could'a said as much from the dock," the captain said.

"She did come out here," Elicasta said to Makk, while the captain turned them around. "More than once."

"How do you know more than once?"

"Same way I know she wasn't in an aero-car over this part of the world when the tech pinged her. She popped because she stopped moving, more than once, right about here."

"But there's nothing here," he reiterated,

"I can see that."

Another couple of days at T'Patto exhausted their possible avenues of inquiry. Then they skipped the next island—Hyjus May—altogether and headed straight to Midgie, the final island in the chain. This was on advice from the captain who took them out to the uneventful location.

"Barely a dock at Hyjus," he said. "It's not a place you live neither, getting a choice on it."

"I've heard good things about the resort," Elicasta said.

"Sure, miss. If you're of a mind for that, it's swell. But the fishers don't pull out from Hyjus May, and that's what you and the mister are for. After the resort, there's nothing there."

What they were talking about was the only five-star rated resort hotel in Canos-Holo. Elicasta didn't even bother hiding her disappointment that they wouldn't be going there.

Makk was pretty sure this vacation wasn't working out as well as she'd hoped. Then again, she *was* going through Veeser withdrawal: Possibly, reality itself was disappointing her, and there wasn't anything he could do about that.

∼

They were only at Midgie for an afternoon before Makk decided this was where they should have headed first. Unlike the other islands, Midgie's entire shoreline seemed dedicated to sport fishing and drinking. The hotel they settled on, while a step up from where they stayed in T'Patto, was a functional but no-frills affair meant for people who would be spending their day on the water.

"I already like the bar scene better here than on the other islands," Makk said, after their second day.

"You would," Elicasta said. "They all feel like the Lucky Twins."

"Better food *here*."

"You just say that because you can identify what you're eating in this place."

"Yes, that's one of my fundamental requirements for food edibility," he said.

They were sitting in the corner of a shack that looked like a stiff wind could take it out any minute, which was interesting because Canos-Holo was in the hurricane corridor; it *had* to be sturdier than it appeared. Makk decided the abundance of windows was a factor: open them all up and there's hardly anything left to blow down.

It was the end of the day. The best times to question charter fishing boat captains was either early in the morning or at sunset, and they'd missed their chance at sunrise. The best *place* to question them was off the dock, in the bars dotting the shoreline. The best *bars* to question them in were the ones tourists didn't spend a lot of time in.

Makk and Elicasta had already eaten their fill of fried seafood —this seemed to be the one thing every bar on every island did well—and were struggling to alternate between strong drink and water, so as to keep their wits about them.

This was another thing that made this less vacation-like. Makk wasn't currently on duty—he could drink as much as he liked—but he wasn't about to relax to the point where he missed a lead because he was insufficiently sober to notice it. Unfortunately, every bartender on Canos-Holo seemed exceptionally gifted when it came to rum drinks in particular, and he didn't want to miss out on that either.

Elicasta both didn't care how much she drank and didn't seem affected by it in the same was Makk was. She drank enough rum that he wondered if she had an extra stomach hidden somewhere.

About halfway through the evening, a local stopped by their table. He had the look of a man who spent most of his time on the water: shorts, worn-out shirt, no shoes, a ball cap, and the kind of gait that indicated surprise that the floor wasn't moving.

Makk had seen him when he first came in, just like he'd seen the last half dozen who looked just like him. The man had gone to the bar for a beer, got a quick talking-to from the bartender, and then looked over at Makk and Elicasta's table.

This had been happening all evening because sometime around the second or third day Makk realized the best way to get the information he was looking for was to drop some coin on the person behind the bar, tell them he wanted to ask local charter boaters a few questions, and make it clear it would be worth their time to swing by his table.

"Itta say you looking to talk to a boater," the fisherman said. "Say it's worth a coin for my time. Izzat so?"

"It is," Makk said. "You handle a lot of for-hire fishing?"

"Sure do. Where you lookin' to go, and when you want to go? I got freedom later in the week, if you here for it."

"We just want information," Elicasta said with a smile. She was no better or worse than the next civilian when it came to eliciting information from people, but the smile had definitely proven to be an asset.

"What kinda?"

Makk opened his voicer and called up an image of Viselle Daska. It wasn't her most flattering photo, but they had limited options. It was pulled from the vid that made her famous. He slid it across the table.

"We're looking for this woman," he said. "We understand she hired someone such as yourself, recently."

"Izzat so?" the man said, without looking down. "She in some trouble, is she?"

"Not with us," Elicasta said.

"We just want to talk to her," Makk added.

The captain looked down at the image then. "Pretty lady," he said. His gaze lingered for long enough that Makk thought that they'd finally found the right guy.

"Tell you what," the man said. "I sit down, you buy me another beer an' we talk. But not about the girl in the image."

"All right," Makk said. "What do you want to talk about?"

"One at a time. I'm Erry Gisador. Who might you two be?"

∿

After introductions and new round, Captain Gisador leaned back, took one more look at the image on Makk's voicer, and started talking.

"Here's the mess, friends," he said. "I been paid extra to *not* sit here at this table wit' you nice folks and talk about that particular lady. Can't tell you when she was here nor when she left, nor what she did in the middle. I can't do that because I'm a man of my word. You appreciate this, I'm taking."

"I do," Makk said.

"But you *have* sat down," Elicasta said.

"Oh, indeed. The company's nice and the beer's free, which is my favorite way to end a hard day a' fishing. And maybe one o' the reasons I'm sittin' is you're not what I was anticipating."

"What were you expecting?" Makk asked.

"Like *you*, but about twenty more. Uniforms and such. The fare we ain't talkin' about seemed the type to attract that sort of attention, you get me? But as I said..."

"...you can't talk about her," Makk finished.

"Exactly. Now, in spite of that, I do have a mite problem the two of you seem like to take care of for me, and on account of that mite problem being the *fault* of the woman I never saw before in that image on your pocket screen...I'm saying maybe while I'm all busy not helping you at all we can still manage to help each other."

"I need a lot more rum for this," Elicasta muttered.

"I cut to the straight, detective man," Gisador said. "I can't say nothing about her. But I can take you to one who'd fill you right up with near everything you need to know with a lot more on top. I get to keep my word, you get your facts, we part as friends."

"That's it?" Makk asked. He was waiting for a price because it seemed like Erry Gisador was drifting in that direction.

"Oh, sure," Gisador said, sipping his beer. "Well, and there's another thing, but I expect you'll arrive at this on your own without my prompt. This fella I'm talking of, he's in a poor place. I feel an obligation to his upkeep, because I mean to get into the Haven after this life, and I'm not wanting an extra mark on my ledger. He's got none else, and he *is* very much the fault of her I can't talk about, and so now he's my burden. But he don't have to be."

"Honus's sake," Elicasta said. "Did she leave behind a *baby*?"

Gisador laughed. "He's a touch too vocal, but you got the right idea. He's adrift, Miss Sangristy. Adrift on land, but adrift no less. Come, let's get another round a drink and then you'll be ready for him. Best not bein' all sober if you want ta get what he say."

~

Gisador led them from the bar down to the docks, along the shore for a time, and then back upland to a nondescript brick building that looked like its heyday had passed sometime in the prior century.

"It's a schoolhouse," Erry said. "Or it was not so far back. Been closed since before my boyhood, but my pap attended, I'm told."

It looked like the sort of place one brought tourists prior to murdering them, but Makk didn't say so.

"I'm surprised this is here," Elicasta said. She glanced at Makk and tapped the side of her rig. *I'm recording*, she was telling him.

Evidently, she had the same concern about the murder schoolhouse.

"How you mean?" Erry asked.

"So close to the water. It looks like prime real estate."

He turned around to take in the view, as if he'd only just noticed there was water nearby.

"It is," he agreed. "But there's no beach and the shoals are brutal in this patch. I 'spect one day every inch of every coastline on *all* the islands'll be ate up by tourism, but we not there yet. Plenty of old muni housing unclaimed, meanwhile. Come on, it's just here."

He pointed to a down staircase along the side of the building.

"What's there?" Makk asked, tacitly not moving.

"Used'ta be the recreational," Erry said.

"In the basement," Elicasta clarified.

"Ya."

"The basement in the abandoned building in the middle of nowhere at the edge of the island," she said.

Erry Gisador realized only then what it must look like, and laughed.

"Oh, no, I'm sorry. Oh, my friends. I been here so many times I don't even see how it look to your eyes. It's a bar, is all."

"We were at a perfectly good bar a few minutes ago," Makk said.

"This one different. You a detective, yeah?"

"Yes."

"You got a place? Your people, outside the regular."

"You mean, a cop bar? Sure. It's not in an abandoned schoolhouse."

"Well that's what we got here. Need a place without you lot."

"Cops?" Makk asked.

"Tourists, Makk Stidgeon," Erry said. "*And* cops," he added, after consideration. "This is no legal place."

"You don't say," Elicasta said.

"All right, come on. Closer, you can see for yourself through the windows. Erry Gisador is an honest captain, he don't play. Ask anyone."

The time for character witnesses had long passed and Makk wished he had his gun, but Gisador seemed trustworthy *enough* to proceed.

The captain led them to the top of the stairs and tapped on the window as he went by. It was dirty so the view was murky, but there *was* light in the basement and there *were* people down there. Makk could make out a bar and a few tables, too. It appeared Erry Gisador was telling the truth.

Erry reached the metal door at the bottom of the stairs, rapped twice, waited, and then rapped three times in a cadenced knock.

"So you know," Erry said, "not supposed to bring off-islanders to *The Wind*."

"This place has a *name?*" Elicasta asked.

"More of a side joke, really, miss," Erry said. "Where's Noddy got off to?' 'Oh, he's in the wind he is.'"

The door opened. A tall, wiry man leaned out and looked down.

"Erry," he greeted in a deep voice. He nodded at Makk and Elicasta. "What's this, then?"

"They friends, Bagga. Step aside."

"You been doin' a lot of that, of late," Bagga said. "Makin' friends. What's the password?"

"Lick my tacklebox is the password, nephew, now get out the way."

It was unclear whether "lick my tacklebox" was actually the password or just an insult—neither men seemed inclined to clarify—but Bagga did step aside and let them through.

The interior was exactly as described: a former school gym converted into a bar. The floor was composed of warped wooden slats whose finish had been rubbed off by years of having sand tracked across it. The bar and the tables looked like they were assembled via some combination of rescued furniture and cobbled-together driftwood. The customers that they could *see*—the lighting was terrible—all bore the same ineffable physical qualities as Erry that marked them as locals. Only, with fewer friendly expressions and more scars.

Erry brought them straight to the bar, behind which was a large woman with a bald head and no left ear, who was busy staring them down.

"You keep bringin' strays, Erry Gisador, I'm like to ban your entry."

"Vira, my love, these are no strays," Erry said.

She said something in another language then—Makk was pretty sure it was Biddobay, the island tongue he'd only heard spoken a couple of times since they arrived—and then they went back and forth a while. It was pretty clear Vira was cursing Erry, but it was hard to figure out much more than that.

Finally, she turned to Makk.

"What's your demon, mister?" she asked.

"Ah, how about just some water?"

"Water here's like to kill you. The whisky's safer."

"Whisky, then."

"And the miss?"

"Um..."

"Everybody drink here, and everybody pay," Vira said. "Here, I got a sweet barrel black rum to pucker your cheeks."

She poured Elicasta an inky beverage and a brownish liquid for Makk, slid a bottle of beer to Erry, and then quoted an outrageous sum for the three.

Makk paid it. "You didn't bring us here to clear your tab, did you?" he asked Erry.

"Only if you see fit to," he said. "Come, my friend is set in the shadows."

He led them past the collection of scowling fishers to a table at the limit of the room's visible light, on which was sitting a man who did *not* look like an islander. Nor did he look like a tourist. Makk's first impression was that he was meeting the survivor of a shipwreck.

With black hair and big black eyes, tan skin and the beginnings of a light beard, he was sitting behind a table that was holding three empty glasses and a set of dirty plates. He clutched a fourth glass—not yet empty—as if he might drown if he let go.

He was Wivvolian. Beyond that, Makk had no idea who he was.

"Hello, friend," Erry greeted. "Brought some people looking for a story."

He looked up, not obviously recognizing Gisador.

*This is a broken man*, Makk thought.

"I have no story," he hissed. "I am no-one."

Elicasta gasped.

"Djbbit," she said. "You're Xto Djbbit."

Something lit up behind the man's eyes. "You know me?" he asked.

Makk had the same question. "You know him?"

"Gods, Makk, consume *some* news. The missing astronaut?"

"No idea what you're saying."

"Wivvol lost one of their astronauts on reentry. It was big news." She turned to the man at the table. "That *is* you, isn't it?"

"It is." His demeanor changed remarkably, on having been identified. "And now I am no longer no-one, though the name you've given me is *shtgl*."

"Sorry, I don't know what that means."

"There is no…common tongue word. Disgraced. Honor-less. Deserving of exile. Shamed by my own actions. You understand."

"Outcast," Makk offered.

"Yes."

"How did you end up *here*?" Elicasta asked. "And how can we help?"

"I am here having foolishly surrendered my birthright," Xto said.

"Ey, that's why these people be here too," Erry said. "They want the one what took it from you. Tell 'em the story."

Xto looked them both over for an uncomfortably long time.

"Sit," he said, finally. "I will give you ownership of my tale, and then you will let me die here, in this hole, where I deserve to stay."

"Don't worry," Erry whispered to Makk. "The bottom of a glass brings out the drama in this one. He's not so bad sober."

"How often is he sober?"

"Not often."

Makk and Elicasta sat. Erry, ever the good host, cleared off the table.

"My story begins two years ago," Xto said. "When a man I trusted spoke a name I'd never before heard, belonging to a man I would never meet, hailing from a place I'll never be. That name was Orno Linus."

## Chapter Two

X to Djbbit had an apartment just past the eastern part of the outer rim of Chnta proper. It was an uncharacteristic residential arrangement for those of his profession, but one he preferred. Involvement in the rocket program demanded a nearly 20/7 commitment already; better to have a location in which to escape in the rare moments of down time than to *live* there as well.

The apartment was still larger than that of most citizens. Not *as* large as the one he would have if he lived on the base, but perfectly adequate to his needs, which were minimal.

Most Chntans asserted a direct connection between apartment size and importance, and it was true that the astronauts of the rocket program were among the *most* important citizens in Wivvol and thus commanded some of the largest apartments in Chnta.

Not that an astronaut with a large apartment made any sense. Once they began their rotation they were *guaranteed* to spend two years away from their preciously spacious residences, which was an excellent reason not to bother to give them so much room. Another was that they'd be *spending* their rotation in severely cramped quarters; better to get used to limited living space on the ground.

Living a distance from the program meant Xto had to ride the electric rail every couple of days, which mandated dealing with the mass of citizenry *not* employed by the program. This was another thing most of his fellow astronauts would just as readily not deal with, because most of his fellow astronauts were too famous for that.

Xto was modestly famous, but more for family connections than for his daring as an astronaut. His fame would definitely rise as the date of his first flight got closer—the state's public relations division would ensure that—but for now, to most, he was just another citizen riding the rail.

Or nearly so. He still wore the uniform issued to all members of the rocket program, and he *was* traveling from the Bnuft Region. Even children knew that the *Extraplanetary Project for the Future of All* was located in Bnuft, and most knew what the uniforms looked like. All of this meant he received plenty of attention when boarding the train, which he resolutely ignored.

The trip to his apartment took the long way, looping counterclockwise around the glut of enormous towers that made up Chnta's downtown. It was precisely eighty-seven minutes from the Bnuft landing to the Vrtl Block stop, the nearest to his apartment. That was provided the train ran on schedule; a reasonable expectation.

In the entire history of the Chnta electric rail, it had gone off schedule only seven times. This was according to the state, and was therefore likely an exaggeration, as the perfection of public services was a fundamental tenet of the public-facing arm of the Chancellery. However, it was also true that Xto couldn't name a single occasion in which a rail line he rode *was* off schedule.

A happy citizen would argue that this meant the state was correct—public services were indeed high-precision mechanisms.

A paranoid citizen would argue that the state adjusted all the clocks whenever a train ran late.

This was, of course, impossible, as the clocks in Wivvol were tuned to the sky itself, which meant in order to adjust the time in the city of Chnta to account for the 4:17 from Bnuft running late the state would have to be capable of altering the stars and the suns. As every citizen—even the *profoundly* paranoid—knew that no government was quite that powerful, the assertion that they did this (again, rather than that the trains really did always run on time) became a joke, and then an idiom.

The idiom was "the dancers are lame today", alluding to the common name for Dib's twin suns. Politely, this meant, *I'm having trouble with this.* In common usage, it was more like, *I don't fucking believe it.*

Ignoring the eyes on him, Xto focused on the view from the window as the train got underway.

The highest building downtown was the spire in the dead-center: Chancellery Main in Lpyk Square. This was the seat of government for the entire country. In the view from above—Xto was one of the few citizens who'd *seen* the view from above, from the cockpit during one of his many wingplane training missions—the Chancellery buildings looked like an enormous infection radiating outward from an originative wound.

It looked much more impressive from the ground. Especially Chancellery Main: a bright, attractive well-lit dagger pointing skyward as if threatening the gods themselves to a swordfight.

*Except we don't believe in the gods here,* he thought.

He sighed, turned from the window and opened his assigned tablet. There was studying to be done—there was always studying to be done—and this was the time to do it.

∾

Roughly thirty minutes into the eighty-seven minute journey to his stop, Xto realized someone else in the train car was fixated on him.

The back half of the train car's seats faced the same direction in which they were traveling, while the front half faced opposite. Xto had taken a free forward-facing seat three rows from the center, on the left, where he could see the cityscape through the window.

In the first row of opposite-facing seats, on the far right (from Xto's orientation) sat a man next to a window displaying the urban sprawl of the outer ring, i.e., nothing in particular. That he was disinterested in looking out on this was unsurprising. What was *very* surprising was that he chose instead to stare unswervingly at future astronaut Xto Djbbit.

Xto stared back, for as long as he could. His silent interlocutor was a modest-looking person of modest height wearing a baggy suit. He had one leg crossed, displaying a leather shoe in need of resoling and a fresh polish. He wore a neck kerchief loosely. Everything about him, from the color of his clothing to the cut of his hair suggested a drab citizen, instantly forgettable.

All except for his eyes. They sparkled with life, fixed as they were on Xto. The eyes contradicted everything else. *This is a costume*, they said. *I have better clothing*.

Xto broke his gaze, and tried to control his breathing even as his heartrate jumped.

Xto had been stress-tested extensively since entering the rocket program. He was proud of the fact that his pulse didn't elevate in the face of high risk circumstance. Yet one overcurious stranger on the electric rail and his heart lost all discipline.

It couldn't be helped.

*He's Council Seventeen*, Xto thought.

Council Seventeen was the Chancellery's private investigative unit. They were known to intervene in matters deemed a threat to the greater good, to root out subversion (by their own malleable definition) and to enforce, in general terms, the rule of *thought* the Chancellery deemed correct.

They also provided security though, and once Xto calmed down he allowed that this was as good an explanation as any. It was expected that once they formally announced that Xto Djbbit, (son of none other than the great Mondr Djbbit,) would be the next astronaut into space, he'd be assigned a C17 agent. This would be both to ensure Xto didn't come into contact with some manner of subversion and to act as bodyguard.

However, it was also the case that when Xto's flight schedule was announced he would no longer be riding the rail to his apartment but staying in the quarters reserved for him on the base and *then* that a C17 agent was to be assigned.

That was what he'd been told.

Therefore, this man was either Council Seventeen and Xto was theoretically in some trouble, or he wasn't Council Seventeen and Xto was being paranoid.

It perhaps wouldn't have been quite as frightening a prospect to consider if Xto had no reason to fear a C17 investigation. However, there was likely no citizen in Wivvol who felt this comfortable about their own lives and he was no exception. Everyone had secrets. Xto could think of at least two which could in theory disqualify him for the rocket program—and certainly *would* if he had a different family name—and perhaps even a total disappearance...something Council Seventeen was known to have a talent for.

At the forty-three minute mark, the train stopped at the landing for the Mzch Block, and several riders disembarked. The man got to his feet, tantalized Xto for a moment with the thought that he might get off at Mzch as well, and then took the seat directly behind Xto.

The doors closed, and the train glided back to traveling speed.

Xto wavered between standing and confronting the man, and holding his breath until he lost consciousness.

"Xto Djbbit," the man whispered. Xto checked the man's reflection in the window; he was leaning forward to speak in Xto's ear.

"Yes," Xto said. "Are you Council Seventeen?"

The man shook his head. "You need not fear them today," he said. "I come with a message from your uncle."

"Tbyct?"

"Yes, that uncle. He wishes an audience."

Xto fought the urge to simply turn around and speak to this messenger, but now that he knew the nature of the encounter he recognized that their *not* being seen talking was of great importance.

"And who are you?" Xto asked.

"A friend."

"A friend would not endanger my standing by approaching me in such a manner. Nor would my uncle send someone so clumsy."

"He appreciates the risk, as do I. But this is a matter of great import, and it cannot wait. Word is, your flight will be booked within the month."

"All the more reason for me to have nothing to do with uncle."

"One meeting is all he asks."

"It's impossible," Xto said. "For all I know, I'm being followed already."

"You are not," the man said. "I've made sure."

"*You* have. And who are you that can guarantee such a thing?"

"A friend, as I said. One who is very good at his job."

"An adherent," Xto said.

"I am that as well."

"I still cannot risk being seen with Ghn Tbyct. He knows precisely why."

The man sighed.

"I had hoped not to do this," he said.

He slid a piece of paper around the side of the chair.

"What is this?" Xto asked.

"Take it."

Xto took the paper and unfolded it. Then his heartrate jumped again.

"Where did this image come from?" Xto asked.

"That hardly matters," the man said. "Know that I captured it myself and that you are the only citizen to lay eyes on it. Know also that this will not *remain* the case if you fail to do as I ask."

"So it will be blackmail, then," Xto said.

"As I said, I had hoped we would not arrive here. I take no joy."

Xto folded up the paper and slid it into his pocket. "When?" he asked.

"Tonight."

Xto laughed. "Impossible."

"*Tonight*, you are not being followed, except by me. I can make no guarantees for other nights and as I said, the announcement will be soon. We've made all of the arrangements; you needn't worry."

"You come bearing evidence of my compromise and ask for trust? Fine. Tonight, then. Where?"

~

The man identified himself as Citizen Drk. No first name was provided, which was perhaps just as well: *Drk* was likely a made-up name.

Drk told him to go home as planned. Then he handed over a buzz-box.

"When this thrums," Drk said, "take the rear exit to your apartment building. We will be ready."

It was the lowest of low-tech devices, only slightly more advanced than rapping on the floor with a broom-handle. Xto found this comforting, somehow. Since the buzz-box's sole function was to vibrate gently upon receipt of a nearby signal of the correct frequency, he needn't worry about any secondary function. Likewise, if he was found holding it, there was no way to trace its origin or discern its purpose beyond one-way signaling. It was just this kind of detail he'd expect a state-run entrapment operation to get wrong.

He didn't think Citizen Drk was part of a state op to root out subversives, but he knew such operations existed. (If Drk *was*, he had all the material he needed already.) Still, the first thing Xto did when he got back to his apartment was to take apart the buzz-box to make sure it truly was as crude as it looked.

It was, and so he reassembled it and slid it into his hip pocket.

The next three hours were uniquely unsettling.

Xto had a meal of freeze-dried rations first. It was the same manner of meal he'd be eating for his extra-planetary rotation, so an argument could be made that getting used to it was an aspect of his training, but that wasn't the truth. The truth was, the ration was a step *up* from the standard-issue meals available to most residents. To him, then, it was a treat.

Likewise, the small bottle of undiluted beer was most appreciated. He'd grown to like alcohol, and expected to miss it a good deal while off-planet.

After the meal, there was nothing to do but concentrate on his studies. When this didn't work—he was retaining nothing—he activated the wall screen for the state-stream news.

As was the case with all forms of official news, the state-stream managed to be uniquely uninformative while managing to give the impression that it was the precise opposite. The problem was that the Wivvol depicted in the news didn't bear any resemblance to the everyday Wivvol its citizens occupied. At best, it was an astoundingly rosy version. At worst, it was altogether fictional. In either case, nobody watched it to find out what was *actually* happening; they watched it to find out what was *going* to happen, per government edict.

When the news also failed as a serviceable distraction he turned off the state-stream and settled down at his window, which offered a semi-decent view of late-night Chnta.

Xto's experience with his city and his country was less sheltered than most. He'd seen, for instance, still images of a number of other cities. Velon, in Inimata, was the one that most often came to mind, especially when he looked out his own window. The image he'd seen as a child was that of a gaudily-lit metropolis with flying cars and lewd advertisements, captured through a greasy window. It was *intended* to give the impression that the world outside of Wivvol was grimy, disordered, and dangerous in the abstract. Instead, the young Xto mostly felt a sense of awe and wanting. This quality resurfaced whenever he looked at Chnta's dull, grey cityscape. Here, there were no flying cars, and the only lighting at this time of night came from the Chancellery buildings and the streetlamps.

Had the box not vibrated, Xto likely would have spent the entire evening at that window, wondering what mess his uncle was about to get him involved with. But then, at just past twenty, it thumped.

Xto closed his curtains and turned out his light for the benefit of the Council Seventeen member he imagined was watching from a distant building—it would now look as if he'd retired for the evening—threw on a hooded jacket, and left.

The rear exit of the building was tagged with all manner of warnings about its use in the event there was *not* an emergency; per the Chancellery, only the front doors were permitted exits. Conveniently for the building's inhabitants, the signage neglected to define what constituted a permissible emergency. One might presume that the state's definition was fairly narrow—a fire, a structural collapse, an explosive device, and little else. However, sometime in the past dozen years some intrepid apartment-dweller decided to broaden the definition of *emergency* while at the same time making the important discovery that the *alarms* which were expected to notify the city's emergency responders should the door be opened did not in fact exist.

Since that famous (yet unrecorded) moment, everyone in the building had developed a preference for the door. The reason was obvious: the state had no opticals directed at the rear exit.

There was a high likelihood that nobody leaving the building had anything to *hide* from the Chancellery—there simply wasn't that much opportunity to partake in non-permitted acts in Chnta. But it was a demonstrable fact that a people constantly watched will gravitate toward opportunities in which they are not. Even if it's only for a stolen moment of privacy.

Xto stepped out into the cool night, waited until the door had closed behind him—another intrepid resident had long ago disabled the locking mechanism, so it didn't latch—and then waited some more, because he didn't know what he was expected to do next.

He was standing in a narrow alley that opened to main avenues on the left and right sides. Both had roving street-level opticals to capture an image of Xto as soon as he committed to a direction. Such detection would presumably run contrary to this mission.

*What would you have me do now?* he wondered.

Gradually, he became aware of a flashing light to his left. It could have been a silent alarm signal, except it was irregular. More precisely, it was a pattern: someone was behind the light, and they were talking to him in Binarial.

All Wivvolians learned Binarial Code as children, and *nearly* all of them forgot it by the time they reached adulthood. But Xto was fluent; it was part of his training, as a secondary communication method should his comms fail.

*This way, on the mark*, was what they said.

Xto walked to the edge of the alley, about two paces from the walkway and three from the street, and waited. He was still in the shadow of the buildings, well out of sight of all but the most directly-facing of optical devices. (It was easy enough to know this; the state's street-level opticals were all attached to fixed poles either beside or beneath the streetlights. They were not in any way hidden.)

The message repeated, providing him the opportunity to work out that it was coming from the alley across the way and to his right.

Then: *walk even pace, on three...two...one.*

Xto headed across. There was no need to check for vehicles on his way, as the only cars on the road at this time of night belonged to the state police; if he were to encounter one at this moment it would likely be best if he just allowed it to run him over. He likewise didn't need to concern himself with aero-cars or optical devices attached to drones, as neither of those technologies were employed in Wivvol. (The Chancellery formally disallowed zero-gravity tech almost as soon as the technology came into existence.)

The urge to *run* across was great, but unwise. The opticals rotated up and down the street in predictable transits with known gaps. Xto didn't know the timing of the gaps, only because he'd never needed to. (Whoever was leading Xto across, he presumed, *did* know them and was walking him through one at this moment.) But the opticals also had peripheral sensors that were triggered by rapid movement, so it was better to walk slowly and steadily.

Also—and this was another thing people who were constantly watched came to understand innately—looking as if one was in a hurry was an excellent way to end up getting stopped and questioned.

So he walked, holding his breath the entire time, as if a sharp exhale would be enough to bring the state down upon him. He was only out in the open for fifteen seconds, but it was an eternal fifteen seconds.

Drk wasn't the one waiting for him in the alley, which was a surprise. Instead, he was face-to-face with a woman. She was short and young, with close-cropped black hair and large eyes that made her look younger still.

"May the Five be close," she whispered.

"And... with you," Xto sputtered. It was an automatic reply that he couldn't quite stop himself from uttering.

"I am Imbw," she said. "Please follow me."

She began walking swiftly down the alley. Xto had to jog to catch up.

"I have questions," he said. "Before we proceed."

"We've no time for questions. The timing of our journey is very precise, and must be conducted as quietly as possible. You will have to save them for when we arrive."

"And where will that be?"

"We're going to your uncle," she said. "At the House."

Xto grabbed her by the arm.

"There *is* no House temple in Chnta," he said. "Not any longer."

This was only partly accurate. The House's temple remained standing, its center-column Finger continuing to jut out above the low-lying apartment-houses that surrounded it. But the doors had been barred for over ten years, ever since the state formally banned Septalism.

Imbw smiled.

"The House is wherever the High Hat says it is. And the temple isn't as closed as you've been led to believe. Now come. The roving eyes of the state delay for no citizen."

∼

Imbw led Xto through two more alleys, then cut through the ground floor of an unoccupied building and another three alleys. They were traversing the city diagonally, in a roundabout path that brought them to within two blocks of the boarded-up temple. It was only thanks to the Septal Finger looming above the cityscape that Xto even knew where they were; he'd never traveled Chnta by way of the side-alleys before, and never been out at night at *all*.

Now they'd come up short, staring—from a distance—at the impenetrable steel slats that held the temple's doors closed.

"Shall we teleport now?" Xto asked.

"Of course not," Imbw said. "If I could do that, I'd have done it from outside your apartment."

She stepped up to a street-level door near the edge of the alley and knocked arrhythmically. The door opened, a hand's-breadth. Someone on the dark interior was looking at them.

Imbw made a hand-signal familiar to anyone raised as a Septal: an open-palm hand over the heart that was then clutched into a fist. The door swung all the way open and a large man in a proper Septal hood stepped out to let them pass.

"Brother," Xto muttered on his way past.

"May the Five bless you," he said back.

Imbw lit the hand-held light she'd used to signal Binarial Code, the nameless brother closed the door, and then they were standing in a vacant storage room with no evident second exit.

Imbw pulled her own Septal hood up. "If you would, Brother Zyk?" she asked, shining the light at a random spot on the floor.

Zyk stepped around Xto and kicked some dirt away from the center of the floor to expose a metal handle. He knelt down, grabbed the handle and pulled open the trap door. There was a staircase on the other side.

"Come, Brother Djbbit," Imbw said, leading him down the stairs.

"It's only Xto," he said. "I've taken no vows."

"The ways to the House are many," she said, "as are the ways to the Brethren."

"That's all fine, but again, I've taken no vows. Please don't call me that."

"Very well."

The stairs led to a long, extremely cold corridor.

"What is this place?" Xto asked. "Did you build it after the temple was barred?"

She laughed. "Chnta is *rooted* in Septalism. I mean this literally. These tunnels predate the city above us."

"But the Chancellery...?"

"Knows nothing about it. Or they do, and find it easier to pretend otherwise. It's always been so that the secular apparatus of the state fears what the Septals know. Better for them to imagine it can be eradicated from the country by fiat than to engage in direct conflict."

The corridor led to another staircase, a second corridor, and another staircase to yet another corridor. And then they exited the corridor and entered into what felt like a much vaster space. Since the only light they had was from Imbw's electrical torch Xto couldn't properly judge exactly *how* vast.

"I was raised a Septal," he said. "But at no time did I think of our faith as being something worthy of *fear*, certainly not contra the state."

"I know how you were raised. As to what you were and were not *told*... High Hat Tbyct will explain it all, but understand that details have been kept from you since your future as a captain of the sky was assured. And were it not for the circumstance in which we currently find ourselves, the details would continue to be kept from you."

"What circumstance?"

Imbw's light found the side of a machine. It was inactive. Xto wanted very much for them to stop so that he could work out what it was and what it did, but his guide showed no interest in giving a tour.

"Your uncle will explain soon enough," she said, leading him around the machine without commenting on its existence in any meaningful way. "We're directly beneath the House temple now. We go up again from here."

Her light found a doorway, on the other side of which was a spiral staircase. Before beginning his ascent, Xto turned once more to have a look at the machinery hidden by the pitch-blackness of the room.

"You can ask," Imbw said. "But I can't tell you. Not because what it does is a secret I'm keeping, but because I don't know what it does either."

"Does my uncle?"

"Ask him yourself."

~

The spiral staircase went on for longer than seemed reasonable, but they eventually emerged in what Xto recognized as the back room of the temple's main hall. As a child, he attended the ceremonies weekly up until the ban. It was a part of his life about which the Chancellery was well aware, but which had been scrubbed from his biography prior to his formal enrollment in the astronautical program. They couldn't have a citizen who held unsanctioned views representing the state, regardless of who his father was.

At least, not officially. Xto no longer practiced, but he knew of three active adherents in the program, and they hinted at more. But unlike Xto they had kept their faith hidden from the state and would lose their positions were they discovered, if not their lives.

Xto had never felt so strongly about his Septal roots to risk his life in the name of the Five. His uncle likely knew this, which was why he and his people resorted to blackmail to entice Xto to risk so much for an in-person conversation. An order from his High Hat wouldn't have been enough.

They exited the room onto the altar, and then Imbw extinguished her light.

"From here there are windows," she whispered. "Better to not be seen moving about. We're making for the front stairs. We mean to access the upper offices."

Xto wanted to ask what could have possibly compelled Uncle Tbyct to retain the literal office of his title in the face of state oppression, but decided to hold his tongue. Tbyct was a stubborn old man, and stubborn old man did stubborn things, stubbornly.

They walked along the side aisle without a word, until reaching a door on the side near the front of the temple which led to a windowless stairwell. From there, the prospect of detection was reduced to almost zero. A visibly relaxed Imbw relit her torch and up they went.

"It has been an honor," Imbw said, as they climbed, "to guide a national hero."

Xto laughed.

"I am hardly a hero. I'm just a man going into space."

"Yes. Very brave."

"Tell me: is it brave to do something when given no option otherwise?"

She thought about this.

"Yes," she decided. "Because I don't believe you have no options. The alternatives would bring you and your family shame, but they *are* alternatives. This is a kind of bravery."

"You're very generous."

They reached the top floor. Imbw opened it and stood at the threshold.

"Here is where I leave you," she said. "High Hat Tbyct awaits in his office; I'm certain you know the way."

"And when I wish to leave?"

"You will find me at the bottom of these same stairs. May the Five be close, Xto Djbbit."

"And with you."

"Now go."

She shut the door.

Xto turned and looked down the corridor, the memories of a hundred other such occasions in which he looked down this same hallway flooding back. It used to look impressively long; now it was just a regular corridor.

The door at the other end opened.

"Well, come on," the High Hat of Chnta said. "We haven't got all night."

## Chapter Three

High Hat Tbyct—or Uncle Ghn, as Xto knew him growing up—kept a modest office even back when keeping an office and holding his title was allowed; in that sense, very little had changed. The hardwood desk in the corner no longer had papers stacked upon it, the fireplace wasn't in use, and the plush area rug Xto remembered rolling around on was missing, but otherwise it looked about the same.

Which was utterly unreasonable. At minimum there should have been a layer of dust over everything. If discovered, it would take a Chancellery investigator only seconds to work out that somebody was still practicing Septalism in this building, and from there conclude—correctly, it appeared—that the Chnta chapter High Hat remained active.

Uncle Ghn looked about the same as ever. He was in his hood, which only exposed his lower face, so Xto couldn't see the usual indicators of age—receding hairline and so on. He had perhaps put on some weight. Otherwise, there was no difference. Granted, he was wearing simple street clothes rather than his full robe—be-robed was how he appeared roughly two thirds of the time in

Xto's memories—but otherwise it was if no time had passed at all.

Ghn hugged him briefly, closed the door, and gestured to the nearest chair.

"Thank you for coming," he said.

"I hardly had an option," Xto said. "Your man threatened to compromise me. Tell me you knew this."

Ghn sighed. "I did. But you could have called our bluff." He walked around the desk and sat, his grunts betraying a stiff back.

"*Was* it a bluff?" Xto asked.

"Of course. I wouldn't have allowed my nephew to be exposed. Your mother's spirit would never forgive me. But I also expected you to weigh the risks in my favor, as you have."

"I have. Now please tell me why I'm here. And perhaps explain why *you're* here."

Ghn laughed. "Even an institution as stubborn as the Chancellery recognizes that you can't eradicate something people *believe* in simply by making it illegal to hold that belief. They know we still exist in the shadows and don't mind as long as we keep to them."

"You're sure of that?"

"When it comes to the state are any of us sure of anything? I'm not. But if you harbor real concern, know that I regularly hold services with two significant chancel secretaries. As long as I don't announce myself in a way the state can't *deny*, we're left alone."

"Or attempt to overthrow the state."

"That was always the official concern, wasn't it? They don't expect that from this office and likely never have, but you're right in thinking that the Chancellery has *other* fears contributing to their decision to leave us alone."

Xto wondered if the machine in the basement was the basis of one of those fears, and considered asking his uncle what it did. But it was getting late—or rather *early*—quickly. Regardless of how devoted the state was to looking the other way when it came to the House, Council Seventeen would no doubt take issue if one of their astronauts greeted the sunrise on the steps of the temple rather than his apartment.

"The House has secrets," the High Hat added. "Secrets the Chancellery know precisely enough of that they worry about what they *don't* know. This keeps them at bay. It's one of those secrets that brought you here, nephew."

Ghn pulled something from a drawer and dropped it on the desktop.

It looked like a key of some sort, but unlike any key Xto had ever seen before.

"Take a closer look," Ghn said. "It's all right."

Xto picked it up.

Partly transparent, it was tinted yellow and much lighter than it looked. It had the appearance of glass, only it wasn't.

He tried bending it, but it wouldn't give.

"It's as strong as metal, it *looks* like glass and it's as light as balsawood," he observed. "What in the name of the Five am I holding, uncle?"

"It's a key," Ghn said. Which was obvious.

"To what?"

"Many things. You were taught about the Collapse as a child, were you not?"

"I was taught by the Brethren that it happened many, many years ago. I was taught by the state that it never happened at all. I await a third authority to break the tie."

Ghn grinned. What was left unstated was that hardly anybody took the state's version of things to be the *truth*. What one learned from government-sanctioned educational classes was what the state wanted one to *say* when asked. Even if both parties knew what was being stated was a lie.

"Yes, well. On that I can provide proof of the Collapse," his uncle said, "if you really need it. Or I can just refer you to every body of knowledge outside of Wivvol."

"I have no access to knowledge outside of Wivvol. And the state would have me believe such knowledge is incorrect by default. What is this made of?"

"I don't entirely know. It's a synthesized material that includes petroleum, but beyond that I can't say."

"That's rare, isn't it?"

"It's exceedingly rare *here*," his uncle said.

"You mean, in Wivvol."

"No, that isn't what I mean."

"All right, then where did it come from?" Xto asked.

"From the Haven above, nephew. You're holding a pre-Collapse artifact, originally crafted by the Five themselves."

"The gods gave us a key?"

"The gods gave us *five* keys. This one is associated with Javilon, according to our texts."

"That's remarkable," Xto said, putting the key of Javilon back on the desk. He was no longer certain he even believed in the Five, but just in case he thought it best to not handle their stuff. "I was never taught this. Or did I need to take the vows first?"

"The vows wouldn't have helped. There are perhaps a hundred people on the planet that know about the keys. In Wivvol, there are only two."

"And now three."

"No, *you're* the second."

Xto was taken aback.

"This...is knowledge passed to you from the last High Hat, then," Xto said. "And now you're telling me. Are you presumptuous enough to imagine I'll be taking your position? I believe there are others who are more qualified. I met two this evening. Three, if your friend Drk is an adherent."

His uncle smiled gently. "It's nothing like that," he said.

Ghn stood and moved to the window. It was still dark out, so there was little to see aside from a dimly lit city foregrounding the tall buildings of the Chancellery. But he wasn't there to take in the view.

Uncle crossed his arms behind his back and took a deep breath. Xto had seen him do this before, a couple of times, in this very office; it was how he prepared himself to deliver important news that was, generally, also *bad* news. Once, it was to tell a Sister that her family had been denounced. Another time, it was to tell his nephew that he'd be leaving the faith because he was going to be an astronaut, whether or not he *wanted* to be one.

"Your father has the final word," he'd said then. "It isn't my role to counter him. Nor is it yours."

Back then, it seemed grossly unfair. Now, it just looked like the first in a long line of decisions made by someone in authority about Xto's future.

"There was a time," Uncle Ghn said, "when I imagined it playing out that way. That you would take the vows, I mean, and ascend in the ranks to a level where such a transfer would be reasonable. The title is almost never passed on by blood, but... well. This was before your true path became clear."

"My true path," Xto repeated.

Ghn turned.

"I've been in contact with a scholar from outside Wivvol. Don't ask how; just know that the House has its ways. His name is Orno Linus, and he's concerned about the end of the world."

"I expect we should all be *concerned* about the end of the world."

"I'm speaking of the proximate end, nephew."

"I see," Xto said. "Assuming this Linus is a Septal scholar, we're talking now of the return of the Outcast?"

"We are, and we are not. The problem with the Outcast has always been that his return is taken non-literally, as the stuff of myth and hyperbole. In all our other teachings, the influence of the Outcast has been metaphorical. You understand."

"A *literal* end of the world, then," Xto said.

"Yes. By way of whichever term you prefer."

"And soon."

"The Outcast will return within our lifetimes. Or, if that bothers you, the means for our planet's destruction will manifest within our lifetimes."

"I'm less concerned about the principle of naming than by the vehicle of delivery. How might this world-ending event transpire?"

"Brother Linus was less forthcoming on this detail, but no less convincing due to its lack. His *scholarship* is impeccable. And what he's learned is critical to the future of us all. Specifically, he's learned that the gods anticipated this moment in history and gave us the tools to survive it."

Xto rolled this around in his head for a few seconds. He wanted to render it in laic terms, but found this was simply not possible. When discussing something so improbable as the entire world ending, there was simply no way to avoid the House's lexicon.

"You're saying the Five provided Dib-kind with a weapon to fight off the Outcast?" Xto asked. "Is it the machine in the basement?"

"Not precisely," Ghn said. "It's true the engine has a role to play, but that moment is not now."

*The Engine of the World,* Xto thought. *He thinks that thing is the Engine of the World.*

Xto's inner skeptic laughed at the notion, while his inner Septal—having been silent for many years now—awoke and began clearing his throat.

"I mean the key on the desk," his uncle continued.

The key looked no more lethal now than it did a moment earlier. "The key that *unlocks* a weapon," Xto offered.

"Nearly so. As I said, there are five such keys. The Chnta chapter holds one and the Velon chapter another. A third was last known to be in the Middle Kingdoms. The fourth is believed to be in the possession of the High Hat of Pelgut, but the Dunners of Unak are notoriously tight-lipped about *everything*, so it's difficult to say. As for the fifth, it was last seen at the Khiko chapter on Dorabon, but this was before the Unitist schism so who knows where it ended up?"

"But we have *ours*," Xto said. "To defend ourselves with when the Outcast returns."

"Again, *this* is not the weapon. Nor is what it unlocks, precisely. But in order *to* unlock it, all five keys are needed."

Xto sighed.

"We're going to keep going around and around until the suns rise and I'm stranded here for the day, uncle. Is it a weapon or not?"

"It's a *defense*. And it's for the entire planet. Which is why the entire planet must unite in order to defend itself from the Outcast."

"If the keys perform the singular function of saving the world from the Outcast, it seems foolish to have split them up among the Septal chapters," Xto said.

"Yes but again, this isn't *all* the keys unlock. They hold other functions. That said, I've no doubt the Five failed to anticipate our present conditions. I don't mean the politics of the moment —although this is a hurdle as well—but the dissolution of the House as a unifying force. In another time, the High Hats of the various realms would have come together with their keys and done what was needed for the future of the planet. Now, I can't even leave the city, much less attend a colloquium overseas."

"Nor can I," Xto said. "Is that where we're heading with this? I'm not even going to be on the *planet* for the next two years, never mind attending a High Hat Colloquium in Velon or wherever these things take place."

"No, no. There will be no gathering of the High Hats. Not for this. Brother Linus is a man of great conviction, but his work remains ongoing. Not even his own High Hat has been swayed."

"Then...I'm sorry, I have no idea what you're expecting from me, uncle. This is a compelling story, but I see no role in it for myself."

Ghn shook his head. "Your creativity has been dimmed by the program, Xto. You spoke before of being as incapable of leaving the city as I am, yet in another month you'll be doing precisely that."

"Again..." Xto began, rubbing his face. He was starting to wonder if his uncle had lost his mind. "I'll be in *space*. Is there a Septal chapter floating on the ocean in the sky?"

Ghn took the key from the desk and waved it at him.

"Here's what's going to happen, Xto. This is one of the five most important objects in the history of our world. I'm giving it to you, so that you can in turn give it to Professor Orno Linus. And you're going to do this because this is what the gods have fated for you."

"You would have me give it to him in orbit?"

"*Not* in orbit. In the Midpoint, in two years. Do you understand now?"

"Not at all."

His uncle grunted, and returned to his seat, shaking his head. "I *know* you're not this dense, nephew."

"It's that you speak of things which are impossible. I understand what you're saying, but it can't be done."

"The key is no longer than your thigh, Xto. Tape it down before preflight and smuggle it with you into orbit. Keep it safe for two years, and then..."

"...and then I'll return to the touchdown runway with the key still attached to my thigh? The part where I smuggle this into space isn't what I'm having an issue with, uncle."

"You have some control over where and when you come down, do you not?"

Xto stared at the High Hat for a time.

"I see," Xto said. "You're asking me to sabotage my own ship."

"I'm *asking* you, nephew, to effect a landing at a different location: a splashdown landing in the Midpoint where Orno Linus will be waiting. Give him the key so that he can add it to the other four and save us all."

"It sounds as if Brother Linus has *none* of the keys at present," Xto said. "Precisely how much faith are you placing in this man?"

"Enough to risk your life and mine, and to willingly surrender the most sacred relic in our vaults. He *will* get it done, nephew. Now, will you do this for me? Because the day is coming, and we've run out of time."

∼

∼

"Hang on," Elicasta said, putting her hand on Xto's wrist. He recoiled, as if human contact was something he'd forgotten was possible. "There are *five* keys?"

The astronaut looked at the two of them through bleary eyes. "You know about the keys?" he asked.

"We know about one of them," Makk said. He called up the image of the one he still kept strapped to his own leg, on his voicer. "Does yours look like this?"

Xto snatched the device from him, and stared eagerly at the key. "Nearly," he said. "Different color, and the tip looks different. But this looks like the same material. Where do you have this?"

"You first," Makk said. "Where's *yours?* I'm just assuming since you've told us this much that you agreed to take it."

"I did," he said. "My uncle provided coordinates and an arrival window, and when the time came, I disabled my auto-piloting, shorted the communications systems, and crashed the shuttle pod. As promised, I was extracted from the ocean, only not by Orno Linus."

"Linus is dead," Makk said.

"I learned this later. Do you...no, you wouldn't. You must understand that returning to full gravity after two years can be quite ruinous to a person. I was told to *only* give the key to Professor Orno Linus, and also that in doing so I would be completing the set of five. But Linus wasn't at the extraction point; this Daska woman was. And when she told me she was acting on Linus's behalf...I was weak, and tired, and in a fair amount of pain. You see? I could barely breathe. If she tried to take the key by force I was in no condition to fight back. At the same time...I put up no fight at all."

"You gave the key to her," Elicasta said.

"I believed her. She explained that Orno was waiting on the mainland but that she wanted to message ahead, to let him know both that I'd arrived *and* that I had the key. So I gave it to her as evidence that the mission was a success. She never gave it back; as soon as we were tied to the dock, she was gone."

He took a drink then, as if toasting the moment of his greatest shame. Makk wanted to tell him not to beat himself up about it, because Viselle Daska was a pretty good liar. But it didn't seem like he'd be receptive to that argument.

"It was many days before I appreciated the enormity of what I'd done wrong," Xto said. "Captain Gisador helped discern that there was no person on the island by the name of Orno Linus. When we tapped the Stream to see about reaching him in his Velon home we learned that he was dead. And then..."

He looked at Elicasta.

"I know now where I've seen you before," he said.

"On the Stream," she said. "It's where everybody has seen me before."

"You are a...Veeser? Is the word? I saw your exposé featuring the Daska woman. It was how I learned *she* murdered Professor Linus."

"That isn't the most current vid on the subject," she said.

"She didn't actually do it," Makk added.

"But I saw..."

"It's a whole thing," Elicasta said. "We'll get you caught up. Viselle's definitely the wrong flavor, but she didn't kill Orno."

"She might *actually* have been working with Orno," Makk said.

"Then...she spoke the truth?"

"I mean she still skipped with your key and all," Elicasta said. "That was kinda off. In her brand, though."

Xto smiled at her. "I thought my poor understanding of your words was due to a shortness in my education in the common tongue, but you speak strangely, don't you?"

"You get used to it," Makk said.

"It's how they speak on the Stream," Xto said. "I've had little else to do since my splashdown but catch up on the world by way of the Stream."

"And drink," Makk added.

"Yes, and drink. So now Daska has my key and this one," Xto said, tapping Makk's voicer. "I suppose she's collecting all five for herself? For what good it does."

"She doesn't have this one," Makk said. "We do."

"Pretend she *does* have all five," Elicasta said. "And pretend she meant to use them like your uncle said. Where would that happen? Did he say?"

"He did not. Uncle intimated the existence of a sacred location, but not where it happened to be."

"Sounded like he was implying that it wasn't in Velon, Chnta, the Middle Kingdoms, Pelgut or Khiko," Makk said. "Where does that leave?"

"Every other part of the planet," Elicasta said. "Xto, what did you mean by, *for what good it does?*"

"Because none of it matters. I don't know what Linus's true intent was—theft, perhaps. But there is no Outcast, or the Five. It's all a lie. I know that now."

Makk didn't know quite what to say. He never expected to meet a Wivvolian with a faith to *lose*, but now that he had he wasn't sure what to do about it. Makk had himself been arguing much the same thing, pursuing Viselle primarily because she needed to be caught and because he wanted to know more about what Orno told her. But he wasn't doing that because he *believed* the Outcast was coming. What *he* believed was that Orno Linus and Ba-Ugna Kev believed it. And evidently, the High Hat of Chnta believed it too.

If nothing else, it argued that Professor Linus had been an incredibly persuasive man.

So Makk was fully on board with Xto's assertion that this whole thing was ridiculous. This left him temporarily unsure as to where to take this questioning next.

Fortunately, Elicasta was there to pick up the thread.

"Why do you say that?" she asked. "Because Viselle took your key?"

"Before then. I delivered the key as asked because I made a vow to do so. My shame is in not *keeping* it when it was clear the man I promised to hand it to was dead. And it's true uncle considered it the most sacred relic in Wivvol. But I realized before then that none of it was real. Uncle is fooling himself. All of them are."

"*All of them* meaning the Septals?" Makk asked. "As a whole. You're passing judgment on the entire House."

"I'm in a position to. I've seen..."

He stopped himself, and took another good look at Elicasta.

"That apparatus you wear on your head," he said, pointing. "This is how you create for the Stream, yes?"

"It is," she said.

"Is it on right now?"

"There'd be a light," she said, which didn't really answer the question.

Makk knew she had a default panic mode setting that only streamed if the gear was ripped from her head, but using anything she captured in a *non*-emergency situation would cost her the Veeser flag. Xto probably didn't need to know all of that, though.

"Do you want it to be?" Elicasta asked.

"I would only like to know to whom I'm revealing state secrets beforehand: you and the detective only, or the entire world? Unless they aren't secrets at all. How much do you...? We need another round of drinks."

He waved to Vira at the bar, who responded with a nod and an obscene gesture.

"I don't think we *need*..." Elicasta started to say.

"You will," Xto said. "I promise. But, please answer this: how much does the world know about what my country is doing in space? I have the assurances of the Chancellery that *nobody* knows, but it's a fact that the state is fully capable of lying to its people and to itself as well."

"We don't know anything," Makk said. "It's not a secret that you guys go up a lot, but nobody's sure why."

"I've heard a bunch of theories," Elicasta said. "Nothing I'd stake a rep on."

"Very well. Then I will explain, and when I am done you will understand why I drink. It's the only thing that makes sense. Because I have learned that the Haven is empty, Elicasta Sangristy. The Haven is empty and the gods are missing, if they were ever there at all."

# Chapter Four

Xto took the key from his uncle, but he didn't carry it with him into the *Extraplanetary Project for the Future of All;* instead, he hid it in his bedsprings and did his best —during the day—to pretend it wasn't there.

His fear of being detected overrode any sense of fealty to the Septals. Yes, when he took ownership of the artifact, he did swear an oath to do as his uncle asked. And this was no trivial thing. Ghn Tbyct was a father to Xto in all the ways that mattered; certainly more so than his father by blood.

But a lot could happen in his two years in space.

*Maybe this Orno Linus's scheme will evaporate and there will be no need to self-sabotage my reentry,* he thought. *Provided I return at all.*

This was, after all, a simply lunatic story that not even the highest ranking Septals believed, from the sound of it. Surely by the time Xto's tour was up, someone—Linus, or someone else— would work out that the Outcast scenario was off by centuries or wrong entirely.

Why risk having the key discovered, then, if it turned out to be an unnecessary risk all along?

But Uncle Ghn's last words wore him down.

"This is your path, Xto," he'd said. "It's your birthright. It isn't happenstance that you are the only one who can do this; the gods have chosen this path for you. Rejecting the will of the gods invites the Outcast into your heart, and I mean that more literally now than I might have before. Believe that this is real because *I* do."

*My birthright.*

So it was that after two weeks of recalcitrance, Xto removed Javilon's key from the bedsprings and strapped it to his leg.

He was formally reassigned to the base two days later.

~

The *EPFA* rocket compound was a small city unto itself. In addition to the launch pads—of which there were seven—there was a fully operational and always-in-use airfield, an entire warehouse district, three neighborhoods of residential bunkers, and the massive Central Operations with its enormous radio tower.

The tower was what caught the eye first. It was the tallest structure in Wivvol and the second-tallest in the *world* after the Tether in Velon. Its tip touched the clouds, from where it could line-of-sight communicate with two-thirds of the sky. (Wivvol's string of orbital satellites could do the same—and actually covered 100%—but the state didn't own the sky, and so mistrusted it.)

After that, it was the warehouses that drew the most attention, and the most questions...even if those questions were only ever directed inward. Trucks arrived weekly with raw material that was then loaded into the warehouses, to be employed in some way that wasn't obvious to anyone interested in examining it critically. There were sometimes active building projects taking place at the rocket compound, but those projects didn't justify the quantity of material. *Nothing* did, seemingly.

Whenever Xto approached the campus on the train, he wondered what the satellites thought of all of this. Or rather, the owners of those satellites—Inimata, primarily, but also Unak and Ghon-Dik, and the communications satellites of non-governmental corporations. All of them no doubt had at least one eye looking askance at Wivvol to see what the insular nation was up to. What did *they* imagine was going on?

The state's formal answer to the question of what the rest of the world knew and did not know about the inner workings of Wivvol was brilliantly contradictory. It was sometimes the case that the state justified absolute control over its secrets because Wivvol was surrounded by cunning and treacherous enemies. Other times, it was said that the state was *so* much smarter than its imbecilic and inferior neighbors that even if those neighbors were told *exactly* what was going on with the rocket program, they were incapable of grasping its genius.

That these managed to both be true at the same time didn't evidently bother anyone but Xto.

His assigned apartment was in the VIP section of the compound, in a row of two-level buildings set apart from the denser four-level structures housing the majority of the staff. It was twice the size of his permanent residence downtown, with a view of the distant launchpads and the sunset, a fully stocked kitchen, and—a big deal, as Xto had never owned or used one—a full bathtub.

Nearly every square centimader was on optical. They didn't even try to hide it; tiny black domes behind which was a lens rested in recessed points all over the apartment.

Like everyone else on Wivvol—save perhaps for certain cabinet members—Xto had spent his entire life under passive observation from the state. It was something he was so accustomed to he never even thought about it...until now. *Now* he had something to hide.

*How am I going to do this?* he wondered. Then he thought again about not doing it at all.

But the time for that was past. He'd already brought the key in with him; leaving it behind in the state-owned apartment on the state-owned compound would be worse than taking it off-planet, even if after two years he simply touched down where he was supposed to and ended up back in this same apartment with the artifact still on his person.

As he sat on his new bed, staring at the one bag he was allowed to bring—a mixture of personal items and off-duty clothing—feeling the dressing on his thigh that held the key in place itch suggestively, there was a knock on the door.

It was Trebnvto, with a bottle of potato wine in his hands and a smile on his face.

"Xto!" he declared. "Finally, you've decided to bunk with the rest of us plebes."

"Oh shut up," Xto said, "and get in here before the entire building hears you."

There was little real risk of this, as the majority of the building was empty. With another astronaut going up every month for a two-year tour, at *least* thirty-two of the apartments were vacant at any given time. Add in the number that were vacant because the occupant never returned at all, and it felt like Xto was residing in an unused building.

Trebnvto sauntered past Xto and into the kitchen, where he proceeded to correctly locate the knife drawer and the cabinet with the glasses—the furnishings were standardized—and went about opening the bottle.

"That doesn't look like a Wivvolian brand," Xto noted.

"It is not! It's from Botzis, by way of Lladn, I believe. They do not, to my understanding, grow potatoes on Botzis."

"And how did it arrive in my kitchen?"

"I have ways!"

"I don't doubt it," Xto said. "My concern is that, given where you're standing right now, I've inadvertently taken possession of contraband. On top of which, alcoholic consumption is strongly condemned by the program at *any* time, daylight or no."

Trebnvto laughed, and filled the glasses. "You are being ridiculous," he said.

"I am being practical."

"They won't do anything. Here I'll show you."

He held the bottle up to the nearest optical, close enough so that the observer presumed to be on the other side of it would have no trouble reading the label.

"La, la, look at the Lladn label!" Trebnvto said, performing a brief, unsanctioned dance.

"Treb..."

"No, hold on." He froze where he was. "I hear no approaching army, do you?" he asked.

"That proves nothing," Xto said.

"But it does!"

Trebnvto put the bottle down, picked up the glasses, and handed Xto one of them.

Xto just stared at the glass.

"What is it?" Trebnvto asked. "Don't say it's not your drink; we both know this is untrue."

"My security being jeopardized by others telling me not to worry has become a problem of late," Xto said.

"What does *that* mean?"

"Nothing." Xto downed his wine in one gulp. "Thank you for the potato wine. It's very good."

"Ahh. You're not any fun." Trebnvto snatched the glass from his hand and refilled it. "Come on, let's *really* celebrate. You don't report until the morning and your dietary panel doesn't begin until next week."

"I shouldn't."

"This is your problem, Xto. I've been telling you, but you weren't listening to me. The *reason* to move to the compound as soon as it's offered is this: *nobody cares* what you do here. You can no longer embarrass the state with a public error, because there *is* no public in front of which to err. Twice the eyes but half the concern. You see?"

To illustrate this point, Trebnvto finished his glass, refilled it, and finished it again.

"You would not be the first to report for duty still drunk from the nighttime," he said. "And you know it. Remember Plzi? He was tipsy every morning before his scheduled. You saw it yourself."

"I remember," Xto said. "He may have been drunk the *day* he was scheduled. I recall he barely made orbit safely. But Plzi is the son of the transport chair. They would have sent him up unconscious if they had to."

Treb laughed. "Look who's talking."

"Point taken. I would still rather not test the fences. Nor should you. You've not gotten scheduled yet, and you've been waiting longer than I have."

"I'm marked to follow *you*, actually, but we'll see if that comes true," Trebnvto said. "My time will come as soon as they run out of legacies to send first. Come."

"Come where?"

Trebnvto put his glass down and gestured grandly to the room. "I have to give you your tour."

"The apartment isn't *that* large, Treb," Xto said.

"Yes, but there are certain nuances you may not yet appreciate. Have you seen the bathroom?"

"I have."

"No, you have not. Rather, you haven't seen all there is to see in there."

"Honestly, I don't..."

"Oh just follow me, Xto, Honestly."

Xto put down his glass and followed his friend into the

spacious bathroom, which looked precisely the same as it had the last time Xto had been in there.

"Now then," Trebnvto said, "look up in the corner. What do you see?"

"You mean, the dome for the optical lens?"

"That *is* what I mean. Note that it is over the toilet, which means it cannot see you *on* the toilet."

"I've already noted this, yes. Thank you?"

"It *can* see you at the sink, and...have you *looked at* this tub? Is it not magnificent?"

"Treb, really..."

"Hold on."

Trebnvto opened the mirrored cabinet over the sink, such that the mirror faced the door, and also the optical. Then he stepped past the tub, in a space roughly one mader square.

"Come, stand next to me," Trebnvto said.

Xto did; now they were chest-to-chest. Trebnvto took him by the shoulders and spun him around.

"With the design of the bathroom and the positioning of the optical," Treb said, "the only way to see into this corner is to use the reflection from the mirror. Which means that right now, we are blissfully unobserved by the state."

"I see," Xto said, turning. "I assume they know of this."

"I'm sure they do. But there's no exit here, so what's the worst that could happen?"

"Thank you," he said, thinking again of the key bound to his thigh, "this *is* useful."

"You're welcome."

Then Trebnvto turned Xto back around and kissed him on the lips.

For three seconds of weakness, Xto let him do it. Then he pushed away.

"No," he said. "We cannot."

"We can do a *little*," Treb said with a smile. "They can't see and they don't care."

"They care about *this*," Xto said. "My family connections might save me, but not you."

Treb shrugged. "It's the risk that makes it fun," he said.

"Not for me."

Xto stepped out the corner, closed the mirror cabinet, and left the bathroom. Trebnvto followed, sulking all the way.

"I'm sorry," Treb said. "I was just having fun."

"I know."

"I've upset you."

Xto returned to the table, and poured himself another glass of his friend's contraband.

"It isn't you that's upset me," Xto said. "We can't *do* any of that here, and you know it, but that isn't why either."

"I'm only being a tease, Xto…"

"There are images, Treb. I've seen them."

"Images? Of what?"

"Of *us*."

Trebnvto laughed. "Doing what?"

Xto just stared at him.

"No," Treb said. "There couldn't be. Not *that*."

"No," Xto said. "*Not* that. But sufficiently compromising that *that* is fairly implied."

"Who has these images?"

Xto downed his glass and capped the bottle before he felt compelled to keep going until he'd discovered the bottom. "It doesn't matter who has them," he said. "They exist, and that should be enough to worry us both. I don't believe the owner of these images intends to use them against us, but you should know. And, we should stop our promiscuousness now and count ourselves lucky."

"That's the word you would choose?" Trebnvto asked. "Promiscuousness?"

"It's the word I'm choosing right *now*, Treb."

"Well," he said. He stared at Xto, who couldn't bring himself to maintain eye contact. Treb reached out, halfway across the distance between them, waiting for Xto to meet him there. When he didn't, Treb's hand fell. He looked unbelievably sad, and—given he was facing an optical Xto had carefully put to his own back— didn't appear to care who noticed.

"It used to be a different word," Trebnvto said.

"We were being foolish," Xto said.

"You really believe that?"

*No,* Xto thought.

"It's for the best," Xto said.

"Of course," Trebnvto muttered. "Then... Welcome to the base apartments, Citizen Djbbit. Enjoy the gift. I look forward to tomorrow's training, as always."

Treb left then, expressing his dissatisfaction by aggressively closing the door on his way out.

"It's for the best," Xto said again, only this time for his own sake.

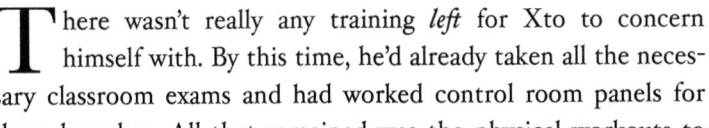

∼

There wasn't really any training *left* for Xto to concern himself with. By this time, he'd already taken all the necessary classroom exams and had worked control room panels for three launches. All that remained was the physical workouts to maintain his fitness-for-departure and the weekly extreme-G training. (The latter was literally designed to force him to vomit after high-gravity compression; the G-force applied was greater than he'd face at any point in his two year off-planet cycle. Xto's greatest accomplishment to this point was that he was the only person in the history of the *EPFA* to have never passed out during this test.)

He spent his morning working out enough to get his pulse rate up and push the alcohol out his pores before reporting to what would be a bystander of an afternoon: Tbux Opygy's launch was on.

Tbux was supposed to have gone up a week prior, but the weather had been less-than-optimal during the favored windows, so she was held back. Now, on a glorious blue-sky day, her mission had been approved to proceed.

They were already midway through a ninety minute countdown by the time Xto reached the control center, located on the fourth (and top) floor of the Central Operations building beside the majestic radio tower. Central Operations was an artless square of a thing, an aesthetic surrender to function over form. At least on the outside. Inside, it was polished metal and glass under high ceilings and bright lights. The grand hall of the entryway featured half-sized mockups of the rocket program's most memorable landmark vessels dangling from above. It was designed to impress, although *who* was supposed to be impressed by it was an unanswered question.

Outside of non-rocket program affiliated chairs, the *EPFA* entertained no guests and new recruits didn't see the inside of Central Operations until they'd passed their first practicum more than a year in, which was well beyond the impressionable stage of their involvement. The logical conclusion, then, was that the grand hall was designed so that the heads of the rocket program could begin each day *self*-impressed.

Xto had stopped looking up on his way down the hall some time ago. The last time he *did*, he noted that none of the admirable failures of the program—*failures* in the sense that the mission was unsuccessful, *admirable* in the sense that much was learned by said failures—were represented. The models were more than just a celebration of the program's history, then; they were a rewriting of it.

Not that this was a surprise. Up until his second year, Xto didn't even receive intelligence on the failed missions, and then it was only the ones from which lessons could be gleaned. They were portrayed as foredoomed, accounting to a weakness on someone's part, rather than as the unavoidable accidents they were. Which meant Xto ended up taking another lesson from those failures: Regardless of why, should his own mission fail history will record it as an error on his part. Provided history recorded it at all.

Past the grand hall, it was an unceremonious hike up four flights of stairs on an ID-card-only stairwell that happened to be the fastest way to the top. Xto emerged in a corner of the control center.

The floor was already a bustle of motion. Two dozen citizens occupied rows upon rows of control panels, each displaying readouts from some minute portion of the rockets, the shuttle riding the top of the rockets, the astronaut within the shuttle, or the cargo crate at rest between the astronaut and the rockets. One wall of the room was taken up by a macro view of the entire mission, quite literally: the rocket was on a launching pad less than a kalomader from them, visible through a large window.

There were *better* views of the launch; most obviously the screen hanging from the ceiling just before the window, featuring the launch platform up-close and at multiple angles. Xto preferred to watch from the window. It was easy to forget this was *really happening* when looking at it through the lens of an optical.

"Xto!" Plaquib Mh declared loudly from across the floor. "Get over here."

Plaquib was the head of the command center and a minor legend within the *EPFA*. He'd done five tours before retiring from active aeronautics to run Central Operations and—presumably, given his current girth—to overindulge in the dining largesse accorded to a minor legend.

Xto wove his way to the back of the room. The floor was raked slightly, so that each row's occupant had a clean look at the viewscreens. Plaquib's station sat in the center of the highest point in the room. From there, he could speak to anyone else, eye-to-eye, and/or hurl projectiles as appropriate.

"Come on, come on," Plaquib barked impatiently.

"We're forty minutes from launch," Xto said. "Surely there is no crisis for which I'm the solution."

"It's ever so with you Djbbits, thinking you know better."

Plaquib handed Xto a headset.

"Where do you want me?" Xto asked. For the last launch, he took a position at attitude. His role was to stare at a screen to observe the main thrust rocket's micro-adjustments in response to atmospheric randomness. Should a divergence of greater than two factors manifest, Xto was expected to *do* nothing, aside from announcing that this had happened. It was, in short, a task that could be handled by a sensor attached to an alarm.

"Right here; Citizen Opygy awaits. Or did no-one tell you that yours is the next mission?"

"Ah."

For a country that considered religious belief antithetical to the interests of the state, Wivvol certainly had a lot of faith-centric rituals built into the day-to-day. The most obvious example: the number eleven was considered bad luck, so none of the trains had arrival or departure times ending in 11, and children born at that time of day were considered unlucky. Less obvious were rituals like the one Citizen Mh was tasking Xto with now.

It had been a normal thing for some time for the astronaut about to depart to share words with the one scheduled to follow him or her into orbit. This had been going on since before Xto was born, and probably before Plaquib was born as well. But where it went from *a thing we always do* to *an honored ritual* was a conversation that failed to take place.

Xto didn't even know when this happened or which astronauts it involved, for the simple reason that both the impending flight and the subsequent one ended in tragedy and since the *EPFA* didn't discuss these things, the details were lost to history.

That's provided it happened at all, about which Xto was supremely skeptical. But as was often the case with ritualized superstition, skepticism hardly mattered in the face of the *why take the chance?* counterpoint.

He took the headset from Plaquib and slipped it on.

"Hello, Tbux," Xto said. He hit a button on the console that switched the conversation to a private line. Hardly anybody believed it was *actually* private, but they acted like it was anyway. "How are the bugs treating you?"

"They've left me alone, blessedly," she said. "But thanks for asking; you've no doubt awoken them."

"The bugs" was what they called it when, after spending too much time in the spacesuit one's body starts to sweat. It wasn't so bad as long as one didn't think about it, but Xto had just made sure she *was* thinking about it. It was a mild act of familial cruelty he had no doubt would be visited upon him in some form when it was his turn atop the rocket.

"How do you feel?" he asked.

"Ready to get off this damned planet, Xto, if you must know. You'll feel the same, especially after quarantine. I think that's the entire point."

"The *point* is to make sure you go up healthy."

"That's a lie. It's to ensure you're so terrifically bored you think of nothing better than to jam a rocket up your ass."

Xto always liked Tbux. One of only seventeen women currently active in the ground program, Tbux was possibly the most graphically colorful person he knew. *Dissident-mouth* was what she called it. They bonded to a certain extent thanks to their (very private) proclivities: she greatly preferred the company of other women, and Xto greatly preferred the company of other men. Thus, when they went out together, their socializations with others looked collectively heterosexual.

"Well, as long as you don't *mind* having that rocket up there," he said, cleaning things up on his end given he was in earshot of a number of people.

"Provided my ashes still leave the stratosphere, I'm happy," she said. "Are you ready for your turn, Xto?"

"When it happens, it will happen."

"Even-keeled as ever, Citizen Djbbit. When I was where you are a month ago, Zga Tze told me the dirtiest joke he knew. He claimed it was told to him by Elvtol Mnopitat, and so on. The *idea* is to make it difficult for the one on the ground to keep a straight face. Problem is, either the joke isn't funny or Zga told it wrong. But I'm gonna tell it to you anyway. First though, I need you to do me a favor. There's an envelope stuck in the box spring in my apartment. If me and the rocket up my ass don't survive our rapid departure from this miserable globe, I want you to find that envelope and make sure it gets to the addressee."

Xto thought of all the ways what she was asking was completely impossible, beginning with gaining access to her apartment in the first place. Thanks to his family connections, everyone assumed he had more flexibility than he really did. He probably *did*, but not enough to get into her box spring without anyone noticing.

"Of course," he said. "But it will never come to that. You're going to greet me at the dock in the skies a month from now."

"I will indeed," she said. "Now: Three Kvaltian pirates walk into a Dorabon whorehouse..."

~

Tbux Opygy's takeoff was uneventful. The rockets performed as expected and in short time her shuttle and the attendant freight had made it into orbit, the boosters had been ejected and were disintegrating on reentry, and Xto wasn't facing the prospect of trying to keep his promise to a fellow astronaut.

This was hardly a surprise. The *Extraplanetary Project for the Future of All* was currently on an accident-free streak of over a hundred; although it had to be said that this was a streak relating specifically to takeoffs. The official consecutive record for astronauts returning home at the end of their two years was smaller.

The *actual* number was smaller still. On many occasions, the *EPFA* staged a return that never happened, although not necessarily due to a fatality. Some who went up simply never came back down again.

Xto waited until Tbux formally verified that she was safe to begin the next phase of her mission, and then he abandoned the control center, anticipating a light afternoon of text review.

He was met by two guards in the hall.

"Citizen Djbbit?" one asked.

"Yes. Is there a problem?"

"We've been tasked with escorting you to the chair's office. Please follow us."

"I have no open matters with the chair," Xto said. As if this would help.

"Please come with us," he repeated.

The guards flanked him, and together they marched to see the chair. It wasn't far; Ayk's office took up half of the third floor of the same building, so it was only a matter of going down a flight and turning left.

"You can go in directly," Ayk's scheduling assistant said, from his desk in the antechamber. "She's expecting you."

One guard opened the door while the other stood behind Xto, in the event he chose this moment to run or required a shove to cross the threshold. He stepped in, and felt the door close behind him.

Xto had met rocket program chair Ebt Ayk in person on five occasions prior, and conversed with her a dozen other times via optical. She was an elderly citizen, stooped by time and often seemingly adrift in minor confusions. But at least some of that confusion was an act; Citizen Ayk was dangerously clever.

Her office was large but mostly empty. (As was the case in most of Wivvol, it seemed, one's significance was measured in square maders, and not by the objects that filled up those square maders.) She was standing before her desk at the other end of the room, speaking to a man Xto didn't recognize.

Nobody else was in the room, which Xto interpreted to mean that he was *not* in some manner of trouble.

"Astronaut Djbbit, good," Ayk said. "Come."

"Humbly, it's Citizen Djbbit for now," Xto said.

"Yes, yes. The honorific is a few weeks premature, yes. But time is the only remaining obstacle, is it not?"

*A lot can happen in a few weeks,* he thought.

"Yes, Chairwoman Ayk. Of course."

"I would like you to meet Citizen Jrgap."

"Commerce chair Idlo Jrgap?" Xto asked. Given the company, this qualified as an impertinent outburst.

"The same," Jrgap said, stepping forward to shake Xto's hand. "It's a special honor to meet you, Xto Djbbit."

Xto didn't know whether to bow—the appropriate greeting given their respective stations—or return the handshake. He opted for the latter, and hoped it wasn't a grave insult.

"The honor is entirely mine, Citizen Jrgap."

"The chair is here today to let the both of us in on a secret, Xto," Ayk said. "Chairman Jrgap will be retiring next month."

"I... see," Xto said, his confusion obvious. "Your wisdom will be missed, I am certain."

Xto had literally no idea what the responsibilities of the commerce chair were, nor what would happen if one was replaced. This was true for essentially every government position except possibly the position of rocket program chair and even then, the nature of Ebt Ayk's duties eluded him almost entirely.

All he'd ever heard her do was agree with whatever consensus had already been reached by others beforehand.

Jrgap laughed, which was unexpected. "As always, Ebt is prolonging your discomfort on a whim. You want to know why *you're* here."

Ayk smiled, which Xto didn't realize she knew how to do.

"Citizen Djbbit," she said, "you remain top-grade in wingplane piloting, do you not?"

"I do."

"Excellent. Chairman Jrgap has a favor to ask of us before his retirement is official."

"I wish to see the stars in the daytime," Jrgap said.

"And you're going to take him there," Ayk said.

## Chapter Five

There were a dozen pilots at the center who were as qualified as Xto to take the honorable chair on his honorable joyride. Two of them were in the astronautical program, only slated to go up later. Which meant there was a reason Xto was doing this, specifically, rather than someone else.

He didn't know what that reason was, nor how to ask, so he didn't.

The flight was scheduled for the following morning.

"That is a beast of a wingplane," were the first words out of Jrgap's mouth, when he met up with Xto beside the steps leading to the plane. He'd changed from the drab formalwear of his council seat into an ill-fitting flight suit.

"Yes, sir," Xto said. "It's a Khth class. Very powerful."

"*Very* large for just two people."

"The middle chamber is mostly empty. We use it for zero-gravitational exercises. But we could take one of the speeders if you prefer. They *also* seat two and will get us there in half the time."

"No, Citizen Djbbit. This is the plane I requested. A speed-wing would likely kill me before we reached the troposphere. I just didn't realize how massive the Khth was."

"Sir, if it's comfort you're seeking, I could recommend an inflatable. The Middle Kingdoms have many dirigibles to spare, I'm told."

Jrgap laughed. "And that would take *too* long," he said. "Besides, those don't get nearly high enough, do they? Now, enough of this 'sir' and 'citizen' and 'honorable chair'. As long as I am your copilot you will call me Idlo."

"Are you... do you mean to take the stick? Have you any experience?"

"No, and no. But there is only two of us and *you* are the pilot. By elimination I must therefore be the copilot. Don't be so nervous, Xto, I guarantee there is no way for you to wrong-foot so grievously with me as to harm your standing. Now, let's get going."

~

The runway had been cleared well in advance; all incoming and outgoing flight schedules had been adjusted to accommodate the commerce chair's special request. This meant the most time-consuming element of in-atmosphere flight—waiting for the traffic controller to show favor—had been eliminated from the equation. Once Xto had completed his checklist, it was under an hour before they were airborne.

Idlo Jrgap was belted into the copilot seat. He looked as out-of-place in the chair as he did in the flight suit. Xto wondered if the helmet and oxygen system attached to his collar even worked.

The older man managed to tolerate the strain of their initial climb without complaint. Mindful of the brittleness of his passenger, Xto tried to make it a smooth transition, but there was really no way to avoid the high G-force entirely. Regular passenger wing-planes, or the more common helos couldn't compare.

"This was nearly the way," Idlo said, once they'd leveled off a bit. They were now soaring above the farmland of northern Wivvol.

"What was?"

"Planes. Back before you or I were born. Before my *parents* were born, when the idea of exploring space first blossomed in the recesses of the Chancellery...they thought they could do it with wingplanes."

"We nearly can," Xto said.

"Yes. *Nearly*. Nearly is the best I can expect at my age. I wanted to do it *all*, of course. When I was a child I wanted nothing but to be one of the *paltxmxflutz*. Don't look surprised; nobody *aspires* to be commerce chair. Not in their youth."

"It's not that. I've not heard the archaic in some time."

"*Paltxmxflutz*? I know. We borrow 'astronaut' from the common tongue instead. Easier to say, but so mundane. You know the roots?"

"I don't believe I do, no."

"Ah! *Paltxt, mxflah,* and *utz*," Idlo said.

"Captain of the vessel on the ocean in the sky," Xto translated.

"Precisely! The compounded word is ungainly, but there's such poetry underneath, don't you think?"

"Yes, I see what you mean."

They were above the clouds now. Xto kept them on a gradual incline. If he did this right, they'd reach the plane's vertical limit in plenty of time to return to base before the continent spun away beneath them.

"I imagined your father would have shared that with you," Idlo said.

"He did not."

"Ah," Idlo said. He fell silent for a few beats. Then: "I knew him. Your father. Or, I guess I should say, I *know* him; it's only that we've not spoken for twenty years. We were close one time."

Xto strained to imagine his father being *close* to anyone, but he'd only ever known him to be either distant or absent entirely.

"Were you?" Xto asked.

"Very much so. We both strove to enter the rocket program, but...it was my eyesight, they said. And my wind. I argued that the eyes can be corrected and I've no cause to run when in space, but I was serenading the deaf. And so it was that the name Mondr Djbbit became synonymous with the rocket program, while I got to hold his purse."

Xto laughed, which was inappropriate. "You hold the entire country's purse, chairman," he said. "Not just that of the *EPFA*."

"These days? There's hardly a difference."

"An interesting perspective," Xto said.

"It's not merely a *perspective*, young man. I grant that it qualifies as an *exaggeration*, but not a tremendous one."

They were coming up to the point where it felt as if the planet below them was falling away. Dib's curve could be seen on the horizon.

"Your wish to see the stars in the daytime is about to be fulfilled," Xto said. "We're close to our nadir."

"Very well, thank you. As I told Ebt, my dreams of space flight are long gone, but at least I can get close this one time. Before they take my chair from me."

"Forgive me if this is impertinent, but I thought you were retiring."

"Oh, yes. I am. It's a curious word, though, isn't it? The implication is that the retiree initiates the process. Like, *volunteer*. You are, technically, a volunteer in this program and yet I believe it was your father who *volunteered* you, long ago."

"You're *being* retired," Xto offered.

"That would be more accurate," Idlo said. "You know, I admire you, Xto."

"Thank you for saying so."

"I mean it. You could have been utterly unqualified for space flight and they would have sent you anyway. Instead, you've made yourself into a prime candidate. I imagine you'd have made the program regardless of your family name."

"Not much good in making it to space if I'm not fit enough to survive the journey," Xto said.

Idlo laughed. "Well, that's true. Ah! Here we are!"

The nose of the plane poked up through the top of the stratosphere, and for the merest of seconds, they could see stars.

"Beautiful," Idlo said.

They floated at the edge of the sky for as long as they could, but then the groaning from the wingplane—which was at the very limits of its design specs—became too great to ignore.

"I have to turn back now," Xto said.

"Of course. Would that I had the appropriate device to capture an image of this moment."

He meant a voicer, which was not *entirely* prohibited for use among the citizens of Wivvol—not in the same way as they were in the Middle Kingdoms, for instance—but *effectively* so. There was the state-run Stream that carried information nobody trusted with no private use—no Streamers, verified or otherwise—permitted. No citizen within Wivvol could access the outside Stream. Not even on a pirated device.

Despite all of that, Xto was surprised the honorable chair had nothing he could use to capture an image. Xto had no need for a voicer, but surely high members of the Chancellery did.

Xto leveled them off and brought the nose down, and the stars disappeared behind the wisps of the upper atmosphere; they were on their way back to the surface.

"If the experience of weightlessness is on your agenda, now would be the time for it," Xto said.

"It is!" Idlo said. "Will you join me?"

"For a time." Xto set the Khth dash into an auto-function that would send the craft into a steady corkscrew dive, and then he set an alarm. "I'll have to return to the controls after three minutes of weightlessness. It can continue for another two, but not safely without someone at the stick."

"Excellent."

Xto unbuckled his harness and waited for Idlo to do the same. Then he pushed the *initiate* button, led the older man into the barrel-shaped main section of the plane, and closed the door behind them. In another ten seconds, they felt the plane's trajectory change into a rapid plummet.

"Oh," Idlo said, holding his stomach. "I feel it here. How interesting."

"I'm told the transition to weightlessness in this simulator is more drastic than in space flight."

"I've heard much the same." Idlo pushed off the wall he was against and floated into the middle of the cabin. He reached up at one of the grips on the ceiling and held on. "Marvelous."

"You handle yourself well," Xto said, staying against the wall near the door. He'd trained a dozen times in this very space and had no interest in doing so on this occasion.

"Thank you."

It was curious, Xto thought; the older man didn't appear to be deriving any joy from the experience for which he'd no doubt spent a good deal of political capital to arrange.

Something felt off.

Idlo headed to the far end of the cabin.

"I wonder if you could deliver a message for me, Astronaut Djbbit," he said, his back turned. "To your father."

"I've...not spoken to my father in some time, sir," Xto said. "We don't...we are not close."

"I understand. That's why this is a favor. You *don't* speak to him often, this I already know. But you *can* and *will* be speaking shortly. And because you are his son? Hopefully he will listen."

"I suppose. But you are old friends, as you've explained. You're also the commerce chair. Surely you have the necessary influence to compel him to answer a message."

"I'm afraid none of us have that power." Idlo smiled. "You know so little. I forget sometimes that our public face is the only one most ever see. Even for someone as connected as yourself."

His eyes drifted to the digital clock counting down the time they had left in the cabin, and then back to Xto.

"I will be blunt, Astronaut Djbbit. According to your father, the grand plan of which you are a part has *found* something. We don't know what it is or where in the sky it's located, and we don't know this because he has refused to provide us with that information. Unfortunately, we also don't know if what he's reporting is even *true*, or merely a story to compel us to continue to fund the project."

"Is there a risk that the project will be discontinued?" Xto asked. It was the first he'd heard of any such threat.

"Politically? Not at this time. The majority of the Chancellery continues to believe Mondr's wild assertions. But politics isn't the only consideration. Politics can't alter reality, much as my cohort largely believe otherwise, and the reality is, our country is facing an economic catastrophe."

"I don't understand."

"We can't afford to keep sending raw material we *could* be selling on the international market into space."

"But, our economy is the greatest in the world!" Xto said, and then felt embarrassed for having regurgitated Chancellery propaganda to a member of the council.

"It *was*," Idlo agreed, patiently. "In the days when our shipping vessels rode the Great Current with goods from one end of the globe to the other...it was. Back then, a scheme to explore the *next* vast ocean for even greater riches made sense. But nothing we've sent *up* has translated into value coming back *down*, and now the surplus is gone. The world has changed, Xto. You know it. There are now great ships using null-gravitational technology our own government refuses to leverage for itself. They no longer need our ships, and the Chancellery refuses to believe it."

"This is the message you would have me take to my father? How do you imagine he can help?"

"If even a third of the raw material he's demanding for his great adventure was redirected to exports, it might be possible for the country to right itself. Failing that, a sincere effort to monetize what he has found somehow—assuming *that* much is even true and not a ploy to leverage more goods—might make a difference. Mondr's ignored the realities of the country feeding his program for too long."

"I see. Well. I will tell him all of this when the chance arises."

Idlo smiled. "That is not the message, my young friend. It's only the context."

The three-minute alarm was sounding now. Xto would have to return to the cockpit.

"Very well," Xto said. "What *is* the message?"

"They blame me," Idlo said, "for the economic downturn that is their own doing. Much easier to accuse the sitting commerce chair of failing to massage reality to align with their outdated conception of it than to adjust their understanding to the new reality."

He reached into a pocket of his flight suit and pulled out a projectile gun.

"Sir!"

"Don't come closer, Xto," Idlo said. "You don't have enough time to cross the cabin to grapple with me and still reach the cockpit."

"Firing one of those in a wingplane is a great danger to us both."

"Only to you. But do not worry; I won't put a hole in your outer wall. Besides, I am told you're a top-grade pilot."

"Chairman Jrgap, please..."

"*This* is my message to your father," Idlo said. Then he stuck the barrel of the gun under his chin and pulled the trigger.

The bullet tore through the commerce chair's head and out

the back. Blood spattered out of the skull along with bits of skin and bone and brains, some of which spread backwards and painted the wall. The spent slug continued along a trajectory the older man clearly chose with some forethought; it terminated harmlessly in an internal support bulwark, rather than in one of the windows.

He died instantly, his body carried in a gentle somersault with blood from the headwound rolling out and collecting in midair globules. It was so interesting that, after adjusting to the shock of the act, Xto lost several seconds he should have been spending in the cockpit just watching the aftereffect of a suicide in zero gravity.

The second alarm woke him from his reverie. That was the alarm caused by the wingplane's auto-function, notifying whomever that circumstances had arisen which were beyond the program's capacity to cope.

Xto opened the cockpit door and drifted to the front, maneuvering expertly in the zero-gravity until he was back in the seat. He strapped himself in, put his hand on the stick, and deactivated the auto-functionality.

Pulling the plane from the dive was like waking abruptly from a nightmare. Gravity reasserted, his ears popped, and everything was somehow louder, brighter and harsher. He'd left the door to the main cabin open so in addition to all of the alarms of displeasure he was getting from the plane he had to endure the sound of Idlo Jrgap's body as it dropped to the floor with a wet thud.

"Flight KH-1, please respond," the base controller said over the radiograph. "Please adjust your angle of descent. We have you coming in too steep."

"Affirm, control," Xto said. "Correcting now."

"What's happening up there, Xto?" The voice belonged to Oplwaa; she knew him well enough to break to the familiar.

*My passenger blew his brains out,* he thought.

"My apologies," Xto said. "I'm afraid we lost track while in the zero-gravity exercise. It's my fault."

"Affirm. Looking true now," Oplwaa said, adding, "you should know better, Xto. And in front of your honored guest, no less."

He closed the channel, made a few more adjustments, and plotted in a course for the base runway. Then he reengaged the auto-function and took a look in the cabin.

The entire chamber was bloody. Idlo's corpse lay in a jangled heap in the middle of the room, having slid there from the rear when Xto had begun to pull them out of the nosedive. The trail he'd left behind looked disturbingly as if he'd been dragged there.

"What am I going to do now?" Xto asked himself.

This was *not* his fault. That much should be obvious to anyone. Unfortunately, it might also be irrelevant. What *was* relevant was that Xto Djbbit had departed the surface of Dib with a living council member and returned with a deceased council member. Worse, the death was not of natural causes, and there really wasn't any way to make it look otherwise.

*There has been an accident* wasn't going to cut it.

"But you had no doubt I'd still be able to see my father," he said, to the dead man. "How could you be so sure?"

*It's because of who I am.*

This was the same thing Trebnvto had been saying, and maybe it was true: Xto not only underestimated the importance of his family connection, he failed to leverage it in situations in which he *could*.

"And perhaps this is as embarrassing for them as it is for me," Xto said. Then he knew what to do.

He returned to the cockpit and opened a channel.

"Control, this is KH-1," he said. "Affirm."

"Affirm," Oplwaa said, "go ahead, KH-1."

"The honorable commerce chair has requested that Chairwoman Ayk meet us on the runway."

"Understood. I'll pass the request forward."

"Oplwaa," Xto said, "it's not *really* a request. You understand?"

The line was silent for a moment, and then: "Understood. I will pass that forward as well."

~

"Gods, what a mess," Ayk said. She'd only just sufficiently overcome the shock of discovery to form words; the insertion of the gods in her speech—even as an epithet—indicated she was still adjusting.

Just getting her to board the wingplane had been a challenge. Xto had to exit the craft and explain—several times—that Chairman Jrgap demanded a private audience and nothing short of that would be suitable. Xto did this while the whole time convinced someone would notice the droplets of blood on his boots.

Only once it became clear that "Idlo" was precisely stubborn enough to hold up all air traffic (because the Khth was blocking the main runway) did Ayk cave to the demand and follow Xto into the cabin.

"How did this happen?" she asked.

"He shot himself," Xto said, although surely this was obvious.

"I grasp that. I mean, how did you *allow* for this to happen?"

Her tone caught Xto short. She was angry.

"Had I known his intention I would perhaps have acted differently," Xto said. "I think we can agree that this was an outcome that couldn't have been anticipated."

"You *think?* You're not trained to *think*, Citizen Djbbit, you're trained to *know*."

"I assure you, this is not one of the scenarios I have been prepared to anticipate."

Ayk approached Idlo's body, slowly. The chairwoman walked with a cane these days, which she was now using to poke at the body, as if he might rise from the dead—despite missing the back half of his head—if nudged in the right spot.

"Well this is a disaster," she said. "No way around it. Citizen Djbbit, I'm afraid you're grounded until we can complete a full inquiry into your actions here. Alert the guards outside so we can get this mess cleaned up and then confine yourself to your barracks. I'll have to call the council myself; they will need to be made aware of the vacancy at commerce immediately. And his family, of course."

"No," Xto said.

Ayk stood silently at first, as if she hadn't heard him. "No to *what*, Citizen Djbbit?"

"I'm not going to be grounded over this, chairwoman. I'm going to depart in twenty days, as scheduled."

"I see. Is it *possible*, Xto, that you believe you have nothing more to lose at this time? Because you're gravely mistaken."

"What I believe is that the honorable Chairwoman Ayk has no desire to put me at the center of an official inquiry. In such a position I may have no other choice but to mention that the last thing Idlo Jrgap said before he killed himself was that he was only *on* this plane thanks to the direct assistance of his good friend Ebt Ayk...and that she not only knew of his plans, she helped him secret a gun in the pocket of his flight suit."

"That is a *lie*!"

"What it will *be* is an official statement from the son of the great Mondr Djbbit. Do you really think its veracity will be challenged?"

Xto was trying, very hard, not to allow his voice to quiver as he spoke. He was playing a game he'd never played before which *had* to lend some credence to what he was saying.

"You could also simply disappear, boy," she hissed. "Don't for a moment think you're above such outcomes."

"Honorable chairwoman, the amount of political capital you

would spend to accomplish this is far greater than the alternative."

"What alternative?"

"Chairman Jrgap died of a brain hemorrhage. It was the sudden shift in pressure did it. Tragic, but impossible to foresee."

"You imagine this is what a brain hemorrhage looks like?"

"I *imagine* that you have a half dozen men outside who will swear that it *is*, if that is what you tell them."

Ayk stared at him for an uncomfortably long time.

"It will be a stain," she said finally. "On our entire program. A leading member of the Chancellery died while in our hands."

"A retiring member. Whom I understand wasn't retiring voluntarily."

She smiled thinly. "Did he tell you this? What did the two of you discuss?"

"Our conversation was of course entirely appropriate at all times, chairwoman. But a man who is content with his station in life doesn't put a gun under his chin, does he?"

She nodded. He could see that she was coming around to his way of thinking. This was fortunate as he was nearly positive he was bluffing.

A future in which he never went into space and instead spent months if not years playing political games in order to stave off personal dishonor, imprisonment or death did not appeal to him in the slightest. He had no stomach for that kind of ruthlessness. But he also knew that would be where he ended up if she postponed his scheduled flight.

"But why *now*, Xto? I've known Idlo for many years, but I never…I knew there were issues at commerce, but still. This feels personal. Was this for me? What am I not seeing?"

*It's personal, but not for you,* Xto thought.

"I think he wanted to die happy," he said.

"And with honor," she added. "Fine. We'll give him that much."

81

Xto wondered if an aneurysm was a more honorable death than a bullet but definitely wasn't going to wonder it out loud.

Ayk walked up to Xto and held the pommel of her cane under his chin. "I have decided your plan of action is correct, Citizen Djbbit. But I will not forget the impertinence with which you expressed yourself today. Your father's name doesn't protect you as well as you think it does."

"I understand."

"I'm not sure you do. Let me put this plainly: once you have left it would be better for you to not return at all."

Then she turned around and opened the wingplane door.

"Come quickly," she said to the men outside. "There has been a terrible tragedy."

# Chapter Six

As Xto predicted, it took hardly any work to alter the story of Idlo Jrgap's final moments. Ayk simply told members of her security team that the chairman had died from an aneurysm in flight, brought them inside the cabin, and dared them to contradict her.

None did.

Xto was released to return to his apartment. Later that day, he sat for an interview with a man from Council Seventeen in which Xto repeated the lie, adding that their in-flight conversation concerned nothing but Jrgap's curiosity about space travel.

"Why did you not notify control about the chairman's condition before landing?" the man asked.

"I was unsure as to the appropriate way to proceed," Xto said, which was the truth.

"Why was that?"

"It was not an event anticipated by my training, and…I am embarrassed to admit, but I was worried that some might *blame* me in some way, for something I surely had no control over. I was unaware of chairman Jrgap's *condition* prior to departure, you see."

"As were we all," the man (who never gave a name) said.

"I landed, and immediately sought the wisdom of Chairwoman Ayk," Xto said. "Thankfully, she knew how to proceed from there."

"You had some issue on your return, did you not? The records show the flight diverged. You claimed at the time that you 'lost track'. Was *that* when you realized Chairman Jrgap was dead?"

"It was, yes."

"And yet, you informed control that *he* was demanding to speak to the chair of the rocket program. How could he make such a demand, if he was already dead?"

Xto smiled. "Then I am perhaps mistaken."

"Yes," he agreed. "I'm sure you are. Clearly, the honorable chairman's request to speak to Chairwoman Ayk was conveyed to you prior to his unexpected death but not *reported* by you until *after* his passing. Is that how you remember it?"

"Why yes," Xto said. "That's precisely correct."

"Very good. "The man closed his note pad and stood. "I suggest you keep your recollection of this day's events fresh in your mind going forward, citizen. It would be best for everyone if it remains unchanged, should you be questioned in the future."

"I understand."

Then the unnamed man from Council Seventeen left, and that was the end of the matter.

∽

"Did he tell you why?" Trebnvto asked, three nights later.

Xto was only hours from the start of his mandatory quarantine, seven days after which he would be suited up and sitting atop a rocket. This, then, was the last time he and Trebnvto would be breathing the same air for quite a while.

"Why what?" Xto asked.

"Why he killed himself," Treb said.

"The honorable chairman died of a brain aneurysm," Xto said flatly. "As everyone knows."

Trebnvto laughed.

They were at Xto's dining table, sharing a meal that was one part goodbye, and one part binding of the wounds inflicted their last time together.

Treb had sulked for a good week, awaiting an apology for Xto that was never going to come. (Xto would absolutely have gone into space without mending things, as a preferable alternative than admitting he was wrong. He and Trebnvto were equals when it came to stubbornness, but Xto's resolve was greater. Also, he wasn't wrong.) Then one day he started talking to Xto as if the entire thing had never happened, and soon after that they were making dinner plans.

"Literally everyone knows that to be untrue," Treb said. "Whether it's said aloud or not. He *did* say something, I can tell! What was it?"

Xto squirmed uncomfortably. Threading the line between what was factual and what was "true", was always a challenge in Wivvol. He was almost never certain which side to stand on in private.

"He complained about his position," Xto said.

"Then he could have simply retired on schedule," Treb said. "It had to have been more than complaints. Come, you can tell *me*. I've kept more of your secrets than anyone; what's one more?"

Xto laughed. "Please do not present yourself as the living model of discretion, Treb. You have the subtlety of a butterfly trapped in a jar. Very well: the chairman's death was as you described, and he did have words to share before he did it. But those words were for me alone."

Treb grunted. "Sure."

"We both know if I said more, the information exchange wouldn't end here."

"*Nobody* is listening," Trebnvto said.

Xto hesitated, because the last thing he wanted to do was start a new argument. There wasn't enough time left for Treb to traverse an entire sulk cycle before Xto left the planet.

"Treb, you are not the intended recipient of his final message. The chairman went to great effort to guarantee *I* would be that person, and I alone. I mean to honor that."

Trebnvto stared at him for several beats, to measure his earnestness. "Fine," he said. "Although I've just lost a bet with Qsarn; I'm very cross with you now."

Xto laughed. "She knows me better than you, clearly."

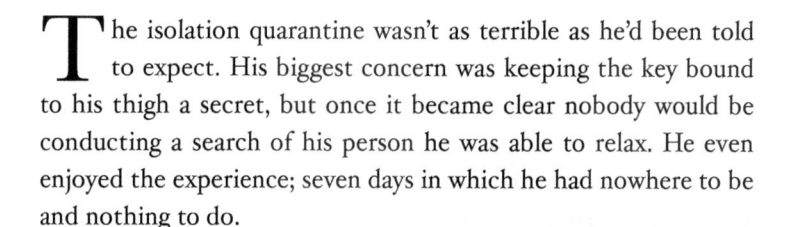

⁓

The isolation quarantine wasn't as terrible as he'd been told to expect. His biggest concern was keeping the key bound to his thigh a secret, but once it became clear nobody would be conducting a search of his person he was able to relax. He even enjoyed the experience; seven days in which he had nowhere to be and nothing to do.

When the day came, he suited up alone. Then two women in epidemic-resistant outfits helped him with his helmet and gloves and he was ready to face the world, as reasonably germ-free as the system allowed. He was driven in an electric cart to the launch pad, rode an elevator to the top of an enormous rocket so that he could sit in what was likely the least-safe place on the planet: the tip-end of one of the most powerful chemical rockets ever designed.

It should have been a matter of great seriousness and ceremony, except that everyone around Xto had done this once a month for several years; the expressions on the faces he passed were similar to that of bus drivers and utility workers.

"Don't look down," the man waiting at the hatch recommended, using a hand-held microphone that Xto picked up on his helmet radio. It wasn't terribly difficult for Xto to not look down, because looking down meant tilting his head forward too far. He knew he was standing on a metallic gangplank with nothing beneath, and the drop to the ground was over a thousand maders; he didn't need to look to verify that.

"I would rather look skyward, citizen," Xto said.

The man laughed, as he took Xto by the elbow and helped him inside. (It was a heavy suit. It was expected to be perfectly reasonable in zero gravity, but otherwise was very hard to move around in.) "The call of the ocean in the sky, as the poets say."

"Indeed," Xto said.

The top of the rocket consisted of a cockpit embedded in a shuttle that could move independently once it had been liberated from the pull of Dib's gravity and untethered from the booster rockets underneath. It would be Xto's home for the next twelve days.

He climbed into the chair, settled down in a position facing the ceiling, and waited for his helper to strap him down and check that everything was in order.

*This is so unnecessary*, Xto thought.

It was a surprising thought at a surprising time, but no less the truth for it. Incomprehensibly, Wivvol—or rather, the Chancellery and the *EPFA*—refused to embrace null-gravity technology. True, they had developed space travel before null-gravity was feasible, using semi-reusable chemical rockets. Also true, there wasn't a single element of the program that relied upon imported goods, meaning every aspect of the mechanism that would shortly put Xto Djbbit into orbit, from the mathematical formulas to the rubber seal on the shuttle door, was birthed in Wivvol. It was appropriate to be proud of this. However, just because newer technology was established elsewhere didn't mean that technology had to be rejected out-of-hand. Not when that newer technology was a demonstrable improvement.

"You're set," the man said, on inspecting Xto's last buckle and latch. "How do you feel?"

"I have an itch on my backside," Xto said.

The man laughed again. "Too early for the bugs, Citizen Djbbit; you're two weeks from scratching it."

The man was supposed to leave then, seal the hatch from the outside, signal control that this month's astronaut was properly lashed to his personal rocket, and maneuver the elevator system away from the launch pad. Instead, he leaned in and spoke to Xto without the benefit of his hand-held microphone.

"Your uncle sends regards," he said. And then, "Do you have it?"

Startled, Xto hesitated with his reply.

"Shuttle this is control," Plaquib said over the microphone. If Xto was capable of jumping in surprise, he would have. "How are we doing, Astronaut Djbbit?"

Xto looked the man in the eye, and nodded slowly. "I do," he said, off audio.

The man smiled and clapped Xto on the shoulder. "May the Five be with you."

"Affirm, Astronaut Djbbit," Plaquib said.

Xto turned his helmet microphone back on. "Affirm, control," he said. "Waiting on the hatch seal and then we are ready."

"Well get on with it, man," Plaquib said. "We don't have all morning."

~

An excruciating two hours followed, during which Xto could do nothing but sit on his rocket and wait for someone to give him permission to go. About the only thing that happened which he didn't expect was when the next astronaut in line to go after him got on the radio…and it was Kly Ghalkk.

"Oh, hello Kly," Xto said, as calmly as possible. Hopefully nobody registered a significant spike in his heart rate. "I was expecting Trebnvto Pna."

"He's been bumped again," she said. "Our friend is on track for the record."

Xto laughed, but only because anybody listening would be expecting him to. "Longest career as an almost-astronaut," Xto said.

"Indeed.".

*Your father's name doesn't protect you as well as you think it does*, Ayk had said. What if she decided to express her displeasure with Xto by punishing Treb?

"Did they say why?" he asked.

"If they did, they didn't say it to me," Kly said. "Don't worry about Trebnvto, Xto; he always lands on his feet. And we will take care of him for you. I promise."

"Thank you for saying so."

"Xto. I mean this. Do not fill your head with concern about what's behind you and forget to worry about what's ahead. We take care of our own around here, my friend."

"I...will endeavor to."

"Eyes skyward, astronaut. Now, I understand you have a dirty joke for me."

Xto told the joke, badly. Kly Ghalkk laughed anyway, promised to tell it better when it was her turn, and then it was time to go.

~

Leaving the planet was a terrible experience. The g-force was tremendous—his *eyes* hurt from the pressure—and there were three occasions in which Xto became convinced the tiny wayward wobble he was feeling in his tailbone was the precursor to a catastrophic failure.

It was, thankfully, over very quickly. It may have taken him the better part of an hour to reach the edge of the atmosphere in a Khth class wingplane, but it was a matter of minutes by rocket.

He detached from the main boosters halfway up, and the secondary boosters once in low orbit. Then it was just his shuttle and the cargo crate.

Xto took a moment to maneuver around so as to get a good look at Dib from space. It wasn't, strictly, part of his flight plan to do anything of the sort, but extra time had been built in.

They'd taken off in the daytime, as was typical, and so Xto didn't have to contend with the biggest (assumed) threat to Wivvol's dominance of the ocean in the sky: Lys. A part of him wanted to take his shuttle past the secret haven for the wealthy, even though that would mean definitively breaking a number of important rules, the largest being: do not actively engage non-Wivvolian crafts. He just wanted to know what it looked like.

After a few minutes to appreciate the view, Xto toggled until his nose was pointed toward his destination.

"Control, I'm ready for the handoff," Xto said. "Affirm."

"Affirm, shuttle, this is control," Plaquib Mh said. "Handoff confirmed. We'll see you in two years, Astronaut Djbbit."

"Affirm."

*Take care of the planet while I'm away,* Xto thought.

The channel's signal vanished into static for about thirty seconds, which was long enough to be alarming. Then, the signal cleared up.

"Shuttle, this is command platform one," a familiar voice said. "We're prepared for your arrival. Welcome to the ocean in the sky, Xto."

"Thank you, father. I'll see you in twelve days."

# PART II

House Secrets

## Chapter Seven

Although it had never been a pressing question for them, Dorn Jimbal had begun to understand how the very wealthy could end up out of touch with the day-to-day of the rest of the planet.

Especially on Lys, with its make-believe sky and make-believe gravity.

It was distressingly easy to lose all track of time on the space station, which Dorn knew because they already *had*. They thought they'd probably been there for only a month but it could have been two months. It could also have been two weeks.

Losing track of things like this made them acutely aware of how they used to tell time on the surface: by the accretion of successive obligations. On Lys, in their corner of the Demara estate, Dorn's only obligation was to the parsing of Professor Linus's notes, which they did at their own pace. There was an *urgency* to it, but it was an urgency on the scale of decades, not days.

At least, that was how Dorn had approached it initially, and how their *other* host—Ba-Ugna Kev—had framed it. Kev was also warm to the notion that whatever he was expecting to get out of

Linus's copious notes, Dorn would find it quickly. Why? Because he thought Dorn already knew the answers; they just had to *see* it in the way Linus had.

"I'm told your work has proven much of what Orno concluded based on his research," Kev had said, which was a preposterous assertion. Dorn's "work" consisted of proving the long-term orbit of Dibble was fundamentally unstable and would eventually spin away from its twin suns. However, this wasn't something happening *soon* from the perspective of anyone on the planet. (Cosmically? Fairly soon.)

When Dorn asked who gave Ba-Ugna this impression, he explained that the source was Orno himself, by way of Viselle Daska (who was, Dorn also learned—in this same conversation—Kev's semi-estranged daughter.) Dorn tried to claim that this was clearly a matter of mistranslation: a third party receiving information from a second party who heard a slightly different version of it from the first party. It wasn't fundamentally accurate.

Kev insisted Dorn was wrong, and just didn't see the connection yet and urged Dorn to dive into Linus's documentation.

It *was* true that Dorn was likely the best person to look at their former professor's notes, as there were few better qualified to understand what was in them... and all of the other possibly qualified persons were a significant distance away.

Dorn simply couldn't see the link. Especially once it turned out fully three-quarters of Professor Linus's notes pertained to religious studies, while Dorn's expertise was in astrophysics.

Additional non-academic complications emerged, especially after the news that Viselle Daska—who, again, was Kev's daughter—was the one who murdered Orno Linus. This would have led to a tense confrontation, had Ba-Ugna Kev been available for Dorn to confront. He wasn't; Jig kept Dorn politely but firmly distanced. And then Calcut Linus was arrested instead and Dorn didn't know what to believe, so they just went back to the room with Orno's notes and never brought it up with Kev.

Then came the day that *should* have changed everything.

One morning, Exty Demara showed up in the doorway of the room in which Dorn was working. She looked upset; her eyes were red and her cheeks wet. As her face was generally all smiles, even something as mild as a frown would have come across as evidence of a tragedy.

"I think you should know," she said, "Ba-Ugna is dead. He was killed."

"*Here*? When? Are we in danger?"

She laughed gently. "You're so cute. No, he was on the surface. He surrendered to the police last night; didn't he tell you?"

"No," Dorn said. What *had* happened was that Jig requested they stick to the upper floor for the evening, a request that might have come off as weird had it not happened multiple times before. Given Dorn still considered themself a fugitive, it was the kind of instruction they were willing to follow, no questions asked.

"Did the police kill him?" Dorn asked. "I don't understand."

"No. Do you remember that detective in charge of your case? Stidgeon? He picked up Ba-Ugna. Him, and Elicasta Sangristy, who is only my *favorite* Veeser... Anyway they were here, and they took him down, and...There's actually a vid of the murder if you want to watch it. Or I can just tell you. Calcut Linus killed him."

"The brother."

"Mm."

"I thought he was arrested for Professor Linus's murder," Dorn said.

"Nope. He's *still* not, either. Oh, but don't worry; he definitely doesn't know you're here."

Up until she's said that, Dorn *hadn't* thought to worry.

"All right," they said. "What happens now?"

"I don't understand."

"I'm only here... I'm only doing this because Mr. Kev asked. What happens now?"

"Oh," she said. "Keep going! Please! And don't think you're not welcome here; I'm happy to have you around for as long as you want to be around."

"Thank you, Exty," they said. She smiled, and Dorn blushed a little, then became embarrassed at the fact that Exty could *see* them blushing inasmuch as they weren't hooded.

One thing Dorn had become accustomed to, while hiding away in the upper recesses of the Demara family guest wing, was going face-naked. Given the scars on Dorn's face—and milky left eyeball—and the Septalist oath, it was supposed to be the case that only a fellow monk was allowed to see their entire face. But a formal Septal hood was out of the question from the moment Dorn fled the campus until they reached the privacy of the Demara estate. After that, it seemed there was no point. Literally only three people were in a position to see Dorn unhooded. Once that had happened, it didn't matter that much. (Non-trivially, Dorn was also not the most devoted of Septals. They wore the trappings of fundamentalism, but that was to get out of having to remove their hood among other Septals. Taking the oath had always been a practical decision for Dorn, not a religious one.)

Despite all of that, and despite their continued hospitality, Dorn still felt like a commodity more than a guest. They expected to be traded for something else at a later date.

To that end, Dorn remained uncertain about their future.

"But, this work," Dorn said, to Exty gesturing to the room. "Should I continue?"

"I don't understand," Exty said. "Of course you should continue."

"And should I find something... to whom should I tell?"

"You can tell me!"

"All right."

She laughed. "I know," she said. "Ba-Ugna was the one with the ideas and the plan, and Orno before him. Just do the work.

Someone looking for the answers you find will eventually come along."

"Who?"

"I don't know! Someone."

The problem with just doing the work was that their former professor was surprisingly scatterbrained. Or more precisely, he was supremely organized in a way that only made sense to him.

There *was* a historical order to the boxes, but it took Dorn a couple of weeks to understand that order, because the history being honored was the history of original documents. It was difficult to see this because Orno had almost no *actual* original documents to work with, because nearly everything in the Septal vaults was a copy of an original, and often several iterations (as in, a copy of a copy of a copy) of an original. Those copies had dates, but what was important to him was the inferred date of the source text. Consequently, Dorn's first few times through the boxes it looked as if there was no order when that wasn't the case at all; Orno was tracking the genesis of the data.

But working that out wasn't the end of Dorn's difficulties, because they weren't clear on what Professor Linus's *thesis* was.

Clearly, he was seeking to *prove* something, and that something had to do with the Outcast. Orno went from vault to vault looking for every mention of the Outcast, logging what volume he found it in, what page, and so on. If he was looking at a text from one vault that was purportedly an identical copy of a text from another vault—which was the case most of the time—he concentrated on everything that was different.

The differences were rare, which made them notable. But what they *meant* to Orno remained unclear. It had been Dorn's understanding that Professor Linus's goal was to determine which of the many Septal vault texts scattered across the globe were *truly* original, which were direct *copies* of true originals, and which were copies of the copies.

But if that was the case, his obsession with the Outcast mythos in particular was a curious way to go about it.

~

"Can you use some help?" Exty said one day. This was a few days (or a week? Perhaps?) after she'd told them about Ba-Ugna's death, and of course she startled them by speaking.

"How long have you been standing there?" they asked.

"Not *too* long," she said. "Not like an embarrassingly long time. Long enough to realize you weren't going to notice I was here if I didn't say something."

"I'm sorry."

"No, don't be; you must be used to working in solitude."

They smiled. "I always have done. This is a task to which I'm unusually suited."

"Even if you don't understand any of it."

"I wouldn't say that."

"You don't have to," she said. "Your face says it for you." Then she laughed, because apparently Dorn's face told her something else after that. "No, it's okay. You're cute when you're...what's the word I want? Befuddled."

"And you thought you could help."

"Couldn't hurt. I'm here."

Dorn put down the copied manuscript text they were in the middle of. "Can you read Eglinat?" they asked.

"No."

"Then...? I don't know how you can help."

She nodded slowly. "All right," she said, turning to go.

"Wait," they said. "I'm sorry. You're right, I'm not used to working with someone else and that was rude of me."

"It's okay," she said. Her expression said otherwise, so Dorn tried again. "*How* do you think you can help? We should perhaps start there."

"Not sure. Organizing? This room is a wreck."

This was a reasonable assessment. Dorn had been given a small office area in which to work. It contained an antique desk that was likely more valuable than the farm they grew up on, two windows they'd never looked out of, three chairs and a fireplace that wasn't in use. Dorn had stacked folders on the desk, two of the chairs, and half of the floor. Like their former professor, Dorn was applying a sorting method that was difficult for anyone else to discern.

"I actually know where everything is," Dorn said.

"Well...okay, how about if you talked some of it through?" she asked. "I mean it, Dorn, there are days when you just sit in that chair for an hour and stare at the wall. I can tell you're trying to work something out. Unless it's a secret?"

"You said you hadn't been standing there for long."

"Not *today*," she laughed.

Dorn realized they liked the sound of Exty Demara's laugh. This was something they probably should have worked out sooner.

"Professor Linus was looking for something," Dorn said. "I don't know what, but it had to do with the Outcast myths."

"Myths, plural? How many are there?"

"In broad strokes, very few. In detail, there are hundreds. He wrote a scholarly synthesis of the myths already."

"*The Outcast Ascendant*," she said.

"Yes," they said, surprised. "You've read it?"

"No, but it's on a shelf downstairs. Want me to go get it?"

"I'm familiar enough. He argued that the number of sources of Outcast myths inferred that there was a historical basis to them."

She was nodding before he finished the thought. "Ba-Ugna said the same thing. He told me a few times that the Outcast was coming. Legitimately coming, not metaphorically. It stuck out because he didn't seem like the type."

"Neither was Professor Linus," Dorn said. "My understanding

was that the idea of a *historical* Outcast was what his scholarship led him to conclude. That it was the *only possible* conclusion. But I never heard him speak about the return with the sort of certainty you're describing."

"Which is funny, because Ba-Ugna said it was Orno who convinced him."

Dorn stared at her. "I didn't know that," they said. When Kev introduced the idea of having Dorn—at the time fleeing an impending arrest for murder—go through their professor's archives, Dorn agreed immediately, thinking it was a condition of their staying at the estate. Kev's talk about the impending arrival of the Outcast and how Dorn was *important* to somehow stopping it didn't have much of an impact on their decision at the time. Nor did they spend any time wondering where Ba-Ugna Kev's end-of-days ideas originated.

"See?" Exty said. "Talking it out helps! Is that what he was looking for?"

"Perhaps, but I don't see how. When would it make sense to look at the past for an event purported to happen so far in the future?"

She smiled. "Well I don't know. Was there something about how it was described in the past that would make him think that?"

"Enh. All the different myths really have in common is the Outcast rising up out of the ground and destroying nearly all life before being conquered and banished to the Depths by the Five. But the professor's prior work focused on what all those stories had in common. His *current* work—if what's all over this room can be defined as a cogent exercise in scholarship—cared about what was *different*. He was doing it to figure out which came first. Or, I think he was. It's how this is ordered."

Exty looked around the room, as if by staring at it long enough, the word "order" would make some sense. "But the ways they're different isn't telling you anything?"

"They're observations that don't add up to anything. There's a repetitive notation that I can't make sense of, referring to another text but that text isn't *here*, and it isn't directly identified or sourced. It's possible if I had that text I would understand the notations, and hence the larger thesis, but I don't."

"Text."

"I think it's a book from one of the vaults. If not, it's a notebook he didn't leave with the rest of his research. I'll show you."

Dorn grabbed a sheet that was an image reproduction of a text from the Septal vault in Elioth, in western Mursk. Orno had circled a passage and drawn a line to a margin note, which read, "ref. pp32 p2 l7, ck wd?"

Exty looked it over. "Okay, I can read this," she said. "He didn't take notes in Eglinat, huh."

Dorn laughed. "No, it's not a good language for shorthand notation. There are too many letters assumed, not apparent. Especially in archaic."

"I was kidding. All right, he's saying to reference this passage to one on page thirty-two, paragraph two, line seven. Yes? And then he says there's something wrong with a word?"

"That's how I read it as well."

"But page thirty-two in what?"

"Precisely the problem. He's performing a metatextual analysis —*that* I understand—but his notes don't illuminate *what* is being compared to *what*. I'm *hoping* it's a single text and not multiples, and I hope that because otherwise I don't see how Professor Linus could have possibly succeeded with such a vague system. Either way, I can't see what he's seeing with only these notes."

"So far."

"Yes. I'll keep working."

"What does the passage say?" she asked.

"Which passage?"

"The one he circled."

"Oh, it's..." Dorn took the sheet back and read the archaic

Eglinat a couple of times, translating it as best they could in their head before speaking. Reciting it *in* Eglinat wouldn't do Exty any good. "It's, 'Foreseen above and below, the Five cannot wage alone.' It's about fighting back the Outcast. In some versions, the Five are joined by their subjects on the field of battle."

"I don't remember that version."

"It's not in the generally accepted account." By that, they meant the common translations taught by most of the Septal chapters. This was a simplification, since all of the House chapters had their own canonical texts to start with, and what was embraced as canon was subject to change whenever a new High Hat was appointed. Still, there was general agreement regarding most of the details.

"It is, however, an *earlier* version," Dorn continued. "And in the *early* common texts, Professor Linus found that telling of the tale to be much more frequent. There's an earlier version still in which the gods didn't step up to fight the Outcast at all; they stepped *back* and allowed the fight to proceed."

"That's definitely not right."

Dorn smiled. "Right or wrong isn't the point. Closer to the source text is."

She looked at the passage again. "Any idea what word he's talking about?" she asked.

"No, but it points to this being a later copy than whatever he's cross-referencing it with."

"How can you be sure?"

"I can't. But he said *this* had a wrong word. Not different: wrong. The implication is that the *other* version, the one we can't see, holds primacy."

"That's really interesting," she said. And she seemed to mean it, which was sort of amazing. "Meanwhile, you're an astrophysicist."

"Yes," they said. "But I can read Eglinat, so that's useful."

Exty laughed again. "I feel like we're getting somewhere now. What other passages did he call out?"

"They're all over the room," they said.

"Great! Show me a couple. Maybe there's a pattern!"

∾

If there had been a pattern, Dorn would have already discovered it, but they showed Exty anyway.

They decided they didn't just like Exty's laugh; they liked Exty. She was easy to talk to and pleasant to be around. Also, she was correct: talking out some of what was going on in their head *did* help. Dorn got no closer to solving the mystery by doing this, but they no longer felt as if they'd accomplished nothing at all.

But after the many hours spent explaining everything Dorn had managed to deduce thus far, Exty had to agree with them that there was no apparent pattern.

A breakthrough—or, the closest thing Dorn had experienced that could qualify as one—came a few days later, at a time when Exty was unavailable.

Dorn frankly didn't know what Exty's regular responsibilities consisted of, nor where she went when not hanging out in the guest wing of the mansion. Dorn had never left the guest area, but inferred the existence of other members of the Demara family in residence elsewhere and thought that a part of what she did consisted of dealing with them: she appeared to occupy the position of *head of the household*. For a clan this wealthy such a responsibility was no doubt similar to being the chief executive of a large company, but since Dorn also didn't know what a chief executive did, the comparison didn't help.

Regardless, her duties were many, so she was only ever able to swing by Dorn's "office" now and then, which was why she missed their first breakthrough.

It wasn't much: just a note in a margin. It was in a copied

image from a post-Collapse text that was widely considered to be a copy of a *pre*-Collapse text called *Parieaum Ejukatesi*, or *In Preparation for the Outcast*. The passage Orno circled—beside the note—was unremarkable. It detailed how the answer to stopping the final days of Dibble-kind lay with the gods in the Haven. It was such a common passage, in all versions of the text to which Dorn was familiar, that it had become an aphorism: Our salvation lies in the Haven.

What Orno wrote next to this version of the phrase was: "Note the tense."

The word "tense" was underlined three times.

One of the things that made Eglinat in general, and the archaic texts in particular, difficult to follow, was that the language had verb tenses for an unnecessarily large range of time periods. Yes, it *was* nice, when reading a sentence like, "He arrived," to be able to tell whether this arrival happened a moment ago, a day ago, months ago, or a lifetime ago, simply by the verb tense used. But it wasn't useful if the reader hadn't managed to memorize all possible verb-tenses for the word, which —Dorn assumed—happened a lot.

The verb in the passage was *prahab*, or *to stop*, in archaic Eglinat. What Orno was calling attention to was that the tense employed in this translation indicated that the act of stopping would have to be *soon*. The word was *prahabito*, which—if Dorn was recalling their tenses correctly—was the tense form of the verb for a *near*-future event: weeks or months.

Which could mean nothing. It could be that the scribe responsible for this copy got their tenses confused, or it could mean that the early editions of this text had a baked-in flair for the dramatic. Still, finding this sent Dorn across the room in search of the same passage from other copies. They finally found one, after two hours. In it, the word used was *prahabitat*, which jibed with the common version of the passage. It meant, roughly, *not at all soon, but someday*.

"It's probably just a mistranslation," Dorn said to themself. It's what they would have thought if finding this on their own. But Orno Linus clearly felt otherwise. And if it *wasn't* a mistranslation, it meant the original document was written by someone who expected to see the Outcast *within their lifetime*.

Dorn did not, at first, see this as a particularly revelatory discovery. Clearly, the source text scribe was *wrong* or there would be nobody around to read their words thousands of years later.

Then Dorn got an idea. It was probably wrong, but just coming up with it made them cold.

"When would it make sense to look at the past for an event purported to happen in the future?" they asked. It was the question that had come up when Exty first offered to help. But now they had an answer: "When what's about to happen has happened before."

If the Outcast truly was *real*, and truly did return within the lifetime of the original scribe, and Dorn *was* around to read about it...

"It would have to mean they stopped the Outcast."

# Chapter Eight

Exty wasn't as impressed as Dorn expected her to be.
"You got that from *one* bad verb tense?" she asked.
"It...sounds worse when you put it that way."
"I'm not saying you're *wrong*, but it could be you've been in that room for too long, sweetie."

Dorn must have made another expression that caused alarm, because Exty back-tracked almost immediately.

"Oh, no, I'm sure it means something, I'm not saying it doesn't," she said. "It's just..."

"Thin," they said.

"Very thin. *Promising*, though. I bet if we ever find that missing text you were talking about, we'll get the whole story."

"True, but I don't know how. He doesn't have a copy of the text here and the original volume would have to be in one of the Septal vaults. Probably the Velon House vault, since that's the one to which Professor Linus had routine access. And it may as well be on the moon, for the good that does."

Exty frowned.

"You know what you need?" she said. "You need a break. Come on."

She took them by the hand and led them out of the room, then down the hall in a direction Dorn had been told not to wander: toward the main house.

"I thought I wasn't allowed this way," Dorn said.

"For your protection, sure," she said. "You understood that, right? Fewer people who know you're here, the safer you are. Even if we're just talking about my relatives. *Especially* if we're talking about my relatives."

This wasn't something Dorn *had* understood, but it did explain why nobody was treating them like they were a prisoner. Kev established in Dorn a sense of traded favors, in which they were allowed to remain safe, as long as they continued to work on Linus's documents.

"And the help?" Dorn asked. "They know I'm here."

"The help is pretty much full-time residential. We even have a couple of families on staff. But I'm less worried about one of them communicating your presence down to the surface than I am my family."

"I'm not sure what that says about your family."

She laughed.

"Not like they would *mean* to expose you."

They stopped at the end of the hall, in a rotunda with a downstaircase. On the other side of the rotunda was a set of double doors leading to the main section. Exty took a moment to look down the stairs, as if expecting to discover a spy.

"It's a funny thing," she said. "Having money, I mean. You've experienced a version of this, I'm thinking. Take away the *need* for a paycheck and the mind looks for other kinds of scarcity to trade. For my family—and pretty much everyone else up here—their currency is gossip."

"Why would you think I have any experience in this?" Dorn asked. They'd never discussed their family with Exty, but it wasn't a secret. Dorn grew up on a farm in Punkoah. Their family was wealthy when compared to the local non-land owning transient farmhands, but not at all in contrast with the Demaras.

"Because the House works the same way," she said. "Doesn't it? After taking the vow you have no need for a *job*, because the House provides room and board and a living stipend. It's not a *lot* different from living off the fruit of a family estate. Only the House trades in knowledge instead of gossip."

"I never considered it in that way before," Dorn said. In truth, they thought it was a weak comparison given the outrageous trappings of wealth surrounding them, but they understood what she was getting at.

Exty led them around the rotunda and through the set of doors. There was a notable change in the air as they crossed, as evidently the oxygen system in the central mansion differed from the one in the guest wing. It was lightly perfumed with the scent of wheat fields.

"Anyway, nobody else is home right now, so there's not as much of a risk. Also, to be honest? I'm not sure anyone's looking for you."

"There was an All-Eyes bulletin."

"Sure, but the murder was solved, right? And it's not like they announce when they've canceled those bulletins. I think everyone assumes Viselle killed you and dropped your body in the Moilen River."

"That's...alarmingly specific," they said.

"It *is*, isn't it?" Exty said with a smile. "I saw it come up as a theory on a Veeser stream a few days back; thought it was cute. My point is, the Veesers are the only ones still looking for you, and only because you're the one piece of the mystery for which there's no firm explanation."

"Because gossip is also a currency on the Stream?"

"Now you're getting it."

Aside from the air, Dorn's first steps into the main house felt no different. The cornice work was perhaps more elegant, the carpet pile slightly higher, but that was all. They'd passed two doors on each side in the time it might have taken them to pass four in the guest wing, so perhaps the rooms were twice as large.

"But the police?" Exty said. "I don't think they want you, aside from to make sure you're still alive. When this is over, you may even be able to go back to your life as a Septal."

"When this is over," Dorn repeated.

"Right."

They didn't need to ask what she meant. There was a third interested party, after the police and the Stream, regarding Dorn's whereabouts: the Linus family.

It hardly made sense, given Calcut Linus's indictment for the crime of murdering his own brother, but according to Exty the man still blamed Dorn for Orno's death. It was as if, once having attempted to sell that false accusation, Mr. Linus saw no recourse except to continue trying to sell it. This was even after he'd been witnessed by millions murdering Ba-Ugna Kev.

Unless he'd decided Dorn was responsible for *that* too.

In any case, it would be some time before they felt comfortable returning to the Septal fold. They doubted they *ever* would.

On the other hand, the charity of Exty Demara might have limits; it may soon be the case that Dorn would have no other option.

When they reached the end of the hallway, Exty paused in front of a set of enormous gold-inlaid dark wood doors. She stood before of Dorn and leaned up against the doorknobs.

"I told you we've rebuilt this place a few times, right?" she asked. "Since Archeo's days."

"You did. You would have had to. There used to be no gravity on Lys, isn't that the case?"

"Exactly. But we didn't rebuild *all* of it. We kept one room as it was, which wasn't an easy feat. It's one thing to build around a ground floor room, but this one's on the top floor in what used to

# THE OCEAN IN THE SKY

be the dead center of the mansion. But it was Archeo's favorite place. Also, he insisted in his will."

She turned around and pushed the doors open. On the other side was a large, round room with a massive telescope of brass, steel and glass under a domed ceiling.

It looked like a museum exhibit rather than an active piece of scientific equipment; not because of the age of the device—although it *was* quite old—but because there was nothing to look at. The ceiling was slate-gray and decidedly non-transparent.

"How thoroughly impractical," Dorn said.

"But pretty, right?" Exty asked.

"It's very attractive. I'm not certain of its functional value in this age; there's more to learn from interrogating the sky in the non-visual spectrum."

"Sure, but not as much poetry."

"If poetry is what one seeks from the stars, yes. But there are no stars to see here in either case. The ceiling's opaque, and it's daytime."

Exty laughed.

"You've been here too long," she said. "It's whatever time we decide it is."

This was true, but skirted the point. Yes, Lys in its fixed orbital position never *had* a daytime, because the space station never faced the suns. But regardless of whether it was "day" or "night" on the grounds of the Demara estate, the *sky* that they could see from the windows wasn't the real sky. The ceiling above the telescope could just as easily be transparent, but it didn't change the fact that the domed sky on the other side of that ceiling was not.

"I didn't set up the room properly," Exty said. "Hang on; you still have a chance to be impressed."

She hurried over to the base of the telescope, sat in the chair attached to it, and activated a control panel. After a few seconds, the slate gray ceiling blinked.

"Oh," Dorn said.

"Yeah, it's a screen," Exty said. "Sorry, I bet that's jarring. Here we go."

The ceiling screen blinked again, and went black. Then a bunch of pinhole-sized stars began to appear.

"It's a *planetarium*," Dorn said. They walked around the room to get a better look, nearly running into the railing that encircled the telescope as they went. "Is this...this isn't our night sky."

"It is and it isn't. This is the default setting. Archeo set it up to look like the part of the sky he couldn't see. We actually lost the original ceiling in one of the rebuilds; this is a reconstruction from the original design specs."

"Where are the dancers?" Dorn asked.

"Diminished. Hang on." Exty pushed a button and the twin stars appeared, dimly, directly overhead. "If I bring them up to full brightness they block out half the stars."

"As they do currently," Dorn said. "We have technology to filter out the brightness of the suns with our orbital telescopes, but that wasn't the case in Archeo Demara's day. This is a sky that never actually existed, for him."

"Yeah, I think that's why he liked it. He even said that this was why he built Lys."

"To look at a sky he couldn't see? That makes no sense."

"I know. Nobody else understood it either. My great grandfather was a visionary in a lot of ways, but he was lousy about metaphors. Anyway, to answer your earlier question, the ceiling *has* a transparency setting, and we can do the same with the outer dome. And the optics on this thing actually work. So if you wanted to look at the real sky with it, you could. But there are better ways."

"Yes, as I said before. The nonvisible spectrum is more useful."

"And that is *not* what I meant, Dorn. Again, think more like a poet."

"I'll try."

She dove back into the control panel. The ceiling blinked once more, and then a new set of stars appeared.

"Does that look more familiar?" she asked.

"It does. It's a copy of the night sky above us."

"Yes and no. It's the night sky, but it's a live feed. It's what you'd see if we *did* make both of the obstacles transparent. We're getting it from a bank of orbiting telescopes owned by the Demara corporation. Now come up here and sit down."

Dorn stepped onto the slight platform on which the telescope rested. Exty got up and guided him into the seat, and then put her hand on his back and leaned next to his ear. Dorn was glad for the dim lights, as their face was hot; they were blushing.

"Now look in the telescope," she said into their ear. They leaned forward, closed one eye, and peered through. The view was indistinguishable from that of a standard telescope looking at a true night sky. But that only meant the screen's resolution was uncommonly high. They were looking at a star called Divus-13B. Dorn knew it well, having done a luminosity study on Divus-13B at age seven. It was one of the stars astronomers used to measure the distance of *other* stars.

"All right," Dorn said.

"Let's get a closer look at that star," she said. She reached around Dorn to get to a dial on the control panel. When she spun it, the image of Divus-13B grew.

The outcome was unexpected. If Dorn was looking at a screen, focusing on a detail on that screen would only result in a blurrier image, but that hadn't happened. Yet, they *were* definitely looking at a screen, and not at the actual sky.

They pulled away from the eyepiece and looked at the ceiling with the naked eye. The entire celestial image had moved.

"Explain," they said.

"The orbital telescopes providing the image are slaved to this control panel. When you focus the optics *here*, you're actually focusing the optics *there*. See, there's no need to make the ceiling transparent and turn off the outer dome. You've got the most interactive planetarium in existence here."

"And Archeo built this?"

"He *thought* of it but most of the technology was theoretical at the time of his death. *His* ceiling was the one I showed you before, only in his day it wasn't a screen. If he wanted to use the telescope like a telescope he opened the roof. The outer shell was transparent by default back then. Still think a radio telescope is a better idea?"

"I do, but this is a very good alternative. It has... poetry."

She laughed, and hugged his shoulder. "There you go," she said. "Okay, I have one more thing to show you."

Reaching around once more, she pushed a series of buttons on the console. The sky switched back to what looked like Archeo's false sun-facing sky.

"I've seen this already," Dorn said.

"You have, but you haven't. Look more closely."

Dorn took that literally, moving the telescope around until they discovered another distant star. This one was called Mnatta-2. Then Dorn took a hold of the knob they'd seen Exty use, and tried looking more closely at the star.

"Oh," Dorn said, pulling away from the eyepiece. "This is the real sky, isn't it?"

"The family owns sun-facing telescopes too," Exty said. The light from the Dancers is being filtered, so the stars behind the corona are mostly best-guess; if you focus on one of those and it'll get a little blurry. The rest is live-feed stuff. *Now* are you impressed?"

"I am," Dorn said.

Exty wrinkled her nose at him. "You are *so* hard to read sometimes, Dorn Jimbal." Then she clapped them on the shoulder and headed for the door.

"Okay, I'm gonna leave you here to play. I bet there's a thousand things you've been dying to get a better look at, and you didn't even know it before now."

Dorn actually wanted to get back to their room to continue working on the puzzle Orno had left them. But they didn't feel comfortable saying so.

"Absolutely," they said. "I can find my way back. I'm sure you have other responsibilities to return to."

"Actually, yeah. I forgot to mention. You're invited to dinner tonight. We're having a guest."

"I...thought it was best I stay away from anyone aside from you and the staff," Dorn said.

"Still true! Do you trust me?"

"I do."

"Then don't worry; I would never endanger you. But I *do* have to run. The shuttle should be landing shortly. I'll send Jig around when it's time."

~

Dorn was still in the planetarium when Jig came for them, some three hours later. They didn't actually own a watch, but the transit of the real-time stars served as a decent enough timepiece.

"Your presence is requested at the pavilion, Other," Jig said, upon arrival. Jig called Dorn "Other" after having already worked out that all of the other appropriate titles were gender-specific. The butler also refused to simply call them "Dorn". So for a week, he called them "Other Jimbal", before eventually just dropping the last name.

Dorn had been conducting a deep-dive on a region of space just to the left of the Daughters. There wasn't anything in particular in that part of space on which to focus, which was the point. Dorn wanted to know how good the telescope array really was. They were so preoccupied with this that they didn't even hear Jig enter. Thus, Dorn's first reaction was a startled cry.

"Yes. Yes of course," Dorn said, after recovering. "The pavilion. Dinner?"

"Yes."

"I, um, I do not know where that is."

"Understood. Follow me?"

Jig headed for the doors opposite the ones Dorn entered through. This was not readily apparent from within the room, as the doors looked identical and it was extremely easy to get turned around while working the telescope; it, and the platform on which it rested, rotated 360 degrees. Dorn only worked out they were going in a new direction after passing through the door and finding an unfamiliar corridor.

Jig led them down a mahogany-paneled hallway to the kind of open staircase people getting married posed upon: white stone, brass railing, giant works of art curling up the wall, and so on. It led to a massive space with a vaulted ceiling and a crystal chandelier that looked to Dorn to be about the same size as the shuttle that brought them to Lys.

From there they passed through a series of themed rooms evidently dedicated to artifacts from different parts of the world. Dorn again had the weird sensation of walking through a museum.

"Jig," they said, jogging to catch up to the long-legged butler. "I'm feeling extremely underdressed right now. Should I go back and find something else to wear?"

Jig stopped to look them over. "You *have* nothing else to wear," he rightly pointed out.

"I have nothing *better* to wear, but something cleaner, perhaps. Or, my Septal robe. Or one of the staff could lend me a jacket."

"If the lady of the house shared your concern, she would have provided clothing for you," he said. "Don't concern yourself."

Inasmuch as Exty had provided Dorn with *all* of the clothes at their disposal this was probably an accurate statement, but it didn't make them feel any better. Jig, mercilessly unconcerned with Dorn's general comfort, kept walking anyway.

After another set of stairs (slightly less ornate) they walked through what appeared to be a small casino to reach an atrium, and then to a set of glass doors leading to a grass lawn. At the far end was an arbor on a wood deck.

Beyond the arbor was a small river, on the other side of which was a breathtaking open valley that reminded them of some of the nicer parts of Punkoah. The river was real, the valley an illusion, but it was nearly impossible to tell.

Exty was sitting at a table under the arbor, talking to someone Dorn couldn't see; they were obscured behind one of the supports. Two members of the staff were walking to the table with large trays on their shoulders with enough food to feed a dozen.

*How* many *guests are we expecting?* Dorn wondered.

"Come along," Jig said. "Or the first course will get there before you."

This was evidently bad form or something. Dorn picked up their pace to match Jig's.

"There you are!" Exty said, jumping from her seat as soon as she saw Dorn. *She* had managed to change, into a pretty lavender suit. Her attire was so distracting that Dorn didn't even think to get their first look at the guest until all the way to the table.

"Hello, Dorn Jimbal," Viselle Daska said, standing. "It's good to see you again.

## Chapter Nine

Dorn's first instinct was to turn and run, which—while understandable—was self-evidently foolish. There was nowhere to run.

Exty grabbed them by the elbow before they got two steps anyway.

"No, no, it's okay, it's okay." She held Dorn's head in her hands and forced them to look at her. "Didn't you say you trusted me?"

"Yes."

"And didn't *I* say I wouldn't put you in danger?"

They looked back across the table at Viselle, who remained standing.

The first time Dorn met her she was in a tailored pants suit and expensive shoes, flashing a badge, long blonde hair and a smile. Now, she had on an ill-fitting t-shirt, old denim pants and rubber shoes, her hair was cropped short—it was no longer blonde—and she had an uneven tan. She looked like she'd been through a lot recently.

She also looked unarmed.

"You dyed your hair," Dorn said.

"I did," Viselle said, smiling. She remained—when smiling—

the most striking woman Dorn had ever seen. That somehow made being afraid of her much worse. "And you've dispensed with your hood," she added.

All at once, Dorn was self-conscious about being face-naked. They fought the urge to reach for the hood that came with the shirt they were wearing, and cover up.

"I have, yes."

"That's a great defense you have there," she said, pointing to his eye. "Probably would have helped prove it wasn't you in the vid if you'd taken off the hood earlier."

"I think we can agree that there were many things that could have gone differently, and in my favor," Dorn said, "had certain events not happened."

Viselle smiled thinly. "Yes. On that we agree."

Dorn pulled Exty away from the table and more importantly, away from Viselle Daska.

"Please explain what's happening right now," they said.

"She's a friend," Exty said. "One of my *oldest* friends. I trust her with my life. You did too, when she brought you here."

"That was before I knew she was the one who put my life in jeopardy in the first place."

"She didn't actually do that. Ba-Ugna did. Well, and I helped."

"What?" Dorn asked.

"A little. With the vid spoof of you at the scene. Not the making-of, but I had the contacts to get it out on the Stream untraceably."

"I can't believe this is happening."

"Look, it was a weird time for everyone, okay?"

Dorn laughed. "Exty, I like you very much but your existence up here is more cloistered than mine was in the House. A 'weird time' isn't a remotely adequate rejoinder."

She smiled. "You like me very much?" she asked.

"This is the part you heard?"

"I felt bad about your situation, okay? So did Viselle. That's why we did what we did to protect you after the fact. And you're not having a *terrible* time up here, right?"

"I'm...it's more *interesting*," they said.

"Then you're having an *interesting* time."

"She murdered people. On vid. The whole world saw."

"I feel bad about that," Viselle said.

"She feels bad," Exty said.

"They *were* hired killers and they were about to shoot my partner," Viselle said. "*And* my best friend's favorite Veeser."

"I can't believe you almost got 'Casta killed," Exty said to Viselle. "I'm still mad about that."

Dorn began to wonder if they were losing their mind.

"Come on, Jimbal, there's nowhere to go," Viselle said. "I mean, jump in the river if you want, it'll just take you back here. And you probably know the valley's fake. Plus the food's getting cold. Promise I won't hurt you."

Dorn returned to the table, reluctantly, and sat. They didn't like any of this, but the part they liked the least was where it turned out Exty wasn't nearly as worthy of their trust as they had thought. It was a jarring discovery on which Dorn was trying hard not to dwell.

One of the servants, who had evidently been standing at the end of the table this entire time with his plates of food, set one down in front of Dorn, then did the same for the others. It was some kind of stew; Dorn's portion appeared to be meatless, which was appreciated. Not that they had any kind of appetite at the moment.

"All right," Dorn said, looking at Viselle. "Why are you here?"

"Didn't have anywhere else to be," Viselle said. "Figured I'd check on how you were doing."

"With?"

"Orno's notes. Oh, and I wanted to show you this." She reached down into the bag at her feet and extracted something, waited a few seconds until she was certain the servant was no longer nearby, and put it on the table.

It looked like a short staff of yellow glass. The corners were squared off, it had a small loop at one end and an irregular pattern of bumps and indents on the other. They picked it up, and was startled to discover how light it was.

"What do you make of it?" she asked.

"Not glass," they said.

"Nope. Couldn't tell you what it *is* made of. Just where it came from, and possibly what it does. You might know too."

Dorn whacked it on the side of the table. It was stiff and sturdy; it felt as if the wood of the table might surrender before the object did.

"It's a *key*," they said. "But to what I can't imagine."

"I don't know either. Not literally. Metaphorically, maybe. But I do know that there are five of them. And I know they're the most important five objects in history."

Dorn put it down gently then. "History," they said. "This came from the vaults."

"Very good."

"I've heard stories about objects like this; rare artifacts stored deep within the House. But none who might talk have access, and none who have access would ever talk. How did you learn that there were *five*?"

Viselle just looked at him.

"Professor Linus," Dorn said. "Did he give this to you?"

"No. He was *going* to smuggle out the key from the Velon chapter on the night he died. Either he didn't manage to do it, or he did and someone else has it. I don't."

"Then where did *this* one come from?"

"The Chnta vault," she said. "Long story."

"I didn't know there was a House still standing in Wivvol."

"Only barely. Two years ago, Orno arranged for this to get smuggled out. I was just there to pick it up. Unfortunately, it's the only one I've been able to get my hands on, and I need all five."

"Why is that?"

Viselle didn't answer.

"Well," they said. "I can tell you what it's probably made of. Some kind of synthetic petroleum compound."

This piqued everyone's interest. "Petroleum?" Viselle said. "I'm not even sure what that is."

"I've heard of engines made using it as a fuel," Exty said. "But not practical ones."

"That's because it's a rare substance," Dorn said. "Some early House texts include diagrams for machines—as you say, Exty—that use it as a fuel. It's been called the blood of the gods."

"*That* I have heard," Viselle said. "I didn't think it was a literal thing."

Dorn nodded, enjoying being the one with the answers for a change. "It is," they said. "This is a true thing for a great many in the faith: we treat as metaphorical things with a literal antecedent. My understanding is that a number of the pre-collapse artifacts in the House vaults are synthesized the same way, with petroleum as a base. Nobody knows why. Possibly, it wasn't *always* rare."

They picked up the key again.

"I'm beginning to see that this object has a similar path, from metaphorical to literal," Dorn said. "You've stated you know what it might do, only not in a literal sense."

Viselle nodded. "I do, but it will sound…when I first heard it, I thought it was ridiculous."

"Ba-Ugna thought the Outcast was coming back," Exty said. "It can't sound *that* much crazier, right?"

"Right," Viselle said with a sigh. "He got that from Orno, and I got *different* information from Orno, because—and I don't know if you knew this about him, Dorn—Orno was kind of an asshole about information."

"He was my professor," Dorn said. "I of course found him generous in that regard."

"I'll bet. But how much he told whoever he was talking to depended on how badly he needed them, and how much detail he thought it would take to get them to agree to help. With my father, it wasn't all that much; just enough to convince him to involve *me*. *I* needed more. But all right; Supposedly—and this is where the metaphor comes in—the five keys unlock the power of the gods themselves."

"Enough power to stop the Outcast?" they asked.

"That was the implication."

Dorn stared at her. "I understand now," they said. Because there was something about Viselle's demeanor in all of this that had been difficult to read, until this moment.

Viselle looked perplexed. "What is it you understand?" she asked.

"I understand that you're doing this out of an obligation," they said. "You're attempting to accomplish something for reasons you do not yourself believe. That must make all of this difficult."

She nodded slowly. "I think you're half right; I don't know *what* I believe. But my father *did* believe it, all of it. *I* believe the keys unlock something, and that the something will turn out to be important. Like, a universal free energy source or whatever. But if you're asking me if I think that finding all five keys will mean we'll be able to, I don't know, shoot a holy ray gun at the physical manifestation of the Outcast? I guess my answer depends on how my day's going up to that point."

"How about right now?"

"Today I think it's ridiculous and I don't know why I've ruined my career for this. Orno Linus was chasing a child's nightmare story, he somehow managed to convince my father to chase it too, and that's all. But tomorrow morning I'll wake up remembering that both of them thought it was important enough to lay down their lives, so maybe I'd better take it seriously. I'm going to keep going with this. Just as soon as I figure out what I'm supposed to do next."

Dorn fell silent for a time. Their understanding of who Viselle Daska was and why she did the things she did was being rewritten on the fly, which was somewhat jarring. Dorn was seeing the person Exty called friend, evidently for the first time. They didn't yet know if this meant they should trust Viselle more, or Exty less.

"Your retrieval of this key..." Dorn said. "You said Professor Linus arranged that."

"He did. He left behind a couple of other leads as well, but this is the only one I was able to follow. Aside from the key he was going to hand over directly on the night he died, this was the only other sure thing."

Viselle looked at Exty.

"I have to locate a couple of people," she said. "Ba-Ugna's equipment is still here?"

"His gadgets?" Exty asked. "Yes. I haven't touched any of it."

"Good. He's got a program that might help."

"Who are you looking for?" Dorn asked.

"Another professor," Viselle said. "Damid Magly. You wouldn't know him; he's not a Septal. Orno seemed to think Professor Magly had a way into the Middle Kingdoms. I'll have to find him, to see if he did or if he can. He's my best bet for a next step right now. After that? Nobody's sure where the last two keys are. And again, Orno's stolen key is still missing."

"I think I know who has that," Exty said quietly.

"What? Who?"

"Um... Ba-Ugna was *so* odd sometimes, wasn't he?" Exty said.

"Sure. He also had a bad temper and he was rude, and he sucked at raising children. What's your point, Ex?"

"The...night he died. He was being weirder than usual. He insisted on turning himself in to the police, and I don't know if you even know this but he did that so they'd clear the charges on you because he was *sure* you knew everything he didn't about the...whatever, anyway, so then he demanded that Detective Stidgeon and Elicasta show up here to bring him down, but first he was going to *talk* to them, and he *insisted* this be a conversation alone. He didn't want there to be any chance of someone overhearing. He told me this himself."

"I see," Viselle said. "And you couldn't resist."

"I hid an electronic ear in his pile of junk."

"Did you *record* it?" Viselle asked, hopefully.

"I just listened. But anyway...I'm pretty sure your former partner has the stolen key."

Viselle erupted in laughter. It was so abrupt that it gave Dorn a start.

"Of course," she said, shaking her head. "Of course. Makk, you gods-damned *Cholem*. Well I guess to get that one I just have to tip him off on my location."

"Won't he arrest you?" Dorn asked.

"Possibly, yes. One thing at a time."

"All right," Dorn said. They weren't ready to discuss next steps yet, as they remained fixed on the need for this odd quest at all. "Now you know of two keys. Imagine you've successfully collected all five. Where do you go to activate this godly power? What do they unlock?"

"I don't know that either," Viselle said. "But Orno claimed to. He said he found it in a book. Which brings us back to your research, Other Jimbal. What breadcrumbs did your former mentor leave behind?"

Dorn sighed. "I'm afraid you're going to be disappointed."

~

Dorn broke down everything they had discovered so far, which didn't take long.

They felt as if they should have been reluctant to provide

Viselle with *all* of the information. Dorn couldn't speak definitively to Professor Linus's state of mind when being—as she put it—an "asshole about information," but they understood the impulse. Ba-Ugna Kev and his daughter were dangerous people; deliberately withholding details and making it *known* one was doing so may have been a survival mechanism. It didn't *work,* but not because of Viselle or Ba-Ugna. (The same could not be said for Dorn's predicament, as they were directly responsible for that, as was—apparently—Exty Demara.)

There was a competing instinct, however. Dorn thought it possible that, upon admitting there was a limit to what they could learn from Orno's notes and further, that they were likely *at* that limit, might lead to a circumstance in which the people who turned Dorn into a fugitive could undo that damage and give them back the life they had before all of this.

Provided Dorn even wanted that. They still weren't sure.

But there was another reason it made sense to simply tell Viselle everything: Dorn had withheld nothing from Exty. She would know if they were holding back, and while a few hours earlier Dorn would have assumed her to be trustworthy enough to hold her tongue, now they knew better.

Viselle listened without comment until Dorn finished. Then she drank a good portion of the wine in her glass, which appeared to be a statement all its own.

"You're missing a book," she said. "That's what you're telling me."

"It appears so," Dorn said.

"And with our luck, it's the same one Orno mentioned to *me*. I hadn't even considered it."

"I don't understand," Dorn said. "Considered what?"

"That the book could be *this* important."

"You know where it is!" Exty said.

"No," Viselle said. "But I know who had it last. Makk and I found it hidden in Orno's house on the first night of the investigation. He made me swear to secrecy and kept it out of evidence."

"Are you saying Detective Stidgeon recognized, that night, the book was important and *you* did not?" Dorn asked. Given how much Viselle knew at that stage, it seemed unlikely.

"He didn't know anything. He still doesn't. But Makk has an unerring talent when it comes to fucking up things for everyone else. I don't really believe in a *Cholem* curse, but if I did, he would be exhibit one. For my part, I figured it was important, but that the same information in the book was also in Orno's notes. Plus, there was no way to get it out of Makk's hands without raising his suspicion, so I let him keep it."

"But why did he even do that?" Exty asked.

"Makk has a healthy distrust of the House. Entirely warranted, mind you, especially when it came to the Linus murder. He thought if it was checked into evidence, it would just go straight back to the Septal vault and out of our reach. But if he kept it, and the House had something to *do* with the professor's death...maybe someone would come looking for it. They did, too. And they didn't find it, which is great for us but also not so great. He hid it and I don't know where. I tried to get him to tell me but he never did."

"I see," Dorn said. "So if I have this correct, if you wish to continue, you need to get both a second key and an ancient manuscript from your former partner, while he means to arrest you at the first opportunity."

"Yes that's exactly right," Viselle said. "Like I said, Makk Stidgeon has a gift." She looked at Exty. "Before I try reaching out to him by voicer...should I assume he's still in the city? Or is he busy trying to hunt down my father's murderer? That seems like something he'd do."

"I don't know," Exty said. "But Elicasta's gone dark. The whole Stream's humming on it, actually. She's never gone without a new live drop this long before. The buzz is, she's left Velon."

"Perhaps they've chosen the safety of relative anonymity over having their lives threatened as a matter of routine," Dorn offered.

"That's definitely not Makk's style," Viselle said. "But neither is chasing down someone like Calcut Linus with an untrained Veeser as his only backup. Okay. I need to trace this Magly guy and Makk both. Hopefully, my father's toy is where it's supposed to be."

∼

Dorn left the table shortly after, returning to their office space with a little help from Jig, who recognized right away that his guest would not be able to find their own way back.

They didn't get anything done; not really. The conversation over dinner was something that took longer to digest than the meal itself. By the time Dorn successfully excised it from their head for long enough to concentrate on the work at hand, Exty was standing in the doorway.

"You're pissed at me, aren't you?" she said.

Dorn didn't answer right away. They were looking at a sheaf of notes Orno took some five years prior, on a manuscript he came across on the island of Botzis. The notes weren't terribly illuminating, but once again Dorn came away impressed at their professor's world-traveling propensity.

"What do you *do?*" Dorn asked, eventually. "What's your job, Exty? I appreciate that you 'run' the family business, but in what sense? And why someone so young?"

"Oh," she said. "Well." She'd been leaning against the door jamb, affecting a casual pose, but as soon as Dorn asked the question she shifted into a more defensive posture. "I do it because someone has to and nobody else wants to."

"Do *you* want to?"

She shrugged. "It has to be done. And I'm good at it, I guess.

But the companies...I don't *run* the companies, like, directly. There's a battalion of CEOs and CFOs and COOs who pilot the ships, as it were."

"But you own the ships," Dorn said.

"The family trust does. And I run the family trust. So to answer you, my job is to sign things lawyers put in front of me. Sometimes I read them and sometimes I don't. A couple of times a year the Demaras host a fundraiser for charity so I get to do the organizing for that. And I handle this mansion, which is a little like managing an exclusive hotel. That's the main stuff. How long have you wanted to ask me that?"

"Do you ever *leave* Lys?"

She wrinkled her nose in something like a frown. Dorn was coming to realize there were many versions of Exty Demara, and they only ever knew one of them. The *something like a frown* was a perfect example: A mild expression of distaste packaged in a polite delivery system that masked whatever true emotion was coursing underneath all of that posturing.

"Sure I do," she said. "But that's probably not what you mean, right? You're talking about, do I know what it's like to *not* have all this money and of course I don't. But if you met basically any one of my relatives, you'd see that...I guess the 'but you should see the other guy' point is a weak one, but that's what I mean. I think I have my feet firmly planted, compared to essentially everyone else I know. Except Viselle, maybe. But she wasn't truly raised by Ba-Ugna so her connection to this kind of life isn't as direct. Why is this important to you?"

"Did you hesitate at all when it came time to frame me for Professor Linus's murder?"

*I didn't do that* was what she nearly said. Dorn could see it in her face, which had—for the briefest of seconds—displayed a real emotion. "No, I didn't," she admitted. "But that's why I took you in. I know what happened was pretty awful for you, but this isn't so bad, is it?"

That *smile* came back, and they forgot themself for a moment.

"Forgiveness isn't just another thing you can expense," Dorn said. "And being kind to me so that *you* can feel better only succeeds in making me feel manipulated."

They'd gone too far. They knew it as soon as they said it, but by then it was too late. Exty's expression went cold, and Dorn saw something genuine in her eyes for possibly the first time: hurt.

"I'll leave you to this," she said.

Then she left before Dorn had a chance to take back any of it.

∽

Dorn couldn't sleep at all that evening. Their bedroom was situated across the hall from the office holding Orno's things—both of these were technically guest bedrooms, but the latter didn't have a bed in it at the moment. This was just as well; Dorn needed the work space and the sleep space separated or they'd do too little of one and not enough of the other.

They gave up and got out of the bed at a little past twenty, but rather than return to the office, they wandered down the stairs to the wing's main rooms where Ba-Ugna's nest of electronics lived. Whether this was Dorn's intended destination or not, it was hard to say.

Viselle Daska was at one of the desks, watching silently as a computer completed a search.

"Dammit!" she exclaimed loudly, slapping her hand on the table. Then she realized she wasn't alone.

"Oh," she said. "It's you. What, did I wake you? I'm not being *that* loud."

"No," they said, taking a seat in one of the few chairs not covered with fragments of electronic devices. "I take it whatever you're searching for is eluding you."

"That's one way to put it. Another would be that my father found a new way to fuck me over from beyond the grave."

She got up and crossed the room to an open wine bottle on the edge of a table. She filled a glass.

"It's Lladnian wine," she said without turning. "Want some?"

"No thank you," Dorn said. "What is it you're trying to find in here?"

"She genuinely likes you, you know," Viselle said, which wasn't an answer to the question.

"Exty?"

"I can see it. You should be nicer to her. And I'm looking for a program my father built. It leverages every Stream-connected electronic device in the world to track the movements of anyone attached."

"The GPS in the voicers?" Dorn asked. "It looks for that?"

"No, no, no. You can turn off GPS tracking and it'll still find you. It's not fully real-time, but it's pretty good. Not good enough to know where to drop a seeker missile maybe, but enough to know which neighborhood to canvass. It's *wildly* illegal, in case you were wondering."

"I can imagine. But illegality doesn't appear to matter to anyone up here."

Viselle held up her wine glass. "We do tend to make up our own rules as we go. I'm with you there. And you're right, but you're also wrong. My father's approach was to invent something first, arrange for the laws that would allow it to exist second, and sell it third. He was about halfway through the second part. Meanwhile, it exists and I need it."

"And you can't find it."

"I think he took it with him. Which means the police probably have it now. I doubt they appreciate what it is they have."

"I don't understand," Dorn said. "Is it a physical device? It sounds like a computer program."

"It *is* a computer program. An incredibly complex one that uses backdoors only he knew about to look at data with an algorithm only he understood. It's impossible to duplicate, if that's what you're thinking."

"I'm thinking we're in a room full of computers owned by your father. Where else would it be?"

"Ah. That isn't how he operated. Ba-Ugna was supremely paranoid about intellectual theft. He'd never store something like this on one of these. I mean, I'm checking, but I'm kidding myself. What he would do is store it on a memory chip and keep it on him. If he needed to use it, he'd pop it into whatever device was handy and when he was done he'd burn the device's memory…if not the device itself."

"I see," Dorn said. "Then if it's anywhere…"

"It's with his personal effects."

"At the police station."

"Last I knew, yes," she said. "Not that I'm in a position to claim the body, but that's what I *would* be doing."

Dorn wondered who there was in Ba-Ugna Kev's life that *could* claim the man's remains, but this didn't seem the time to ask.

"So," Viselle said, emptying her glass, "I'm screwed. Or rather, my father's master plan to save the world is screwed. Or, I guess, Orno's plan to have my father save the world is. It's hard to tell whose ghost I'm disappointing."

It was becoming evident that Viselle Daska had had more than her share of the Lladnian wine.

She walked over to the chair opposite Dorn, pushed something that looked like the neural net of a Veeser rig onto the floor and sat down, bottle and glass in hand. "What did my father tell you, anyway?" she asked.

"About what?"

"How you ended up here. The frame-up. I'm assuming he blamed me for that."

What Ba-Ugna did was make it sound as if Dorn was the luckiest person in the world.

"He never took the blame for doing it," Dorn said, after

consideration. "And there was the un-doctored Stream vid showing you entering in my stead along with the footage of you killing those men...I would say Ba-Ugna allowed my assumptions to go uncorrected. His degree of complicity was unclear to me until today, I suppose."

"That sounds like him."

Dorn looked around at the undifferentiated piles of electronic scrap—this is what it looked like to them—for evidence of a memory fob that might have eluded Viselle, but there was no point to this.

"You can't find and use this program," Dorn said, "but there was a second option if I'm recalling correctly. What about the book?"

"To get that I'd have to convince Makk to help us," she said. "Not sure I have that in me."

"How do you know? He might surprise us, and just contacting him would do no harm."

She smiled. "It could do all *kinds* of harm. Here's the way I look at it: what would it take to convince *me?* The answer is, I don't have enough yet. And if I go in short, it'll just harden his resolve, make it even tougher to convince him later. If I go through with this I'm gonna need his key; I can't afford to alienate him."

"*If* you go through with this?"

"Sorry, Other Jimbal, I'm back in the 'this is ridiculous' mindset right now. If the end of the world is around the corner and *I'm* the only thing in its way, we're in a lot of trouble. On the other hand, my father had a god complex, which I'm sure was Orno's way in. This would be just like Ba-Ugna, sticking me with this when there's nothing there."

"With the book," Dorn said, "it's possible we would have enough information to convince Detective Stidgeon. And yourself if you've failed to tap into your *own* god complex by then."

Viselle laughed. "She *did* tell me you were funny," she said. Which was amusing only because Dorn wasn't trying to be funny.

"You said Detective Stidgeon hid it," Dorn said. "Which implies he doesn't have it *with* him right now."

"Hidden, yeah but not in his apartment, I can tell you that," she said. "The House's Sentries tossed it about an hour before I had a chance to. He seemed pretty tight with the guy who owned the restaurant under his place; it could be hidden there. But that... I don't know, leaving it with *anybody* seems like a risk. This was a pre-Collapse text; it'd go for a ton of Credits on the Black Market. How many people would *you* trust with something like that?"

"I know nobody that well. Outside of Lys."

She smirked. "You think Exty would keep it safe?"

"I think anyone for whom a Black Market windfall would be trivial could be trusted with such an object."

"Great point. Makk doesn't know anyone like that, I'm pretty sure. No, I think he stored it someplace where only he has access."

"A bank vault?"

"Maybe. Wait. Pant City."

"What?"

"The Pantolinar Quarter."

"I know of where you speak; I don't understand the relevance," Dorn said, but Viselle had already leapt from her chair and resettled at one of Ba-Ugna's computers. She put down the alcohol and started typing.

"The same night the Sentries were tossing his Kindontown apartment, Makk didn't go straight home from the station," she said. "He had a uniform drive him to Pant City. I'd already left the precinct and headed directly to his place to look for it. But when Makk didn't show up when I expected him to I checked the auto log of the car he took and it stopped outside of Pant City before heading back downtown. I didn't think too much of it at the time, because there's a lot of things a guy like Makk might appreciate about that part of town. But maybe I was wrong."

Dorn got up and joined her at the computer. "How do you know the Sentries didn't find the volume that same night?" they asked.

"Maybe they did," she admitted. "But they didn't act like it. And they weren't really looking for the book; they wanted the key."

"Which he *also* had."

"True, but possibly not then... No. No, I don't think the found the book. If they had they could have used it as leverage to get what they *really* wanted."

"I understand," Dorn said, although they didn't entirely. If the Sentries were powerful enough to credibly threaten a civilian police detective with a vault theft accusation, they were more fearsome than Dorn thought.

"I'm thinking Makk dropped the book off somewhere in Pant City that night," she said. "And not in a bank vault."

"Why not?"

"He wasn't there during banking hours. Also, if he wanted to rent a vault box, there are plenty of banks to choose from in Kindontown. Makk didn't even own a car; that kind of detour makes no sense."

"I see," Dorn said. "I believe you're piling unsupported guesses atop one another, but I see how you've arrived there."

"No, no, this is good. I can feel it."

"Then if you're not searching Pant City banking centers, what are you looking for?"

"Following a hunch," she said.

Dorn decided against pointing out that she was on her third or fourth hunch just getting this far. And possibly her seventh or eighth glass of wine.

Viselle tapped a few more commands into the computer and then sat back and watched as result began collating...or whatever was going on within the machine. Computers were not a major component of Dorn's scholarship; they didn't use them much.

"I know Makk's history backwards and forwards," she explained, after refilling her glass. "I committed to a deep dive on his personnel file downtown once it became clear the only way to get where I wanted to be was to partner with him, and it's easier to make friendly with someone you know everything about already. Right?"

"Yes, that makes sense."

"You're sure you don't want any wine?"

"I don't drink. Did the information become useful?"

"Not as much as I thought it would," she said. "I got most of the way there by putting on a decent suit and low heels and smiling a lot."

It was Dorn's turn to laugh. This was precisely how she got *them* to talk as well, in the diner. Dorn recalled being dumbstruck that a police detective could look like she did. Makk Stidgeon, on the other hand, looked as if he'd been birthed from a generic detective vending machine.

"It comes back to, who would you trust with something like that?" Viselle said. "My first thought was, Makk didn't have anyone in his life that fit that description so he must have hidden it. But he was also an army man at one point."

"I see. One of the men he served with. Someone with whom he'd entrust his life."

"Exactly. And there's only one man to search for," she said. "Everyone in Makk's platoon died in the same accident except for Makk and one other guy: A Corporal Lemaighey Witts. My hunch is that Corporal Witts lives somewhere in the Pantolinar Quarter, and he has our book."

Viselle's search was something a touch more advanced than a simple address search. She did *that* too but it took under a second to return zero results so she tried something more complicated instead.

Dorn didn't understand *how* it was more complicated; just that it *was* more complicated. She described it as a metadata search utilizing some of the backdoor access she mentioned previously when describing Ba-Ugna's device. "Only, simpler and more brute-force," she added. This did not illuminate things as well as she thought it did.

Sensing, perhaps, that Dorn wasn't following, and also having nothing else to do while the search was going on, she tried explaining it a second time. "Everyone using anything associated with the Stream leaves an ident stamp behind. Like DNA, only electronic," she said. "And there are only so many ways for data to enter and exit Pant City. What I'm doing is targeting the pinch-points so I can isolate to just the quarter and looking inside the bubble. The short of it is, if this guy has left behind any record of his existence, we'll find it. I used to use the same technique in cyber before I transferred to homicide. Only, you know, at cyber these searches were done behind legal warrants."

It made sense only to a limited degree. If Corporal Witts was to be found in Pantolinar Quarter, he was there without a legal address. This could mean he was staying with someone else, or it could mean he didn't want to be found. (It could also mean he wasn't there and this was futile, but they suspected Viselle Daska was many hours away from accepting this conclusion.) If he didn't want to be found, it surely followed that he wasn't using his own name when accessing the Stream. How much good could a search like this actually do?

When Dorn posed a version of this question to Viselle, she said that there was only so far anyone could get on the Stream without there being *some* connection to a real person in the world.

How long it took to find that connection said a lot about the proficiency of the target.

After two hours of searching, it began to look as if Corporal Witts was either *highly* proficient, or legitimately not in the Pantolinar Quarter.

Then something peculiar happened. Dorn happened to be watching the screen—Viselle was across the room, stretching her legs—when the search window disappeared.

"Detective Daska?" Dorn said.

"What's wrong?" she asked.

A message box popped up on the computer.

WHO ARE YOU AND WHY ARE YOU LOOKING FOR ME?

"I think you've found him," Dorn said. "And I think he doesn't appreciate being found."

## Chapter Ten

Leemie Witts had been having an entirely normal day.
First, he spent the morning scoping gigs on the Black Market for the right combination of bid min, complexity, and degree of criminality. What he was looking for was something difficult, posted by someone who knew enough to recognize that it *was* difficult (which the minimum bid figure would tell him,) and that fell on the good side of illegal.

The latter was an incredibly vague metric that changed daily based on the mood of the city in general and Leemie's comfort level in particular, but measuring it was probably the most important part of the job.

Basically, there were some laws that could be broken and some laws that couldn't. For example, there were certain perishables that were either not allowed into Inimata without the levying of a high tariff or were not in allowed at all, period. In the former case, someone who managed a way around the tariff would have a huge market advantage when it came to underselling the competition (who presumably *was* paying the tariff.) In the latter case, the forbidden items were—*because* they were forbidden—hugely valuable to a certain kind of person.

Getting around these regulations meant hiring someone to break into the tracking system used by customs, which was a violation of a decent number of federal laws. But it was quite literally the case that nobody cared. Leemie could walk into County Attorney's office, admit to being the guy who backdoored the customs main for a shipment of Kindonese pufferfish or Wivvolian cigars, and the very worst that would happen is that the C.A. would take his contact information and tell him he'll be in touch later about pressing charges. Then the County Attorney would close the door to his office, light a Wivvolian cigar, call his wife and tell her he's in the mood for Kindonese seafood.

Probably. The point was, these were goods everyone wanted, the people supplying those goods had by now factored the cost of hiring a cybercrimer in with the rest of the overhead, and their customers were the exact well-to-do types who were supposed to be enforcing the laws being broken.

But then there were the laws that could *not* be broken, either because they would definitely send too much attention in Leemie's direction or because he was opposed to them on moral grounds. He drew the line, for instance, at most acts of terrorism, and had a big problem with drug smuggling and child smuggling.

The problem was that almost none of the posted gigs were as obviously benign as eluding customs or as obviously pernicious as child slave labor. They all fell in-between, so Leemie spent a *lot* of time stress-testing his moral compass.

On this day, he felt comfortable with only two gigs. One was perfect: a hack into a corporate database for a shipping manifest. It had a high minimum bid, and the only challenge to it was it had to be accomplished without the target corporation ever knowing it happened.

It took Leemie about ten minutes to work out who the "anonymous" client was: a high-ranking representative of the target's marketplace competitor. Leemie didn't know why a manifest could be so important to *either* company but that didn't matter. He was almost always morally unopposed to corporate espionage.

*The more time they spend destroying each other,* he thought, *the less time they have to control* me.

The second gig was slightly iffier: somebody wanted to clone an ident badge for a government-secured location. *Which* location wasn't revealed in the gig text, and the client did a much better job of anonymizing themselves before posting it—so Leemie couldn't tell who was asking—but the price was good. It felt right *enough* that Leemie took the gig.

It turned out the ask was to get into a surplus grain warehouse on the docks, which was fine. Also, whether the client knew it or not the cloned badge would only get them past the first set of security doors. Leemie didn't know why they only wanted that one door opened, or why they needed access to a grain storage depository, and he didn't care as long as their C-Coins cleared.

Either one of these gigs would have been a heavy lift for someone without Leemie's degree of experience; for him it was only a couple of hours. Then he was free to deal with the pre-Collapse manuscript hidden in his desk.

Leemie's computer-work area was a cockpit-shaped section of his apartment featuring six screens tied to three computers on a table that was threatening to collapse, a squeaky office chair, and a reconditioned Streamer rig with double opticals.

The book had its own corner of the room. It lived in a drawer at his desk, in a sealed poly-cloth sleeve. Every day that the morning jobs didn't bleed into the afternoon or evening, Leemie spent the rest of his time attempting to teach himself archaic Eglinat.

Unsurprisingly, he was getting nowhere. Possibly his biggest accomplishment was realizing that there was a faded title on the spine that was now only visible in the ultraviolet end of the spectrum. But the only word of the title he recognized was *Outcast*, so that wasn't really much of an accomplishment at all. Beyond that, he'd cracked another five words since the last time he'd spoken to Makk Stidgeon (the man who, theoretically, the book belonged to) which was certainly not enough to evaluate the significance of the contents.

Why he was still bothering to translate the text was an open question. Makk originally gave it to Leemie for, A: safekeeping, and B: to figure out how to read it. Both of those goals were premised on the book being important in solving the murder of Orno Linus, but that murder had since been solved. Yet Makk still checked in occasionally to see if Leemie had gotten any farther while at no point indicating he planned to swing by and retrieve the volume.

Which was fine. Leemie had stopped waking up in the middle of the night convinced the Allimites were storming the apartment. It was just like Makk said: nobody was looking for it.

Unless he was wrong about that. Leemie had just slipped on his gloves and the off-brand Septal hood (he found it easier to read Eglinat with the hood on) and cracked open both the ancient volume and his notebook when the alarms started going off.

"Here they come," he said, to the pre-Collapse book. "Like we always knew they would. Didn't we, old man?"

The book didn't answer.

～

Leemie wasn't registered as living at the Pantolinar Quarter address. The name on his rental agreement was Noht Lyngso, an entirely real person who died some ten years prior in the same transport accident that killed the rest of Leemie and Makk's unit. Despite being legally dead in the eyes of the Inimatan government and its corporatized military adjunct, resurrecting him for the purpose of property leasing ended up being a simple matter. (Leemie also had C-Coin accounts in the names of three other deceased comrades-in-arms. Those accounts were supposed to be impossible to trace back to an owner, but he didn't believe it.)

Noht's rental contract was the closest thing Leemie had to a legal footprint in Pant City. Meanwhile, to find anything under the name Lemaighey Witts—in Pantolinar or elsewhere—one had to look at the travel and postal records, where it would appear that he'd retired to an island on the coast of Botzis two years after his discharge from military service. That was the best anyone could expect from a front door search.

A backdoor search might end up being more promising. There were the things Leemie knew about—facial recognition bots riding street-level drones, true-ID DNA registers, and retinal database records were three quick examples—and also things he only suspected. He was pretty sure the government tagged him with an isotope while he was serving and had been employing micro-opticals to keep an eye on him since. That was why even though he took every precaution imaginable, from foil-lining his apartment to violently deactivating every front-facing optical lens on his devices and never exiting the apartment without a disguise on, he was pretty positive they knew where he was. And in knowing, they could come for him at any time.

The best he could do about *that* was make sure he was ready when they did.

The alarms were coming from his main computer rig. It constantly monitored Stream traffic using a recursive algorithm Leemie stole from an antitheft program that had been designed to catch cybercrimers like Leemie. (He managed to evade it, but in doing so found it to be elegantly constructed. Not a surprise; it had DNA from the Kev Cyber Initiative.) Evidently, someone was performing multiple backdoor searches for Lemaighey Witts, and not across the entire Stream: they'd only hit five nexus points, but they were the five nexus points that handled all traffic from the Pantolinar section of Velon.

They didn't know Leemie was living in Noht Lyngso's apartment, but they knew enough to narrow their search to Pant City. That was not good.

He shut off the alarms (five of them, one for each nexus point) and opened up his extensive library of stolen code until he found what he was looking for: a backtrace trick criminally misapplied by a beverage wholesaler who used it to confirm that people voting for their favorite flavors only voted once. Once Leemie had stripped it of the anonymizers—which the company had to install to make it complaint with regulations—it worked incredibly well. Which was to say, it worked the way the original designer clearly intended for it to.

The backtracer jumped into action and within about an hour Leemie had an answer. It made no *sense*, but it was an answer: the search was coming from off-planet.

This wasn't a logical conclusion, so he spent another half an hour rechecking the results.

It looked like the initiator hit a global satellite first, which could have meant that it either began from somewhere on the surface or from another global satellite and *then* somewhere else on the surface. But there were special nodes on the satellites reserved for space-to-Dib communications and it was one of those nodes that was being used.

That left only a few viable options for the ultimate source: a ship in orbit; the moon base; or Lys.

The moon base was probably out of the question, only because the signal delay would cause problems with the search. A ship in orbit also seemed unlikely; that would be like someone in a car suddenly deciding they had to find Leemie immediately.

It had to be Lys.

Leemie could think of a few good reasons why somebody would want to find him, provided that somebody worked for a government, the House, the police, the Allimites, the military, the Unitists, the League of Countries, or the Linus family. (There were others, but those were the first ones he could think of off the top of his head.) But he drew a blank when it came to someone on Lys needing to locate him, for any reason.

Lys was where the truly elite lived, sure. And as a true believer in roughly a dozen conspiracy theories, he firmly believed that the people up there ultimately ran *everything* on the surface. (This was a component of half of the aforementioned rough dozen conspiracy theories.) But he *also* believed that none of them got directly involved; not at the "must locate Leemie Witts" level.

He just wasn't that important. He couldn't be.

He *had* to know who was doing it, and why. So he did the thing he absolutely should not have done: he lit up a location-masking algo—so it would look like he was talking to them from that island off Botzis—and then he opened up a direct message and asked them who they were.

∼

"What should we say?" Dorn asked.

Viselle stared at the message for several seconds before answering. "I don't know. But I'm going to have to adjust my thinking about this guy; what he just did is very difficult. Hang on."

She slid into the chair at the computer and began tapping away rapidly at the keys. All the screens save for the one with Corporal Witts' message underwent a series of transformations in response.

"He's supposedly written to us from Lesser Calus," she said, after some time.

"Is that a part of the Pantolinar Quarter?" Dorna sked.

"It's an island on the tip of a chain in the Norton. Tax haven. Very popular among certain types."

"Then if this is the man we're looking for...he's not where we thought he was. Which would mean he doesn't have our book."

Viselle Daska laughed gently. "Lesser Calus is basically two goats and a bank on top of a rock. It's not where you retire to. It's where your fids retire to."

Dorn had to run this through their head for a moment. The fid was Inimata's government-backed currency. (Fid was short for fiddlach. It was the base currency of a country that no longer existed, also called Fiddlach. The country was now northern Inimata.) As an inanimate thing, it made little sense to Dorn why it would need to retire anywhere. But economics wasn't one of their areas of study.

"He's not on Lesser Calus," they said. "This is what you're saying."

"I am. Honestly, not sure much of anything exists there anymore. The C-Coin pretty much took out the need for fiscal paradises."

Her hands appeared to be divorced from the rest of her, as they didn't currently require the use of her mind in order to continue with whatever they were doing.

"Why is that?" Dorn asked.

"It's almost impossible to source C-Coins. If you happen to be a lot wealthier than you're supposed to be you no longer have to find a way to hide it or justify it. At least, that's the case right now. Expect that to change in another five or ten years; these things go in cycles. There."

She stopped typing.

"Okay," she said. "He *is* in Pant City. I have him narrowed down to three blocks. If I try to trace him any closer he'll know it."

"I thought his computer said he was somewhere in the Norton Ocean."

"It did. But the command to tell us that had to come from somewhere, and *that* command came from somewhere else. I used to do this full-time, and it's looking like our friend is the kind of person I used to hunt. I think *you* should answer him."

"I don't understand."

Viselle got up and surrendered the chair. "I mean, tell him who you are."

~

It was a few minutes before Leemie got an answer. In that time, he triple-checked his various security systems to make absolutely sure there had been no significant breaches.

Physically, he appeared to be okay; nobody was trying to break through the walls of his apartment-building. Stream-wise, there were a number of low-level tickles, but nothing that couldn't be explained by a slightly higher-than-normal search activity. It was the kind of noise where, if he panicked about it, he'd always be panicking. Even as a self-acknowledged high-functioning paranoid, Leemie didn't panic at anything that was less than two standard deviations from the norm.

When the reply came through, Leemie nearly fell over.

MY NAME IS DORN JIMBAL AND I NEED YOUR HELP.

"No fucking way," Leemie said.

DORN JIMBAL IS DEAD, Leemie typed. WHO IS THIS REALLY.

I ASSURE YOU I AM NOT DEAD.

Leemie picked up his voicer then. The best person to clear up any confusion regarding the current wellbeing of the ex-Septal Other who went by that name was Makk Stidgeon. However, the last thing Makk told Leemie—on the same night Calcut Linus murdered Ba-Ugna Kev—was that he was headed into the deep weeds and to not expect him to be available for a while. (He meant this in a non-literal sense. In the war, the going into the "deep weeds" meant rough-traveling behind enemy lines.)

Leemie could *try* reaching out to Makk with a direct message, but there was a real risk that in doing so he'd be putting his friend in jeopardy. (Because you needed it quiet to survive in the deep weeds.) More likely, the direct wouldn't connect.

He put the voicer back down.

I NEED YOUR HELP, the sender restated.

For a hot second, Leemie was reminded of a popular scamblast. *Just give me your wallet address, send a few thousand credits, and in a month's time my father's fortune will be yours.* He knew a handful of gray-moral Black Market coders who specialized in that kind of gig. But whoever was on the other end had gone through too much effort to find Leemie for it to be something that basic.

After much consideration, Leemie responded: PROVE TO ME YOU ARE DORN JIMBAL AND THEN WE'LL TALK.

Then he dropped a skiplink at the end of the message. It led to his own private Black Market barter room. The place was heavily masked and not more than a little expensive but it was worth it; the security encryption was the best on the planet. Nothing that went on in the room could get out, and nobody who wasn't supposed to be there could get in.

Leemie shifted to another screen, opened up the room, and waited. It took about thirty seconds before he was joined by his mysterious guest.

I'M HERE, they said.

"Audio is enabled in this space," Leemie said. "Turn on your aud."

Hesitation, and then: "All right."

"Now turn on your optical," Leemie said. On a different screen, Leemie called up two images: the still of Dorn Jimbal's full face from the Linus murder vid, and a second still of Other Jimbal under the Septal hood.

"I'd rather not do that," was the response.

"We're not going further without a visual, friend," Leemie said. "There's no audio record of Dorn Jimbal's voice or I'd do a vocal ID. And before you ask, I'm not going to be turning on my optical. You don't need to know what *I* look like."

A long pause, and then the optical on the other end of the communication popped to life and Leemie was staring at the face of a stranger. The person before him had short-cropped black hair, a round face, and only one functioning eye. The left was milky white, no doubt thanks to the same trauma that gave them the scarring on the rest of that side of the face.

Behind them was a well-appointed room that told Leemie almost nothing. He saw gold trim along part of the top of a doorway, wood paneling on one wall and a section of red brick along another wall.

It could have been someplace on Lys but it could have been just about anywhere else too; Leemie knew exactly as much about what the interior of the properties on Lys looked like as the next person, which was to say he knew almost nothing.

But, the background was no doubt a choice.

"Now what?" the person claiming to be Dorn said.

"You don't look like the vid still," Leemie said.

"That's because the vid wasn't me; it was spoofed. You know this."

"Yes I do. Hold still."

"What?"

"Just hold still," Leemie repeated. He triggered a facial scan algo, took the results, and ran them against both of the images on the other screen. It came back with an 89% match on the spoofed face. On the hooded image—with the algo adjusted to anticipate disparity from the Septal hood—Leemie got a 97% match.

Good enough.

"All right, you have my attention, Dorn Jimbal," Leemie said. "You wanna explain to me how you ended up at Lys?"

There were already two dozen theories tumbling through his brain. Half of them were preexisting, predicated on the concept of secret organizations ruling the world from—literally—on high. Dorn could be an unwitting pawn in a greater game or a willing participant. They could even be the orchestrator, with Dorn's retreat to Lys simply being a return to home base.

Dorn had also been a Septal, and Leemie was quite positive the House secretly ran everything too. (There was no inherent contradiction to the idea that both the House and the shadowy elite living in Lys secretly ran the world. These were not mutually exclusive concepts but indications that there was a higher order still.) Dorn could be acting in that capacity.

But there was their face... Something about Dorn Jimbal's scarring shook Leemie Witts, for reasons he couldn't pin down. It didn't fit the narrative, somehow.

"I am not in a position to confirm my current location," Dorn said.

"Yeah okay. Are you alone?"

"Yes. As you can see. I am alone."

"I can see what the optical is showing me, which isn't much. Crappy old inbuilt fisheye lens, too. Bet if you panned around we'd find a device with a better rig."

Dorn looked impatient. Notably, their eyes—well, the one with a pupil—kept flicking up and to their right. They were looking at someone or something that was behind the screen, out of Leemie's view.

"That may be so," Dorn said. "But I've met your conditions. Am I speaking right now to Corporal Lemaighey Witts?"

"You are," Leemie said. "Why did you want to?"

"I'm told you have a certain book," Dorn said.

Leemie was glad he wasn't on optical, because he undoubtedly looked like he was suffering a cardiac event.

"I don't know what you're talking about," he said, unconvincingly.

"It was given to you by Detective Makk Stidgeon of the Velon homicide department. It's an artifact from the Septal vaults."

"I'm sorry," Leemie said quickly. "I can't help you."

"Please! Please don't disconnect. What's in that book is...it *may be* of grave importance."

*It's a trap*, Leemie thought. *Confess to nothing. Burn the book. Go dark. Run. It's over.*

"How do you know about the book?" he asked.

"Makk Stidgeon told me," Dorn said.

Leemie laughed. "You're overplaying your hand, Dorn Jimbal. When would he have done that?"

Dorn looked beyond the screen again. Then: "The...the night he came to Lys. To arrest Ba-Ugna Kev. That's when he told me."

"I'm sorry, no. You're a terrible liar. Goodbye."

"Wait! I can read it!"

Leemie's finger hesitated over the disconnect.

"It's in the archaic," Leemie said. "And you're a fourth-year Septal. An *ex* fourth-year Septal."

"I'm not as talented in it as Professor Linus," Dorn said, "but it *is* one of my fields of study. And I would have a better time of it than you. That *is* what you're doing with the book, isn't it? Trying to translate it?"

Leemie didn't answer. He also didn't sever the connection like he should have.

"Don't you want to know what it says?" Dorn asked.

"Makk said it was important. But he didn't know why," Leemie said. "All right."

"All right? You'll help?"

"All right I'm sending you an address. You come to that address alone and I'll let you see the book. But it doesn't leave with you, do you understand? You help translate it and then you go and we're done."

"I...yes. Yes, that will be fine."

"Because I promised Makk it would never leave my possession," Leemie said, "and I'm not going anywhere."

"I understand."

"Another thing. Tell whoever is in that room with you that

they're not welcome. I don't care who they are; they can be a living incarnation of Honus himself and they'll still draw fire. Understood?"

Jimbal's eyes drifted beyond the screen again, for a heartbeat.

"Yes," they said.

"Come at night," Leemie said. Then he disconnected.

## Chapter Eleven

The trip to the surface consisted of a sequence of surrealistic experiences that left Dorn shaken and disoriented.

To begin with, the path back down didn't involve the Tether, despite that seemingly being the most effective way to reenter Velon from Lys.

The timing even worked out. They'd spoken to Witts at what felt like the early morning hours, but that was because the Demara mansion's local time was set to match Wivvol local time rather than Velon. (Wivvol local time—or WLT—was the standard for ships at sea. There was little reason for it to be the adopted standard for the Demara family estate, although astronomical observations were also recorded in WLT and Archeo had that big telescope, so this could have been why.) The point was that it was actually late afternoon in Velon itself, which meant the Tether shuttle was already past the clouds. They could very easily have packed up and made it to the departing shuttle.

That didn't happen. Instead, after a robust debate as to who would *actually* be going, what they would be bringing with them, and what would be happening if it all went asunder, Dorn, Viselle

Daska and Exty Demara took a ride down an elevator from the bottommost point of the mansion. At precisely the halfway point, they went weightless, turned completely upside-down (in respect to their prior orientation) and proceeded up to the ship dock about which Dorn had previously heard a great deal. Exty would often mention shipments of this or that, and how they attached to the "underside" of the station, but it never occurred to Dorn that this underside would have inverted gravity (again, in comparison to their prior orientation.)

There was something that looked like a regular aero-car waiting for them. An *expensive* aero-car, certainly—they were *all* expensive, but this looked excessively so—but still just an aero-car. And if there was one thing Dorn thought they knew to be true about aero-cars, it was that they couldn't travel into space.

"How did that get here?" Dorn asked. They knew the answer, but since the answer was nigh impossible, they wanted to hear someone else say it.

"I drove it," Viselle said. "This is how I got here."

"Wow, that's pretty," Exty said. "Ba-Ugna outdid himself."

Dorn took a look at the interior, the glass windshield, and the undercarriage. It made no sense.

"He invented teleportation," Dorn said. "That's right, isn't it? This is lovely, but it couldn't survive in space. And reentry? Out of the question. I'd rather let the corporal burn the book."

"Oh it works," Viselle said.

"I've never heard of such a thing," Dorn said.

"You wouldn't have," Exty said. "This here's the prototype."

"You really got here in this?" Dorn asked Viselle.

"I did. But I can see why you're skeptical; you're not seeing it with the hard candy shell."

"No, definitely not," Dorn said. "I'm staying here."

Exty laughed. "They're joking," she said to Viselle. "Didn't I say they had a dry sense of humor?"

"I'm really not," Dorn said. "How many times have you taken this into space?"

"This was the first, but it worked great," Viselle said. "Dorn, it's our only option. We went over this."

"We did, but that was before I saw what the third choice looked like."

The problem, as they all saw it, was this: There was no way to get from Lys to Velon without being noticed. Taking the Tether shuttle down was a big risk in that regard, because Veesers and UnVeesers camped out with drones on the regular, looking for a shot of someone famous. And even if they managed to evade the attention of a drone optical—Viselle and Exty insisted they had a way to do this—there were still plenty of naked eyes that could ID either Dorn or (more likely) the infamous Viselle Daska.

They could take an exo-vehicle down instead, but they were strictly regulated, meaning even if they were scheduled to land on a private pad, that descent had to be logged by someone, somewhere. And, perhaps mindful of how her father died, Viselle was unwilling to risk ending up in the wrong place with the wrong people waiting for them.

Option number three was evidently an aero-car that would burn up on reentry and kill everyone inside of it.

"We don't have to take this if you don't go down with me," Dorn said, for perhaps the fourth time. "There's a high likelihood I will be able to travel unrecognized, especially with no hood. You can't say that, and you know I'll just use the Tether."

"We're not doing that," she said.

Also previously ruled out was sending Exty down with Dorn. This was somehow interpreted by Viselle as a *worse* option than sending Dorn alone, possibly because Exty Demara was in most respects more famous than either of them and would inadvertently draw attention no matter how well she disguised herself. Dorn didn't think that was the reason, or rather not the main one. They thought the main reason was that Viselle Daska had a blaster she wasn't shy about using and Exty did not.

Dorn didn't think Lemaighey Witts was actually dangerous, but was willing to admit there were things about the man that they didn't know, and that Viselle might.

Viselle opened up the doors on the aero-car—they slid up—and climbed in. It was a tight fit in there, with room for only two, something Dorn found modestly encouraging: perhaps there was unseen equipment in this vehicle that might help. Like an actual spaceship hidden beneath the floorboards.

"Are you getting in willingly, or do I have to threaten you or something?" she asked Dorn.

"No, I'll get in."

"Honestly, if I thought there was a chance this wouldn't work I would find another way down," Viselle said. "I don't want to burn up in the atmosphere any more than you do."

Then began the even *more* surreal portion of their journey. After waving goodbye to Exty (who insisted she would see Dorn soon, something Dorn seriously doubted at this point) Viselle started the engine and they lifted off.

Exiting the Lys docks involved taking the ship through a giant airlock first, which kept the surface from being exposed to space. They reached that airlock, waited for it to close behind them, and then Viselle said, "here we go," and pushed a button.

There was a loud hiss on all sides of the vehicle. At first, Dorn thought they were hearing the initial indications of explosive decompression, but that wasn't what was happening at all. A *foam* was being emitted from various tiny orifices in the shell of the car.

"What is this?" Dorn asked, as the pinkish substance began covering the windows.

"Heat shield," Viselle said. She pushed another button and the dashboard popped open, revealing a second control panel.

"We're to be protected by soap bubbles?"

"It'll harden in a sec."

Shortly, all the windows were covered and they had nothing by which to see except for the internal dash lights.

There was a loud beep, accompanied by a green flashing light.

"There, see?" Viselle said. "Hard candy shell, like I said. And we're ready to go."

"What is it *made* of?"

"It's an incredibly heat-resistant polymer. My father invented it a while back for use as an emergency coolant for nuclear plants. It diffuses heat really well, but unfortunately it had other flaws that made it too dangerous for its intended function."

A new alarm sounded indicating the outer airlock door was open. They were now exposed to space. Using the secondary dashboard—which was intended for sightless piloting—Viselle nudged them toward the planet.

"What sorts of flaws?" Dorn asked.

"It's not so great with radiation," she said. "It was supposed to contain without retaining, which it doesn't do. That's a problem when it melts."

"I'm sorry, did you say 'melts'?"

She laughed. "I know it doesn't seem like it, but we're surrounded by like three maders of this stuff on all sides. We'll be fine. But anyway, yes. It melts, but heat doesn't do it. It's water-soluble."

"Oh. Then let's avoid clouds."

"By the time we hit the cloudbanks we're going to want this stuff off of us. Otherwise, I'll have to splash-land in the nearest ocean and that'll just wreak havoc on the paint job."

"You're joking, aren't you?"

"Partly. If this all works like it's supposed to, we'll read to anyone watching like a meteorite that burned up on the way down. It'll be easier if the foam is falling apart by then. But you're correct that I'm not genuinely concerned about the paint job."

They didn't manage to shed all of the foam on the way down. Nor did they succeed in ridding themselves of all the velocity that came with plummeting to the surface from space. Viselle had to perform a number of wide loops on the way down, and then plunge the aero-car into the ocean.

"How did you get rid of this on your way up?" Dorn asked.

"I landed with some of it on," she said. "But I wasn't worried about sneaking into a city looking like a regular old aero, so it was no big deal. We washed it off with a hose."

They were ultimately able to do precisely that: sneak into the city. At a little past one in the morning, Viselle set the aero-car down a few blocks from the edge of the Pantolinar Quarter, looking like every other car on the street.

Viselle pulled a hood over her head, checked her blaster, and unlocked the doors. Then she took a small, round device from a pocket and turned it on.

"Are you ready?" she asked, holding up the device.

Dorn fumbled around in their pockets for the one Exty gave them.

"Yes, I think," they said, activating it. For some reason, they expected to feel differently with it on, but of course they didn't.

"Good."

"Are you sure this will work?" Dorn asked.

The devices were supposed to make them invisible to all optical feeds, be they state-run or private. As difficult as it was to believe such technology was real, Dorn knew the entire case proving Calcut Linus murdered Orno hinged on it being so.

"Of course it will," Viselle said.

"Then if you don't mind my asking, why didn't you use it when going to see Orno?"

"Why was *I* visible when Calcut wasn't?" she asked. "Because I didn't have access to the tech. I didn't even know it existed at the time. Not sure Ba-Ugna did either. *Exty* did, but she kept it to herself."

"Even knowing it might help explain what happened?"

"Not sure she made that connection. Even if she did...she probably still would have kept it to herself. Exty holds a lot of secrets for a lot of people. If it hadn't come out of Makk's investigation already I think we still wouldn't know about it."

"Do you have difficulty trusting her? Knowing this?"

*Because I do*, Dorn thought.

"Of course not. If anything, I trust her more for it. Besides, if it's a real problem, she'll just put two people with complementary secrets in the same room together until it pans out. Now come on; I want to be headed back to Lys before the suns come up."

Dorn put up their own hood and got out of the car.

The hood wasn't nearly as comforting an accessory as the Septal hoods to which they were accustomed. The House version included a band of fabric that covered the top half of the face, such that only the mouth and chin were exposed. It had the dual effect of masking most of the wearer's visage while also turning the world on the other side of the veil a little fuzzy. Dorn failed to appreciate, until this moment, how distancing that view had been for them; it had made the world a little less colorful and vibrant, certainly, but also consisting of events that transpired at a great remove.

It likely also didn't help that Dorn had been in isolation for an extended period, well away from the bustle of a major city.

In short, there were seemingly hundreds of people between them and the arch signifying the formal border of Pant City and Dorn was having trouble coping.

Really, it was only a couple dozen people. But there was no reason for this many to be out at this hour.

"Are you all right?" Viselle asked.

"No," they said. "Do they not all have jobs?"

"Sure. Probably on their way to them. Or from them. Or

doing them right now." She nodded to a woman in scant clothing, walking back and forth along the curb. "Velon doesn't have a bedtime."

"The House's schedule was strictly diurnal," Dorn said. "So I *did* have a bedtime."

"Well. You aren't a Septal any longer, Dorn Jimbal. Let's go."

She took them by the arm and started walking.

They dove into the stream of rapidly transiting locals, through the gates and into Pant City. There, the scene worsened somehow.

"How long would it take us to get back to Lys?" they asked.

"A few hours. Why?"

"We agreed to come at night, but not necessarily *this* night, yes?"

"Calm down. We only have a few blocks to go."

They passed a street vendor hawking wallets, a purveyor of Kindonese pastries, a woman who believed it was appropriate to rub her thigh against Dorn's leg while speaking nonsense, a man wielding a butcher's blade who inexplicably sold kittens, dozens of heavily inebriated packs of people traveling between establishments, five vagrants who were either sleeping or dead, and more. It all left Dorn with the impression that, A: if this was the alternative, they would gladly return to life as a Septal, provided the House accepted them back, and B: it really was a good thing Viselle insisted on coming.

They finally reached their destination after a seemingly endless journey. Blissfully, the street on which the address was located was less crowded than the roadways near the gate.

"This is it," Viselle said, at the top of a down staircase. Corporal Witts evidently lived in the building's sublevel. She leaned over to get a better look, without also going down. "All right, you'd better turn off your thing."

"Why?"

"He's got a security optical. He's gonna be pretty confused if you ring the doorbell but don't show up on his vid. This is perfect, actually."

Dorn pulled the device from their pocket and pushed the button to turn it off. They felt silly about this, because again, there was no external indication that it was doing anything whatsoever. "Why is it perfect?" they asked.

"Because he won't know I'm here until he shows up at the door," she said. "All I have to do is keep mine on."

"Or, you could wait out here," Dorn said. "Like we agreed on."

"I'm not feeling right about that now," she said. "I..." she trailed off, her eyes going up the street. Dorn followed her gaze.

"What is it?" they asked.

"Not sure." She looked up, left and right. There were pedestrians on the sidewalks on both sides and a few cars transiting the road, but none of that was what had caught her interest. "Something feels wrong," she said.

"Should we turn around?"

"It's too late for that. Come on, let's get inside. He'll just have to live with me."

Dorn and Viselle went down the stairs. An overhead light flickered on, either triggered by their motion or turned on by someone watching. It illuminated a door that was papered with legal passages."

"Oh, great," Viselle said. "He's one of *those* people."

"What do you mean?"

"Dorn Jimbal," a voice announced, far louder than Dorn was personally comfortable with. It came from a speaker next to the optical above the door.

"I'm here," Dorn said.

"You were told to come alone."

Viselle, confused, rechecked her own pocket invisibility device while Dorn felt vindicated. *They* don't *do anything*, Dorn thought.

"It's a bluff," she whispered. "No way he can see me."

Dorn shook their head. She was wrong. "I, um, this is just my, uh, bodyguard."

"No, dammit," she muttered.

"I can see you, woman," Witts said. "And I can hear you. Our deal is null. Please leave."

"No, wait," Dorn said, lowering their hood. "Nothing's changed. You still need my help and I still need yours."

The silence that followed was long enough that Dorn thought it was too late, and Corporal Witts had receded into his private little basement hole.

"Take off your hood too, lady," Witts said.

"I don't think that's a good idea," she said.

"Go ahead and try breaking in if you want. Trust me that this is the easier way."

Viselle sighed, lowered her hood and looked directly at the optical.

Another long silence followed. This time Dorn was pretty sure their host was filling up the time with a variety of curses.

"Are you here to kill me?" Witts asked.

"What? No, why would I want to do that?"

"Good. Please leave."

"Corporal Witts..." Dorn began.

"Now, or I'll be forced to open fire."

Dorn looked around for evidence of a protruding gun barrel. Viselle, meanwhile, stepped in front of Dorn and spoke directly to the optical.

"I think you need to let us inside, Lemaighey," she said. "They already know we're here."

"*Who* already knows? You're being followed??"

"I think so. I've seen them. You know who I'm talking about."

"Then go! Quickly! Before they track you here!"

"I think we're going to wait, Dorn and I," Viselle said. "Right here on your stoop. When they arrive we'll just tell them who you are and what you have. You know they've been looking for you, right?"

Witts didn't respond. Viselle was holding her breath, and Dorn realized they were holding theirs too.

Then the door buzzed. Viselle grabbed the knob and pushed it open.

"Hurry," she said, pushing Dorn through, "before he changes his mind."

The door closed and locked behind them. Then they were stuck: the door at the other end of the room—heavily reinforced from the look of it—was locked.

"They who?" Dorn asked.

"What?"

"You said *they* were coming and *they* were looking for him. Who is 'they'?"

"Oh," she said. "No idea. I let him fill that in for himself. Maybe you can ask; I'm curious what he comes up with."

There was a metallic clang at the inner door. Then it flew open and Lemaighey Witts stepped into view, holding a double-barreled shotgun. He was a tall man, skinny in a way that indicated a nutrient deficiency, and he looked genuinely manic. It was not the sort of expression one hopes to see at the trigger end of a shotgun.

Dorn raised their hands.

"I should shoot the both of you right now!" he said. "I'd be in my rights!"

"But you aren't going to," Viselle said mildly. "Here, I'm going to take out my blaster and hand it to you, all right? It's our only weapon."

"I'm not armed," Dorn said quickly.

"Stay right there!" Witts said to Viselle. "Okay, draw it. Butt-first. Put it on the floor and kick it to me."

She did as directed and then lifted her jacket to show her belt and turned around slowly.

"No other weapons, okay?" she said.

Witts put his foot on her blaster and dragged it through the doorway and out of view, while keeping the barrel of the shotgun leveled the entire time. It seemed as if he was mostly interested in keeping it pointed at Viselle, but if Dorn's understanding of the mechanics of shotguns was accurate it didn't much matter which one of them the barrels directly faced; in the narrow entryway, they'd both be hit by approximately the same amount of shot.

"Pants," Witts said.

"You...want me to take off my pants?" she asked.

"Raise the legs."

Viselle knelt down and lifted one pants leg, and then the other. Both ankles were free of weapons.

"I also don't have anything in my sleeves," she said, rolling them back. "There are probably a couple other places we can check if you want, but I'm not sure we have that kind of time."

Witts looked at Dorn. "Now you," he said.

Dorn performed the same acts as Viselle, save for the one where they slid a blaster across the floor, as they didn't have one of those.

"Now can we go inside or do you really want to do this out here?" Viselle asked.

Lemaighey Witts remained uncommitted for a lot longer than made sense to Dorn; it was evident the man was only barely holding it together. Dorn wondered if the war made him that way or if this happened later.

"All right, walk to me," he said, finally. "Slowly."

Hands raised, Dorn walked through the inner doorway with Viselle trailing. When she was halfway through, Witts grabbed her by the elbow and pulled her in violently. She stumbled and landed on a collection of papers stacked on the floor near a couch that was being used for more papers. It looked a lot like the office where Dorn had been attempting to decipher Orno's notes only Witts had a larger collection, and it looked as if many of these stacks had existed in their current form for a number of years.

Viselle remained where she'd landed, hands up, while Dorn tried to figure out what to do with themself. Witts slammed the door and slid five bolts into place. Then he picked up the blaster and slid it into his belt.

"All right, congratulations, you tricked your way into my home and led them to me in the bargain. Who is it? The House? Allimites? Who?"

Viselle laughed. "The *Allimites?* There's no such group."

"You're Ba-Ugna Kev's daughter. You have access to the wealthiest people in the world, you're a cop, and you tracked me down from a terminal on *Lys*. When it comes to the existence of Allimites, you're literally the least credible person on Dib. Your father's definitely an Allimitist. And don't think for a second that I believe he's really dead."

Dorn's head was spinning. They didn't know what an Allimitist was and was afraid to ask, but they were as certain as they could be that Kev was deceased. The vid of his murder left no room for equivocation, in no small part because over a dozen drones captured it as it happened, from multiple angles.

"Great," Viselle said. "If you know where he's hiding, let me know. Can I get up?"

"Who's coming?" Witts asked again.

"Nobody's coming, corporal. I just needed a way to get in."

"What?"

Witts took two giant steps toward Viselle, thrusting the barrel aggressively as if it was sharp and capable of impaling her. She didn't move, which was wise, and also didn't look terribly worried.

"I said something I knew you were prepared to believe so that we could get inside," she said. "And you're still not going to shoot me."

"You lied??" he said.

"Sure. But you expected me to."

Witts held still, Dorn held his breath, and Viselle remained where she was, all for an interminable period.

Then Corporal Witts laughed. "Clever!" he exclaimed. "I can either be a fool or a paranoid, is that it?"

"Excuse me," Dorn said.

"No, excuse *me*. I'm going to need both of you to leave my home immediately. And I'm keeping your expensive blaster, Detective Daska."

"I'm not a detective any longer," she said.

"Excuse me," Dorn said again.

"I heard that!" Witts said. "I believe it as much as I believe your father is actually..."

"You want to know what the book says!" Dorn shouted. This snapped Witts out of whatever lunatic reverie he was about to embark upon. "Don't you?" they added.

"I do," Witts said. "And if I could trust you to tell me the truth about its contents, I'd show it to you."

Dorn chanced a look around the room; specifically, the desk area. There were bits of scrap attached to a corkboard and loose piles of paper on the desktop and the floor. To someone else it would have probably just looked like doodles.

"You're attempting to translate it yourself," Dorn said.

Witts nodded. "I've gotten pretty far, too."

"Have you? I've found the past participles in archaic extremely challenging. What do *you* think?"

"I'm making progress!"

"I'm sure. But I can make *faster* progress. And I'll be happy to share what I've learned with you the moment I learn it. Since I don't know *which* parts of the text you've already translated, testing my veracity should be a simple enough matter."

"Look, no bullshit," Viselle said. "We're pretty sure that book is the key to understanding how the world ends. Of all the people who'd appreciate that..."

"Don't patronize me!" he snapped. To Dorn, he said, "top drawer of the desk. Translate the title for me and then we'll see."

Dorn stepped around the stacks of files and slid into a creaky chair. They noticed, sitting atop the desk, a fake Septal hood. They held it up, quizzically.

"I thought it would help," Witts said.

Dorn tossed it aside, pulled open the drawer, and found the book.

To his credit, their host had kept the book sealed in a polycloth bag. Ideally, it should have been held in a cool, dry, antiseptic room as well, but there wasn't one available.

Dorn started to take the book out of the bag.

"Gloves!" Witts barked. He pointed to another part of the desk where, indeed, a set of gloves rested. Dorn slid the gloves on, then extracted the book.

It was *old* all right. Hidebound, tied closed with straps, Dorn had seen maybe four other examples of such volumes in their time in the House. (And always, before now, separated from them by glass.) It was so old, there was no evidence of lettering on the cover at all.

"Do you happen to have an ultraviolet lamp?" Dorn asked, after examining the spine from several angles."

Witts smiled. "There's a scanner in the drawer on the left."

Dorn, feeling as if they'd passed some sort of test, found the device, activated it, and dragged the light along the spine.

*"Parieaum Ejukatesi,"* Dorn said. "It means, 'in preparation for the Outcast.' Is that what you came up with?"

Witts lowered the shotgun, finally. Dorn exhaled even though the gun hadn't been pointed at him.

"Yeah," Witts said. "Well, half. So what's the book about?"

"I can tell you what later editions are about," Dorn said. "But this one is exceptional for preceding those. Provided this is what I believe it to be."

The corporal walked over. He'd apparently forgotten about Viselle Daska entirely.

"So it's important," Witts said. "I thought it might be."

"Possibly," Dorn said. They flipped to page 32, paragraph two, line seven.

U*nforeseen above and below, the Five cannot wage alone*, the passage read. That one word Professor Linus called out was the first word of the phrase. The later copies of this manuscript had what some intrepid scribe no doubt assumed was an error, which was corrected: for surely, what could be considered unforeseen to gods who know everything?

*Except that's not precisely correct either,* they thought. *If the Outcast was stopped, it was with our assistance. That is what was unforeseen.*

"Is it what you'd hoped?" Viselle asked.

"I think it is," Dorn said.

Witts looked between them. "What? What is it you hoped? You promised..."

"There's an exceptionally long answer to that question, Corporal Witts," Dorn said.

"To...how the world ends?" he asked. "In preparation for the Outcast, you said."

"Possibly. Or the key to how to stop it from ending."

"Right," Witts said. "Right, right. Makk said it might be a key."

"How do you mean?" Viselle asked.

"He said the Sentries were looking for one and thought it was the book...hang on."

There was a red flashing light in the corner of one of Witts' computer screens.

"No, no, no," Witts muttered, running over to his nest of computers. He typed a series of commands at great speed.

"What's the matter?" Viselle asked. There was a steel in her voice that Dorn last heard in the vid where she attempted to murder her former partner.

"I thought you said you were bluffing!" Witts said.

"I was," she said. "More or less."

Lemaighey Witts spun around in his chair. "*More or less??*"

"I picked up a tail," she said. "But I wasn't sure. You know how it is in Pant City this time of night. It could have been a horny tenner."

"But you knew it wasn't."

"I suspected it might not be. But as for *who* was following us and why, I didn't know. There's no way anyone could have known we'd be here, not unless they managed to tap into your private room when we spoke."

Witts hit a button on his keyboard. One of the screens shifted to what appeared to be the live feed of the optical above his front door.

"My room's security is pristine," Witts said.

There was a Septal on the vid. He was wearing an unusual hood, with a wraparound front-piece—tinted glass instead of fabric—that preserved his peripheral vision.

It was a Sentry.

"He's here for me," Dorn said.

"Doubtful," Viselle said. "They don't care about you."

The vid toggled to another optical showing the left and right sides of the building around the down steps to the front door. The Sentry at the door wasn't alone; four more were along the wall, probing the inset windows to get a view inside the sublevel apartment. Dorn could see no opportunity for natural light within the apartment; Witts had boarded them up.

The man at the door was staring directly at the lens as if daring someone inside to look at him. He even waved for it.

"Thinks I can't see him," Witts said. He looked at Viselle. "You've got the same tech, don't you? Thought you were invisible."

"I did," she admitted. "Why wasn't I?"

Witts laughed. "I bought the fix on the Black Market two

weeks ago. Cost a bundle of coin, and most everyone thought it was fake. All I had to do was take my opticals apart and kill a redundant circuit. Call *me* paranoid all they want but I know." He turned to Dorn. "And they're here for *me*. They've been hot to find that book since the day Makk brought it to my door. Now they've followed you two here."

"That isn't it either," Viselle said. "They don't think they even know the book is missing; it didn't come from the local Septal vault. They're here for me."

"Terrific. Why's that? Are the Sentries arresting murderers now?"

"Because of what they *think* I have."

"And what's that?"

Viselle ignored the question. She was pacing the room, looking for some other way out. It didn't seem like there was one. It felt as if they'd landed in a grave site for clerical files, and graves didn't tend to have multiple exit points.

"If you want a way out of this, you're going to have to give me the story," Witts said.

"Way out," Viselle said with a laugh. "The man at the door is named Corland. He's competent, which is all he needs to be. We're not going to be able to shoot our way through his team, if that's what you're thinking."

"There's a back door. Talk."

Viselle turned a couple of times, looking for the aforementioned back door. Dorn stood and did the same. The closest was a back stairwell but it led to a brick wall.

"Honest," Witts said. "I have one."

There was a loud buzz. Dorn jumped at the sound.

"That's the doorbell," Witts said. "He'll start knocking next. Figure an hour before they bring out the heavy artillery. What do they think you have, detective?"

Viselle sighed, reached back under her shirt, and pulled out the key from between her shoulder blades.

"They're looking for one of these," she said. "Not this one; the one Orno Linus took out of the Velon House vault before he died. It's all they've ever cared about; not Other Jimbal and not the professor's killer. Just the key."

"And that *isn't* the one they want?"

"No, but I'm sure they'll be happy to have it all the same. They *thought* Makk had it. Now they think I do."

"But you don't."

"This one came from Wivvol. Makk actually *does* have their key."

"Makk thought the book was the key," Witts said.

"The book isn't a key; the book is just a book."

"Can I see that?" Witts asked.

"Yeah if you give me back the blaster," Viselle said. Witts made a face. "Whether we're shooting our way out or not, better to have two of us armed than just one," she added.

He shrugged. "Yeah, okay," he said, tossing the blaster to her.

Viselle in turn handed over the key. Witts held it up to the light, waved it around and used it like a sword; all very un-key-like things, but it was an unusual key, in fairness.

"Pretty cool," he said. "Any idea what it unlocks?"

"That's another very long conversation," Dorn said.

"Hello?" Brother Corland said, over the open audio from the front door.

"Corporal Witts," Dorn said. "Lemaighey. Can we call you that?"

"Leemie," Witts said. "Nobody calls me Lemaighey."

"Leemie. You mentioned a back door?"

"I did, yes." His attention was focused on the end of the key meant to be inserted into whatever lock it was supposed to work on. "Can you flip to page forty-nine?"

"What?" Dorn asked.

"Page forty-nine. In the book."

Dorn turned to a two-page spread of a diagram. It showed

what looked like a rectangular control panel with lines drawn away from it, and little holes in the center of the panel. One got the impression from looking at it that this was representing a small part of a much larger object. Five lines were hovering in front of the panel, in front of five very faded dots in the panel.

Beneath this strange object was the legend, in archaic: *Ngni Mmnidi*.

It would be *Engni Ammunidi* in modern Eglinat.

"I didn't know what I was looking at until now," Witts said. "You said there's more than one of these. How many?"

"Five," Viselle said. She stepped around the desk to look at the diagram. "Five keys."

"Tell me those five lines aren't keys," Witts said, pointing.

"They certainly look like they're supposed to be," Viselle said. "Dorn, does it tell us where that is?"

"Only *what* it is," Dorn said. "It says this is The Engine of the World."

Leemie Witts laughed again. "Even *I* know that's not a real thing," he said.

"Orno Linus thought otherwise," Viselle said. "Show us this back door, and maybe we'll have a chance to find out who's right."

## Chapter Twelve

Leemie didn't think of himself as legitimately paranoid and/or crazy, but recognized long ago that his perspective on the world could be *viewed* that way by someone who bought into the standard worldview. This wasn't anyone's fault; people just preferred the standard worldview because—however false—it was soothing. It was *designed* to be.

He also appreciated that for those who'd known him a while—family members, old classmates, former coworkers, none of whom he still spoke to—it may have seemed as if he'd "deteriorated" over the years. In truth, he'd always been making connections nobody else saw; it was just that he used to be quieter about it. More than that, he just assumed eventually everyone would catch up to him. When they never did he went from waiting to lecturing. Which didn't help at all.

Makk was probably the only person who saw Leemie more or less the same way Leemie saw himself. But Makk was coming from a different place than most. It takes an outcast to understand another outcast.

All that said, the idea that the patently mythological Engine of the World actually existed physically somewhere was too much even for him... but if the deceased Professor Orno Linus legitimately thought otherwise? If nothing else, that was *exciting*.

Leemie had been proven right more times than he could count (annoyingly, hardly ever getting credit for it) but he'd never been proven wrong before in a situation where *he* was the one holding onto the less outlandish possibility.

"Hello?" the man at the door repeated. "I'm here for Viselle Daska. I know she's inside. I've come alone; nobody else has to be involved. Just open up and we'll be on our way."

Leemie laughed because this Brother Corland had turned off his making device while instructing the rest of his team not to turn off theirs, so when he said he was "alone" it was while standing next to two other Sentries. The rest of his team—which appeared to grow in number every time Leemie checked on them—was still circling around the building, looking for another way in.

He heard a theory once that the House had developed teleportation technology, which would explain how the team outside kept growing but not why they were flummoxed by a door. Maybe they needed a receiver device on the other side and they couldn't just teleport *anywhere*.

Or they didn't have any such technology. It was probably that.

"Corporal Witts," Daska said. "We need a way out."

"I was thinking about teleportation," he said.

"That is not a viable option," Dorn Jimbal said.

"No, no, for them...never mind. I'll get you out but I'm coming with you."

"All right," Daska said.

"I mean, all the way up to Lys," he said. "You've just adopted me."

She looked perplexed. "I can't...it's not my..."

"Our host isn't here," Dorn said. "We would need to speak to them first. It's not our invitation to extend."

"That isn't my problem. This place is about to become inhospitable to life, and I don't have a lot of fallbacks."

"We'll make sure you're taken care of," Daska said, in a way that made it unclear whether she meant that in a good way or a bad way. But it was the best promise he was going to get and they were running out of time.

Leemie pulled out a steel box from beneath his deask, unlocked it, and extracted a large collection of data shards.

"What's that?" Dorn asked, as Leemie held up the collection. It was attached to a chain that he looped around his neck.

"This is *everything*," Leemie said. "Everything computer-based. Pack up that book."

"What about your notes?"

"I have the important stuff digitized. Oh, but grab that hood for me, would you?"

"What do you want *me* to do?" Daska asked.

"You, talk to the guy at the door. See if you can delay the antimatter cannons."

"There's no such thing as an antimatter cannon."

He laughed. "Sure. Look, your name's the only one he's mentioned. They probably know all about Other Jimbal being here and they definitely know about me, but just in case I'm wrong I'm not about to introduce myself and neither should the Other. So you have to be the one to talk to Corland."

"Yes, I understand," she said. "That makes sense."

She seemed surprised that Leemie came off as lucid. (He got that a lot.) She stepped around three of his info stacks—the only interesting one concerned exobiologicals, but he had most of that saved off elsewhere—and landed in the chair in front of the screens. He was about to tell her how to activate the voice-response to the security rig when she did it on her own. She knew her way around his setup.

It was only then that Leemie realized she was the one who tracked him down initially and not Dorn or some other party. He shouldn't have been surprised—she *was* Ba-Ugna Kev's daughter—but he was.

"Hello, Corland," she said. "Long time."

"Detective Daska," Corland said. "Good. Let's be civil, shall we?"

"We can *try* that, sure. Do you want to tell me how you found me?"

"I'm not going to do that."

"No," she said. "I didn't think you would. Thought I'd ask anyway. I'm ready to negotiate the terms of my surrender."

Leemie wordlessly directed Viselle to the skull rig hooked up to the screens. She nodded. A second later she was in a closed audio loop; Corland would only be hearing her.

"All right, let's get to work," Leemie said to Dorn. "Help me move the couch."

~

There was not, strictly speaking, a "back door" to the apartment. Legally, every residential space in Velon proper (and probably in Inimata as a whole, although Leemie wasn't familiar with all of the federal statutes in this regard) had to have multiple points of egress in the event of a fire. And he did, after a fashion. It's just that the second exit after the front door was not the *intended* one. He'd bricked up that one—the rear door at the top of the stairs—a long time ago.

Leemie paid his landlord considerably more than he could otherwise get for such a crap place in such a crap part of a crap quarter, and in return his landlord ignored Leemie's non-standard adjustments to the property. Every few years a building inspector would sniff around, and then Leemie would have to either kick in a bribe or find some other way to incentivize the inspector to leave them alone, but that was the worst of it.

So they weren't getting out the back door, but that didn't

mean the Sentries wouldn't try to get *in* that way. The steel inner door at the front of the place could take a direct hit from a drone missile, but the brick wall at the back wouldn't. Neither would the windows Leemie had boarded up.

They had to use a different second exit to escape...Leemie just had to create it.

After he and Dorn got the couch out of the way—scattering files everywhere—Leemie rolled back the threadbare rug to reveal what appeared to be a solid concrete floor, with an X painted in the middle.

Dorn stepped back. "Perhaps you should have painted a door instead," they suggested drily.

"Funny. Come on."

Leemie led Dorn to the "bedroom" portion of the basement. He lifted and tossed the small cot on which he (occasionally) rested. Underneath it was two large bags. He lifted one and handed it to Dorn.

"Guns," he said. "They're loaded and ready to go. I'm giving them to you to carry because I don't think you know how to use them."

"You're correct," Dorn said.

"Keep them safe, dry and away from fire."

"Will...will there be fire?"

Leemie ignored the question. He lifted the second bag and carried it to the X in the floor, unzipped the bag and pulled out one of the shaped charges.

Viselle Daska saw the explosive, muted herself, and said, "Honus's balls, you're going to kill all of us with that."

"I know what I'm doing," he said.

"Your plan is to blow a hole through the foundation rock?"

"I am not fond of that plan," Dorn said.

"We only need to go down a half mader," Leemie said. "That's the depth at the X. It's thicker everywhere else, and yes I know this for sure."

Daska's eyes were fixed on the charge in his hands. "And you know how to use that?"

"This is a Barlis grade three doorbuster. Black Market surplus. And yes, I know what I'm doing with it. Now mind your job and I'll mind mine."

"All right, but I'm running out of demands. I just told him I wanted to surrender to Duqo Plaint himself. Doesn't sound like they're going for it."

Leemie knelt down and attached the doorbuster to the floor at the center of the X. It clamped in place, sending up a cloud of cement dust.

"Seen any heavy artillery yet?" he asked Daska.

"Not yet, but I think he figured out we can see his team. Whoop. He just kicked down the outer door."

"That's all right; that one's meant to be easy. Okay, I'm ready here."

"What's on the other side of the half mader?" Dorn asked.

"A tunnel," Leemie said. "Now stand back."

"Sorry, hold on," Dorn said. "How do you know this? Because the moment that device goes off, whether it also blows us up or no, they're going to hear it outside and if they *do* have their own heavy artillery as you keep suggesting, nothing Viselle can say will dissuade them from using it. Before we reach that point, I'd like to know how you conceived of this."

"There are tunnels all over the city," Leemie said. "Everybody knows it. They were left behind by the Duggerdos."

"The...Dugger...dos?"

"Ancient sentient race. They lived here before we did, but underground. The city planners sealed up most of the tunnels, but it's not hard to find them. I figured a *Septal* would know this; the House is who's keeping it secret."

"Gods," Daska muttered. In the audio she said, "Corland, stand down; we're coming out."

"What are you doing?" Leemie asked.

"Leaving. Dorn, you have the book?"

"Yes," Dorn said, putting down the bag of guns.

"Wait a minute, you're not going anywhere!" Leemie said.

"The Duggerdos are as imaginary as the tunnel you think you're going to find, Corporal Witts. We'll try our luck with the House. What we're doing is too important; maybe they'll listen." She drew her blaster. "Now step away from that explosive."

"You can't do that," Leemie said. "You won't even make it out of Pant City alive, you've gotta recognize that. You *know* too much. And so do I."

"I'm sorry," she said. "I realize that us being here imperiled you but there isn't anything I can do about that now."

"Leemie," Dorn said, "I think she's right."

"There *is* something you can do about it, Detective Daska," Leemie said. "You can step back a couple of paces."

"Witts..." she began. Whatever else she was planning to say got drowned out by the terrific sound of the Barlis grade three doorbuster rending a hole in the floor.

Daska and Jimbal were knocked backwards, with the detective inadvertently firing her blaster into the ceiling, causing a portion of the metal-lined wood to collapse, albeit on the other side of the room where it couldn't hurt anyone. Leemie, who'd never stood that close to a detonating grade three doorbuster before, had his legs knocked out from under him by the force of the explosion. He landed five maders away, borne aloft (seemingly) by a cloud of particulates.

It was astonishingly loud. He had eardrum guards in the bag with the explosives which, had Daska allowed for the opportunity, they all would have been wearing before the blast. Absent that, it was several seconds before his hearing returned in any meaningful way.

Or, it *felt* like several seconds. It was probably longer. In fact, it soon became clear he'd lost consciousness for at least a minute. Either that, or Viselle Daska was uncommonly fast.

"You idiot," she said. Her voice sounded like it was passing through ten layers of cloth. She was standing directly over him, her blaster pointed at his head. "I could have talked us out of this."

"Never trust the Allimites," Leemie said.

"Shut up." She jerked him to his feet. The room spun a bit before settling down. "I'll turn you in and claim to be a hostage. Probably won't work but I'm gonna need something."

"Viselle," Dorn said. They were standing beside the spot where the X used to be. It was now a hole. "Take a look at this."

Grumbling, she took Leemie by the collar and dragged him along to the opening. She looked down, but there was nothing to see.

"So it's a hole," she said.

"Smell," Dorn said. "Fresh air."

She shoved Leemie to the ground, pulled out a voicer, and activated its torch function. There was indeed a tunnel down there.

"I told you," Leemie said. "Why doesn't anybody ever believe me?"

"Where's it go?" she asked.

"I don't know," Leemie said. "But if the air smells fresh it must go *somewhere*."

"That's not good enough for me. Did you discover this on an old map? Where's the map? I want to see it."

"I told you, the Duggerdos..."

"Dammit, I need a real answer before I go down there!"

There was a loud thud then; it didn't come from the front.

"They've discovered the easiest way in isn't through the door," Leemie said. "I'm going down the hole. You should too, if you want to live."

"They're not going to kill us," Daska said. "We're too important to them."

"You're a disposable piece to the Septals. Both of you. But that isn't what I mean."

He pulled a remote device from his pocket and pushed the button. It set off a series of small incendiaries ringing the room. In seconds, the fire was tracing lines across the walls and the ceiling along the path of the flash paper Leemie had embedded there.

"We have about thirty seconds before the fire reaches the main stash," he said. "You won't even make it to the door."

Realizing she was out of realistic options, Viselle holstered her blaster and pulled Leemie to his feet.

"Now I understand why you and Makk get along," she said. "You're even crazier than he is."

She grabbed the gun bag Dorn had discarded, tossed it into the hole and waited to hear how long it took to find the bottom. It wasn't long.

"Go," she said to Dorn. They jumped down, rather reluctantly, while Daska lunged for the desk and the key they'd nearly left behind.

"What are you waiting for, corporal?" she asked, sliding the key down the back of her shirt. She dropped into the hole.

Leemie grabbed his bag of explosive devices and then took one last look around the place he'd barely left since the war ended.

"I knew you'd fuck me over eventually, Makk Stidgeon," he said. "I'm actually surprised it took this long."

There was a puff of smoke from beneath the computer rig. That was where the largest charge was.

*Time to leave.*

He jumped into the hole.

Their first task was getting as far away from the building as possible before the place went up. That meant caring less about where the tunnel they were heading down went than that it was going *somewhere*. Unfortunately, in his haste, Leemie neglected to pack a means of illumination; they had nothing to work with aside from Viselle Daska's voicer, so they could only go so fast. (He had also been under the impression they wouldn't need one. Duggerdos employed electrochemical technology that required no external energy source; the tunnels *should* have glowed and he was disappointed that they didn't.)

By his guess, they were only about a city block away when the eruption happened. The explosion was sufficiently powerful to send a fireball shooting down the corridor, forcing them to dive to the floor. It fortunately died out before reaching them.

"All right," Daska said, getting to her feet again. "Not the worst plan ever, Corporal Witts. They'll be sifting through rubble for a week before realizing we weren't there. Did you bring down the whole building?"

"I might have," he said. "Hard to say."

"You arranged that in advance," Dorn said. "Why would you do this?"

"You never know when they're going to come for you, Other Jimbal," Leemie said. "I prepared. But I don't believe for a second that they think we died up there. We just made it harder for them to follow, but they'll keep on tracking our movements. We need to get someplace they can't touch us or this'll just be a temporary setback for the House."

"Someplace like Lys?" Daska asked.

"I'm going to keep suggesting it until you get us there," he said.

"Wait," Dorn said. "How *did* they track us? Viselle, nobody knew we were coming here."

"I don't know," she said. "Maybe they were watching Corporal Witts already when we showed up."

"That doesn't sound right," Dorn said. "Leemie, you think they're tracking us *right now*. How do you imagine they're doing that?"

"Dorn, honestly," Daska said. "He'll give you five answers and none of them are going to be reality-based."

"The tunnel's real, isn't it?" Leemie said.

"It's real, but Duggerdos had nothing to do with it," she said.

"I'd like to know what his answer is," Dorn said, interrupting what was bound to be a lengthy argument. "How are they tracking us, Leemie?"

"How can they *not?*" Leemie asked. "They've got spyware in half of the world's tech."

"And they somehow monitor all of it, all the time?" Daska said. "I really don't have the patience for this."

"No, hold on," Dorn said. "They don't have to monitor *all* of it. Just...oh. Oh, I understand. Corporal Witts, we *did* lead them right to you."

Leemie laughed, because he didn't think this was even in dispute.

Dorn held up a small, round button. "Viselle," they said, "the Sentries only knew as much about Detective Stidgeon's movements as we did. Right? They didn't know where to find Leemie or what he had or didn't have. Or even who he is. They just knew that Detective Stidgeon showed up in Pant City at around the time he would have had the missing key. Then one night we show up using rare, expensive cloaking technology developed by the House..."

"Shit," Daska said. "Throw it on the ground."

Dorn did as she asked and Viselle Daska threw hers down next to it. Then she drew her blaster and fired a pulse at them.

"All right," she said. "*Now* can we get moving?"

They headed in the approximate direction of fresh air at first. But that approach didn't make as much sense once they either ran out of fresh air or lost the capacity to detect it, because soon enough it all smelled stale and they had no clue where they were.

"According to the map, we're below Jambus Street," Daska said. "Which is hard to believe."

"You don't believe enough things," Leemie said. "What's wrong with Jambus?"

"All the major roads run above the main sewer lines; there should be pipes where we're standing. You can argue Jambus is the exception if you want, but since it runs straight to the harbor I'm going to have a hard time believing that too."

"We must be below the piping," Dorn suggested.

"Sure we are," Leemie said. "Duggerdo tunnels run deep."

"Just stop with that," Daska said. "My point is that I'm finding it hard to believe there's an entire tunnel system beneath Pantolinar that nobody knew about. How was this not discovered already? Someone had to dig for the sewers." She shined her light on Leemie's face. "How did *you* discover them?"

Leemie resisted the urge to bring up Duggerdos again. The truth was, he knew about the tunnels because he knew the lore, but now that he was *in* one of the purported Duggerdo burrows he was having second thoughts. She was right; someone else built this.

"Ultrasound," he said. "Building contractors use the same equipment."

"This is my point," she said. "The city would have at least *known* there was hollow ground down here."

They'd encountered three rooms so far, separated by long corridors. Everything was solid, with high ceilings and dry walls and floors, which was something one didn't expect to encounter in a structure this deep. And the last room they came across implied a much larger network; it had four entrances.

Rather than electrochemical paneling Leemie had expected, these spaces were meant to be lit by torchlight, as the many empty sconces indicated.

"I think I understand," Dorn said. They were examining the corridor wall. "Bring the light here."

Daska did so. Dorn was tracing a carving in the wall with their finger.

"It's an arrow," Daska said.

"It is. Now look above the arrow," Dorn said.

"Is that..."

"Yes." Dorn waved Leemie closer. "Take a look."

"That's Eglinat, isn't it?" Leemie said.

"What does it say?" Daska asked.

"That's the interesting part," Dorn said. "It's directing us to the northern concourse, whatever that is, but the word for 'northern' in modern Eglinat is *aquilitis*. This word here is *aquitis*; it's the archaic version. This tells us two things. These tunnels are *very* old indeed, and the reason a city planner hasn't exposed them to the world is that the House is keeping them hidden."

"You're starting to sound like him," Daska said.

"Not at all," Dorn said. "I had a roommate who was studying architecture and according to him *all* major construction projects are vetted by the House. I think you'll find most of the city planners are also Septals, which I used to think was an odd factoid. Now I think there's intent behind it."

"But why?" Daska asked. "Why would they want to hide this? Especially if it's as extensive as it looks like it must be."

"The reason's simple," Leemie said. "They don't want us to know about it because we're not meant to benefit. That's how it always is with you people."

Daska looked confused. "Do you mean, 'us' rich people, or 'us' Septals?"

"Both," Leemie said. It could have been the case that what he really meant was what they represented (the wealthy, the House) and not Viselle Daska and Dorn Jimbal personally. The calm, rational side of him, the side that Makk was always telling him to listen to more often, thought this. The *creative* side, the one that made all the right connections and figured out the things that made the rational side go, *but that's crazy*... that part was starting to think Jimbal and Daska were manipulating him for to some nefarious end.

He was considering taking his bag of guns and running. He didn't know where he'd go; *away* was the only imperative.

But Daska had the only light source at the moment, and it was very dark in the tunnels.

"Lemaighey..." Daska began, "Leemie, why don't we assume, just for now, that neither Dorn nor I have any more information about this than you do. Pretend if you have to. And tell us what you mean by 'benefit.'"

"I mean that these tunnels aren't just to get around in. You know how every year there's a proposal to move the Hyperline underground?"

"Actually, I don't."

"Every year. Mainly petitions from the neighborhoods living directly under the existing Hyperline. City beautification they call it. I follow these things because you know who opposes it, every year? The House. And any time the House is against something... the people who're paying *attention* to things, we care too. They could easily build a rail line using these tunnels if they wanted to. They don't, because the tunnels aren't here for getting from one part of the city to another part. The House is hiding something else."

Daska didn't look convinced, but that wasn't a surprise. "All right, well, if these tunnels *do* belong to the House we have a new problem," she said. "They know how to find us down here."

Leemie laughed. "That's what I've been saying. They probably used one of these to get to Pant City in the first place."

"You're right," she admitted. "I didn't see any Septals on the street until right before we got to your block. They could have come up from here. Which also means there are in-use exits. So let's find one to get out of before they use one to find us." She illuminated the tunnel in the direction of Dorn's found arrow. "I'm guessing the northern concourse has one."

∼

They reached what the signage indicated was the northern concourse at around the same time they heard the first noises indicating they weren't alone in the underground.

The concourse ran perpendicular to the corridor they'd been following. It was about twice as wide as any channel they'd come across, and the ceiling was high enough that Daska's light couldn't reach it.

It also came with echoes. At a distant point to their left, somebody was moving. Daska's initial reaction was to kill the light on her voicer, pull Dorn to the wall—she left Leemie to his own devices, which was fine—and wait.

"I don't think they're nearby," Leemie whispered, after about ten seconds.

"Yeah," Daska said. "Yeah, you're right. This is...vast. I'm having trouble believing there's this much room beneath a city built on a river delta. The ground shouldn't be firm enough for all of this."

"House tech," Leemie said.

"I think that we have been heading down steadily," Dorn said. "The ceiling here is much too high. In the basement we were able to jump down without harm. I get the sense if we did so here, we'd break a leg."

Daska opened up her voicer again to look at the map function. "Wow, all right," she said. "If we go left we'll end up at the House temple."

"There has to be a way out of the tunnels in that direction," Dorn said.

"Sure, but it'll be crawling with Sentries," Leemie said.

"Quiet," Daska said. She crouched down and put her hand on the floor. Then: "Against the wall, everyone. Now something *is* coming."

The something was an actual *truck*: a big flatbed that ran almost entirely silent. It had faint yellow lights around the trim that that was more for the sake of people outside of the vehicle while the headlights, such as they were, barely showed more than what was directly in front of it.

"That was riding low," Leemie said after it went past. "Anyone see what was in the back?"

"I did not," Dorn said.

"Crates of something," Daska said. "Come on, Dorn is right; there has to be an exit this way. We'll worry about dodging the Sentries once we've found a door."

"Actually, I'd kind of like to know where the truck was going," Leemie said. "Wouldn't you?"

Daska sighed. "I'm armed," she said. "You're *very* armed. We get up there, ambush a couple of Septals, swap clothes with them and walk out. I make a direct to a friend, and we're heading back to Lys. That's what you want, right?"

"There may be an exit this way too," Leemie said, pointing in the direction in which the truck went. "One that's less busy."

"*Our* goal was to get the book," she said. "We got the book. We're not here to fulfill your itch for a good conspiracy and you don't have to come with us."

"Actually," Dorn said, "I too would like to know where the truck is going."

"Seriously?"

Leemie knew exactly enough about Viselle Daska to be afraid

of her, which was why for about three seconds he considered drawing down on her, because for that same three seconds she seemed ready to pull out her blaster and take the book from Dorn Jimbal.

The moment passed.

"*Fine*," she said to Dorn. "But when this goes sideways, I'm telling her this was your idea."

She marched past Leemie and Dorn, heading west in the direction of the truck.

"'Her' who?" Leemie asked Dorn.

"Our mutual benefactor," they said. "Someone you probably won't trust."

"Gods, that could be anybody."

~

The concourse had multiple corridors breaking off from it, underscoring the vastness of the underground network. It was possibly the first time Leemie thought he had perhaps been too *conservative* in his suspicion of the House. Granted, the enormity of what they were hiding had so far proven to be a largely *empty* enormity, but it was still enormous.

There were also exits along the way. Dorn found the first one by accident; they had been sticking to the wall as much as possible, instinctively, and they ran right into it.

"Ow," Dorn said. "Hold up. I've found something. A protrusion."

Daska went over and used the light to discover a metal ladder attached to the wall. The light didn't reach the top. She checked where they were. "We're beneath Mahlio," she said. "A couple kalomaders from Kloget airfield. This is our best way out if you want it."

"Remember this spot," Leemie said. "We can come back."

"Dorn?" she asked.

"Yes," they said. "We can come back."

"Hope so. Because the stakes are higher here than your curiosity."

"Explain why," Leemie said.

"Just keep moving, I want to get this over with," she said. "And this gets dumber the longer we stay in these tunnels."

*How important is the book*, Leemie wondered, not for the first time.

His hope was that it was important enough to make detonating his entire life worth it, since that's what ended up happening.

The concourse terminated at a closed steel door.

"There," Daska said. "Now can we go?"

"Doors open," Dorn said, placing their hand on the steel. "Should we look for an access panel?"

Leemie crouched down in the center of the path. There was a grooved channel in the middle that he recognized. "You know what, I think the truck was following a lead."

"How do you mean?" Dorn asked.

"We used to use leads in the army to automate supply runs between two points in secured territory. Trucks would follow a track just like this. I bet there wasn't anyone in the cab."

"Like an app-car?"

"Lower tech, but yeah."

The door rumbled.

"Get to the side," Daska said. She lit the way for them to do so, and then put out the light from the voicer.

Red lights flashed near the base of the door, and then with a loud hiss the steel door retracted into the ceiling. The truck—now facing the other way—rolled out. Leemie noted with some satisfaction that there was, in fact, no driver behind the wheel. That was the good news. The bad news, someone on the other side of the door unloaded the truck; the bed was empty.

Leemie took a step through the open door. Daska grabbed his

elbow. "No guarantees we can open the door again from the inside," she said.

"I didn't use *all* my explosives," he said. "We have options. And we've come too far to turn around."

Dorn Jimbal, evidently unbothered by the potential risk, stepped across, and then Detective Daska followed.

It was dark on the other side of the doorway, and since Daska hadn't relit her voicer, they didn't know anything about where they were standing or if they were alone. The red warning lights on the floor stopped flashing as soon as the door was completely open, so the good news was that if there was someone inside they probably didn't know about the intruders at the door, either.

Leemie got down on the floor and unzipped his gun bag, feeling around until his hand found the butt of the spray gun.

The door slid closed again behind them. As soon as it was secure, overhead lights came on.

They were in a long, narrow warehouse of sorts. There was an open aisle down the center with rows of stacked crates on both sides. At the far end of the room was a circle for the truck to turn around in.

The crates were the interesting part. There were far too many to count.

*The great takeover,* Leemie thought.

There was a theory that one day the House would rise up and seize all the governments of the world, impose strict religious laws and execute anyone who refused the oath. In practical terms —and Leemie Witts approached all of these theories with the practicality of a man who'd strategized for the war effort—they didn't have nearly enough numbers to do such a thing. But it was possible they didn't need them; House-born tech could simply stop working for everyone not a part of the effort. And they had a hand in a *lot* of tech. They also owned the politicians. And the super-wealthy were on their side.

But they would still need munitions. Surely, that was what was in these crates.

Someone emerged from an aisle about halfway down the room. It was a Septal. She was counting crates and recording the information on a hand-held tablet.

Leemie acted in a way that could have been construed as rash; not thinking so much as reacting.

He fired the spray gun over the Septal's head. Spray guns fired projectiles by the dozen, which was why he liked them. They had greater range than any shotgun and they could be aimed in a way shotguns couldn't, but they were also generous to someone who wasn't the world's greatest shot.

"You!" he shouted. "Don't move!"

"Gods," he heard Daska say. Leemie ran in the direction of the terrified (probably; it was difficult to tell what they were thinking under those hoods) Septal, while Daska fell in behind. Jimbal was probably still at the door, shitting himself.

"Are you alone?" Leemie barked.

The Septal Sister was doing her best to not move. She'd dropped the tablet at the sound of the gunshot and she'd raised her hands, but had otherwise remained still.

She shook her head. She was *not* alone.

Leemie put the barrel in her face.

"How many?"

"F-five," she stuttered. "On the loader."

"What are they packing?"

"...packing?"

"Tell me what guns I'm up against and maybe you'll make it out of this alive."

"I...we don't have guns, sir. We're just, I mean..."

"Look at her, Witts," Daska said. She had her hand on his shoulder. "Sentries have tactical hoods. She's just a regular member of the order."

"No such thing."

Leemie switched out the spray gun for his handgun, spun the

Sister around and pushed the barrel up against her temple.

"The Sister here says there's another five of you!" he shouted. "Come on out. You have ten seconds."

Slowly, another five Septals emerged from an aisle further down the warehouse. They had their hands in the air.

They looked harmless. That just made Leemie more suspicious.

"Put your guns down on the ground," Leemie demanded. "Now!"

"We don't have any guns," one of the Brothers said.

"You're in a warehouse full of guns and none of you is armed? How stupid do you think I am?"

They looked at one another, possibly wondering if this was a rhetorical question.

"These aren't guns," their spokesperson said.

"Sure," Leemie said.

"He's telling the truth," Other Jimbal said, from behind Leemie.

Dorn tossed a package on the ground. It was a nutrient pack. Leemie hadn't seen one since the war—and the ones he got back then were of far lesser quality, if the flavor description was anything to go by—but he knew what he was looking at.

"I checked five crates," Dorn continued. "It's all food."

This didn't scan at all. "Why would the House be hoarding food?" he asked. "That doesn't make any sense."

"Why don't you let her go," Daska said. "Then everyone can calm down and we can ask them."

Leemie turned in her direction, expecting that she'd have her blaster trained on the five Septals. She didn't; it was pointed at his head.

"Yes, all right," he said. "Good idea."

"Dorn?" one of the five said. It was a Brother standing in the back. He stepped forward. "Other Jimbal? Is that you?"

"Oh," Dorn said. "Hello, Pyt."

## Chapter Thirteen

It had become clear to Dorn that as insightful as Corporal Witts could be, his capacity for unbalanced behavior was becoming a liability. Although if Dorn was being fair, they had encouraged him more than was wise.

Viselle had been correct; they should have taken the exit when they found it. But Dorn *very much* wanted to see what was going on. It felt important. More important, perhaps, than translating Orno's research with the aid of his missing book. However, when they were mentally calculating this, they never considered this might end up being a one-or-the-other circumstance.

Faced with Viselle's blaster pointed at his head, Leemie released the Sister and let her return to the company of the other five brethren.

Brother Pyt, meanwhile, just wanted to catch up.

"We thought you were dead," he was saying to Dorn. "I'm so glad to see you."

"It's good to see you as well," Dorn said. They were blushing, feeling particularly exposed without their hood before Pyt, who had never seen Dorn without one. None of the six Septals had, but they didn't matter as much because Dorn didn't know any of the others.

"Leemie," Viselle said, "why don't you put the gun away. I can keep track of the Brethren."

"I don't trust them," he said. "And I *barely* trust you. I don't think so; not until they've been secured." He turned to Dorn. "And I don't believe there's *only* food here. It makes no sense."

"Check for yourself," Dorn said.

"I will, after... We need to tie them up or shoot them. Probably both."

"We're not shooting unarmed Septals," Viselle said.

"How soon before another truck comes?" Dorn asked.

"Any minute," the talkative one said.

Dorn ignored him. "Pyt? The truth, please."

"Not for another two hours," Pyt said. "It'll have the next shift aboard; we're taking it back."

"Empty your pockets," Viselle said. "All of you." She turned to Leemie. "Go find something to tie them up with. We'll get what we can from them and be gone before the next truck. All right? Look at me. Is that all right?"

Leemie made eye contact with her. "Yes," he grumbled, putting the gun away.

"There's some loose rope on the loader," one of the Brethren said helpfully as Leemie walked past.

"Pyt," Dorn said, "what are you all doing down here?"

"Inventory," Pyt said. "We take the crates off the truck, catalogue the contents and shelve them appropriately."

"Warehouse work," Dorn said. "Explain to me how a scholar of your caliber ended up in a basement tabulating boxes of food."

Brother Pyt, three years Dorn's senior, was a phycologist who'd been published several times. His work on Norton Ocean blue algae blooms was supposed to be groundbreaking. (Dorn didn't know what "groundbreaking phycological research" looked like, but believed what they had been told was accurate.) Finding Pyt in this sublevel made little sense.

"You're young," the Brother standing beside Pyt said.

"What does that mean?" Dorn asked.

"You would have served your time here," Pyt said. "Everyone reaching the third Trycium does."

"Sounds like a prison sentence," Viselle said.

"It's an honor to be entrusted," the Sister who'd only recently had a gun pointed to her temple said.

Dorn looked down one of the aisles. This warehouse space seemed constricted, but that was because of how *much* was already being stored there. *Fifty paces to each wall*, they thought.

Then they wondered if this was the only storage space like it hidden below the city.

"Why are you doing this?" Dorn asked. "How long has this been going on?"

They got silence in return.

"Answer their questions," Viselle said.

The Septals stared at one another, waiting for someone to resolve the problem of the woman pointing a blaster at them.

"Pyt?" Dorn asked. "Just tell us what you know. I'm certain the House will forgive."

"Very well," Pyt said. "But only because it's you. This is preparation for the return. You understand?"

Viselle looked at Dorn. "Gods," she said.

"The return of the Outcast," Dorn said. "The House has known all along."

~

A somehow-disheartened Leemie Witts emerged from the back of the room with rope. He'd conducted an independent search of the crates, he said, and was clearly disappointed to discover that it was in fact only food.

Leemie escorted the Septals to the aisle with the loader—a platform-on-wheels with a base mechanism to lift things—crowded them onto the platform and tied them to one another. Then Viselle raised it to the top and turned off the loader.

Unless they jumped they wouldn't be going anywhere.

"Now we should go," Dorn said to Viselle. Leemie was already at the door, playing with the locking mechanism.

Viselle didn't answer. She was staring off in a direction where there wasn't anything to look at.

"Are you all right?" they asked.

"I'm sorry," she said. "No, I don't think I am. Duqo Plaint lied to me."

"You've met High Hat Plaint?"

"I have, yes. Have you?"

"In a group setting."

"We spoke a couple of times during the Linus investigation," she said. "He was very up-front about Orno's research. I didn't think much about it at the time, but Plaint insisted the correct interpretation of the Outcast myth was purely metaphorical. And you know, until now I didn't realize how much his stated opinion impacted everything *I* thought about it."

"As you've said, your belief vacillates."

"Sure. And Plaint helped seed that doubt. Now I find out he's been preparing for the *literal* return of the Outcast all this time... look at this room. This has been going on for a *while*."

She stared at Dorn. "You really didn't know anything about this."

"It seems the only one of us unsurprised is Leemie," Dorn said.

"Yeah well, he's got a big enough catalog of conspiracies in his head; not a shock when one of two of them land." She turned to Leemie. "Any luck with that door?"

"No," he said. "There's an emergency button but I'd rather not use that."

"Me neither," she said. "That's all right, it'll open on its own."

Their plan was to wait until the truck returned as scheduled and slip out while the unmanned vehicle rolled in. The only thing that made more sense was to somehow get back to the causeway either without opening the door at all or by opening and closing it before the truck got there, with nobody being the wiser. But since there appeared to be no emergency exit and no way to open it without triggering an alarm, they were stuck with the plan they had.

"Yeah. I don't like being trapped in here," Leemie said.

"Same," Viselle said.

"Can that blaster put a hole in the door?" Dorn asked, referring to Viselle's weapon.

"Maybe after ten or eleven shots," she said. "I'd do it if I knew it was never opening again. Otherwise, probably not worth it."

Just then, the lights surrounding the door began flashing, a low alarm sounded, and the lights in the room went out.

"Oh," Dorn said. "The truck's already here."

"Too early," Leemie said. "Way too early!"

"He's right," Viselle said. "Get back from the door; something's wrong."

She grabbed Dorn's arm and yanked them around the corner of the nearest aisle. Leemie scooped up his bags and took cover in the opposite aisle.

There was a loud hiss, and then the door began to slide up again. Something large was on the other side, but it was no flatbed truck. The lighting wasn't great—the flashing lights on the floor were all Dorn had to go by—but it looked as if there was a large gun mounted on the vehicle.

Spotlights came up from a position above the gun. Then six more lights—personal lights carried by what was clearly a team of Sentries—were added from the ground level in front of the gun-mounted vehicle.

"Viselle Daska," a man said through an audio amplifier, "we

know you're here. Why don't you and whoever you're with come on out and we can take care of this peacefully?"

"Hello, Corland," Viselle said. "Took you long enough."

"You missed something in the neighborhood of ten exits to the street on the way here, detective. Our mistake was thinking you were smarter than this. How many with you, and what did you do with the Septals?"

"They're fine," she said. "And I'm alone. You want to tell me what's going on? This is a lot of food; you guys know something the rest of us don't?"

Leemie was signaling from the other aisle. It was hard to see him clearly but it looked like he was holding something metal in his hand; Dorn couldn't make out precisely what it was.

"I'm afraid knowing about this room means you're not going to be able to leave us, Detective Daska," Corland said.

"Oh so you're going to execute me now?" she said. "Not a huge incentive to come out, Corland, if I'm being honest."

"You'll remain alive and very comfortable. We have the means and you know it. You just won't be able to tell anyone about what you've seen. Neither will anybody else who's here with you today. But you *will* all live; you have my word on that."

"That being the case, no reason not to explain what all the food's for," she said. "Since I won't be able to tell anyone else anyway."

Corland laughed. "Viselle, if I knew? I might even tell you. Ours is not to question. Now come on, you've been in enough of these to know they don't work out but one way."

Dorn tapped Viselle on the shoulder and pointed to Leemie.

*She* knew what he was holding up.

"No," she muttered, shaking her head demonstratively. "No, you maniac, don't."

"All right, Corland," she said. "I'm coming out."

"I'm coming out first!" Leemie shouted.

"No he's not!" Viselle said. "No he isn't!"

"To whom am I talking now?" Corland asked.

Leemie stepped into the aisle. His hands were raised above his head and he had no guns that Dorn could see.

"Corporal Lemaighey Witts," Leemie said. "I'm the guy whose home you blew up earlier."

"We didn't do that, corporal," Corland said. "If our scene forensics are correct, you did that yourself."

"Wouldn't have had to if you weren't at my door, Allimite."

Leemie was walking toward the truck as he spoke. Every light at the door followed him as he went.

"Don't know who you *think* we are, soldier, but..."

"Oh, I know *exactly* who you are. Detective Daska needs to hear it from you but I already know what this is about. This is part of the one-world dominion plot between the Allimites, the House, and the demigods of Lys. You're just a puppet. We all are."

"Get ready," Viselle muttered.

"For what?" Dorn asked.

"This idiot is about to give us an opening. We may as well take it."

"There's something in his hand," one of the Sentries on the ground announced. He was right; Leemie had a remote in his left hand. Then Dorn noticed the bulge in the corporal's back and understood.

He was wearing a shaped charge under his shirt.

"But that will kill him," Dorn whispered.

"Very thoroughly, yes," Viselle said.

"Why don't you stop where you are," Corland said, "and drop whatever that is."

Leemie continued walking.

"It's too important, right?" Leemie said over his shoulder. "We're saving the world?"

"That's right, Leemie," Viselle said. It wasn't loud enough for anyone but Dorn to hear, but it seemed like Leemie heard her anyway.

"Drop it now, or we will drop *you*, corporal!" Corland barked.

"Make sure you get it done," Leemie said. Then he pushed the button.

The blast was tremendous. Dorn had only experienced one other explosion in their lifetime—the one that tore through the bottom of Leemie's apartment—but this one seemed much bigger. This likely had more to do with the directionality, which in this case was through a man's body and across open space, rather than into thick concrete.

It popped Dorn's ears and blew air backwards with concussive force...and Dorn was *behind* the blast. The shaped charge was pointed the other way, so it must have had a far more significant impact in the other direction.

All the lights near the door went out except for the ones in the floor.

Then Viselle was grabbing them by the arm.

"Come on," she said. Dorn could barely hear her even though she was clearly shouting. They stumbled forward through the smoke across a floor littered with debris and soft things that Dorn realized were body parts. They were horrified, but since this was no time to stop and process trauma they shoved it away, to be dealt with later.

It seemed Viselle could see better than Dorn, as her guidance through the aftermath of the bomb was true. She did stop once, shout something Dorn couldn't hear properly, and fire her blaster. The pulse lit up the darkness, arced across the tunnel—this was how Dorn knew they'd even *reached* the tunnel—and struck something or someone. Then the two of them staggered along.

They traveled for an eternity in the darkness. It was probably only about ten minutes, but Dorn's sense of time had been damaged in the explosion.

"Please," they said. "I need to stop. Just for a minute."

Viselle stopped. Dorn leaned up against the wall and put their hands on their knees.

"Are you hurt?" she asked.

"No. I may be ill."

"We don't have time for you to be ill."

"I'm aware of that," they said. "However, I'm unaccustomed to having men self-detonate in my presence and so my body is going to react how it's going to react. I believe this is called shock."

"Yeah okay. Sit down. Put your head between your knees if you can."

They did as she suggested. It helped, but they couldn't imagine *why* it did.

"Am I correct," they said, after a few deep breaths, "in being glad that there was no light to see what we just ran through?"

"Yes."

"Why would he do that?"

"I don't think the corporal thought he had any other options," she said. "He was probably right. They were going to keep us for as long as it took to figure out what we knew and who else knew it too, and then dispose of us quietly. As crazy as Leemie Witts was, he read the situation pretty clearly."

"You knew what he planned," Dorn said. "And you didn't want him to do it."

"I didn't want him to inadvertently blow *us* up along with himself. Since that didn't happen? No objections. It worked out."

Dorn considered remarking on how callous a determination that was but decided against it.

*You may decide I'm disposable one day,* they thought. *I need to remember that.*

"Feel well enough to move again?" she asked.

"Nearly. How much farther?"

"The ladder is just up there, but you're going to have to be able to climb it; I can't carry you."

"And then what?"

"Then we call for a ride back to Lys. I'm sure Exty will be happy to hear from us."

# PART III

Dark Sunrise

## Chapter Fourteen

It was a twelve day journey from the surface of Dib to orbital platform one. In contrast, it only took three days to reach the planet's moon.

There were a number of reasons it took longer, the first being the most obvious: platform one was farther away than the moon. Second, the shuttle Xto commanded had only limited propulsive capacity. The bulk of the propulsion used to get it into space was from the rockets that were shed before reaching the orbital plane; what he had after that was sufficient to break free from Dib's orbit entirely and get the vessel pointed in the right direction. Everything else was to be reserved for fractional adjustments, docking maneuverability and emergency corrections if he was knocked off-course.

The third reason was paranoia. It was well within the power of the *Extraplanetary Project for the Future of All* to construct a shuttle with greater booster power so as to shorten the journey. But—and Xto knew this better than most thanks to his special family access—the Chancellery was worried about a shuttle falling (literally) into foreign hands and/or being spotted in transit. They valued low-burn engines that were difficult to spot as they transited the night sky and which, if recovered, looked like something meant to be used only in upper orbit.

This was because Wivvol's space platform was supposed to be a secret.

As far as anyone knew, it *was* a secret, despite being a project that was over a hundred years old. It was either that or none of the other countries cared one way or another.

Orbital platform one (there *was* no orbital platform two) was built behind and atop an asteroid called Shizuna Two. Slightly closer to the Dancers, Shizuna Two had almost precisely the same orbital period as Dib, but its orbital *plane* was roughly three degrees off. A quarter of the time, one would find the asteroid by locating the Dancers and then looking north. Another quarter of the time, one would have to look south. Twice a year, the asteroid transited in front of one or both of the suns, although it wasn't large enough to be noticed without instrumentation.

Everyone on the planet knew about Shizuna Two. A select few knew Wivvol visited it routinely. Fewer still realized there were Wivvolians *living* there. And perhaps a hundred people at any given time knew *why*.

That was, unless Wivvol was collectively fooling itself. "Truth" and truth remained different principles in Wivvol, after all, so it was entirely possible that the other space-able nations of Dib knew perfectly well what Wivvol was up to while Wivvol pretended otherwise. Totalitarian nations were perfectly capable of repeating the mistaken assumptions of the few to the many, and expecting those assumptions to be believed.

Xto thought this likely. There had been a joint international effort to establish a moon base: seven nations, and Wivvol wasn't even one of them. (Almost nobody in Wivvol even knew the moon base existed.) It seemed impossible for these other countries to have advanced far enough in space flight to reach the moon and yet be unaware that the one spacefaring nation they weren't working with was busy sending crafts in the opposite direction.

This was one of the recurring thoughts that came to him during his twelve days in near-total isolation. He had radiographic exchanges with platform one twice daily, but those were very formal—confirmations of heading and gauge readouts—and very brief. They barely constituted person-to-person contact at all, and could no doubt have been conducted computer-to-computer without bothering Xto. (That they were not strongly implied the second purpose, which was proof-of-life.) Other than that, he was alone with his thoughts.

He'd been warned this would be the toughest part of the journey: the total isolation and all that. He was trained on ways to cope, but while training he kept saying to himself that when the time came it wouldn't be an issue because when the time came he would be in *space*. How could *anyone* get tired of that?

The answer was, *he* could, after maybe two days. He spent days one and two simply awed by the entire experience—especially the view of the stars unfiltered by atmospheric interference—but by the third day his attitude was, *oh yes, stars*. And that was that.

He had some room to move around. Not much, but better than what his predecessors had to cope with. (Earlier shuttle flights came with a chair the pilot was meant to remain in for the entire trip, which had to be agony.) Five times a day he'd get up, float to the middle of the open area behind the chair, and perform the zero-gravity exercises his training dictated. He also had two meals a day to look forward to—flavored packages he squeezed into his mouth—and the pills he would have to take after each meal for his two years in space. The pills were designed to trick his body into continuing to produce calcium for his bones, since there would be no gravity telling it to do so on its own. Without them, he could end up too brittle to survive when he returned to the surface.

By day five he decided there was no longer any reason to have the key tied to his thigh, so he unwrapped it and left it to float about the cabin. With no optical showing the inside of the shuttle, there was no harm in it. He just had to remember to reattach it before reaching the platform.

"Trebnvto would never survive this," Xto decided, sometime in day nine. This was after he spent several hours pondering the absurdity of continuing to record his time in space in "days" when this was an artifact of the planet's rotation that no longer applied; for him, suns never set.

This would be equally true on platform one, which also respected the twenty hour day for no good reason.

Then Xto set about designing a new way to tell time in space and made several pages of notes working out the system. He was about to radio the results to Dib in an unsanctioned broadcast when he decided it would be better to stop and double-check his work first. Then he realized he'd accidentally re-proven the merits of synchronizing with the planet's standard.

*That* was when he decided Treb wouldn't do well.

"The last place you'd like to be is alone with your thoughts, my love," Xto said. "It will perhaps be better if you stay where you are."

Day ten, he convinced himself Treb had heard his words and was communicating information back to him by flashing the lights on the shuttle dash in Binarial code.

That was when Xto decided to start taking the *optional* pills; the ones meant to help him sleep.

When he finally made it to day twelve he suddenly had a lot to do: reattach the key to his thigh; get back into his spacesuit; strap down in the cockpit chair; and perform a complex series of maneuvers to get around the rocky backside of Shizuna Two.

The shuttle's programmed trajectory took it directly into the asteroid. This was the *EPFA's* low-cost version of a self-destruct mechanism. If the astronaut was dead or otherwise incapacitated, a default flight path that wiped the craft out on the side of a space mountain resolved any lingering—and still utterly paranoid—concerns by the higher-ups that their technology might someday fall into non-Wivvolian hands. The alternative, where the shuttle overshoots the asteroid and continues on a direct course to deep space wasn't good enough for them. No, another country might have a craft out there. Or—and this was unstated but without question on their minds—it might be picked up by a hostile alien species who could then trace the route backwards to Dib.

Much better to summarily execute the pilot and destroy the ship. Never mind that they also gave the pilot sleeping pills and allowed them to self-medicate as they saw fit, guaranteeing that every now and then one of them would oversleep.

Xto did not oversleep, thankfully. He was at the stick and ready when it was time to commit to his first adjustment: fifteen degrees off plane. This brought him close enough to see the impact crater left behind by the shuttle pilots who failed at this task, but not close enough to contribute to it.

The craft slid below the lowermost point of Shizuna Two. Then came the part they called "turning into the skid". Xto fired the side thrusters to get his nose facing in a direction other than where his momentum was taking him and then tapped the rear thrusters. This took the shuttle into a curl, up and facing the other side of the asteroid. It was his first glimpse of orbital platform one, and Wivvol's greatest accomplishment: the *Zabmez*.

The *Zabmez* was the first of its kind, a massive spaceship intended for long range travel. It was designed following a blueprint that was about a hundred years old, based on a blueprint for a different kind of craft that was significantly older still. This was why it looked an awful lot like a Wivvolian ocean-going sailing ship.

It even had a mast rising up in the middle of the flat top of the deck. It wasn't ornamental, either; it would actually hold a sail. That sail would be square-rigged and attached to both the center mast and additional masts jutting out on the side of the ship (these did *not* correspond to the sailing ship aesthetic) such that when employed it would look like a gigantic hand-held fan.

This was designed to ride solar winds.

The sides of the *Zabmez* were polished steel that glistened in the sunlight. It was prow-forward, so Xto was unable to see what the rear looked like but he knew from the plans that there were permanent rocket boosters back there fueled by a nuclear fusion reactor.

The *Zabmez* had yet to set sail and wasn't expected to for another decade because, while theoretically complete and spaceworthy, the plan all along had been for an entire *fleet* of these ships. That seemed a little more ambitious a century after the hatching of the grand plan, but "more than just one" was still considered a requisite, so the updated scheme was a team of three. But the other two ships—the *Hlyib* and the *Guh*—were still just unfinished shells in the berths beside the *Zabmez*, so it was going to be a while longer.

"Unless the funding runs out," Xto said. "Then not at all."

The shuttle's momentum was still carrying it past the place where he was expecting to dock, so he tapped the side thrusters again until his tail was facing the vector on which he was traveling. He gave the rear thrusters a nudge to slow down and a second to stop.

"Shuttle one, we have you," the command center on platform one said. It was Tbux Opygy, fulfilling her promise to talk him in on arrival. "Well done, Xto."

"Thank you, platform one. Light the dock, please."

A light flickered on and off at the far end of the platform. It looked incredibly tiny from Xto's perspective and gave him a better sense of the scale of what he was looking at.

*I am supposed to fit this shuttle into that little space*, he thought. It looked the same size as the sensor bulbs on his instrumentation panel.

"I have it," he said, and then the light stopped flickering and switched to solid. He set a course.

∼

Docking went far more smoothly than Xto had been led to expect. He lined up the nose to an opening that was actually quite large, brought the ship to a stop (relative to the motion of the asteroid), turned 180 degrees and backed in, and that was that.

He'd heard plenty of horror stories about how this was the maneuver everyone got at least a little wrong, but it wasn't hard; it just required patience. You had to feel for when the shuttle was properly locked in orbital synchrony with the asteroid. Just rushing in meant too many variables to account for. The problem, he decided, was that after twelve days it was easy to become impatient to finally get out of the shuttle.

Once the vessel was secure, Xto powered down and stood.

Shizuna Two had gravity, but it was only about a tenth of the gravity of Dib at sea level. When Xto stood, he settled to the floor—the first time he'd felt the sensation of being pulled in a direction for a while. His body told him he could relax and walk normally, but his head reminded him that he could leap *off* the asteroid if he wasn't careful. He engaged the magnets in his boots to be safe and unlocked the side hatch. There was a hiss—air escaping—and then the door slid open.

He was greeted on the other side by two women whose names he didn't know, in spacesuits because the shuttle bay was open. The nearest of the two took him by the elbow.

"Welcome," she said. "And please step carefully."

"I know how to walk," he said.

"Up here, you do not. Don't take offense; it will be a number of days before you have your space legs."

The other woman disappeared into the shuttle, likely performing an inventory or looking for stowaways or something.

The back portion of Xto's shuttle was already a bustle of activity. He had to back in because half of his purpose on this mission was to deliver supplies, and the crate containing those supplies had to be extracted from the rear of the vehicle. Xto expected this to not happen right away, as he assumed his rear thrusters needed time to cool—they were positioned to the left and right of the rear doors—but on this he was clearly mistaken. He watched as a man no larger than Xto extracted a steel beam that could only be lifted by heavy machinery on Dib, threw it over his shoulder, and walked it to the other end of the shuttle bay where a cart was waiting.

The woman holding his elbow continued to walk with him like he was a child, straight to the nearest exit door. They passed into an airlock. After waiting for thirty seconds for the chamber to pressurize, she took off her helmet and signaled he could do the same.

"I am Opzk. It's a pleasure to meet you finally, Xto Djbbit."

Opzk was blessed with big, brown eyes on a face that seemed like it could have been beautiful. Her cheekbones seemed too pronounced somehow, like she was suffering a vitamin deficiency. He wondered how long she'd been aboard platform one.

"Thank you," he said, wondering if his father had been talking about him or if Opzk was simply being polite.

The inner door opened. "Please come," she said. "We must conduct your exam."

∼

Possibly the most extraordinary thing about orbital platform one was how ordinary it was. After exiting the airlock helmet in hand and definitely still adjusting to the slight gravity, Xto followed Opzk into a dull, cream-colored hallway lit by fluorescents. Save for the lack of carpeting it could have been any hallway on Dib. It even had dust.

It was jarring. Then they passed a couple of crew members who were walking without the use of magnetic boots. They *bounded* along as if it was the most natural thing imaginable, and the sensation of being back on the planet went away.

Opzk brought Xto to an examination room some fifty paces (normal paces, not the big bounding ones) from the airlock. The room had a metal bed, a couple of stools, and a wall-length counter of equipment that was all nailed down. Opzk began removing her spacesuit.

"Go ahead," she said, referring to his own suit.

"You are examining me *now?*" he asked.

"Of course."

"I thought that I would have an opportunity to...to collect my personal things. I expected to visit my private quarters first."

"Your personals are being moved to your quarters as we speak," she said.

"This is not protocol."

"Well," she said, smiling, "it may not be the protocol they're teaching planet side, but we follow our own commandments out here. You're welcome to raise your concerns in two years; I'm sure they'll send a Council Seventeen man up here right away. Now come on, get that off."

He began to do so, slowly, hoping perhaps that someone would barge in and declare that a terrible mistake had been made. "You're a physician, then," he said.

"I am. I've been your father's physician for eight years."

"You've been here for eight years?"

"Ten. I was supposed to *leave* eight years ago but took the long haul instead."

*Taking the long haul* meant electing not to return to the planet.

He'd gotten out of the suit. What he had underneath was an insulated two piece cloth outfit that was standard for every astronaut, and socks. (Opzk did not. She had on loose-fitting pants and a cotton pullover shirt that was tucked in tightly out of respect for the near-zero gravity of the location. It looked stylish by comparison.) Having reached this level of undress, Xto hopped onto the table and awaited the exam.

She stared at him. "You will need to take those off as well for the skin check," she said.

"It can wait."

"It really cannot."

The examination protocol under discussion concerned the establishing of a baseline health metric for the *skin* of a new arrival. Being in space for an extended period behind what was only nominal shielding meant a higher statistical likelihood of being exposed to sudden small bursts of cosmic radiation, which often manifested first as redness on the skin. It was also the case that some were more susceptible than others to rashes from the dryness of the air, both in the shuttle and aboard the platform. This too manifested as redness on the skin. However, skin rashes tended to show up first as a consequence of being twelve days without a bath, and so the sensible thing to do was to examine everyone upon arrival in order to anticipate rashes from skin dryness over their two year tour.

It was important, but it wasn't critical. He expected to be able to change in privacy before having to worry about it.

She shook her head, opened a cabinet, and extracted a number of medical tools that were adhered within. She came at him first with a flat metal stick.

"Open your mouth, please," she said. He did. She pressed the tongue down with the metal stick and thrust it into the back of the throat.

"I cannot imagine," she said, as he fought with his gag reflex, "that this has anything to do with my being a woman. As I said, I've been your father's physician for some time."

She recorded some information on a handheld tablet, then

turned his head and checked his ears with another device. "And I don't believe the prominence of female medical doctors has dropped precipitously on the surface since I last checked. This is surely not your first such exam with one."

She recorded more information, and then stuck a different stick into his mouth. This was to get his body temperature. "Not to mention how much poking and prodding all astronauts have to withstand during training," she said. "I would say you've been naked before more strangers than any man in Wivvol by now, save for the other astronauts and the sex workers."

She checked his heartrate then, which necessitated she stop speaking for the moment. He strove to calm his heart down.

"Mm," she said, "slightly elevated."

She scooped up all the equipment and went back to the cabinet with it. "If it's something else, I have to tell you: Not only am I *in* a relationship but from what I've been told I am not your type."

He gasped. "Well," he said, "now my heartrate *is* elevated."

She laughed. "There are no secrets in space," she said. "Only the things we know but do not speak of, and the things we know but *do* speak of. And now that I am your doctor I can promise confidentiality on the topic of your preferences. Besides, I think you will find things much more relaxed up here. We've no choice but to be."

Xto seriously doubted his father would hew to such a generous perspective, but didn't say so.

"Now," she said, "there is *one* exception to my oath of confidentiality, Xto Djbbit. Historically, we've had issues with astronauts smuggling contraband aboard. If I believe one of my patients has brought in something potentially *dangerous* to the wellbeing of the rest of us, I have a duty to report that. So. Why don't you tell me what's tied to your thigh? Or would you rather I had some men come in and hold you down? I would add that your family connections will not help and also that we *do* have a brig. It was considered a more palatable alternative to jettisoning malcontents into space."

She stared at him, eyebrows raised, waiting.

"All right," he said. Standing, he took off his shirt and then dropped his pants. Naked, he untied the key and put it on the table.

"What is *that?*" she asked.

"What it is not, is a weapon, or drugs, or a prohibited electronic device," he said. "If I'm to understand the rules of confidence as you've explained them, this means you have an obligation to keep it secret."

"Not so fast, Xto," she said, picking it up. "It's still something not meant to be aboard the platform. You wouldn't have hidden it otherwise. It is not, likewise, a medical condition or a body part. What does it do?"

"Nothing," he said. "It's a Septal artifact."

She laughed. "Well, that *is* contraband then, isn't it? Not the kind I'd call dangerous. Fascinating, actually. What do you suppose it's made of?"

"I have no idea."

She handed it back. "If that had been found before you left the surface, you may not have ever left. So why? Why risk so much to bring that here, if it doesn't do anything?"

"It was a favor to my uncle."

She fixed him with a neutral look that betrayed nothing. Did she know that his uncle—her commanding officer's brother-in-law—was technically the High Hat of Chnta? How plugged in was this woman he'd never before heard of, who'd spent the past ten years in space?

"And now that you've gotten it here, you are supposed to do what with it?" she asked.

"Keep it safe and bring it back down again after my tour is up," he said. The answer omitted some important details, but it was true.

"There's more you're not telling me, Xto," she said. She stared at him for a few rapid heartbeats to see if he'd give her more. He didn't.

"All right, fine," she said. "I'll keep your secret. Just don't make me regret it."

"I shall strive not to."

"Now let's have a look at that skin; your father is waiting."

## Chapter Fifteen

Whether one was speaking to an ordinary citizen of Wivvol, a member of the Chancellery, or his son, the great Mondr Djbbit was as much a mythical creation as a real person. He was said to be taller and stronger and more energetic, more fundamentally *vital* than anyone living, which was of course outrageous hyperbole that everyone more or less thought was at least partly accurate.

Yes, he likely did *not* spacewalk without a suit one day to see what it was like because that was absurd. And yes, he probably didn't reinvent the chemical rocket—which had been in use in some form since before he'd been born—to improve the viability of the space program. Also yes, he probably wasn't a polymath genius secretly running the Chancellery from his office (or throne) at the *EPFA*.

Yet again, when the stories were *that* outrageous there was a lingering sense that the kernel of truth which fostered them still had to be pretty fantastic.

Xto barely knew his father. Mondr Djbbit conceived him in between his third and fourth tour and was virtually absent beyond that. Xto's father figure, growing up, was Uncle Ghn, the brother of Xto's mother Dwnet. (Dwnet died when Xto was two; he remembered very little about her.) Mondr was more like a distant god enforcing his will via commandment and sending the occasional birthday gift.

Because of all this Xto's first in-person encounter with the legendary Mondr Djbbit—as an adult—was bound to be *somewhat* disappointing; no one man could possibly live up to the hype built around him. Xto knew this, and yet was unprepared.

Mondr was shorter than he expected, not quite as short as Xto but also not towering above him. His great muscular frame had atrophied dramatically, if it ever existed at all. His face—round and bearded in images—was unshaven and sallow. His cheekbones popped in the same way as Opzk's, meaning this was probably the natural consequence of an extended stay.

His voice, though, was everything it had always been.

Mondr Djbbit had the kind of booming stentorious timbre that could move nations. And, when it came to the latter stages of the Wivvol space program, likely had.

"Let me have a look at you, boy!" was the first thing he said to his son. They were in Mondr's office, a modest place whose most significant feature was the thick glass window that overlooked the dock where the *Zabmez, Hlyib* and the *Guh* were being built. There was a table with several computer screens, set up to look—from one angle—quite impressive. This would be where the great man sat when addressing important people from Dib.

When Xto walked in Mondr was seated at a different table eating something sticky, next to a couch that—despite the lower gravity—had been beaten down quite a lot over the years, across from a bed.

His father slept in his office.

Xto stepped into the middle of the room, still using the magnetic clips on his boots to get around. Mondr reached Xto in two nimble bounds, clapped Xto on the shoulders as if testing the sturdiness of a car, and looked his son in the eyes. He had portions of whatever he had been eating on his chin.

"Yes, I can see much of your mother," Mondr said. "Daresay you look more like a young rendition of your Uncle Ghn."

"This is not so terrible," Xto said.

"No, no, not at all!"

Mondr hugged him briefly, an obligatory gesture rather than a heartfelt one.

"Sit!" he said then, pointing to the couch. He went back to his table and the sticky meal. It was a protein supplement, gelatinous and served in a tube. Xto had his share of the same repast on the trip over, but had been told to expect better food on arrival. Its presence at his father's table meant either someone had lied to him about this or Mondr was eating it as a choice rather than due to a lack of options.

"Your quarters are adequate?" Mondr asked.

"They are fine, yes," Xto said. He had been given a cabin near Zga and Tbux, the last two astronauts to leave the surface prior. This was, he assumed, because familiar faces would make the transition easier. He'd already been greeted in person by Tbux, who told him without elaboration to expect many adjustments and much weirdness.

"Good, good. I told them I wanted you to be treated the same as the rest of your flight cohort for now. You're *not* the same, and we know this, but the best way to understand how a ship works is to start at the bottom and work your way up, no? The best captains begin in the hold, not on the deck."

"Yes," Xto said. "No, I don't think I understand, sir. I *do* expect to be treated the same, but I always have. My tasks are no different than any other citizen's."

Mondr smiled. His teeth were brown.

"We will return to that at a later date. We have plenty of time together ahead of us, you and I."

This was probably meant to be a happy thought, but Xto couldn't imagine another notion as chilling.

"I, um, I was given an interesting message for you, sir," Xto said.

"Please, Xto, call me *anything* but sir. 'Father', or even 'Mondr.' If you *must* engage in honorifics and titles, then 'commander'. What message?"

"You remember Idlo Jrgap? He spoke of you as an old friend."

"*Idlo?* Of course I do. How is councilman Jrgap these days? Still holding to the national purse with both hands, I take it?"

"I...they did not tell you, then. He's dead. He...he died in an unfortunate accident. I was with him when he passed."

"An accident, you say."

Mondr stood and cleaned himself up, then went to the computer table. It was as if he had to formally transition from father to commander by literally shifting positions. He had stopped smiling; his shoulders were back and his spine had straightened. Xto began to understand how he could have been thought of as taller than he was.

"What kind of accident?" he asked.

"The kind that isn't accidental at all," Xto said. He briefly considered hewing to the story they agreed to tell about the councilman's passing, but Jrgap's suicide was *part* of his message to Mondr; not including that detail would mean not delivering it as promised.

"I see. How, then?"

"A projectile weapon," Xto said. "Below the chin."

"Accidentally."

"So it has been said."

"And his message?"

"He wanted to make it as clear to you as possible that the country is at a crossroads. The Chancellery cannot continue sending material here with no benefit. The country, he said, is no longer the economic powerhouse it once was. Even a one-third reduction would make all the difference."

"Hah!" Mondr said. He sank into the chair behind the table and turned to face the *Zabmez*. "The fools. It's their own fault. I told them. Zero-gravity could have been ours, were we not so stuck in the past. It is not *my* program that threatens our collective economic future; it's the Chancellery's antiquated concept of intellectual purity. I am *proud* to know that what built this magnificent vessel, and is keeping us alive right now, began in the minds of our countrymen. But it's a far cry from that and denouncing all non-Wivvolian advancements as flawed and inferior by default."

He turned back around.

"I'm not unaware of the strain the program has put upon the nation's accounts," he said. "But we are the winds in Wivvol's sails, not the stone that sinks us. Never forget that."

"I will strive not to," Xto said.

"Besides which, that message wasn't for me."

"He said that it was."

"Understood. But it was for you. Because he knows, as do I, and as perhaps you do not, that you are my natural successor."

Xto was stuck without words.

"I see you have doubts," Mondr said. "As I told you, we'll discuss it more at a later date. But know one thing, son. I will be too old and frail to take the *Zabmez* on its maiden voyage when the time comes. But a Djbbit must be at the helm. If he wanted to stop that, the truly courageous thing to do would have been to put the gun up to *your* head; not his own. But Idlo always did lack courage and vision."

*You mean for me to stay here*, Xto thought. *How did I not see this?*

"There was one other thing," Xto said. "Councilman Jrgap claimed you...found something. Something important. A discovery you insist on keeping to yourself."

"And he believed this thing would be the key to our economic salvation?" Mondr asked.

"He hinted as much."

"I don't know how true that is because I don't know how it could be monetized. Not yet. But is it important? Oh yes."

"What is it?"

Mondr grinned. "It will be here in twenty-three days. Now I see your examination came back clean; you should report to the dock for your assignment. We will talk more soon."

∽

∽

"That's the meat," Elicasta said, profoundly confusing their new friend.

"There's...meat?" Xto Djbbit asked looking around.

"She means the information is valuable," Makk said. "I think. Try not to speak in Veeser too much, 'Casta, you'll confuse both of us."

"I mean that if I was recording this right now my sub list would blow up. Again. You're telling me Wivvol has been building a space station and a fleet of interstellar ships on the other side of Shizuna Two? That might play bigger than the Linus reveal."

"If anyone believes it, sure," Makk said.

"Hey now, I'm a Verified Streamer talking to the son of the head of the rocket program. That's moonshot gold."

"Whatever that means," Makk said. "I'm saying, I'm here listening to the man now and I'm not all that sure *I* believe it."

Between Xto's on-and-off command of the common tongue and Elicasta's departures into Veeser-speak, Makk felt like he needed a translator for both of them. And probably a nap.

"We are not at the part that is difficult to believe," Xto said.

"Okay but I need some color," Elicasta said. Xto looked to Makk again, a touch of fright behind his eyes. *What is happening to her*, he seemed to want to ask.

"Fill in the gaps," she added. "*Why* the spaceship? Why the secrecy? Everyone knew you guys were sending a lot of launches and I guess nobody worked out that the ones going up weren't the same ones coming back down a month later, but the *scope* is just ultra."

"It's not a thing I ever questioned before," Xto admitted. "It is who we are and always were. When there were no more oceans on Dib for Wivvol to conquer, the ocean in the *sky* was the next logical challenge."

"Yeah but, you guys could turn a profit from the oceans down here."

"That was never the primary imperative," he said. "*Exploration* is our guiding principle. Trade shipping became our excuse. And our funding. But you are correct in recognizing that there is less potential for economic gain in a space program. There has thus far been no discovery of a trade partner or a rare material to mine. But this was not known when the program began. Also..."

He trailed off, as if this next part was either a secret or was somewhat embarrassing. Both, as it turned out.

"There was Elbid," he said.

Makk laughed, but Xto was serious.

"I haven't heard anyone mention Elbid seriously since I was a child," he said.

Elbid was one of those cultural legends that didn't appear to have an origin story. Oft-referenced but never taken seriously, Elbid was supposed to be a mirror planet of Dib, one that had the exact same orbit but was the precise opposite side of the Dancers, which meant it was perpetually impossible to see from Dib-bound telescopes. The first time Makk could remember being introduced to the idea of this imaginary planet was in a book series written for young adults featuring a protagonist who woke up one morning on Elbid. Makk couldn't fathom anyone basing a space program on something that was so clearly made up.

Elicasta's response was somewhat more measured.

"I've seen some deep-Stream theories that take it seriously," she said. "I mean sure, it's *kinda* crazy, but not a lot crazier than anything the House has to offer. Plus it meets the minimum standard for a Stream theory: it's nearly impossible to disprove."

"The dream of Elbid was the driver for the program in the early days," Xto said. "I am sure you see the appeal. If we have no more oceans down here to conquer, let us find a world with new oceans and new continents and continue with our exploration there. We planned to build an interplanetary empire before we even knew if there were other planets."

There *were* other planets in their own solar system. There was Hoa, an ice planet twice the size of Dib, a gas giant named Wintow, and a distant, smaller, ringed gas giant named Bob. All three planets were farther from Dib than Dib was from the Dancers and none appeared capable of supporting the kind of life someone from Wivvol might consider a viable trading partner. Beyond that, there was a planet called Coranova in orbit around a non-binary star called YM-237B that many scientists believed to be the right size and distance from its sun to support life. (There was an equal number of scientists who disagreed, some on the grounds that it was unlikely for life to thrive on a planet in a non-tandem star system.) But Coranova was pretty far away. Makk didn't think Wivvol had the kind of technology capable of making it there in less than a couple of lifetimes.

"I think the worst thing that could have happened to our nation was to run out of places to discover," Xto said.

"Yet you're supposed to take over the whole program from your father," Makk said. "How's that going to work out?"

"As should be obvious now, detective, the Septal artifact wasn't the only birthright I surrendered by splashing down in the wrong place. Whether he assumes I've *actually* perished or no, I'm certain I am now dead to him."

*Welcome to the outcast club,* Makk thought.

"So now I *have* to know," Elicasta said. "What happened twenty-three days later?"

~

~

Xto quickly lost track of the days. It was a combination of (still) being away from the planet's daily cycle and the work calendar aboard platform one.

He was thrust into service the minute it was evident he would not be spending his first week vomiting, as was often the case. They worked in a six hour rotation—six on, six off—performing a combination of tasks only some of which was related to finishing the *Zabmez*, the *Hlyib* or the *Guh*.

Whatever productivity metrics they were relying upon to work out the six hour thing (he assumed there was some science behind it) just the fact that it was impossible to divide twenty by six evenly meant an external timepiece—which he didn't have— was needed to let him know what day it was; there was no way he'd be able to work that out on his own.

As a consequence, Xto had no idea twenty-three days had passed until he was summoned to his father's side.

The meeting wasn't in Mondr's office this time; it was at one of the two observation points atop the asteroid. Getting there meant being excused from his customary duties, which on that day had been to tighten restraining bolts on the third level. It was a task which was evidently performed on a constant cycle throughout the station. Xto was unclear as to why; it seemed to him as if the bulk of the facility was free of the usual stresses buildings that dealt with sea-level gravity had to worry about. *But why are the bolts loose at all?* was one of the questions he promised himself he'd ask, once he decided who would most likely have the correct answer.

Getting to the observation point also meant exiting the main living area—with its pressurized air—putting on a spacesuit and climbing a ladder a half a kalomader in height—exhausting work even in the low gravity. It took Xto well over two hours to do it. This was at least in part because despite being tethered to the pole running alongside the ladder, he went as slowly as he would have had this been a true spacewalk. This just seemed prudent; there was a point above which the modest natural pull of Shizuna Two would be insufficient to keep him from drifting into space. He didn't know where that point was—and again, he was tethered anyway—but didn't want to find out via trial-and-error.

He also stopped a couple of times to take in the view. The station was nestled in a natural concavity on the sunward side of the asteroid. From the shuttle it looked small because he was comparing it to the overall bulk of Shizuna Two. From the *inside* the station seemed massive. Now he was outside and looking down at it, and it again looked quite small.

The ladder terminated at a hatch. Xto spun open the locking mechanism and pushed his way inside to a small airlock, closed it behind him and waited for the room to pressurize. Then it was up another ten rungs on a different ladder to a second hatch and finally he was inside observation point one.

"There you are," his father said. He was halfway out of his spacesuit, leaning on a stool and eating a protein supplement. Beside him was a large telescope.

They were in a large glass bubble on the upper lip of Shizuna Two. No longer obscured by the side of the asteroid, they could see both the Dancers and the planet Dib from this position. It was possibly the best stationary view in the solar system.

Xto was quite taken by the sight. At the same time, he wondered how old this observation point was, whether the glass was sufficiently sturdy, and if it was really a good idea to take off his helmet.

He did, reluctantly.

"It's a long climb," Xto said, in response to his father's goading.

"Is it? I suppose I'm used to it. I've been told you're doing well."

"I've been told the same. I have no metric to compare myself to."

Mondr laughed. "Guarded and pragmatic. They've made you into a fine citizen, haven't they?"

Xto didn't know what his father meant by that but didn't pursue it.

"At any rate," Mondr continued, "I am sorry I haven't had many opportunities to spend time with you, but don't worry; I have been getting regular reports on your progress. And we will have *more* opportunities soon enough."

"Of course," Xto said, having no idea if any of that was true. Mondr unquestionably *believed* it was, but he was known to overpromise. Legendarily so, when it came to the *Zabmez*, the *Hlyib* and the *Guh*. "Now tell me father; why am I here today? What have you to show me?"

"We'll get to that."

Mondr rose from the stool and crossed the room, the magnets on his metal boots clicking and clacking. He was retrieving a cloth bag, from which he extracted a bottle of water.

"Here," he said, pulling out a second bottle for himself. "Always rehydrate after time in one of those suits."

"Thank you."

"And tell me about your friend, Trebnvto Pna."

Xto nearly spit up the water.

"He is...as you say he is a friend," Xto said. "What of him?"

Mondr nodded slowly. "I wonder, my son, if you have been paying attention to how we get along up here, on our own in deep space."

"I'm not sure that I understand."

"Get along. Get by. Coexist. We are many, yes, but not *so*

many. I have found...I would call it the wisdom of an old man but I don't think this is true. It's the wisdom that comes from surviving under exigent circumstance. What I have found is that a larger society—a city, a nation—can *afford* to be intolerant of what it perceives as deviance from the standard. One deviant, labeled and removed, can be readily supplanted by three who are either *not* deviant or who hide it better. But up here? I am telling you that those who elect to stay as often as not have reason to stay. That reason is, they have a place here that they do not have on the surface; the notion of returning to the Wivvolian fold then becomes intolerable."

"For you?" Xto asked. "Is that why you've remained up here as long as you have?"

"Yes. And no. I find the restraint of *thought* in my compatriots at the Chancellery to be an abomination. I was saddened by the news of Idlo's demise, but as I said it wasn't me or this program that killed him; it was their suffocating inflexibility. I would not willingly return to that nest of stubborn vipers. However, setting aside metaphoric suffocation there would also be literal suffocation. I've been up here for too long this last time."

*Most of my life*, Xto thought. Before he settled on indifference toward his father, the young Xto thought Mondr Djbbit remained in space to avoid *him*, specifically. Intellectually, he no longer thought this way, but emotionally it retained some truth.

"You mean that it would be unsafe?" Xto asked.

"I would likely die in Dib's gravity. I maintain the medical regimen needed to retain bone density and conduct the necessary muscle retention exercises but none of that was meant as a permanent substitute. So yes; it would be unsafe. They know this at the *EPFA* and yet they have been attempting to recall me for the past five years."

"I did not know that."

"Oh yes. I suggested they send a team here for my retrieval if they felt this strongly. To date, they have not done so."

"Despite which, father, by all accounts you remain one of the most powerful men in Wivvol. How is this so?"

Mondr laughed. "There are advantages to the paralyzed mindset. I can speak to any member of the Chancellery from here, and I do. Knowing how to play them off of one another is a talent I will teach you. You are correct that the power I wield is largely illusory, but what you will have to learn is that this is true of *all* power."

Xto thought back to when he threatened Ayk and wondered if this was what his father meant. At the time he thought he was bluffing and that Chairwoman Ayk had it within her means to make him disappear should she desire it; he had nothing preventing that aside from his family name. But maybe he wasn't bluffing at all, and the consequence of crossing him was real only he himself didn't know it.

He had been governed by fear his entire life; it never occurred to him that the ones doing the governing were motivated by fear themselves.

"But we have gone astray of my initial question," Mondr said. "About your friend. Would you like for Citizen Pna to join us?"

"He *will* join us when it is his turn in the rotation."

"Ah, but it has *been* his turn for some time, hasn't it?"

"It has," Xto said. "Do *you* have something to do with that, father?"

"Hardly. You must not realize this, Xto, but had Trebnvto made *friends* with any other person—in the astronaut program or in the *country* I expect—he would have been washed out some time ago. I think these days the washouts are sent to the iron ore mines in the northern territories."

"He wasn't, because they're afraid of you?"

"They're afraid of *you*, Xto. Now answer my question. Would you like your friend to join us? He can share your cabin." When Xto didn't answer right away, Mondr added, "You understand what it is I am offering you, son?"

"I do," Xto said.

"Because with one transmission I can have him on the next shuttle."

"I understand, father. What I am unclear on is what I'm exchanging for this privilege."

"I'm offering you the freedom to live as you please, son."

"Provided I remain here."

Mondr shrugged. "I'm not asking for that."

"Then yes, I would like it if Trebnvto were at my side during my stay. All right? Now please tell me why we had this conversation in an observation point instead of your office."

"Yes," Mondr said. He checked the timepiece on his wrist. "It's time."

Setting aside his water bottle, Mondr went to work adjusting the telescope to a specific set of coordinates with a practiced skill.

"There we are," he said, peering through the eyepiece. "Right on schedule. We first spotted it five years ago but have only visited it up close on a limited number of occasions. Here; have a look."

Mondr stepped aside so Xto could lean over and see for himself.

There was an object beginning a transit between Shizuna Two and the Dancers. At this point it was just to the left of Dyhine's corona; it would later be impossible to see with a light-based optic as the suns would wash it out.

It was a spaceship.

## Chapter Sixteen

The ship had a long central tube similar to that of a wingplane, only instead of wings this had a torus structure around its center. Xto couldn't make out more than that, no matter how much he fiddled with the focus dial.

There were no space programs on Dib anywhere close to the scale and scope of what Wivvol was doing. And if Xto's understanding of history was accurate, there never had been. No nation on the planet had the technology to build something like this.

It was an alien spaceship. That was the only conclusion.

"Not possible," he said.

Mondr laughed and clapped Xto on the shoulder. "Now you understand," he said.

"I understand nothing. What is that and where did it come from?"

"Elbid. Or an equivalent. We don't *know*, son."

"How can you not know? Five years, you said."

"I did. Five years of piloting shuttles out there to examine it as best we can. We've collected reams of information about the hull's composition, we've done all we could to guess its age, its means of propulsion...almost everything except where it came from and who built it."

"You can't get inside."

"We haven't figured out how to yet. Not without damaging it. And to your next question, as far as we've been able to tell whoever used to live in the ship died some time ago. It's been adrift in a stable orbit, possibly for centuries."

"Did it luck into a stable orbit or was it put into one?"

Mondr smiled, and shrugged.

"Who else knows about this?" Xto asked. "I expect the Chancellery to keep something like this quiet but the entire *EPFA*?"

"The only ones who know *this* much are the long haulers. And now you. I can't trust anyone on a two year tour with this information. As for the Chancellery, not one of them knows the entire thing. I've given partial information to a few, just enough to keep the shipments coming."

"But why? I don't understand. This is a history-altering discovery. What is the value in secrecy?"

"Information is power," Xto," Mondr said.

"You only just finished explaining that power is an illusion, father."

"I amend my prior statement. Power isn't entirely an illusion but it *is* transitory. If I give up all I know about that ship I will lose leverage. Worse, I'll be forced by one of those fools on the surface to find a way to monetize this. They're too short-sighted, the entire Chancellery."

"Monetize?"

"There's technology on that ship far beyond anything we're capable of. I can't prove that but it *has* to be true. Until we've figured out how to gain access safely without harming it somehow, we will remain spectators."

"But to do that you need to bring it here," Xto said.

"And to have any hope of doing *that* I need all three ships. Now you understand."

"All...how big is it? It's impossible to tell from here."

"Twice the size of the *Zabmez*. Almost half of which is taken up by the ship's engine, according to our sonic scanners. Whoever built it intended to travel a great distance. Wouldn't you like to have a good look at the technology capable of such a thing?"

"Unless it failed," Xto said. "Perhaps the engine malfunctioned and killed the crew on its maiden voyage."

"We can tell whatever story we want about how it ended up here. Perhaps you're right and it literally arrived in this place from the mythical planet of Elbid. Perhaps if we took out the *Zabmez* as soon as it was ready we'd manage the transit to the far side of the Dancers and find out for ourselves. This is what many on the Chancellery want. But ask yourself: if this was but one ship from a planet *that* close..."

"...Where are the rest of their ships?" Xto said, finishing the thought.

"Precisely. I believe this is a ship built for great distances that *traveled* a great distance, at high velocity, using that magnificent engine."

"Are there any markings on the outside?"

"Language? A legend of some kind?"

"A name. Vessels have names."

"None we've been able to find," Mondr said. "The outside is pocked and coated in dust particles from historical collisions with space debris, and charred in a few places, so if words once existed on the hull I don't believe they do now. Not that we would be able to read them."

"But windows? What about windows. You could peer inside..."

"There are heavy shutters on the front, which we think are protecting windows. Xto, we can go on for the rest of the day with your questions but there's no need. We're planning another scout mission to coincide with the moment when it's nearest to our position. One of the shuttles can be yours if you'd like to get an up-close look at it for yourself. But choose quickly. The next opportunity won't be for another six months."

"In exchange for?"

"How do you mean?"

"Everything about this has been transactional in nature, father. You mean for me to stay and take over for you. You've dangled the man you know perfectly well is my lover before me as an enticement. Now you're sharing the most important discovery in the history of the planet and underlining that none but long haulers know of it. Say what you need to say."

"I'm not going to *demand* that you remain here, son," Mondr said. "You're not a prisoner."

"There are plenty in Wivvol who are not prisoners by name but are imprisoned nonetheless. If anything, it would be easier to effectively imprison me here."

"I want you to *want* to stay, Xto. I want you to *want* to be here when we learn all of our alien friend's secrets. And if we are being honest, it shouldn't be that difficult of a choice. You're being offered the freedom to live as you wish and the greatest mystery of all time. So no, I will not *demand* that you accept it, but I would be astonished at your short-sightedness if you do not."

*That* was the Mondr Djbbit he remembered. The one who insisted he estrange his uncle and drop his adherence to Septalism, enter into the astronaut program and follow his father into space. It may have seemed to Mondr that all of these things were choices Xto made for himself, but the truth was nothing that led to this moment had been Xto's decision. Not really. And now the pattern was continuing.

*Everyone says you have power, Xto,* he thought. *Why not use it?*

"I would like to see the alien ship up close," Xto said levelly. "And I would much appreciate it if my friend Trebnvto were to join me. After that, I will give you my decision."

The hangar holding all of the long hauler shuttles was set off a distance from both the bay in which Xto initially touched down and the shipyard-like hangar holding the *Zabmez*, *Hlyib* and *Guh*. In order to reach it, Xto had to walk to the very limit of the pressurized living area, suit up for a tethered walk across (and over) a craggy terrain ill-suited for anything other than puncturing spacesuits, and into another pressurized area—an observation deck overlooking the shuttle hangar.

"There are so many," was the first thing he said to his guide, Opzk, upon arrival.

"One for each long hauler," she said. "in addition to any vessels belonging to the since-passed. You'll have to take one of these as your shuttle is still in the other bay."

The shuttles—along with the very existence of this auxiliary hangar in which to house them—was a consequence of the peculiar problem created by the Chancellery's dual obsessions with secrecy and control. The entire concept of astronauts remaining in space beyond their two year solo exploratory voyage (as it was described to the public) was beyond the ken of most because... where would they *stay*? The station on the sunny side of Shizuna Two was a secret. Likewise, a citizen so great as to attain the rank of astronaut openly defying the *EPFA* to remain in space after their tour was up? This was a huge embarrassment that could never be made public.

Yet, it was also the case that every astronaut departed with great fanfare, lauded as a genuine hero of the nation. The Chancellery couldn't simply pretend, two years later, that they had never existed.

Roughly nine times out of ten they simply pretended they *had* come back. "If conditions are fair," the Voice (the Chancellery's media arm) might announce, "and you are looking in just the right part of the sky, it may be possible to see Astronaut Koqba's glorious reentry this evening."

It mattered not at all that Astronaut Koqba was doing no such thing. If one elected to look at the sky that evening and failed to see the shuttle's return, well, you must have been looking in the wrong place or at the wrong time, because he clearly *did* land. Here is the (spoofed) footage! Koqba's retirement from public life would be announced subsequently and that would be that. Meanwhile, the *actual* Koqba remained in space and was, in fact, on the hangar floor preparing his shuttle at that very moment.

In one of the ten times, the Chancellery would instead declare the astronaut had died due to a tragic accident either in space or upon reentry. These happened strategically, when it was felt that the nation needed a common cause around which to rally. (Importantly, they only did this when it had been some time since an *actual* accident.) There was a funeral and a national day of mourning and it was all very solemn and beautiful.

In his brief time at the station, Xto had already met three astronauts whose funerals he attended, two of whom he didn't know prior to running into them that they were actually alive.

"Welcome to the Haven," one of them, the supposedly long-dead Ay Lbakz, joked upon seeing the shocked look on Xto's face. "This is where we *all* go when we die." He clapped Xto on the shoulder and walked away, still resolutely alive.

Xto wondered what his Uncle Ghn would have to say about that.

"Which one?" Xto asked Opzk, regarding the shuttle he would be using. There were perhaps a hundred shuttles from which to choose. Koqba was standing beside his own, and Astronaut Uywg stood next to *her* own, but that didn't do much to diminish all of the available choices.

"Your father's," she said.

"He is not coming?"

"Only the four of us. I am afraid Mondr is occupied with other duties today."

*More important than an up-close look at an alien spaceship?* Xto thought.

"Which is his?" he asked.

"It should be obvious, should it not?" she asked, pointing to a shuttle at the far end of the bay near the hangar's exit.

It was indeed obvious, in the same way Koqba and Uywg's were obvious: there were words and images painted on the sides of these shuttles. Some of it was functional but basic—Uywg's had her name and a depiction of their system's tandem stars and nothing else—but most were deep expressions of artistic freedom that would not have been allowed on any ship returning to Dib. (Indeed, since most of the return shuttles landed on a pad at the *EPFA*, they were reused. A painted claim of ownership by a returning astronaut would be irrational given a different astronaut would be taking it back into space subsequently.)

The painted shuttles were yet another example of the petty rebellions that marked so much of what day-to-day life was like at the station. Xto imagined he would get used to it eventually.

His father's shuttle was garish and self-aggrandizing. DJBBIT, it read in bold purple lettering, fresh and bright and probably recently retouched. Above it was a word that meant "commander," but it wasn't the modern Ghshtic version of the title. Instead, Mondr had chosen an archaic Ghshtic permutation, which also happened to be the root word for "ruler," "king," and "lord."

Father wanted to be seen as royalty.

"Yes," Xto said, "it's very obvious."

"We will move your shuttle here," Opzk said, "once you've formally declared. And then you can paint it however you wish."

"Prince Djbbit?" he said, laughing.

"If you'd like."

She didn't laugh.

The hangar floor was unpressurized—the exit was open to space—so it took a while for them to get assembled, into their shuttles and underway. It didn't help that the least experienced of them in matters of spacewalking also had to walk the farthest. Likewise, it didn't help that upon arrival he had to familiarize himself with someone else's shuttle.

It wasn't so much that his father's personal shuttle had its own peculiar quirks (although it did) but that it was a *much* older model than anything Xto had previously flown.

But, he managed, and in a little under two hours the four of them were on their way.

Which meant there was suddenly very little to do. Their route was charted by Koqba, who also took the lead. Xto made sure his ship's systems were aligned with Koqba's and then he was done...for the next seventeen hours. That was how long it would take them to reach the "anomalous object." (This was everyone's euphemism for the alien spaceship; quite useful when talking in mixed company around people who might not be aware of its existence.)

For the first six hours he slept. The next six he spent familiarizing himself (again) with all of the information they'd already amassed on the alien ship.

Then he had nothing else to do.

He opened his comms.

"Opzk," he said, to her private channel. "Exactly how sick is my father?"

There was a lengthy pause on the open line, and then: "He told you?"

"He said nothing to me; he's not one to articulate weakness or if he is then I am not the audience for it. There have been signs. Today is the largest but hardly the only; he would surely be here himself if he could be."

"I'm his...physician, Xto. I can only say so much."

"Then don't speak to me as his physician; speak as his friend. Or lover, if that's preferable."

"You observe too much, Xto Djbbit," she said. "As you've raised it, my relationship with your father is not sexual."

"But it wasn't always," he said.

"As I said. You observe too much."

"It should be obvious that I don't care, Opzk. I'm only providing you with a means to answer my question. I am his son and you are a close friend and former mistress who has information for me. So if you would: how sick is he?"

There was another long patch of dead air before her response. She had the channel open—he heard her breathing—but wouldn't speak.

"Your father has cancer," she said finally. "It's a common problem out here, especially for those on extended stay. Right now his is curable, but the cure is on Dib and he refuses to leave. Mondr would rather remain here and die sooner than return to Wivvol and die later."

"How much time does he have?"

"There's no way to tell. I can say that the window of opportunity for him to return to the surface and receive life-saving treatment will close within the year. Beyond that, his survival relies upon far too many variables. It could be five years or it could be eighteen months. I grounded him, which is why he is not here with us. But the very fact that he accepted the grounding—he could have easily chosen to ignore it—should tell you all you need to know. He's frightened, Xto."

"This is why, then," Xto said.

"Why what?"

"He wants me to stay and take over for him. He's offered nothing but carrots thus far but I know this will not last; he'll show the stick in his other hand soon enough."

Opzk didn't respond.

"I am sorry," Xto said. "This is not your concern; it's a family problem. I should not involve you."

"It's all right," she said. "I am *your* physician as well. But know that your father began speaking of the day you would come here since well before his diagnosis. It was *always* his plan for you. The cancer added urgency but it did not create the dynamic."

"Thank you for saying that," Xto said. "I will keep it in mind as I consider my choice. That's provided my father continues to allow it to *be* my choice."

~

Yd Koqba's shuttle had been repainted with a fresh base coat of brilliant lavender sometime recently. It ran contrast to the mustard-yellow letters of his name and the many-hued pastel cockatiel—well, the many-hued *bird*; identifying the type Koqba was aiming for was difficult—near the shuttle's nose.

It was garish, frankly; the colors did not balance well, chosen for their individual brightness with little concern about whether they looked attractive together. To Xto, it looked less like a piece of artistic expression and more like the consequence of a child's tantrum. After a lifetime of whites, browns and grays, perhaps that's exactly what it was: a tantrum.

It was also the only thing Xto had to look at for the bulk of their journey. He was positioned at Koqba's right flank, with Opzk at the left and Uywg taking the rear.

Their path to the anomalous object was slightly indirect; they curled behind it—putting the Dancers on their left—and then accelerated to match its velocity.

Now, after many, many hours in which their prey was a distant and indistinct object, they were finally close enough to see it clearly with the naked eye.

Xto's first thought was, *it's actually real*. And indeed, it was.

The spaceship wasn't traveling nose-first in the direction of its orbit, as one might expect of a vehicle whose vector was intended. Were the rockets to jump to life suddenly, the ship would head away at a forty degree angle from the vertical and thirty-five from the horizontal.

It was massive. Almost from the moment it came into view Xto felt as if he was moments away from being close enough to touch it, yet he was not...and it kept taking up more of the horizon.

Xto got a brief but good look at the ship's rockets from the rear. They jutted out from the back asymmetrically—the central rocket was wider in diameter and extended past the other rockets, which ringed it. They reminded him of the Fingers atop the House temple in Chnta.

He found the ship's torus structure particularly interesting. There was rampant speculation in the documentation as to the purpose of this part of the alien ship: a secondary power generator; a gravity ring; the manifold for a solar sail; and so on. It was the only thing on the ship that had no cognate to a Dib-based vessel, and so it drew the most interest from everyone. There was some evidence that it could rotate when powered, which didn't disqualify any of the theories by itself, but seemed to favor the gravity ring theory. The support struts attaching the ring to the ship even looked large enough to be hollow, which if so would allow someone from the ship's main tube to walk or climb to the ring.

Xto was dubious. The intent of a gravity ring was to provide artificial gravity via centripetal force; a similar design had been considered in the early blueprints for the *Zabmez* before being scrapped. (Mainly for technical reasons, although there was a line of thinking among certain Wivvolians that artificial gravity of any kind in space was a sign of weakness. "Don't go to sea without learning to swim," was the approximate philosophy.)

It seemed to him that a species sufficiently advanced to sail this ship across the interstellar ocean in the sky would be sufficiently advanced to have developed artificial gravity as well. It had to be something else.

"Break formation." Koqba said once they were (finally) close enough to interact meaningfully with the alien ship. "Fall in."

The four shuttles collapsed into a single file, with Xto directly behind Koqba.

Astronaut Koqba steered them alongside the ring until they were within about ten maders of the torus's outer hull. Xto's role at this time was to keep his eyes firmly upon the rear rockets of Koqba's shuttle; their firing pattern told him whether they were heading left, right, up or down, actions he would have to match. It was no time to be sightseeing.

And yet, an up-close look at the anomaly was just a quick glance to his left.

He peeked a couple of times. What he saw was the scarred surface of what looked like steel gray hull plates. The plates were square and appeared to be as long as he was tall. They were fixed in place by rivets along the border. Nothing about the panels screamed evidence of significant technological advances.

But this was perhaps not where he should be looking for that evidence; there were only so many ways to attach a panel.

Once past the outer edge of the ring, Koqba steered them in and alongside the body of the ship.

"Fall back, team," he said over the comms. "Xto, prepare to dock beside me. Opzk, the top. Uywg, the bottom."

Everyone confirmed, and applied their reverse thrusters, settling into a drift alongside the vessel. Then Koqba maneuvered his lavender shuttle sideways and landed on the alien ship's hull.

Then, finally, Xto had something he could use for scale. The ship's body was a cylinder, which meant no matter how he lined up Koqba would be attempting to land a flat-bottomed shuttle onto a curved surface. However, this hardly mattered, as the body was evidently about ten times larger than that of the largest wingplane Xto had ever seen.

The side of the body may as well have been flat.

"Clamps are enabled," Koqba said. "Astronaut Djbbit, proceed."

It took Xto far longer than it would have had he been in his own shuttle. His father's toggle attitude was sluggish and there was a half second delay in the feedback when he made an adjustment. Also, a number of the dials were analog when he was accustomed to digital.

But he got it done, setting down beside Koqba and activating the clamps.

"I am in place," he said.

"Affirmed," Koqba said.

They waited until the other two had docked as well, relying on audio verification as the top and bottom of the body wasn't visible from their perspective.

Then it was time to head outside.

Xto put his helmet back on, stood and stretched in the zero gravity, and then activated the magnets on his boots.

One of the reasons they'd been able to learn what they had—although it wasn't much—was that the aliens had chosen to compose their hull of a material that was at least *partly* ferrous metal. This was important, because what the hull lacked was guide rails or any other protrusion that would be of value to someone looking to anchor a tether.

Xto lowered himself into the shuttle's tiny airlock, sealed off the main chamber and depressurized, then stepped out. He felt the boots adhere to the hull. Satisfied he wasn't going to float away, Xto began walking—slowly, always slowly—beside the shuttle until he met up with Koqba, who was busy attaching a magnetic handle to the side of the anomaly. He had a length of cable over his shoulder.

The purpose of this expedition was not scientific; it was to *enable* future science-based trips. What they would be doing is establishing a series of permanent guide wires at different parts of the hull so that when they came back they could investigate with greater mobility and far lesser risk.

It was a three-person job. Xto had no duties beyond his own curiosity; his role was to look at whatever part of the ship he felt like looking at, within bounds.

*Enflame your interest,* his father had said.

"How are you?" Koqba asked. "Are you stable?"

"I am stable and oriented," Xto said.

"All right. Do not lose your footing and drift away; the commander would never forgive me."

"I shall endeavor not to."

"Line of sight protocols, Xto. I mean that. No matter what you find."

He meant, always keep within line of sight of one of his three teammates. Given how spread out they were, this wouldn't be difficult.

"Affirm," Xto said.

He activated the light atop the dome of his helmet and began to walk along a surface that was closest he would ever get to an alien planet.

∼

For the first couple of hours Xto's primary concern was just getting used to walking. He'd had extensive experience with mag boots, but this was the first time a minor misstep could mean his demise, and so he took the time to automate the process.

It helped that for those first two hours there was little to look at. Without meaning to, he began heading in the direction of the mysterious torus structure, because it was a destination that excited him, but the journey there had hardly anything special to offer. (Also, he would likely not have sufficient time to get close to it. Reaching a support strut was feasible but walking its length to get to the ring was far too great a distance.) Here and there he spotted things that had come up previously in the reports he'd read—a couple of metal shutters, a fist-sized impact crater, and so on—but nothing he didn't already know about.

He reached the base of one of the support struts after another two hours and then looked up to gauge the distance from there to the ring itself. Then he looked back at the shuttle from which he'd walked. He could barely make out Koqba, running his cable up the width of the ship.

*You are the same distance to Koqba as you are to the ring,* he thought. *The ring is four hours of walking; it's too far.*

Still, he lifted one boot and put it on the side of the support strut. He could walk *part* of the way, surely.

Except he couldn't. Whatever the strut was made of, it wasn't the same material as the hull; magnets didn't work on it.

He bent down and examined the strut's connection to the ship more closely. It looked as if there was something sandwiched between the strut's base and the hull. It was a hard thing, about as thick as his arm, with grooves in the side.

"Shock absorption," he said.

Standing, he followed the strut up again with his eyes, noting for the first time the joints at regular intervals, no doubt filled with the same substance.

He wished he'd been allowed to bring an evidence bag and a tool of some kind. If they were looking for alien substances, the shock absorbent material was probably it, because it wasn't rubber, or metal, or wood. Amusingly, the only thing he'd ever seen that was quite like it was the Septal artifact hidden in his cabin. But that wasn't alien; it was just old.

But what, he wondered, was the strut *itself* made of, if not purely metal?

What looked like an opaque surface was in point of fact an unclean one; it was covered in the same space dust as the hull. When Xto brushed some of it off he got a look at the *actual* support strut.

It was partly transparent.

Suddenly, the comparison to this material and the composition of Javilon's key seemed less frivolous.

*A coincidence,* he thought. *It couldn't be anything but.*

He moved around the strut. It took him out of a line of sight with Koqba, briefly, so of course that was when he stepped into a hole.

His forward boot failed to connect with a surface he'd expected to be attaching himself to, and then his leg was flying back weirdly, as if he'd tripped but fallen in the wrong direction.

It was up to the rear boot to keep him from drifting away. It did, but it was a perilous few seconds of worrying that it just might not.

Once stabilized, Xto knelt down to get a better look at the indentation that had nearly caused him to spin off into deep space.

It wasn't an impact crater like all of the others he'd seen; the sides of it were too smooth. It was purposeful.

He reached into the indent and was surprised to find that there was a concavity within the concavity, about the right size for his fingers.

This was a handle.

He pulled, but nothing happened. It had no give to it.

Xto took two steps back and tried to get a better measure of what he was looking it. It *seemed* as if there was an outline of a rectangle.

"It's a hatch," he said.

He bent down and began tracing the barely visible line with his hand, all the way around the rectangular outline, until he'd confirmed as accurate what he'd gone in thinking was probably just his eyes playing tricks. There was an actual rectangular shape in the side of the ship.

He had found an entrance. A real entrance. It was a *locked* entrance, but it was a start.

*They were the same size as us*, he thought. *And they had hands to open doors with.*

*How did they unlock those doors?*

He returned his attention to the area around the handle. Locks were found near handles; was there a keypad, perhaps? Or a long-dormant sensor waiting for someone to wave a hand across them?

He didn't find either of those things, but he *did* find another intentional hole. It was to the right of the handle and the left of the door's edge. It was small and difficult to find at first, but he found it: an odd-shaped hole below the handle.

A keyhole.

"Now all I need is the key," he said, wondering if it might be possible to jam something—like one of the tools he hadn't been allowed to bring on his introductory mission—into the keyhole to get it to work.

Then he gasped, because he recognized the *shape* of this keyhole.

He stood and stared again at the strut composed of a partly transparent, strong but non-metal, non-wood, non-glass substance. It was impossible but at the same time it was true.

The means to open this door was hidden in Xto's bunk.

"Uncle, I've found where your key fits," he said. "By the Five, I wish you were here with me to explain it."

## Chapter Seventeen

By the time Dorn and Viselle reached the surface a non-trivial portion of their exploits had made it to the Stream, albeit in a profoundly bastardized form.

The explosion that destroyed Leemie Witts' basement apartment was the start of a conflagration that ended up consuming half of the building above it and—since all of the buildings in that part of Pant City were atop one another—the apartment houses on both sides. Shortly after the news of the fire broke, one of the more respectable Veesers linked the explosion to the ones that killed Zam the Madman and *nearly* killed Elicasta Sangristy. (*How* they were linked wasn't made clear.) Since those attacks were subsequently connected to both Viselle Daska and Ba-Ugna Kev, and since Elicasta Sangristy was currently considered missing by the Stream at large—and had been since the aforementioned Ba-Ugna Kev was murdered by the also-missing Calcut Linus—there were roughly 1,000 active theories running around the Stream when Viselle and Dorn emerged from their subterranean adventure to find themselves in a vacant office park within spitting distance of Kloget airfield.

Interestingly, despite the roundabout way in which they got

there, the Stream had collectively managed to end up looking for the right person: Viselle Daska. The theories associating her were all profoundly incorrect: the victim was Elicasta Sangristy, or Dorn Jimbal, or Calcut Linus; or Daska was *working* with Linus and the victim was actually the also-missing police detective named Makk Stidgeon; or it was actually *Orno* Linus all along, faking his own death to frame his brother to something something the House, but with Viselle's help surely.

One way or another, the entire city knew to look for Viselle Daska, which made every second she spent on the surface especially perilous.

Fortunately, one name *never* came up in connection with the bombing: Exty Demara. She had no trouble booking an exo landing at the airfield and little fear that when she arrived she would end up surrounded by police and/or House Sentries.

Exty had a *different* problem, which was that she was a famous person who famously hardly ever left Lys. This was what made it possible for her to get a landing pad on short notice, but the downside was that there was no way for Dorn and Viselle to get to *her* without being identified by one of a hundred Streamers (verified and not) vying to catch a vid of the reclusive Demara family figurehead.

It was ultimately decided that Viselle and Dorn would find a position of relative safety, remain there and wait until their savior made it to the surface and figured out a way to get a car to them without herself being followed.

To Dorn, this sounded like an impossibility. To both Viselle and Exty, it didn't appear to be a big deal.

"Evading Veesers is something the Demaras are pretty good at," Viselle had said. "She'll be fine."

The office park felt like nearly as alien a terrain to Dorn as had the tunnels beneath it. They were familiar with office areas and business-related aggregations of services, but always on the Septal grounds. This meant a certain collegiality; one could walk into any room and feel somewhat as if one was in the right place. There, the buildings belonged to Dorn, and Dorn belonged in the buildings.

Dorn got no such sense from these office buildings. This place felt unwelcoming.

No, that wasn't right. It felt like someone else's home: a public space that nonetheless belonged to someone else.

It was difficult to tell if this was a failed office park or a new park that simply hadn't gotten full-time tenants yet. Half of the facades had no signage at all, and the other half had partial signage that looked to be either in the process of going up or coming down.

The tunnel's hatch had disgorged them into an untended atrium of dirt and scrub grass. Viselle, ever mindful of their tactical position, immediately broke into a run for the nearest doorway, stopping only long enough to make sure Dorn was in fact following her lead.

"We have to put distance between us and the hatch," she'd said. "Quickly, before a drone spots us."

The door was open, which made perfect sense given the atrium wasn't accessible from the street; just the other buildings in the compound. Whoever designed it probably didn't plan on anyone coming up through a hidden trap door.

They'd eventually settled in the former offices of what appeared to be a travel agency. *Then* Viselle called Exty. They'd been waiting there since.

Dorn immediately camped out under one of the emergency lights and cracked open their hard-won prize: Professor Linus's stolen archival text. It wasn't an ideal setting in which to solve any great mysteries, but they had nothing else to do.

"Is it all you'd hoped for?" Viselle asked, after about four hours. She'd spent the time pacing, hushing Dorn when she thought she heard something—Dorn wasn't making any noise that mandated a hush command—and staring out the window at the front rotunda, which was where Exty was supposed to show up to retrieve them.

"The book?" they asked.

"Yes, that's what I mean. We risked enough to get it. Is that the answer to Orno's mysteries?"

"Well, I don't know yet, obviously. I need to put it up against my notes, which I didn't bring. I believe it is, though; I've seen many of the canonical texts—rather, copies of them—in the Velon Septal House. This isn't like any of them. It's something unique."

"Unique is good?"

"It could be. The drawback of something unique is that there may be a good reason for it. The most obvious, it's non-canonical, which is another way of saying the House doesn't believe it's true."

"That wouldn't have been Orno's perspective, I'm pretty sure," she said.

"It wouldn't. His perspective was, I believe, that this is *true* but also dangerous."

She laughed. "The House hides uncomfortable truths? Why don't I find that difficult to believe? Why would it be dangerous?"

"Again, I don't know. I need my notes."

"Right. Any guesses? We have time. I won't tell anyone if you end up being wrong."

They sighed and closed the book, holding it up in the light of the emergency exit sign as if it was a sacred object bequeathed by the gods directly.

"This appears to be the oldest known version of the *Parieaum Ejukatesi* in existence," Dorn said. "I believe Orno thought that made it *truer* in some way, and that's possible. But as I said this could also be a non-canonical text, meaning we should discard its textual distinctions entirely."

"This has been a lot of work to uncover the product of a bad scribe," she said.

"I agree, and I don't think we have. Generally, books as well-known as this are rejected from the canon when it can be compared to a contemporary and found wanting. I doubt we have anything to compare this to."

Viselle stepped away from the window. "I remember when we found it," she said. "Makk and I. It was hidden under Orno's bed. We knew it was old, but we didn't know *how* old. How are you dating it?"

"You couldn't have known from looking at the cover. But there are ways within the text."

"Such as?"

"Weights and measures are a good bellwether," they said.

"The mader and so on."

"And so on. The standards we use now were established by the House well before the Collapse, which makes the weight and measurement tables the closest thing we have to uncorrupted knowledge from the earliest of times. I don't know whether this is *true*, but I've heard there are exemplars in existence. A mader stick, for example, made of material that won't shrink or expand with temperature changes...like that key you stole from the astronaut, now that I think of it. That's probably the same substance."

"Sure," she said, making a face. They thought she was probably displeased with their classification of how she obtained the key as *stealing*.

"How does that help us date the book?" she asked.

"While the size of the mader hasn't changed over time—so far as anyone knows—the *word* for it has. Eglinat has a lot of assumed vowels, and the texts we're all working with have been copied by numerous scribes over the centuries so the consonants for common-use words have drifted. This is the essential problem with trying to read archaic Eglinat using only a familiarity with the modern form, and why Corporal Witts had so much trouble; he was using a modern primer to read what was effectively a different language."

"Like Ghshtic," she said. "Assumed vowels."

"I suppose," they said. "I've never tried speaking to a Wivvolian so I don't know."

"The language is one giant glottal stop. Go on."

"When a consonant drifts it can affect the vowel sound," Dorn continued. "Very soon, one has what may as well be a different word. And *that* is what can be useful. The common tongue word 'mader' is also 'mader' in Eglinat, but spelled somewhat closer to M-D-R where the assumed vowel sound between the M and the D is an 'ayy' sound. However, earlier iterations of the word use a consonant *similar* to the modern Eglinat 'M'. It produces the same sound but contraindicates a different vowel sound: an 'I'. So in earlier texts the word is more like 'mider.'"

"All right, I think I understand," she said. "If you can find that word in the text you can determine what era it originated from. Do I have that right?"

"Exactly. Because prior to 'mider' there was 'miter' and 'mater' and—if I'm remembering correctly—'meeder'."

"And in this book?"

"Honestly, I don't think this permutation has been documented before," they said, flipping to the page in question. It was a text describing how deeply to dig a grave so the dead remain uncorrupted from the posthumous influence of the Outcast. It was a grim section that served no use aside from helping modern scholars date the scribe, just as Dorn was doing.

"'Mee'...hm. You understand linguistics was not my concentration."

"Your best guess is better than mine."

"I think it would sound like...'meter'. Yes, that's about right."

"Okay," she said. "And that tells us...?"

"That this is as old as Orno thought it was. Perhaps not *how* old because if there's no other record of 'meter' being the word for mader we have nothing to compare it to. But the date at the front of the manuscript might help."

"The...Dorn, I may just shoot you."

"I don't understand," they said.

"You went through all of that and there's a *date* in the front?"

Dorn laughed. "Oh, yes that sounds worse when you say it like that," they said. "No, no, it's not *nearly* that useful. Remember, this is a pre-Collapse text and our current calendar started counting from year zero *after* the Collapse. There are any number of ways to interpret what the date was for the scribe, but it's not anything like a direct correlation."

They flipped to the front. "It says year 827 of the eighth millennium. This is only helpful once we compare it to another text whose date we've pinned down via other means, and even then we can't be sure because we simply don't know what counting system the scribe was using. *Our* year has 529 days to it, which is sensible because that's how long it takes for us to complete one circuit around the Dancers. But canonical House calendars have a shorter year."

"How short?"

"I don't recall. Less than a full circuit. There's a good deal of dispute regarding what standard was being used, but it definitely wasn't something on the cosmic scale. To worsen the whole thing, canonical house clocks weren't based on twenty hours, either. There's effectively no good way to figure out what the scribe meant—what year it was, objectively, as compared to now—because he may have been basing it on a year with a different number of days and days calculated on a different number of hours. Compounding *all* of that, we don't even know what they were counting *up* from."

"Okay, you win. The date's not useful. I won't shoot you."

"I appreciate that."

"Oh, hello," she said, only now she was addressing whatever was outside the window.

Dorn got up to have a look.

Three black widewagons had pulled into the rotunda near the main entrance.

"Sentries?" Dorn asked.

"Not sure yet."

The wagons opened on the side to disgorge over a dozen people wearing heavy battle armor. No hoods.

"Nope, that's our ride," Viselle said.

"Exty brought an army?"

"It's a private security company. But yes, essentially. She probably engaged their services before she even landed."

Exty climbed out of the passenger side of the first widewagon and looked around...and not for Dorn and Viselle.

"Uh-oh," Viselle said.

Exty was looking up at a part of the sky Dorn couldn't see from their angle. Then she began windmilling her arm quickly.

"They've found us," Viselle said, grabbing his arm. "We have to run now."

Back through the closed-up office building they went, down three flights of stairs leading to a central lobby with an unoccupied front desk, through an unlocked security trestle and up to a set of glass doors. In a day that had already included more running than Dorn was accustomed to, they began cramping before they'd made it as far as the security point, forcing Viselle to slow down.

"Helping you escape custody is becoming a regular job for me," she said, as she helped Dorn through the gate.

"In both instances, my circumstance has been entirely your doing," they pointed out.

"Hey, *I* wanted to come alone."

"Yes. Imagine how well *that* would have gone."

Pausing at the doors, they saw for the first time what had so alarmed Exty: a team of Sentries had rolled up nose-to-nose with her private security widewagons, which was a large problem. Also, someone was landing a helo in the rotunda.

"This is going to be fun," Viselle said.

Viselle pushed open the glass door. Immediately five members of Exty's security detail broke off from the main group (which was currently forming a protective ring around Exty) and sprinted to Dorn and Viselle.

"Move, move, move!" the leader barked.

"Just run straight for the widewagons," Viselle said. "Keep your head down."

The two of them ran, with Viselle pushing Dorn ahead. The five soldiers activated personal shields of some sort (they were electrically generated from devices on their forearms; Dorn had never seen technology like this before) and kept themselves between Dorn and the amassed Septals.

Nobody fired any weapons at anyone. The Sentries appeared content to allow their prey to reach the widewagons unmolested. Dorn did as instructed, kept their head down, and focused on reaching the vehicles. Only once there did they stop to take in the evolution of their situation.

Exty remained standing near the front fender of the first widewagon, flanked by members of her security force. Opposite, and at a distance, was a small army of Sentries—about twice as many as what Exty had available. They weren't attacking, though. Nor had the Sentries taken a position to actively impede their departure. They were waiting for whoever was in that helo to emerge.

"There are no drones," Viselle said, looking around. Dorn looked up and confirmed the same. This didn't seem all that unlikely to them as they were in an unused office park. They'd also spent most of their life in Velon on the House campus, where drones weren't allowed.

"This is unusual?" Dorn asked.

"It is when Exty's in town. I'm just trying to figure out if this is her doing...or his."

She nodded at the helo just as Duqo Plaint stepped out.

263

The High Hat of the Velon Septal chapter looked precisely as inscrutable as every other time Dorn had seen the man. He was hooded but otherwise wearing a normal businessman's suit, and moved with a sturdiness and grace that belied what had to be rapidly-advancing years.

He stood straight up, not bothering to duck like most people exiting helos when the rotors were still moving, and strode purposefully in their direction.

Plaint glanced only briefly at Dorn, ignored Viselle entirely, and concentrated his gaze on Exty.

"Hey, Duqo," Exty said. "Long time."

"*Too* long, Ms. Demara. So nice to have you rejoin us on the surface. Pity the circumstance."

"You're welcome to swing by for lunch anytime," Exty said.

"Thank you! I just might do that."

"But, ah, these guys are friends of mine. They're under my protection. So we're gonna just go. You and me will have to catch up later."

"Your protection?" Duqo looked past her, an exaggerated gesture. "Viselle Daska, wanted for the murder of...how many is it, Detective Daska? Two? Five? What are the charges up to?"

"I haven't checked the total in a while," Viselle said.

"And Dorn Jimbal, who is *either* still wanted in connection with Professor Linus's murder or is currently a *captive* Septal in need of rescue. Which is it, Dorn?"

"Don't answer him," Viselle muttered.

"Other Jimbal, I can't tell you how happy we all were to discover you were okay," Plaint said. "We'd assumed the worst. And I want you to know that if you'd like to return to your studies, you would be *more* than welcome."

It shouldn't have been a tantalizing offer, but it was. Duqo Plaint was the only man who could make it so the past year never happened...well, short of resurrecting Orno Linus. That was likely not within his abilities.

Dorn had nothing but fond memories of their time as a Septal monk, and there were many days—on Lys, in the comfort of the Demara estate—when they thought that they would give anything to return to that life again.

But that was before. Now, all they wanted to do was get back to the study to finally understand what it was that Orno had uncovered. It was already clear to them that if they returned to the fold, the House would *never* let Dorn continue down that path.

"Dorn's my guest," Exty said. "They're not interested in anything you have to offer, Duqo."

"Are you *certain*?" Duqo asked. "I'd like to hear that from them. Tell me, Dorn: are you a guest or a hostage?"

Exty looked at Dorn for the first time since she'd arrived. She was worried. Dorn wondered what would happen to her if they gave the wrong answer.

"I'm a guest, Highness," they said. "But Exty is wrong. I *am* interested in something you have to offer."

"Very good," Plaint said. "What would that be?"

"I'd like for you to tell me what you're doing in the tunnels."

"What tunnels?"

"Beneath the city, Highness," Dorn said. "We saw the room full of provisions. What are you stocking up for?"

Plaint nodded slowly. Dorn got the sense that had they not been *very* specific, the High Hat would have continued pretending he didn't know what they were talking about. "Yes, I understand," Plaint said. "That must have been a jarring discovery. I'd *forgotten* where you left off in your education, Other Jimbal. Your introduction would have been...gentler otherwise."

"Is it really preparation for the return of the Outcast?" Dorn asked. "Or is that just the story you tell the Brethren so they'll do what you ask?"

"No, it's the truth," Plaint said. "One of the House's most important duties is ensuring the continuation of the species,

Dorn. Not just *our* species. We're the guardians of all life and we need to make certain we're here to restart once the scourge is over. The *vast* majority of us never have to worry about this element of the House's duties but our generation is not so fortunate."

"You're talking about surrender," Dorn said. "When you could be talking about fighting."

Duqo laughed. "You sound so much like Orno. Dorn, the Outcast is inevitable. There *is* no fighting. Pray all you want for the Five to come down from the Haven and fight off the malevolent evil bent on destroying us all. We tell children that this is what will happen so that they'll sleep soundly at night. We don't live in a magical fantasy realm and the gods aren't returning. But the Outcast absolutely is."

He looked at Viselle. "If Orno told your father *half* of what he knew or suspected, Ba-Ugna understood this too. Whether or not he shared it with you."

"He meant to stop the Outcast," Viselle said. "They both did."

"Then Ba-Ugna wasn't really listening." He turned to Exty. "Archeo knew it too, although I believe he figured it out on his own. *He* took steps."

"I'm sorry, I can't believe any of this," Exty said. "The imaginary Outcast is *really* coming but the imaginary gods aren't? And we know about it but can't *do* anything about it? You sound ridiculous Duqo, and you're one of the only people in this world that I never expected to say that about."

"Orno found a way to stop it," Viselle said.

"He *thought* he found a way," Plaint said. "He was mistaken. But his *true* genius was in convincing so many that he was correct. Now as much as I enjoy hashing out all of this with you...Exty, these two fugitives have something that was stolen from our vault. Hand that over and I'll be happy to allow you to take them back to Lys or wherever else. I'm not really interested in them. I'll even forgive the seven dead Sentries they're responsible for. Just hand over our artifact."

"He doesn't know about the book," Viselle muttered in Dorn's ear. "Keep it that way." Then to Plaint she said, "I don't have your key. I *never* had it."

"What does it unlock?" Dorn asked.

"You wouldn't believe any answer I gave, Other Jimbal," Plaint said. "And I can't give you any answer. Just know that it's utterly unique, impossible to replace, and critical to the future of us all."

"Oh," Dorn said. "But it's *not* unique is it? There are five of them."

"Five keys, yes, that open five different things. Now...Exty. I'm not going to ask again."

"Here's what I think, Duqo," Exty said. "I think that key means a *lot* to you, but I *know* you realize none of us is stupid enough to be walking around with it down here. So whatever acts of violence you're planning to commit in the next few minutes, it's not gonna get you what you want. Meanwhile, you're about to get into a firefight with one of the planet's most prominent citizens, and I *know* you're a better politician than that. I mean, that's a P.R. nightmare, right? And before you say anything about the drone shutdown you should know there's multiple long-range opticals pointed at us right now and even *you* can't force a satellite to stop looking. You know what I'm talking about; the older satellites, the ones *without* House tech buried in them."

"Pre-digital? Those were retired long ago."

"Were they? Because I own three." She held up a remote device with a button. "You're going to let us go or I'm going to push this button and start broadcasting a live feed directly over the Stream. Try me, Duqo."

Duqo Plaint, a man who had the ability to silence a room with the click of his tongue, looked entirely unsure about what to do next. So after five seconds passed, Exty turned to the private security at her flank and said, "Let's go."

Very quickly, the three of them were ushered into the nearest widewagon. Before Dorn had a chance to find a proper seatbelt, they were already moving.

Exty, crouched in the passenger seat, stared at the Sentries as they stepped aside and let them pass. Then she exhaled.

"Whoa. Guys. I did *not* think that would work," she said.

"Out of curiosity," Viselle said, "what *does* that button do?"

"This? It unlocks the door to my shuttle. Now let's get off this planet while we still can. He's probably already on a direct with Twenty-One Central about a warrant for the estate."

## Chapter Eighteen

Three days. According to Exty that was how long they had before the possibility of escape became problematic.

She emphasized this point before they'd even made it all the way back to Lys in her autopiloted exo.

"There haven't been many precedents for this kind of thing," she said. "Jurisdictionally, everyone on Lys is still beholden to the laws of Velon and the country of Inimata...mainly because it would be an enormous pain to declare ourselves an independent nation."

"The Staipas did it," Viselle said. "For that floating city-state of theirs." She was referring to Asealand, which was indeed a floating city-state recognized by the League of Countries as an independent nation. Dorn had heard of it and seen images on the Stream, but until this moment hadn't really considered it an actual place.

"Coigo Staipa has a significantly different legal relationship with the people of Asealand," Exty said. "He's more like a landlord; on paper, he owns everything. They also have a government structure and taxation to support it. The Lys estates have a complicated entanglement with my family, but it's not nearly as patrician-like. Anyway, my point is the police can technically show up whenever, with a warrant, and expect to be allowed in eventually."

"Eventually," Dorn repeated.

"Yeah, not right away. And there are stalling tactics we can take. It's not like the Velon police force has a fleet of spaceships; they can't surround us and prevent us from leaving the station by means other than the Tether. Actually, the other two times they served a warrant that *I* can remember, they took the shuttle up the Tether rather than taking an exo at all. Which makes sense because we can't do a whole lot if they ride up here on the shuttle and demand to get on the platform. But we *can* close off our exo ports. Anyway. I'm thinking you guys have three days before this gets hairy."

"I need more than three days," Dorn said.

"How much more?" Viselle asked.

"That's impossible to say. It would take three days just to get the work I've done thus far organized and catalogued for travel. This book is critical to understanding Orno's notes, but that understanding could be weeks away." They turned to Exty. "It *took* weeks before they came for Ba-Ugna. Why three days?"

"Well first off, they didn't know he was on Lys," she said. "Or if they did, they didn't know where he was staying. Then when they *did* know it was because he was agreeing to surrender. That meant a lot of lawyers, which slows down everything. I'm nearly positive neither of you are interested in surrendering and they *do* know where you are and who you're saying with. I'm thinking you guys get away from the estate and then I'll just deny you were ever there. It'll take them a week to search the place just to prove that; by then you could be half a planet away."

"That would also keep you out of legal jeopardy," Viselle said.

"That was on my mind too," Exty admitted. "It'll be harder to make a *harboring fugitives* charge stick if there's no proof I was doing anything of the sort."

"High Hat Plaint and an army of Sentries could argue otherwise," Dorn said.

"Yeah but they're not going to. Even if they win, it won't get Duqo any closer to what he wants."

"A key which I, ironically, don't have," Viselle said. "Makk has the Velon chapter key; Plaint is after the wrong detective and I don't think what I *do* have will work on whatever he needs to unlock. What about another estate? Can someone else on Lys take us in? Marthle or Daga-Bo-Haye, they're friendlies."

"Cordial, but I wouldn't trust either of them to commit a crime without a profit angle. I could maybe influence Paiter Elongo to keep you for a few days in exchange for a pass to put in that third deck he's been wanting to build. But I don't really trust him either. Keep in mind, Viselle, Calcut's still at-large and he has influence with about half of the families up here. He may be a better trading partner than I am. A couple of weeks in someone else's pool house and who knows how many people on Lys will know you're here? It's not a good idea. I think you need to go. This whole hemisphere is too hot for you now."

~

Dorn couldn't get them to budge on the deadline, which meant in three days Dorn would be leaving the company of someone they trusted possibly a little more than they should have, to go on the run with someone they barely trusted at all.

They weren't even sure where they were going to end up fleeing to. Viselle was circumspect when the question of where she would take them came up, muttering that she had "a few" safe houses that hadn't been burned yet. Considering she'd fled to Lys at the first opportunity under the premise that she had nowhere else to go, Dorn was dubious.

They also didn't know why *they* had to go anywhere. Viselle was the fugitive. Viselle had the key. Dorn had a book nobody knew was missing and notes that their dead professor wasn't going to be asking for. If Dorn was still there when the police arrived, what harm would that do? Did law enforcement *really* still want Dorn for questioning on a long-closed case?

*I know too much*, they thought as a counterpoint. The police probably didn't care about Dorn at all, but Duqo Plaint made it clear in his own way that *he* cared. In fact, the longer Dorn sat with Plaint's offer of a return to the fold, the less appealing it became. *I would be a prisoner.*

No, freedom for Dorn Jimbal would have to come in the form of the truth, and the truth was hidden in Professor Linus's papers. Until they found it, everything else *had* to be put on hold.

So instead of packing, they got to work with the notes and the book in a marathon study session to figure out what Professor Orno was attempting to tell them.

It didn't go very well. Every time Dorn tried to concentrate the words of High Hat Plaint came back to them: *The Outcast is inevitable. There is no fighting.* The implication was clear, and horrific. The Outcast—whatever he or it actually was—would raze the planet and there was nothing anyone could do about it except die or hide in a tunnel.

This hardly made sense. The canonical texts didn't say the Outcast would return to destroy everyone *except* the ones hiding underground. It was everyone, period. That being the case, if the High Hat council *knew* the Outcast was returning and—as Plaint claimed—also knew the Five wouldn't be returning to Dib to fight back the Outcast and rescue them all, why was *hiding* even a consideration? It couldn't possibly matter how well one hid from a *god*; surely the living embodiment of evil knows how to check basements and tunnels.

Fighting seems like the only viable option. Not only that, it looked as if that was what the House did the *last* time the Outcast returned.

Of that point there could no longer be any doubt. Assuming the text in the book they'd recovered from Leemie Witts was accurate, the fight for the survival of life on this planet took place at least once already, possibly in the lifetime of the scribe.

Dorn also thought it was possible they were holding the *original* version of the *Parieaum Ejukatesi,* which would make this one of the most extraordinary things ever to emerge from a temple vault. A quick comparison between this text and the copies of later versions scattered through Orno's research bolstered this theory a lot, but the most telling piece of evidence was that the book came with illustrations the others simply didn't have.

Generally, when it came to copying texts, illustrations were the first thing to go. The scribes of old were often working rapidly to transcribe from originals so that each House chapter had a copy of the canonical texts, and it took both time and skill to copy an illustration. This was a well-known defect in the transcription process. Most of the time it was harmless. In this instance, it definitely was not.

The artwork was little more than crude sketches—the author didn't have a real gift for drawing—and the ink was faded and smeared, but there was information to be gleaned still.

Possibly the most important illustration showed rudimentary versions of the five keys on one side of the page and a circle—a dial, perhaps—with five holes on the other side. This was on page forty-seven, and it *appeared* to be a close-up of what was also depicted on page forty-nine—the same two-page spread Leemie had directed them to before.

Except it could also be that these illustrations were demonstrating different places where the five keys had to be used in concert. There *had* been a legend beneath the page forty-seven illustration, but it was largely rubbed out. All Dorn could see was *Ducclem,* the archaic word for *Haven.*

That could mean it was a prayer, which made it useless. It was impossible to say.

Then there was the *Engni Ammunidi* on the following pages. If—as seemed to be the case—the Engine of the World was the weapon Viselle was looking for...well that wasn't at all helpful. Dorn had no clue where to locate the engine and was only tentatively prepared to allow that it existed at all. *Engni Ammunidi* was always, at best, a creation myth not intended for literal interpretation.

The possibility that Dorn was reading a text meant for children surfaced in their brain for further consideration, but they shut that down. Harder to dismiss was the idea that *this* was why High Hat Plaint was so dismissive of other options: The plan to fight back required that an imaginary thing *not* be imaginary.

"This doesn't look like packing," Exty said from the doorway. Dorn jumped at the sound of her voice because once again she had startled them.

"Sorry," she said, "if you were going to be here longer I'd install a bell or something so you know when I'm here."

"No, it's fine," they said. "And no, I'm not packing yet. I haven't worked out what Orno was trying to tell me."

"Tell just *you*?"

"It feels that way, yes. Orno cited my research to Ba-Ugna as being of value and...well, look at all of the subsequent circumstances that led to my being here with these notes and this book. If it wasn't all meant for me, then for whom was it meant? And if it *is* for someone else, when can that person get here so I may be excused?"

She laughed. "Fair enough. But if you want to keep going, Dorn, you're gonna have to stop for now."

"When will the next time be?" they asked. "When will I be this settled again? What lies ahead is a life in transit with a woman I do not trust. I'd almost rather wait here to see if the Velon police even care about me. I'm wagering they do not."

"That's a bad wager. And I've already told you, you can trust her. She got you out of Pant City alive, didn't she?"

"Leemie Witts did more to get us out than Viselle. And what you said was that if I trust *you* I can trust *her*. Forgive me for saying so Exty, but my trust in you isn't as firm as it once was."

Exty actually looked wounded by this.

"Oh," she said. "Well. Look Dorn, you can't stay and Viselle is the only ride out of town. You're important to her; you *will* be safe."

They wanted to point out how important Leemie was to Viselle until he wasn't. Or how important Makk Stidgeon was, until *he* wasn't. What was important to *her* was the knowledge Dorn represented. Dorn was otherwise disposable.

They didn't say that, or anything else, which led to an awkward silence.

"So, um, I can help pack everything up if you want," she said. "You might have to decide what you want to keep; not sure you can take all of it."

"Do you know where I'll be going?"

"Viselle's still working that out. Oh, but she said she thinks she found a third key."

"Really? Where?"

"This guy she was looking for. His name was on Orno's list, you remember? Damid Magly? His name came up in an international bulletin. I guess the Middle Kingdoms put out word that he and some local princess...or something...the Kingdoms are weird...the two of them are wanted for murder and sacred theft."

"*Sacred* theft? This is a category?"

"It is over there?" she said with a shrug. "Anyway his last known location was Temple Island. Guess what's on Temple Island."

"I don't have to guess," Dorn said. "I grew up just north of the Manalusium. Temple Island has the largest Septal temple on two continents. She's thinking Magly absconded with that chapter's key? This seems like a reach."

"Reaches are all we have. Besides, this is the first time the Kingdoms have sent out an international bulletin since anyone can remember. They don't like to admit they're anything other than perfect. Whatever those two took, it's pretty important."

"*Murder* was the other charge."

"I know, but when I say the Kingdoms don't like admitting flaws I mean it. They'd absolutely let a murderer go if they made it past the border. They've done it before."

"So our plan now is to find someone every government in the world is actively looking for," Dorn said.

"Look, all I have is bad news and okay news."

"Yes, I know, I'm sorry."

Dorn looked around the room for the hundredth time. *She's right,* they thought. *I need to pack while I can. No delaying this.*

"Why don't you come back in an hour," they said. "I'll have a better idea then of what I'll need."

"Great. I want to build in enough time to give you a proper send-off. It's a Demara family tradition."

"I'm not sure what that means," they said with obvious concern.

"It means a big banquet," she said with a laugh. "Honestly. We're not *that* strange."

"Ah. All right."

"Back in an hour," she said. "Now I gotta return a call to the police commissioner."

The words "Demara family tradition" rattled something loose in Dorn's memory, sparking a question they'd forgotten to ask. By the time the thought was fully-formed, Exty was already halfway down the corridor.

"What did he mean?" Dorn shouted. "About Archeo."

"What?" she asked, as Dorn closed the distance between them.

"High Hat Plaint. He said Archeo knew something. 'He took steps,' he said."

"Oh, that. No idea what he was talking about. My great grandfather knew a lot of things and did a lot of things, but Duqo Plaint never meet Archeo so I don't know what it is he thinks he knows."

"Archeo built Lys. Plaint knew *that*."

"*Everybody* knows that. I don't see your point."

And then, at once, it all fell together.

It was right in front of them the whole time.

*How could I have missed it?* they thought.

"Get Viselle," Dorn said. "Right now. Meet me in Archeo's planetarium."

"Why..." she began to ask, but Dorn was already running in the other direction, down the hall, to the center of the Demara estate.

~

It was twenty minutes before Exty returned, with Viselle in tow.

They found Dorn seated at the telescope. Dorn had spent the time performing some of the preliminary calculations that were going to end up being significantly more important than anything in Orno's notes. They didn't have to do any adjustments to the telescopic array to make their point; it was already facing the right direction.

"All right, I'm here," Viselle said. "What do you have? Because I don't think anything we're looking for can be found in the stars."

"Nothing what you *think* I was here to find can be found in the stars," Dorn corrected. "That was my problem. I became bogged down in archaic Eglinat and mysteries from ancient scribes in old texts when I should have been looking *up* the entire time."

They hit a few buttons on the panel before them, enhancing a portion of the sky.

"Exty, you told me that Archeo had a default directional setting that you've preserved. Do I have that right?"

"Yeah, but it was just...it's just a reset screen. There's nothing to *see* in that direction."

"That would have been true for most of history," Dorn said. "But not in Archeo's lifetime. And not now."

Dorn directed the array to focus more closely on the particular region of space that Exty's great grandfather found so interesting.

"I still don't see anything," Viselle said.

"Very true. That's because we're looking at the visible spectrum."

Dorn switched to an ultraviolet filter, which revealed a faint object not previously visible.

"Okay, now I see something," Viselle said.

"What is that?" Exty asked.

"The evidence that my thesis is wrong," Dorn said. "I'd proven that Dibble's orbit wasn't stable, and in a few million years we were going to fly away from the Dancers due to this mild instability. That *would* have been correct had I been accounting for all of the extraplanetary objects capable of adjusting our orbit meaningfully. I was not."

Dorn played with the telescope some more.

"Here," they said. "There are some gamma radiation sensors built into the satellites."

They switched on the gamma sensors and overlaid the results against the visible spectrum. The object that was barely visible moments ago was now the brightest thing in the sky.

"What did you do?" Exty asked.

"I'm showing you why this object is so important," Dorn said. "What you're looking at is a neutron star, but a particular *kind* of neutron star: one that emits a *tremendous* amount of gamma radiation. And it's coming this way."

"Gods," Viselle whispered.

"But...I don't understand," Exty said. "How could anyone know this was coming? The ancient texts..."

"The scribes of antiquity knew it was coming because it's been here before," Dorn said. "This is not some stray neutron star; it's a *part* of our solar system. It just has a particularly extreme orbital cycle. We even have a name for it."

"Outcast," Viselle said.

"Exactly."

Exty looked stunned. Viselle looked as if this was the news she'd been expecting to hear, perhaps for her entire life.

"But, okay," Exty said, stammering a little. "So what'll happen when this Outcast gets here?"

"To have the effect I expect it to—to adjust the orbit of the planet—it's going to have pass between us and the Dancers. Neutron stars are incredibly dense, you understand? The gravitational influence will pull us minutely closer. This will likely have a small impact on the seasons and also disprove my thesis. None of which will matter, because it will also bathe the entire planet in lethal amounts of gamma radiation, rendering both seasonality and academic pursuits moot."

"*How* lethal?" Viselle asked.

"Every living thing on the surface will die from radiation poisoning: plants, animals, people...everything. The only way to survive would be..."

"...to live underground for a while," Viselle said, finishing their thought.

"Or to be in orbit on the dark side of Dibble," Dorn said. "This is why Archeo Demara built Lys, Exty. It's not a vacation spot; it's a life raft."

"Gods," Exty muttered.

"How much time do we have?" Viselle asked.

"I don't know yet," Dorn said. "Best guess, within the next ten years. The House might have better numbers, although I believe they're working with historical predictions and not astronomical observations; it's still too far away to calculate anything out with precision."

"Duqo seemed pretty sure about things," Exty said.

"Precisely," Dorn said. "That certitude had to come from somewhere. But it's my opinion that the House is acting on faith, not observation."

"All right," Viselle said. "We know what the Outcast is now. How do we stop it?"

Dorn laughed. "You can't *stop* a neutron star."

"Or...prevent it," Exty said. "Or whatever. They already did it once. *We* did. Dibble-kind. We're still here because the last time the Outcast turned up *we* stopped it. Right? Or there wouldn't be a scribe telling us to expect it? Come on, Dorn, you told me some of this yourself."

"I know," they said. "I still need to understand what Orno found. But...whether High Hat Plaint knows what we now know or not, Exty, I'm inclined to agree with him and not the professor. Hiding may be the only solution. Even then, our ozone layer might be insufficiently robust to allow for *any* chance of survival on the planet, underground or otherwise. Archeo's lifeboat might be *it*."

"Until we run out of food," she said, gasping. "All his early plans to grow things up here...no wonder it was so important to him. We just ignored it."

"Only the power of the gods can stop the Outcast," Viselle said.

"You've chosen an interesting time to become religious," Exty said.

"If you can think of a *better* time for a little faith, let me know," Viselle said. "The way I see it the only thing this information changes, is our timeline. We still need all five keys, we still need to find the weapon the gods left us, and we still need to understand what in the name of Nita Professor Linus knew. The *worst* thing that happens if it's all nonsense is that the world still ends."

Viselle looked at Dorn. "Might as well *try* to save the world, right? I wasn't doing anything else anyway. How about you?"

## Chapter Nineteen

Trebnvto arrived at the orbital platform three months later. Xto was in the platform's command center to talk Treb in, which meant that Xto's was the first voice Treb heard after his twelve days of relative solitude.

This was a wise choice, as Treb didn't handle the time alone well and needed to hear the voice of someone familiar.

Treb was an exceptional astronaut on paper, in that he knew all the right answers to all the difficult questions and he graded out with top marks on all of the physical tests. Psychologically, though...as much as Xto loved him, Trebnvto Pna was not a man who should be left alone with his thoughts.

It was this aspect of Treb's personality that made him so compelling to so many people; a character flaw that manifested as a social asset. He always wanted to know about *you*, about what *your* life was like today, yesterday, any day. And he remembered every detail, drilling down into people's lives in a way that was compelling and intoxicating if you happened to enjoy Trebnvto's company, but invasive and borderline toxic if you did not. He was the most extroverted person Xto knew, which was one of the things Xto found so attractive and also what made them such a good match given Xto's comparative introversion.

But Treb's need to fill up his head with the details of other people's lives was just that: a *need*. An addiction, even. Something he had to do to keep noise of personal self-reflection from driving him insane. That he couldn't cope without being around other people would have been obvious the minute he was relocated to the private barracks of the *EPFA* prior to his flight, and was no doubt one of the reasons it took so long for him to make it into space.

Still, however shakily, he got there. Trebnvto's last task as a pilot—steering his shuttle into the hangar—took long enough and was difficult enough that Mondr nearly activated an in-place emergency plan for retrieving a shuttle with a disabled astronaut. Xto had to talk Treb through each step, slowly.

On arrival, he proved unable to walk, and so had to be carried to the medical bay, where Opzk pronounced him malnourished and severely dehydrated. It was another month before he was allowed to leave the hospital.

Only *then* were they permitted their long-delayed reunion. Treb moved directly from the hospital room to Xto's quarters, and for the first time since their relationship began Xto and Treb were allowed to exist openly as a couple.

Somewhat. They didn't *flaunt* it; they just didn't try to keep it a secret. Open displays of affection were generally frowned upon aboard the platform regardless of the parties involved—which was in keeping with the military style of things—so this hadn't changed. (Unsurprisingly given their dynamic, this was a larger problem for Treb than Xto.) But casual references to one another as *boyfriend, love* or—Trebnvto's favorite—*beloved* happened with sufficient regularity to drive the point home. Nobody minded, or even seemed surprised.

It took another six months before Xto began to wonder if he'd made a mistake.

They fought. A lot. Perhaps it was because Xto had never been *able* to spend so much uninterrupted time with Trebnvto before, but he simply didn't realize how passive-aggressive Treb was. And needy. And clingy.

Also, he snored terribly and he could *not* pick up after himself which was a *huge* annoyance when discarded clothing tended to float.

Their arguments were loud, because another thing about Treb that Xto didn't previously realize was that he relied upon volume to drive home his points. These arguments routinely cascaded out of their quarters and into the hall and the rest of their day. Sometimes Treb would even drag some of their fellow astronauts into the disagreement to bolster his need to be correct—another unsavory aspect of his personality. This embarrassed Xto mightily, which became another thing about which they argued.

Opzk, by then serving the role of therapist more often than doctor, urged Xto to be patient and let the relationship find a new balance.

"You never really had this before," she said. "Either of you. You didn't have a proper relationship together on Wivvol, I am assuming. Unless much has changed down there since I left."

"We did not," Xto confirmed. "We had stolen moments in the dark when we thought nobody was looking."

"There you go," she said. "You saw the best of one another because that was all the time you had to give. And...I only mention this because I have heard this before from other transplanted couples in your circumstance...is it possible *some* of the attraction was because of the danger?"

"If so, the resolution would appear to be asking my father to give us separate quarters and to forbid us from seeing one another."

He said this as a joke, but she didn't take it that way.

"I'm sure he would be happy to do that for you. Do you want me to ask him?"

"No, no. That would be ridiculous."

His relationship with Mondr, meanwhile, had gotten quite icy. By the time of Xto's one year anniversary in space, his father had stopped bothering with subtle clues that it would be *nice* if Xto formally announced what *everyone* already knew, i.e., that he would be passing up his return window and remaining on the platform. He began to ask, outright, at every opportunity.

"Much work has to be done to plan for your transition to long haul residency," Mondr said on one occasion. "I don't want to, but I fear I may have no option but to impose a deadline, my son."

This was, to Xto's understanding of how things worked, simply not true. In conversation with other long haulers Xto confirmed that all that was required was to simply not return to the surface when it came time to do so. Given it took nearly two weeks to get back to Dibble from the platform, the act of *not* leaving on schedule allowed the *EPFA* ample time to decide which of the standard cover stories they would employ this time.

Also, if some of Mondr's other assertions were to be believed, everyone on the surface *already* assumed they would not be seeing Xto down there again. So what "work" was his father talking about?

Xto began avoiding Mondr, as much as was reasonably possible on a small space platform in which the man he was avoiding was the commander of the thing. This no doubt contributed to the iciness of their interactions but it couldn't be helped. As much as Trebnvto might be incapable of extended isolation, Xto began to *long* for it…and he couldn't find it anywhere on orbital platform one.

~

There was another pressure weighing Xto down, one that was almost entirely self-applied.

He'd elected not to notify anyone of his discovery of a *door* on the side of the alien vessel. If this was a conscious decision, Xto couldn't identify at what point he made it.

First, there was the opportunity he had to call out the door to his fellow astronauts— Koqba, Uywg and Opzk—while they were all still attached to the side of the ship. But his head was still swimming with the impossibilities at that time, and this state of mind caused him to hold his tongue. Xto didn't *know*—then or now—that the key his uncle had asked him to smuggle out of the country truly fit the keyhole in the door, but at the same time he was positive that it did...he just couldn't justify that understanding with anything empirical.

If it was true that the key was an artifact of the five gods of the Pentatheon then the alien vessel was an artifact as well, and if *that* was true...this was where Xto's speculation always got stuck. All the implicit outcomes from that conclusion were improbable and/or impossible. More to the point, there was no reason to speculate. All Xto had to do was get the key, go back to the ship, unlock the door and get his answers.

Again, provided the key hidden in his quarters was indeed *the* key.

*There are five keys*, he reminded himself somewhat often. *No reason to think this is the one that unlocks that door.*

Xto kept the information to himself when the team got back to their shuttles and said nothing on the return trip. By the time they reached the hangar again it felt as if it was too late.

Except it wasn't. There were more missions planned. The trip that Xto had gone on was only to establish a tethering system so as to enable more long-term study of the ship. All Xto had to do was get invited on one of those later missions and "discover" the door then.

Or, he could simply tell someone what he saw, show them the key, and go from there. Xto had no doubt that the next time it was possible to visit the ship, they would bring along Xto and his key to show them precisely where the door was and to see about getting inside.

This was perhaps the real source of Xto's paralysis on this matter. The key was a secret. Opzk was the only other crewmember who knew it existed, and Xto had every reason to think she'd forgotten about it already. (Treb didn't know about it even though the key was hidden in their shared quarters. If he *cleaned* he might find it, but that wasn't likely to happen ever.)

Although less omnipresent, the pull of duty he felt toward Uncle Ghn was perhaps stronger than the duty he felt he owed to his father. Ghn did more to raise Xto than Mondr, and unlike Mondr never arranged the trajectory of Xto's entire life. Really, the Ghn only ever asked one thing of Xto, and that was to deliver the House artifact to a Septal monk named Orno Linus. Deciding *not* to do this seemed like a significant betrayal. And he knew as soon as he mentioned that he had a key that *might* fit into that door, the key wasn't going anywhere...whether Xto long hauled or not.

He could only answer his many questions about that key and that door by unlocking the door (or trying to) and going inside. But in doing so, he would be guaranteeing that whatever information he gleaned—along with the key itself—never left Shizuna Two.

And so, he was stuck. He had hoped that a decision could be forced upon him somehow, but two factors that would have made that possible never materialized. First, after that initial trip to the alien ship Xto wasn't invited to return. This wasn't obvious to him initially, because he didn't know how many times various long haulers visited it while it was in range and also hadn't calculated how frequently it came into range. But then one day Xto asked Koqba when he thought they would be returning and Koqba, looking surprised, said, "Only long haulers make that trip, Xto Djbbit. You know this." Then he walked away, shaking his head.

The message was clear: Mondr wouldn't let Xto go back to the ship until Xto agreed to stay.

Second—and he had to infer this—it appeared nobody else had discovered the door yet.

This *had* to be inferential because in the same way only long haulers were allowed to see the alien vessel, only long haulers were allowed to access the data collected about the ship. (The password on the data files was changed a month after Xto returned from his trip. This was another unsubtle message from his father.) However, anyone examining that particular section of the anomaly would see evidence of someone having been there before. The particulate matter clinging to the hull had been amassed over a timespan measured in centuries; it would be a long time before evidence of Xto's disturbance of it was wiped away.

Surely upon discovering the door, the first question anyone would pose would be: who *else* had been there and why hadn't they said anything?

Inevitably, someone would have come to Xto to ask this. Nobody had.

The paralysis of indecision made Xto short-tempered and irritable, which no doubt impacted how he related to Trebnvto and Mondr, along with anyone else in his immediate orbit.

Then one day, roughly six months before Xto's scheduled departure, he was given a clarity of purpose. It began with Mondr, and it was entirely unintentional.

~

Xto was working on the aft section of the *Hlyib* when the summons arrived.

After the *Zabmez*, which from the outside already looked ready for its first voyage, the *Hlyib* was the closest to being finished. Its hull was all but done and the interior was starting to take form. The *Guh*, meanwhile, remained largely a skeleton.

Progress on the *Guh* was the only thing holding back a deep space exploratory mission, and only because of Mondr's demented insistence on having a fleet. (Never mind that three vessels was no more a "fleet" than one vessel.) In fact, were they to stop work on the *Hlyib* and the *Guh* immediately, they could probably have the *Zabmez* out of the dock in six months.

Xto's job that day was to rivet a steel panel into place from within the confines of a portable pressurized bubble. The bubble was meant to make work easier given the dock was exposed to space, but this was only barely true. He still had to wear a bulky spacesuit with its thick gloves and heavy layers of material impeding the flexibility of his joints. He *could* take off his helmet, which made it easier to *see* what he was doing, but this was a trivial benefit. A greater benefit, perhaps, was that the rivet gun he was using didn't work in the vacuum of space. They *had* guns that did, but not many.

"Coming in," someone announced at the flexible outer door of the bubble.

"Affirm," Xto said. He put down the rivet gun and put his helmet back on. It wasn't necessary to do this—the double doors used for passage to the interior would prevent the breathable atmosphere from escaping in sufficient quantities to be life-threatening—but he felt better. Xto didn't trust these bubbles at all.

Astronaut Avx entered. Avx was a long hauler two years past her return date. Xto remembered pretending to welcome her back; it had been a lovely ceremony.

"I'm to take over this task," she said. "You've been summoned to the command deck."

"I see. What does my father wish of me today?"

"He didn't say."

"Very well." He handed off the rivet gun. "Mind the recoil," he said. "These older models have a kick."

"I'm well familiar, thank you," she said.

He headed for the door flap.

"Xto," Avx said. "One thing you should know. When getting these orders...on my way to see Mondr I passed Trebnvto."

Treb was supposed to be working on the platform extension, which would put him at the opposite end of the habitable zone from the command deck.

"How curious," he said. "Thank you for letting me know."

It was an hour's worth of work to get from the *Hlyib* to his father. Movement of any kind on the dock was necessarily slow, and the distance from the half-completed deck to the airlock was substantial. Once there he had to remove his spacesuit, which was arduous. Finally, getting from the lower level changing area to Mondr's bird's nest of an office was aa long trip, and mostly uphill.

Xto spent that entire time concocting esoteric and borderline-paranoid explanations for what Trebnvto was doing talking to Mondr, with each theory more demonstrably absurd than the one that came before. By the time he reached his father, he was half-expecting to find his uncle's Septal artifact on the desk, a team of armed security officers, and a sack to put him into prior to tossing him from an airlock.

It was however—and of course—just Mondr.

"I'm here, father," Xto said. "What is it you want?"

Already, Mondr looked pained. "Please sit, Xto," he said, gesturing to the chair facing his desk. "It's time you and I got past this."

Xto sat in the offered chair while Mondr sat behind the desk. It felt like two soldiers taking positions before the start of formal hostilities.

"Got past what?" Xto asked.

"You know precisely what. I need to know that you're staying. There are things to be set in motion..."

"There are no things," Xto said, cutting him off. "When it's time, should I choose, I simply won't leave. You've told me this yourself."

"Javilon's balls, you ungrateful..." Mondr throttled the rest of the sentence in his throat. "I'm sorry," he said.

"No, no, go on, you were telling me I was ungrateful," Xto said. "I'd like to hear more of that."

"I have given you *everything* you could possibly need, Xto. You have an opportunity here to live out a life of *meaning*. You're being offered command of the first Wivvolian space fleet. When we learn what technology to exploit in that orbiting anomaly of ours, *you* could be here to take advantage. *You* can be the one to tell the *world* that we're not alone and you have the proof. And your lover..."

"Yes, how *is* Trebnvto? I understand the two of you had a long chat."

Mondr sighed. "There are no secrets in this place. Yes, I spoke to Treb, and yes it was a long conversation. He's worried about you."

"Is he."

"He can see the strain this decision is putting on you as well as I can. He knows you *very* well, Xto. Also...I'm sure he'll tell you this himself, but you should know he means to long haul. He's made it formal."

Xto was stunned. He and Treb had talked about this before, when they weren't arguing, but at no point did Treb indicate he'd come to a final decision.

"So I ask you again, Xto," Mondr said. "Are you ready to declare *now*? Because I have nothing left to offer."

Xto got out of the chair and walked to the window. The view of the three ships from this angle was truly breathtaking. Part of him *did* want to stay; the part that wanted to look out this window any time he felt like it.

"You called me ungrateful," Xto said.

"Son, I didn't..."

"No, it's all right. I can see how it looks that way from your perspective...up here, isolated from the rest of the world. For most of your life. I expect everyone on the surface looks like pieces on a barik board to you. Just things to move around into advantageous positions. You're bankrupting the nation, but that doesn't matter because it's *down there*. The country will starve, but *down there*. And I'm just one of your pieces."

"I have given you *every* advantage."

"You've given me the chance to do whatever I want to do with my life, father, provided what I want to do is what you want me to do. Perhaps it seems as if *I* chose to become an astronaut but I didn't. And before you ask what it is I wanted to do instead, the answer is that I don't know; I was never provided the air to decide that for myself. You want to know why I haven't given you an answer yet, it's because all you have to offer is what you *think* I want, so long as it falls within the confines of what *you* want, and then you frame it as if I had a choice. But I've had no choice about the trajectory of my life since I was four. You're much too late."

Mondr nodded, largely expressionless. "So this is spite," he said.

"It's not spite, it's..."

"No, I'm sorry, I take that back. All right, Xto. There's someone else here I think you should talk to."

Xto turned to look around the room. They were alone.

"Not here literally," Mondr said. "I don't often use this technology. It's difficult to arrange as the timing has to be just right." He looked at one of the glass screens on his desk. Xto could only see the side of it from where he was standing.

"Are you still there, Ghn?" his father asked.

"I'm here," a familiar voice said over the audio feed.

Xto stepped behind his father, looked over his shoulder and there he was: Uncle Ghn Tbyct, the itinerant High Hat of Chnta.

The signal was weak; his uncle's face—his entire face, with no hood—was blurry with some parts of the image failing to refresh at the same rate as other parts.

"Hello uncle," he said. "I did not realize I was speaking to both of you."

"Mondr has his dramatical flair to consider," Ghn said. "Step closer, I can't see you."

His father took the cue and got out of the chair so that Xto could sit for the optical.

"You look thin," Ghn said. "From what I can see at all."

"The connection is poor," Mondr said. "And it will deteriorate from here. In another twenty minutes we'll lose it entirely."

Ghn looked thin as well but from age, not the rigors of an extended stay in low gravity.

Xto looked at Mondr. "Why did you do this?" he asked.

"I thought you would benefit from speaking to the man who *was* there to raise you," Mondr said. It was, for him, a remarkably generous and insightful gesture, which had to mean that it wasn't his idea originally. "Now I'm going to leave the two of you alone. Ghn? It was a pleasure to see you again, old friend."

"And you," Ghn said.

Xto waited until Mondr had left the room before returning his attention to the screen.

"Did he actually *leave?*" Ghn asked.

"He did," Xto said. "What's going on, uncle? Where are you right now?"

"I'm at the *EPFA*. Mondr had me brought here. I thought for certain I was being arrested for criminal assembly or whatever their excuse is these days."

*Someone will be listening,* Xto thought. This was already a foregone conclusion, as there was no private entity in Wivvol capable of establishing a vid hookup with the orbital platform, but the fact that uncle was *at* the center rather than in a room in the Chancellery somewhere... Xto imagined half of the control center standing behind Ghn, outside of the optical's range. That may not have been true, but it was wise to talk as if it was.

His pulse rose. He was no longer accustomed to being spied upon.

"I'm very glad to see you," Xto said. "I just do not understand my father's motivation in arranging this."

"Mondr believes *I* am the source of your displeasure with his future plans," Ghn said. A tactful way to say this, as the allowance for long hauling was not a formalized thing. Just knowing that Mondr Djbbit was actually in space and not occupying an office at the *EPFA* likely put uncle in jeopardy. "He thought I could offer you guidance. Help you clear your head."

"Spiritual guidance?" Xto asked.

"If need be. In a...secular sense, of course. Mondr's correct that I helped raise you in ways he could not."

Xto had a lot to share with Ghn, none of which he could state directly. Talking about it *indirectly* might take far longer than the twenty-odd minutes they had, but it was worth a try.

"What if my needs were not *strictly* secular, uncle? Because I think you *can* help me to decide some things...but what is weighing on me right now pertains to some of the matters about which we once spoke in your office."

Meaning—to Ghn—the day he gave Xto the Septal artifact. To everyone else listening this likely would have been interpreted as a reference to Xto's childhood, when Septalism hadn't been formally banned yet and the office of the High Hat still existed.

Ghn looked to the side at one of the people with whom he shared the room. Whoever it was, they evidently assented.

"Go ahead, Xto," he said. "Tell me what's burdening you."

"You spoke that day of the parable of Nita's locksmith," Xto said. "I'm sure you recall it."

There was no such parable in any canonical teachings. Hopefully, none of the observers would realize this.

"I do, yes," Ghn said neutrally.

"The lesson or...what I took to be the lesson...was that in many ways I am like a key, and my goal in life is to find the thing that the, uhm, the holy locksmith means for me to unlock. Metaphorically."

"Metaphorically, yes," Ghn said, warming up to the imaginary lesson. "And sometimes you find that it is not just you that is necessary to unlock this. Nita's locksmith may have forged you for a particular purpose but there are five gods, and five locksmiths. And it remains critical, even now, to fulfill that purpose. For what good is a key without a lock?"

*You still need to bring the key back, so it can be joined with the other four keys*, Ghn was saying.

"I understand, uncle," Xto said. "But what if...What if I found that lock in an *unusual* place. A place where the gods were not expected to be?"

Ghn laughed. "There is no such place, Xto. Nothing on Dibble, in Dibble or above Dibble is beyond the reach of the Five."

This was an actual passage from the weekly services. The rest of it was, "For the Five also rule the suns, the moon and the stars. None but the Outcast can pass beyond their reach."

"I understand," Xto said. "But imagine... All right, I am still a key. *As* a key I have been led to believe that I fit in a particular place, a place where other keys also fit. We could, these other keys and I, unlock something...or turn something on. A machine, say."

"Metaphorically."

"Yes. Now imagine discovering *another place* I, a key, can *also* fit. Only it's not where I was taught I would fit, it's a...vast distance from where I was taught I would fit, and I don't unlock a machine at all. Now it's a door. And I want to go through that door, but I don't understand how the door can exist in the first place. Do you understand my problem, uncle?"

Ghn Tbyct *did* understand, finally. And he was speechless.

"Where...is this door?" he asked.

"It's difficult to describe, uncle," Xto said. "A new place, but also a very old place. I'm wondering if there's anything in the canonical texts that speaks to this dilemma."

There was a moment when it looked as if his uncle was about

to drop any pretense that this was a non-literal conversation about a non-literal key that opened a non-literal door.

"Not in the modern *canonical* texts," Ghn said. "But there *is* a minority interpretation of the *Tracta Duccaleo* that could be interpreted in a *quite* interesting way. I, ah, I think we may find the guidance you seek *there*."

Xto knew only a little Eglinat, but there were some landmark texts in the canon of which nearly anyone versed in Septalism knew the translation. *Tracta Duccaleo* meant "treatise on the Haven" and it was far afield of anything they'd been discussing to this point.

"I am less familiar with the teachings of the *Tracta Duccaleo*, uncle, canonical or otherwise. Can you enlighten me?"

He was looking off to the side again. "I'm being told we're about to run out of time, Xto," Ghn said. "But know that a key can fit many locks. You can both open doors and start machines if you are the right key. For the locksmith is clever. Your way to the Haven may be through that door; embrace it."

"Metaphorically," Xto said.

"Yes," Ghn said. Only this time, he was shaking his head. *Not metaphorically*, he was saying. "Of course."

"Thank you for your guidance, uncle."

Then the signal disappeared into static.

Mondr was back in the office a moment later, not even bothering with the pretense that he hadn't been listening from the other room.

"Did Ghn help you settle matters, my son?" he asked.

"Actually yes, father," Xto said. "His instructions were helpful indeed. I understand my purpose now, and I know what I must do."

"And?"

"You can tell the surface that I'm staying." Xto said. "For a key can fit in many locks."

297

## Chapter Twenty

Much changed in the weeks that followed. Xto learned that his father had been keeping *many* things from him. In addition to the data files collected on the alien anomaly (and the long hauler rotation going out to see it, and the orbital schedule of the object) there were sections of the platform's habitable zone off-limits to anyone on active return rotation. Included in this area was a library with texts that were unavailable anywhere in Wivvol, a commissary with *slightly* better food rations, and—somehow—alcohol.

It didn't seem possible for them to have alcohol of any kind in space as it was definitely not part of the normal provisions sent up every month by shuttle, yet there appeared to be an ample quantity on hand. When Xto asked around he was told that this was where confiscated contraband ended up, as evidently it was commonplace for astronauts on rotation to bring liquor for personal use. Only, again, there was *entirely* too much of it for that to explain things.

The mystery was sufficiently confounding that Xto nearly asked his father about it. (Which was a risk, as he wasn't 100% certain his father knew about the alcohol.)

It was Treb—who was possessed of a far more sophisticated palate when it came to liquor—who worked it out.

"They've built a still," he said. "I thought that was obvious!"

"Not to me," Xto said.

"Oh yes. This is potato liquor. Impressive they figured out how to distill it with almost no gravity. Amazing feat of engineering, really; I hope they named a wing after whoever managed it."

"But the bottles..." They were *in* the bar (or what they called a bar—it was a room with a long table and a wall of tied-down bottles on shelves) having this conversation. Xto could see an array of liquors of different color and origin.

"I'm guessing they just refill them. Cut the alcohol with water. Food coloring and flavor packets makes up the rest. Easy enough to forget what the real stuff tastes like out here, right? Or maybe they know it's off and don't care. It doesn't take much to get drunk in space."

Xto's relationship with Trebnvto had turned a corner in the days since his long haul declaration. There were too many variables in play to work out which change was the one that did it—from them finally reaching that point of equilibrium Opzk told Xto to expect, to the reintroduction of alcohol—but Xto's sense was that Treb calmed down once there was evidence that Xto was committing to him long-term. And Xto calmed down once he'd decided what he was going to do.

Unfortunately, what Xto had decided was the opposite of what Trebnvto and everyone else aboard orbital platform one *thought* he'd decided. Because he wasn't staying at all.

~

Xto wasn't inserted into the rotation for the alien vessel—he didn't have pertinent expertise for their immediate research needs—but was told to expect that to change as soon as they'd found a way inside. But he did get an opportunity to look at all that had been discovered in the year-and-a-half since he'd been locked out.

The answer was: very little.

It had been confirmed that the hull's exterior shell was composed of a steel alloy, which wasn't really news. But there remained a debate as to whether it would be worth trying to cut through the steel to get to the interior without permanently damaging other parts of the ship. To that end, they'd conducted ultrasound experiments on different sections of the vessel to ascertain how *thick* the outside was.

At its thickest points—the nose, and the flat bottom—it was more than two maders. This would be the parts of the ship meant to absorb the heat of reentry into an atmosphere, which said a great deal about the builders.

It meant, for instance, that while they may well have built this ship in space it was *designed* to land on a planet rather than dispatch smaller vessels to accomplish this task. (This was in contrast to the *Zabmez*, which was designed exclusively for space.) It also meant that—like Dibblings—the builders were of a species that responded poorly to extreme heat.

The composition of the two maders was the subject of a lusty debate in the research logs. It wasn't all steel or a steel alloy like the hull; it wasn't nearly as dense. The debate was whether it was a semisolid fibroid substance, a liquid, or some combination of the two.

The sides of the ship were one mader thick, on average, with the thinnest point being under the latticework that supported the ring. There, it was steel alloy only with no secondary layer of insulation. This was also the location of Xto's door.

He was surprised to read that they *had* found it, not long after Xto did. They just didn't think very much of it, in the same way they thought little of the windows with the shutters on them. Until someone worked out a non-invasive way to use the door it was as useless as any other part of the exterior. However, it was also the current favorite entry point candidate for those promoting a controlled detonation or a cutting torch as a means to get inside.

Peculiarly, there was no mention of the keyhole. It didn't seem as if they'd even looked for one.

Aside from efforts to get into the vessel, the bulk of the studies concentrated on the rear of the ship. This made sense; if the aliens really had built a propulsion system capable of interstellar travel, the value of that technology was incalculable. Even without talking to his father about it, Xto could imagine what Mondr might do with such information: hoard it first, sell it to other nations later.

Idlo Jrgap had been right. Mondr really *had* found a solution to Wivvol's economic woes.

*Hopefully*, Xto thought, *the country can remain solvent until that windfall is realized.*

The ship's rear thrusters looked like the largest part of the ship. (In truth, the torus encircling the middle of the vessel was larger in terms of total mass, but as its function was neither obvious nor obviously exploitable, most analyses ignored it.) The thrusters' peculiar design—one large central column ringed by smaller ones that didn't extend as far—baffled the available experts in the mechanics of propulsion. The current theory was that the design was an aesthetic choice rather than a practical one, although *whose* aesthetics were being catered to was a good question.

"Perhaps the aliens found this pleasing to the eye," speculated one baffled long hauler in the textual analysis. "Or whatever optical nerve cluster they used to see."

Xto couldn't shake the similarity to the design of the House temples: one large central column ringed by eight smaller ones. Granted, the nine column design on most temple roofs didn't form a ring, but the commonality was there all the same. Xto didn't dare add this observation to what was already written but all the same he wondered if he was the only one who saw it.

The most daring exploration of the vessel thus far had taken place six months prior, when Astronaut Twlo Kp traveled down the central thruster on a long tether. It was a task that would have been conducted by a drone if they *had* drone technology available to them on the platform, but as they did not it was up to Kp to do the exploration.

They knew in advance that there was no active radiation, so it was nominally safe, but nobody liked the idea of it. "Akin to traveling down the barrel of a projectile gun to see what the firing mechanism looked like," was one particularly vivid description.

Kp emerged unscathed but with scant additional information. She said it looked somewhat like the tail of a chemical rocket, that there were locked exhaust panels that likely opened when the ship was traveling, and that there was no way to get into the ship from there.

Everyone agreed that the means of propulsion was likely *not* chemical—the mass-to-energy ratio for chemical propulsion was too high. It *had* to be nuclear...or something new.

Overall, the new research on the anomalous object was underwhelming. Xto expected more, but was also *glad* there wasn't. It only reinforced the growing sense that what he planned to do was meant to happen. Also—and others had made this point in the notes—they would probably have accomplished more by now if they'd shared what they'd found with the surface. There were people in the *EPFA* with scientific expertise that far outstripped anything available on the platform. It was Mondr's stubbornness (which his father would call political savvy) as much as anything that was dooming them to fail.

Meanwhile, Xto's exploration of the suddenly-available library yielded a surprising discovery: a number of Septal texts were archived there.

Most of the volumes were dry recitations of standard ceremonial practices: less theological texts than instruction manuals. But there was a core of modern-translated canonical texts too. They were sufficiently anodyne to fit on the shelf of any chapter—all the parts that were disputed canon had been removed or so watered down as to no longer resemble the controversial source phrasing—but the fact that they were there at all was remarkable.

A common-tongue translation of the *Tracta Duccaleo* was among the volumes. This was the text Uncle Ghn directed him to review. At the time, Xto thought there was no chance of that ever happening given his lack of access to the *Tracta Duccaleo*. But here it was.

Assuming Ghn even understood what it was that Xto had been trying to tell him, his uncle implied that the answer to Xto's question was contained therein. (That question was: "How is it possible that I've found something in space that I can unlock with this key you've given me?" Again, Xto could only hope that this was the question Ghn *thought* he was answering.)

It seemed improbable that there could possibly be anything in the *Tracta Duccaleo* that would address this, because to Xto's understanding there was nothing in any of the canonical texts that addressed non-planetary objects.

And after reading the *Tracta Duccaleo* from cover to cover, Xto didn't feel any differently. The volume's subject was the Haven—obviously—and its lessons weren't remotely controversial. Lead a good life, denounce the Outcast, and the Five will reward you in the Haven. "Be one with the Five to defeat the One" was the book's takeaway motto. There was perhaps more nuance to it in Eglinat, and more nuance still in archaic Eglinat, but Xto had access to neither (and couldn't read them if he did.)

Whatever Ghn was thinking of when he mentioned the *Tracta Duccaleo*, Xto couldn't see it.

Xto continued to maintain the fiction that he was remaining aboard as a long hauler right up until the week before his two year tour was up.

By then he'd made all of the arrangements he could think of making. He had manipulated his schedule in such a way that it looked as if he was working shifts in two different, equally remote parts of Shizuna Two for the better part of two weeks. The built-in rest periods he wouldn't be taking were scheduled for times when Trebnvto was working his shift in the shipbuilding dock. His monthly dinners with Mondr (in which his father went over the things Xto would need to know in order to run the platform one day) was put off until the next month for a reason Xto felt was sufficiently plausible. Likewise his monthly medical checkup with Opzk.

He had also managed to arrange it so that nobody would be going out to the alien ship during that time. This was a masterpiece of manipulation. Xto thought it was unfortunate that he'd never be able to properly take credit for.

The ship was in position again. Ordinarily, a new fleet of shuttles would be dispatched to the ship as soon as it was in range—which was around the same time Xto's two years was up. Xto had to make it known that he wanted to be a part of the first mission of the new cycle, and then he had to also make it known that this first mission should—for symbolic reasons—definitely not take place until after he was officially a long hauler, i.e., until *after* his two years was up.

When this didn't quite do the trick, he pulled the rough equivalent of a tantrum. It was along the lines of, "I am going to be in charge soon enough and you would do well to respect my wishes even if my wishes are idiosyncratic."

This worked. Possibly, it only worked because Mondr stepped in and told the mission planners to keep his son happy, but it worked nonetheless.

When the day came, he said goodbye to Trebnvto as he would any other day, expressed some regret that they would hardly see one another at all for the next couple of weeks, and left.

Treb gave no indication that anything was amiss, which Xto took to be good news. If Xto had fooled *him*, surely everyone else was equally deceived.

"I'll hold our table," was the last thing Treb said. "In case you find an opening in your day."

Xto probably should have felt some regret or remorse (even if his plan hinged on not *showing* regret or remorse) but the truth was that if he'd decided to stay in space it would have been separate from Treb. At this stage in the relationship their compatibility depended on a regular influx of alcohol and Xto biting his tongue. Were this anything like a normal circumstance he'd have dissolved things months ago.

And ultimately, Trebnvto belonged exactly where he was. Xto did not.

After they parted Xto headed to the topmost part of the habitable zone, put on his spacesuit, and joined the team that was busy building out the platform's latest extension. This was slow work that in these early stages mainly consisted of clearing rocks. It was also very dangerous, as one untethered misstep could send you into low orbit or (much worse) free floating away.

Importantly, it also featured extended periods of total isolation.

When the opportunity arose, Xto positioned himself on the other side of one of the asteroid's many craggy outcroppings and —as quickly as was safe—walked to the far ledge. This put him only about a hundred maders above the shuttle hangar.

Xto fired an anchor into the lip of the ledge with the compression gun he was carrying for just such a purpose, tied the end of the length of rope that came with the compression gun to the anchor and attached the other end to his belt.

Then came the difficult part. Xto walked as far from the ledge as the rope would allow and then did the one thing one is never supposed to do in space: he ran.

Sort of. The gravity on the asteroid was barely adequate for keeping him on the surface, so what he was really doing was trying to create horizontal forward momentum without also generating vertical momentum...until he needed to.

At the right moment—meaning, the moment when he was uncertain that the next step he attempted to take would meet with the surface at all—he pushed off. Then he was heading face-first on an upward diagonal.

He would have continued on that path for the rest of his life were it not for the tether, which stopped his progress. The remaining momentum carried him in a downward arc toward the open hangar, precisely as he'd hoped it would.

The scheme worked almost perfectly. The one problem he had not planned for was that he still had some velocity when he crossed the mouth of the hangar, and he was also upside-down in respect to the floor

Xto waited until the rope was taut—hoping to burn off some of his remaining momentum energy—before untethering. Then he was adrift, roughly two maders above the hangar floor, about to land helmet-first and looking foolish for it.

Via some combination of twisting, activating his magnetic boots, and slowing down due to the nominal gravity, Xto managed to right himself and get his feet down before striking one of the shuttles or an interior wall.

*Well, I'm glad nobody saw that*, he thought.

He checked for the end of the tether. If that was left dangling it might tip them off that something was amiss, but he didn't see it anywhere. Hopefully, there had been enough energy left for the rope to make it all the way back over the top of the ledge, but if it didn't, he was in no position to do much about it.

His shuttle was easy enough to identify. They began pressuring him to paint his ship the very day he formally declared his intention to stay. At first, he couldn't understand why this was—surely there were other, more important matters to attend to—but then he realized it was an insurance policy. Anyone deciding *after* having declared that they didn't want to stay would have to return in a painted ship, which would go over quite poorly on the surface.

Xto had to paint his because until he did none of the long haulers would trust him.

So he painted it. Being neither artistically inclined nor artistically curious, he slapped some blue paint on the side, added white clouds and two yellow suns above his name, and that was that. When people asked he lied and said it reminded him of the view of the sky from a hilltop back home.

He opened the shuttle door and climbed in.

The only way this plan could go awry was if the shuttle wasn't fully stocked. The last time Xto was in the hangar—ostensibly to see off another team traveling to the anomaly—he took the opportunity to fill his personal shuttle's stores with enough food and water to last twenty days, which was five times the amount of provisions he'd otherwise need for a round trip to the alien vessel.

If someone discovered this it would ruin everything.

They had not. The supplies were still there. With a soft exhale and a prayer on his lips, he reached down to close the ship's hatch. It was time to go.

"You aren't as clever as you think, Xto," someone said over the helmet audio.

His heart jumped up into his throat. He climbed out of the shuttle and turned to face the observation deck. Opzk was looking back at him.

"I am *nearly* as clever as I think," he said. "If you are truly here alone."

"I am for now," she said. "What are you doing?"

"That should be obvious. How did you know?"

"Your artifact. You said you promised to bring it back down

again. Although you never said why."

Xto decided he had nothing to lose by explaining himself at least partly. Despite being his father's former lover Opzk had proven to be someone he could trust. So far, she still was, as surely otherwise Mondr would be standing beside her in this moment.

"It belongs to someone else," Xto said. "I'm bringing it to them."

"But how? You will only be landing...ah."

"Much can go wrong in reentry, especially on a planet with so many oceans."

"Yes," she said. "I understand. And what of Trebnvto?"

"Treb knows nothing. Please make sure everyone understands this. He should not take blame for this."

"You'll break his heart is what I mean, Xto. He already suspects and told me as much. That's why I'm *really* here. His concern inspired me to check your schedule and I found the hole you built for yourself."

"Did you... you didn't tell him? Because again, he *can't* know, Opzk. It's the only way he'll be protected."

"I did not. I was hoping I would not have to, because either he was mistaken or you had come to your senses. This will destroy him."

"Treb will be fine," Xto said. "Not right away, but eventually."

"And your father? What of him?"

"He went most of his life without a son; I'm sure he can continue on the same way."

She grimaced, as if he'd said this about her and not Mondr. "That's cruel," she said. "And untrue."

"I'm sorry. I'm sure this looks as if I'm going against the wishes of my father but the truth is I'm honoring the wishes of the man who *raised* me over the one who sired me. I had to choose."

"Except it's your *actual* father that's dying from cancer," she said.

"I know. But I can't live my life as if it was nothing more than an extension of *his* life, whether he dies in six months or six years. I don't expect him to ever understand that."

Opzk nodded, her eyes drifting down to the observation deck's control panel. He was pretty sure there was an alarm button on that console.

"Opzk," he said. "You *know* if you force me to stay, things will be much worse, don't you? Once it's clear how unhappy I am?"

"If you give up voluntarily?" she said. "And we forget this entire thing? They don't need to know."

"That isn't going to happen," he said.

"No. I can see that."

She reached out and pushed a button. Xto felt the floor beneath his shuttle tremble. "What did you just do?" he asked.

"Released the docking clamps," she said. "Since your clever escape plan didn't account for it I assume you didn't know they existed."

"I didn't. Thank you."

"Don't thank me. I was never here. Goodbye, Xto Djbbit. I hope that you find a way to return to us again."

"Perhaps I will," he said, climbing back into the shuttle. "Oh, and Opzk? Even though you were never here, it would be preferable if nobody realized I was gone for a little while."

"I won't tell," she said. "But I won't do anything to prevent someone *else* from discovering your deception. For all either of us knows that could be happening right now."

"Then I'd better hurry."

He closed and sealed the hatch, lit the engine, and began initiating the departure sequence, holding his breath the entire time. He didn't begin to relax until after he'd put some distance between the shuttle and Shizuna Two.

*She didn't know*, he thought, marveling at his good fortune. *She thinks I'm heading straight back to Dib.*

## Chapter Twenty-One

There were a discrete number of ways a shuttle could be tracked while transiting across open space. One was by pinging the onboard transponder. Both the platform on Shizuna Two and the satellites operated by the *EPFA* would be doing that to track Xto's progress back home—a use Xto largely approved of. However, it would also notify anyone who was checking that he wasn't going directly back to Dib; he was taking a four-day detour to intercept the alien spaceship.

The orbital platform would know what this meant immediately, but for the *EPFA* it would likely be the first clue that there was something out there at all. The *EPFA* had access to long range telescopes that were perfectly capable of seeing the ship; they just had to know where to look.

But he didn't want *anyone* to know where he was going, as much as that was in his control at all, so at the same time he restocked his shuttle he disabled the transponder.

The second way was to spot the shuttle as it traveled. The craft had running lights, but they were designed to perform an up-close review of the hull and weren't powerful enough to be visible beyond a few kalomaders. But the thrusters were plenty bright, and unlike the running lights (which he turned off) Xto couldn't operate without thrusters.

For this reason, he spent a week plotting an interception course that required as little adjustment as possible. It meant an extended burn within an hour of leaving the hangar (when there was likely nobody looking for a missing astronaut yet) to reach a velocity that would get him *ahead* of the craft by a few thousand maders. He would then slow gradually—the front thrusters were weaker and would not be facing Shizuna Two for this maneuver—to intercept speed. It would be impossible to do this without using the rear thrusters at all, but he hoped that the usage would be brief and would occur at a time when nobody was focused on the anomaly.

Although by then, assuming he had avoided prior detection, anyone from orbital platform one who was thinking about interfering with Xto's plan would be two days away from doing so.

The third way was by communicating to him via radio. This was the easiest method to confound; all he had to do was not answer. He could even turn the radio *off*, but felt it would be the most effective way to know that he'd been discovered—this would surely be the first thing anyone tried after finding that both Xto and his shuttle were missing—so he left it on.

∼

The two days it took to travel the distance between Shizuna Two and the alien ship went by perfectly uneventfully. Xto whiled the time away re-reading a digital copy of the *Tracta Duccaleo* and wondering what was happening at that very moment on the orbital platform. If his plan was going perfectly, nobody was looking for him at all. But Opzk's cleverness put all of that into doubt. Nobody tried to *reach* him though, and when he trained his opticals in the direction of the asteroid he saw no evidence of a team of ships moving to intercept. (Although, he likely wouldn't, for the same reason they likely couldn't see him.)

His copy of the *Tracta Duccaleo* continued to be of no particular use. He hoped that after all of this was over he'd have an opportunity to ask his uncle—in a setting in which they were *not* being listened to—what prompted the High Hat of Chnta to mention the text in the first place.

Then he decided he'd likely already spoken to Uncle Ghn for the last time. They would punish him for Xto's actions, whether or not he was directly to blame. That would be the case even if Xto opted to eventually return to Wivvol...which as each day went by he became less certain of.

His plotted trajectory worked perfectly. The momentum from that initial long burn took him right into the orbital path of the anomaly and would have—had he not intervened—carried him past it and perilously close to Hadrine, the smaller of the two suns, which was currently foregrounding the larger Dyhine.

Xto committed to an hour's worth of adjustments until the nose of his shuttle was facing in the same direction as the nose of the alien ship (which was a half a kalomader behind him.) Then he began to slow.

In another two hours he had the shuttle running beside the ship. He was forced to fire the rear thrusters then, to match the speed.

*Hello to anyone looking,* he thought.

He managed to set the shuttle down on the side of the vessel, tucked in just ahead of the torus's support struts and a short walk to the door. Then he shut down the engine.

"Good morning, friend," he said to the alien hull. "I've returned."

The hardest part was working out how to carry the key. He couldn't tie a rope to the end of it because the loop at the end was too small for a rope. It was lightweight (although he was in a weightless environment so that didn't really matter) and easy to wield and manipulate with a bare hand, but the big, bulky gloves that were a part of the spacesuit simply didn't pair well with fine motor skills.

He was, in short, afraid of losing his grip on the key and watching it drift away forever.

In the end he decided to attach it to his right glove using the same tape he would use to patch the suit in the event of a tear. It was a risk of a different kind—now he *and* the key were in danger of drifting away forever with one bad handhold—but he felt better about it.

Helmet on, key taped to glove, he opened the hatch to the shuttle with his free hand and walked back out onto the alien hull.

Since the last time he was there, the teams from the orbital platform had established a system of tethers about ten paces apart —exactly wide enough to land a shuttle between—along the entire front half of the ship. Xto didn't bother tying himself to one, but he did grab onto the nearest rope to the door with his left hand upon arrival. It meant if the door swung out he'd be in the wrong position to enter, but one thing at a time.

They'd cleaned off the hull around the doorjamb, he noticed, but the panel to the right with the keyhole was largely undisturbed. There was scoring around the handle, though; they'd tried to force it.

He brushed the keyhole with the side of his right arm to expose the opening.

"Now to find out if I've been wrong this whole time," he said, inserting the key.

It fit into the hole...loosely. The shape of the end of the key didn't align exactly with the keyhole. He continued to push it in until he couldn't any longer. Then he turned the key counterclockwise.

Nothing happened.

Disappointed, he tried to pull the key back out, thinking he could perhaps start over again and have a different result. But it wouldn't come *out* either.

"I have engaged *something*," he decided.

He pushed the key again and this time it gave another three centimaders or so before hitting another stop. He attempted to turn the key counterclockwise again—the strain on his wrist was becoming a problem as he was trying to rotate it from 30 degrees to 60 degrees—but it wouldn't move. He turned it clockwise instead.

The door *sank*, about a hand's width. It so startled Xto he nearly lost his grip on the hull completely. The key slid out—freeing his right hand—and he let go with his left. Only the fact that he'd wrapped the tether around his left wrist (automatically; it was a safety step he no longer did consciously) kept him from soaring away.

*All right calm down,* he thought. *So you opened the door. Get a hold of yourself.*

After a little repositioning, he got into a better angle to interact with the door—the right hand and key were now wrapped around the right-hand tether, leaving his left hand free.

The indent he took as a door handle was not, as it looked, a way to swing open the door. Instead of opening out, the door slid to the left. As soon as this happened the chamber on the other side lit up with a dim glow from indirect lighting.

The ship had power.

Xto took hold of a conveniently-located strap running along the ceiling of the inner room, freed his right arm, and pulled himself in.

The magnet cleats on his boots locked onto the metal floor with a satisfying thump. A panel to his left lit up as soon as he was in its proximity—motion-detection tech, clearly. One of the panel's buttons would seal the door, but since he couldn't read the words beneath the buttons he had to go with best-guess. This wasn't difficult: only one of them was flashing.

The door slid closed and he lost his view of the stars. Xto Djbbit was now fully immersed in an alien world.

The chamber was narrow but long, with a door at the other end. He began walking towards it. As he went he began to encounter something he'd not experienced in two years: gravity. Real gravity, not the gentle kind like what they had on Shizuna Two.

If the ship was mimicking the standard gravity of the alien home world, it was entirely possible Xto was about to be crushed to death.

At about the same time the artificial gravity began applying force to his body, he heard a hissing noise. His immediate reaction was to check his suit for leaks, but none of the risk sensors were going off. This was the sound of the room pressurizing. As with the gravity, if "normal" for the aliens was a highly pressurized atmosphere, Xto was a couple of minutes away from being popped like a fly between a thumb and forefinger.

*Perhaps,* he thought, eyeing the exit door, *this is as far as I go.*

But then a different sensor in his suit caught his attention. It was the atmosphere detector on his left sleeve, blinking to notify him that it was safe to remove his helmet.

Either the aliens breathed the same kind of atmosphere as Dibblings or the ship's sensors were adequately sophisticated to identify the appropriate mixture of gases for Xto's respiration. Both possibilities seemed equally improbable.

Extending a long streak of foolish decisions, he took off his helmet. His training—and he actually *did* have training for this incredibly unlikely scenario—was to keep breathing his own oxygen because there was no way to devise a sensor that could detect an alien pathogen. But the way he saw it, given the age of the ship if there was a living pathogen inside it had more than earned the chance to infect him.

The air smelled stale but was definitely breathable, and the room was comfortably cool. (This answered yet another concern he'd been harboring about his alien hosts: what if they liked it intolerably hot or cold?) It nearly felt like he was back on Dibble...all except for the gravity. It felt too strong. Not murderously so, but not good either. He was worried that if he spent enough time there he'd end up too exhausted to make it back to the shuttle.

This didn't mean the gravity was *stronger* than what he grew up with. It could just as easily mean that he was suffering from the same weakness he would have to endure when he returned; two years in weak-to-no gravity did that to a body. But he'd have someone taking care of him on the surface. Here, he was alone in a locked ship with the only key.

There was probably a way to deactivate the artificial gravity, but to figure out how to do that he'd have to turn into a linguist first.

When he got close enough to the inner door another wall panel lit up with another button flashing suggestively.

"One moment," he said to the impatient ship. He pulled off his left glove, worked the tape off his right glove—freeing the key—and removed that glove as well. Meanwhile, the ship decided it was time to talk to Xto, seeing as how Xto was talking to it.

In a soothing tone that sounded like it belonged to a Dibbling female, the ship's computer offered some manner of greeting. He could only go on tone to determine if it was a welcome and not a warning.

"I don't speak this language," he said. "I don't suppose you speak mine?"

The ship repeated the same alien phrase.

"I didn't think so."

He clipped the gloves and helmet to his belt, gripped the key like it was a weapon, and pushed the flashing button.

The door slid open. He took a deep breath and stepped through.

∽

The ship lit his way with each step. The lighting was a gentle yellow-white and hidden behind ceiling panels in the corridors, perfectly bright enough to see by and not blind him. *Their eyes are like ours*, he thought. This was added to other significant observations such as: *they are around the same height as us* and *their doors work with hands like our hands* and *they were probably bipedal*.

The first door Xto walked through from the airlock led to a corridor that seemed to run the length of the ship. He headed in the direction of the nose of the vessel, which was where he assumed he'd find the main bridge, provided the aliens were enough like him to design an interior the same way he would.

So far, every indication was that they were.

He walked past another door every ten paces, and each time he did another wall panel lit up inviting him to hit a flashing button. Meanwhile, the helpful alien computer speaking an alien language continued to fail to communicate with him.

"I can't understand you," he said. "But I'm sure you are very nice."

He wondered if the computer was self-aware.

Twice, he decided to stop at a door and see what was on the other side. The first time, he wandered into the middle of what looked like a library, only the things on the shelves weren't books. They were book *shaped*, though: clear, glassine rectangular boxes holding tiny vials. The precise contents of the vials were documented in glowing lettering along the spines.

All he could tell about the language so far was that it seemed like a combination of pictographic lettering and the kind of standard letters-representing-sounds symbology he was familiar with. A *few* of the letters of the latter kind looked familiar, but he was ascribing that to the fact that there were only so many two-dimensional shapes available.

The second room he stopped in was someone's private quarters. He stayed long enough to note that the aliens slept like Dibblings and sat like Dibblings. Then he briefly considered lying down in the bunk to recover from the gravity, which meant it was time to move on.

By the time he reached the bridge he *did* have to stop and sit. He'd begun seeing bright patches of light flashing on the periphery of his vision and recognized this as a precursor to passing out.

Fortunately, then, the bridge had plenty of chairs to choose from. Five, to be exact: two at a front console, a raised chair in the middle of the room, and two in the back. Without thinking about what he was doing, he staggered to the raised center chair and sat.

Panels embedded in the chair's arms lit up immediately, and the computer voice asked him a new set of questions.

"If you can understand me, computer, I would appreciate you reducing the gravity," he said. "Otherwise, just be quiet and let me sit here."

He leaned back. The chair, which had not been sat in for perhaps an eon or two, creaked gently.

*Captain's chair*, he decided. *Behind helm control. Elevated view through the windows. Their eyes were front-facing. They had two arms.*

"Perhaps they weren't just *like* us," he said—to either nobody or to the ship's computer, depending. "Perhaps they *were* us."

But there was no version of Dibble's history in which that made sense. He knew it two years ago, when first seeing this ship in the telescope with his father, and he knew it now: at no time was there a nation sufficiently advanced to build such a thing as this.

319

Facts were facts, though. Self-evidently, this was a spaceship intended for use by beings almost *entirely* identical to Xto Djbbit.

*What about a pre-Collapse nation?* he wondered. Was this one of the House's many well-kept secrets? Would he have learned of it had he taken the oath? Did his uncle know?

Another button was flashing at him, this one on the arm of the chair. There were no obvious doors in need of opening; he had no clue what the computer was suggesting he do.

Xto pushed it anyway.

The entire room jumped to life. The front console, which had been an angled piece of black glass, was now a massive illuminated control panel with optical screens, arrows, buttons, gauges and meters. The centerpiece was a large circle that looked a lot like the face of an analog clock except it had only five markings along the circumference instead of twenty. Straight ahead, the metal shutters that had been blocking the front viewing windows slid up. A legend in alien text appeared in the center, just above the windows. The entire room became brighter overall, with the other four chairs now flashing information on their arm displays. The computer made a firm announcement.

He wondered if the engine was going.

The ring in the middle of the center console flashed a slow, steady cadence. In time with the flashing, the computer began repeating the same set of instructions. It wanted him to do something with the ring, but he couldn't begin to guess what that might be. What *he* wanted, meanwhile, was to make everything stop doing what it was doing and go back to sleep. He was all in favor of being the first person to explore an alien ship but he did *not* want to be the first to inadvertently steer one into a sun.

His eyes drifted past the flashing ring, to the legend on the wall above the window.

It was entirely possible his mind was now officially suffering from the effects of gravity sickness but he realized he could *read* one of the words.

It looked a lot like a word that was on the cover of more than one of the texts in Uncle Ghn's library—what he called his Septal vault, but what was really just a locked cabinet in his home. All of the books in that cabinet were written in archaic Eglinat, which meant they were twice removed from being anything Xto could read himself. But he remembered three or four words as reappearing more often than the others. As a young boy thinking his future was that of a Septal monk, Xto used to pester Ghn to read from the books, imagining that he'd grow to understand the words osmotically over time. Ghn never did it, but he *did* tell him what the words on the cover meant.

That was what Xto was reading now. One of those words. Or, *nearly* one of those words.

*Dclm*, he thought. *That's what it says.*

In the same way that a Septal artifact could somehow open the door to a spaceship—designed for people who were *clearly* from the planet Dib even though they couldn't be—this was simply impossible. This word didn't belong where it was.

It could have been a coincidence. But as Xto sat in the captain's chair, trembling—either from gravitational sickness or a visceral reaction to the word—he concluded that the outlandish explanation was the more likely explanation.

The legend on the control panel was the name of the ship. That name was *Dclm*. In modern Eglinat it would be *Ducclem*. They both meant the same thing: Haven.

And *that* meant everything Septalism taught him had been a lie.

"Uncle, I have found the Haven," Xto said mournfully. "And it is empty. The gods are not here."

∼

∼

Astronaut Xto Djbbit closed his eyes and rested his head on the table, as if the effort of imparting this story had been physically exhausting.

"Wait," Elicasta said. "Wait, that's not..."

She looked to Makk as if he had an explanation. He was busy wondering how much of it he was prepared to believe, and couldn't help her. He took a long sip of his drink and waited for the astronaut to talk again, but it didn't look as if he was prepared to do so.

"What happened next, Xto?" Makk finally asked.

Slowly, the Wivvolian raised his head again. "What happened next was that I left."

"But the info was *right there* for the tap," Elicasta said, drifting back into Stream-speak. "This wasn't the time to bug."

Xto seemed to get the gist of what she was saying. "Had I stayed any longer I would have died there," he said. "It would have been three days before I was acclimated to the gravity but by then I would have been too weak from dehydration to save myself. No, it was either escape at that moment or die—ironically—in the Haven."

"But not really *the* Haven," Makk said. "Not the place where all the good people go when they die. You were in a place where you saw a word that looked like the archaic word for Haven. That's all."

Xto just stared at him silently, dispassionately. *I have already had this argument with myself*, he seemed to be saying. *Why do you think I've been drinking so much?*

"I did my best to power the ship back down," Xto said, deciding to skip the theological discussion. "And then I returned to the shuttle. I think you know the rest."

"You were reported missing," Elicasta said. "Your country hardly ever does that."

"I suspect that's my father's doing. And not out of concern for my wellbeing, although that would be nice. When I shut off the ship I couldn't work out how to close the shutters on the windows. They remain open, which means by now Mondr has figured out that I found a way onto the ship. Even if I never return to space he needs for me to tell him how I did it...only I no longer have the key to the door, so it hardly matters. Let them find me; I will explain that I surrendered the legacies of both Mondr and Uncle Ghn on the same afternoon. If I am lucky, *all* they will do is hang me."

~

With an assist from Erry Gisador, Makk and Elicasta managed to get Xto out of the corner of the makeshift tavern and down the road to their hotel. They didn't know what they were going to *do* with him after that, but it didn't seem right to leave him where he was either.

Xto got the bed, which was fine with Makk. He didn't expect to be sleeping any time soon.

The suns were coming up by the time they got Xto settled in. Makk sat on the beach and watched them rise on the horizon.

Elicasta joined him a few minutes later, with two coffees and some fried dough. He grunted a thanks and consumed the dough in two bites.

"So how much of that are we going to believe?" she asked, after a time.

"Not sure."

"I mean, I'm all in on a secret alien spaceship. Who'd have thought *that* to be the easy part of the story?"

"*He* believes it," Makk said. "A guy who was raised a Septal and sounds like he still *is* one, who was suffering from gravity-induced exhaustion when he suddenly decided he could read archaic Eglinat on the wall of an alien ship...? He has every reason to doubt that what he saw was real. Instead he's drinking himself to death because he's decided the place we've all been told was our reward in the next life is actually just a vacant orbiting spaceship. Maybe instead of asking whether *we* believe it we should be asking why Xto Djbbit does."

"*I* don't believe it," she said. "I wasn't raised like you were and I'm not sure we go anywhere when we die, but that doesn't mean I'm down with this spin. On the flip, I'd Stream that in a heartskip."

"Nobody would believe it on the Stream, and you have no proof."

"Got lots of proof. I got *him*. I bet sober he's even credible. Plus all we gotta do is point a telescope in the right place. The proof is in orbit between us and the Dancers. Skip that, there's enough meat around the space station on Shizuna Two to take over the whole Stream for a week, solid. Besides, I think you're underestimating what people on the Stream are prepared to believe."

"You're right," he said, laughing. "I probably am."

"Real question, babe," she said. "What are *we* doing now? We can spend a week getting our new friend sober and prepped for his moment on the Stream if that's all we have left. My 'cast needs an infusion so I'm down. But we're no closer to Viselle, and our pet astronaut has more people looking for him than Calcut Linus does."

"No idea," he admitted. "But getting him sober will be a good start."

∼

The next few days weren't particularly fruitful. They failed to get Xto Djbbit entirely sober—although he was *more* sober than when they met him—or to lighten his overall mood. He seemed to think he'd be discovered by Wivvolian authorities in a matter of minutes and also like he was looking forward to being punished for what he believed he'd done. Meanwhile, Elicasta had decided that in the absence of a plan of attack from Makk (who was the attack planner) she would focus her energies on finding ways to prove Xto's story without using Xto to tell it.

Although he didn't ask, Makk assumed she was doing this because Xto had declined to help her directly.

For his part, Makk wasn't working on a next step because he didn't see one. He also wasn't worried about that.

*One will present itself*, he thought. *It's worked out that way so far.*

He spent his time doing a little of what he should have been doing all along, considering this was a vacation: relaxing, drinking, watching the ocean and so on. Touristy stuff. He even considered hiring Erry Gisador for a fishing trip, even though he didn't much care for fish.

Five days after they first met Xto, Makk was alone at the shore drinking coffee and watching the tide come in when Elicasta ran up.

"We have a ping," she said.

"A what? A ping?"

"Viselle. She's surfaced."

"Oh," he said. "I forgot we could do that. Where does Ba-Ugna's device say she is this time?"

"It wasn't the algo that found her," Elicasta said. "She's in Velon. Streamers are putting her at the scene of an explosion in Pant City overnight."

"Pant City? Are you sure?"

"Pretty sure," she said. "I trust the Veesers with the deets. There's something else. They're saying Dorn Jimbal is with her. I thought they were dead."

"We *all* thought they were dead. How solid is this really?"

"If I were there I'd be tailing this Stream."

"That means very solid?"

"It means very, yes."

His mind jumped to a conclusion that wasn't completely rational. He remembered, when listening to Xto's story, that the leap Xto took from finding a keyhole to concluding that he had the key which fit into it was too vast to make sense. But then Makk had moments like this one. Sometimes you just know.

"Exactly *where* in Pant City?" he asked, pulling out his voicer.

"I dunno, some apartment building. You want an address?"

"Yes."

"I'll get you one. Gimme a few."

She dove into the Stream through the rig on her head while Makk directed Leemie's voicer.

It buzzed and buzzed, but wouldn't connect.

"Come on, Leemie," he muttered, trying another address. Leemie had seven voicers that Makk knew of, and probably a dozen others that he didn't. But considering his friend never left the apartment it shouldn't have mattered which one Makk was trying; Leemie would be near *all* of them.

"I've got the *block*," Elicasta said. She tapped it up on her voicer and showed him the map. "Does that help?"

"Yeah," he said, disconnecting his own device. "Yeah, that helps."

"Whoa," she said, seeing his expression. "A friend of yours?"

"Old army buddy. He was holding something of mine and I think she went there looking for it. I might have gotten him killed."

~

In the hours of Stream news coverage that followed, the name Leemie Witts never once came up. Makk wasn't surprised; his friend wasn't on any official records as living at that location. There were a dozen *other* victims of the fire that engulfed the building (and half of the block) after the explosion, but Leemie wasn't among them.

Aside from a running list of victims, there was effectively

nothing new coming out of the scene. Makk saw a lot of the placeholder statements he was used to making himself when dealing with the media in the middle of an active investigation. "Pursuing all leads" and so on. He could tell they didn't have anything.

They didn't even have Viselle and Dorn listed as anything more than "wanted for questioning." There was an All-Eyes out on both of them, but only as persons of interest.

So, Makk spent the rest of the day plugged into the Stream and learning all the different ways Veesers had to say, "We don't know anything new."

The information Elicasta was getting was slightly more compelling, but it was much more poorly sourced. With Makk concentrating on the well-verified news, she decided to skim the UnVeesers for dirt.

"You can't take anything they *say* seriously," she'd explained, "not individually. But if you pile them together you'll still get a fuzzy vid of the truth."

What came out of her analysis was that the House was definitely involved in whatever was going down in Velon. *How* they were involved was difficult to figure out.

At the end of the day, Viselle popped up again.

"She just used a voicer," Elicasta shouted from the other side of the hotel room. "Nowhere near Pant City. Ba-Ugna's program pins her out by the airfield."

"That's a long way from Pantolinar Quarter," he said.

"Sure is. Oh, and this might be a thing too. Buzz is, Exty Demara's coming down from on high tonight."

"That name sounds familiar."

"It should; we were in her house."

"Right."

"I'm thinking if Kev was sheltering there, maybe his daughter was too."

"I would've killed for this kind of data when I was on duty," he said. "Maybe we can direct an anonymous tip to Twenty-One Central."

"That depends," Elicasta said. "You sure you *want* them in custody? Don't think we'll get any answers from her and Dorn if they get picked up. I'm saying maybe they've been under the optics on Lys this whole time and now we know it. It's a place to go, I'm saying."

"Sure," Makk said. "We'll just drive on over to Lys."

She laughed. "We do *know* an astronaut."

～

The lack of hard news continued through the night and into the early hours of the next morning. All that changed was the number of fire victims and the escalation of interest in Viselle Daska and Dorn Jimbal—now both wanted for a *crime* rather than just *questioning*.

Makk found the inclusion of Dorn interesting. Not only was Other Jimbal supposed to be dead in an unmarked grave somewhere, they were definitely *not* supposed to be involved in acts of violence. Makk only spoke with Dorn one time, but the Septal monk he met didn't strike him as capable of harming someone. (Dorn's roommates had the same opinion, if memory served.) It was also incredibly unlikely that Twenty-One Central considered them a main actor in the Pant City events. Which meant they named Dorn as a means to apply pressure *on* Dorn. And *that* meant they saw Dorn as a means to get at Viselle.

That was *also* interesting. Makk imagined a lot of hypotheticals about Viselle, but working with Dorn wasn't one of them.

*Was I wrong about Dorn?* he thought. *Or was I wrong about Viselle?*

Then, at the end of the day, an opportunity to get some answers arrived in an entirely unexpected way.

He didn't respond to the direct right off, because he didn't recognize the voicer address it was coming from and he'd been ducking messages from the entire Velon police force for well over a week. But then he thought it might be Leemie, reaching out from a new device, so he opened the line.

"Leemie?" he asked. "Is that you?"

There was a moment of silence from the other end, and then: "No," Viselle Daska said. "I'm sorry, Makk. Leemie didn't make it."

"Viselle. What did you do to him?"

"It wasn't like that," she said. "I didn't go there to hurt him and I *didn't* hurt him. He was working *with* us, Makk. If you want to blame somebody for his death you should blame the House. He died helping us escape from them."

"I don't believe a word of that," he growled.

"I know. You have every reason not to listen to me, but you *have* to because I need your help. We have to save the world."

"The world. Really."

"Yes, really. Dorn found the Outcast. It's real, and it's coming, and the only way to save us all is to use the five keys."

The words of Xto's uncle, the High Hat of Chnta came to mind: *saving the world from the outcast in our lifetime*. Ghn Tbyct wanted to unite the keys too.

"Don't pretend you don't know what I'm talking about," Viselle said. "You have one of the keys now, and so do I."

"I heard that," he said. "You stole it from an astronaut."

"He gave it to me." She hesitated again, no doubt putting some things together in her head. "You found him, didn't you?" she said. "You went looking for me and found him instead. How is he?"

"Not great. I'll tell him you said hello."

"He may...come in handy. Why don't you bring him along?"

"On my way to arrest you?" Makk asked.

"We're *way* beyond that now, and if you stop for just a second to think about it you'll realize that yourself. Look, I can explain *all* of this, but Dorn and I have to get off of Lys and I need you to figure out where we're going next."

"I don't understand."

"My father had a device that could track nearly anyone in the world. I've been looking everywhere, but today I realized the reason I couldn't find it was that he *gave* it to someone. He gave it to *you*, I think, for the same reason he sacrificed himself. He knew you had a key and he knew better than either of us did at the time just how important the keys are. So what I need you to do is stop using that toy of his to track *me* down and use it to find someone else."

"That doesn't make any sense at all," he said.

"It will, Makk," she said. "I know you have no reason to believe me but you have to. The world is at stake and I swear that's not an exaggeration."

Improbably, he *did* sort of believe her.

"Who do you want me to find?" he asked.

"His name is Damid Magly. He's a fugitive from the Middle Kingdoms and I believe he's in possession of the third key. Tell me where he is and we'll meet you there. Then you can decide if you still want to arrest me."

He looked at Elicasta, who was busy fiddling with her rig on the other side of the room.

*She'll never trust Viselle enough to do this*, he thought. *But she also can't resist a good story.*

"I'll get back to you as soon as I have a location," Makk said. "See you soon."

# About the Author

Gene Doucette is a hybrid author, albeit in a somewhat round-about way. From 2010 through 2014, Gene published four full-length novels (*Immortal*, *Hellenic Immortal*, *Fixer*, and *Immortal at the Edge of the World*) with a small indie publisher. Then, in 2014, Gene started self-publishing novellas that were set in the same universe as the *Immortal* series, at which point he was a hybrid.

When the novellas proved more lucrative than the novels, Gene tried self-publishing a full novel, *The Spaceship Next Door*, in 2015. This went well. So well, that in 2016, Gene reacquired the rights to the earlier four novels from the publisher, and re-released them, at which point he wasn't a hybrid any longer.

Additional self-published novels followed: *Immortal and the Island of Impossible Things* (2016); *Unfiction* (2017); and *The Frequency of Aliens* (2017).

In 2018, John Joseph Adams Books (an imprint of Houghton Mifflin Harcourt) acquired the rights to *The Spaceship Next Door*. The reprint was published in September of that year, at which point Gene was once again a hybrid author.

Since then, a number of things have happened. Gene published three more novels—*Immortal From Hell* (2018), *Fixer Redux* (2019), and *Immortal: Last Call* (2020)—and wrote a new novel called *The Apocalypse Seven* that he did not self-publish; it was acquired by JJA/HMH in September of 2019. Publication date is May 25, 2021.

Gene lives in Cambridge, MA.

*For the latest on Gene Doucette, follow him online*

genedoucette.me
genedoucette@me.com

# Also by Gene Doucette

## SCI-FI

### The Apocalypse Seven

The whateverpocalypse. That's what Touré, a twenty-something Cambridge coder, calls it after waking up one morning to find himself seemingly the only person left in the city. Once he finds Robbie and Carol, two equally disoriented Harvard freshmen, he realizes he isn't alone, but the name sticks: Whateverpocalypse.

But it doesn't explain where everyone went. It doesn't explain how the city became overgrown with vegetation in the space of a night. Or how wild animals with no fear of humans came to roam the streets.

Add freakish weather to the mix, swings of temperature that spawn tornadoes one minute and snowstorms the next, and it seems things can't get much weirder. Yet even as a handful of new survivors appear—Paul, a preacher as quick with a gun as a Bible verse; Win, a young professional with a horse; Bethany, a thirteen-year-old juvenile delinquent; and Ananda, an MIT astrophysics adjunct—life in Cambridge, Massachusetts gets stranger and stranger.

The self-styled Apocalypse Seven are tired of questions with no answers. Tired of being hunted by things seen and unseen. Now, armed with curiosity, desperation, a shotgun, and a bow, they become the hunters. And that's when things *truly* get weird.

∽

### The Spaceship Next Door

*The world changed on a Tuesday.*

When a spaceship landed in an open field in the quiet mill town of Sorrow Falls, Massachusetts, everyone realized humankind was not alone in the universe. With that realization, everyone freaked out for a little while.

Or, almost everyone. The residents of Sorrow Falls took the news pretty well. This could have been due to a certain local quality of unflappability, or it could have been that in three years, the ship did exactly nothing other than sit quietly in that field, and nobody understood the full extent of this nothing the ship was doing better than the people who lived right next door.

Sixteen-year old Annie Collins is one of the ship's closest neighbors. Once upon a time she took every last theory about the ship seriously, whether it was advanced by an adult ,or by a peer. Surely one of the theories would be proven true eventually—if not several of them—the very minute the ship decided to do something. Annie is starting to think this will never happen.

One late August morning, a little over three years since the ship landed, Edgar Somerville arrived in town. Ed's a government operative posing as a journalist, which is obvious to Annie—and pretty much everyone else he meets—almost immediately. He has a lot of questions that need answers, because he thinks everyone is wrong: the ship is doing something, and he needs Annie's help to figure out what that is.

Annie is a good choice for tour guide. She already knows everyone in town and when Ed's theory is proven correct—something is apocalyptically wrong in Sorrow Falls—she's a pretty good person to have around.

As a matter of fact, Annie Collins might be the most important person on the planet. She just doesn't know it.

~

**The Frequency of Aliens**

**Annie Collins is back!**

Becoming an overnight celebrity at age sixteen should have been a lot more fun. Yes, there were times when it was extremely cool, but when the newness of it all wore off, Annie Collins was left with a permanent security detail and the kind of constant scrutiny that makes the college experience especially awkward.

Not helping matters: she's the only kid in school with her own pet spaceship.

She would love it if things found some kind of normal, but as long as she has control of the most lethal—and only—interstellar vehicle in existence, that isn't going to happen. Worse, things appear to be going in the other direction. Instead of everyone getting used to the idea of the ship, the complaints are getting louder. Public opinion is turning, and the demands that Annie turn over the ship are becoming more frequent. It doesn't help that everyone seems to think Annie is giving them nightmares.

Nightmares aren't the only weird things going on lately. A government telescope in California has been abandoned, and nobody seems to know why.

The man called on to investigate—Edgar Somerville—has become the go-to guy whenever there's something odd going on, which has been pretty common lately. So far, nothing has panned out: no aliens or zombies or anything else that might be deemed legitimately peculiar... but now may be different, and not just because Ed can't find an easy explanation. This isn't the only telescope where people have gone missing, and the clues left behind lead back to Annie.

It all adds up to a new threat that the world may just need saving from, requiring the help of all the Sorrow Falls survivors. The question is: are they saving the world with Annie Collins, or are they saving it from her?

*The Frequency of Aliens* is the exciting sequel to *The Spaceship Next Door*.

∼

### Unfiction

When Oliver Naughton joins the Tenth Avenue Writers Underground, headed by literary wunderkind Wilson Knight, Oliver figures he'll finally get some of the wild imaginings out of his head and onto paper.

But when Wilson takes an intense interest in Oliver's writing and his genre stories of dragons, aliens, and spies, things get weird. Oliver's stories don't just need to be finished: they insist on it.

With the help of Minerva, Wilson's girlfriend, Oliver has to find the connection between reality, fiction, the mythical Cydonian Kingdom, and the non-mythical nightclub called M Pallas. That is, if he can survive the alien invasion, the ghosts, and the fact that he thinks he might be in love with Minerva.

Unfiction is a wild ride through the collision of science fiction, fantasy, thriller, horror and romance. It's what happens when one writer's fiction interferes with everyone's reality.

∼

### Fixer

*What would you do if you could see into the future?*

As a child, he dreamed of being a superhero. Most people never get to realize their childhood dreams, but Corrigan Bain has come close. He is a fixer. His job is to prevent accidents—to see the future and "fix" things before people get hurt. But the ability to see into the future, however limited, isn't always so simple. Sometimes not everyone can be saved.

*"Don't let them know you can see them."*

Graduate students from a local university are dying, and former lover and FBI agent Maggie Trent is the only person who believes their deaths aren't as accidental as they appear. But the truth can only be found in something from Corrigan Bain's past, and he's not interested in sharing that past, not even with Maggie.

To stop the deaths, Corrigan will have to face up to some old horrors, confront the possibility that he may be going mad, and find a way to stop a killer no one can see.

*Corrigan Bain is going insane ... or is he?*

Because there's something in the future that doesn't want to be seen. It isn't human. It's got a taste for mayhem. And it is very, very angry.

## Fixer Redux

*Someone's altering the future, and it isn't Corrigan Bain*

Corrigan Bain was retired.

It wasn't something he ever thought he'd be able to do. The problem was that the *job* he wanted to retire from wasn't actually a job at all: nobody paid him to do it, and nobody else did it. With very few exceptions, nobody even knew he was doing it.

Corrigan called himself a fixer, because he fixed accidents that were about to happen. It was complicated and unrewarding, and even though doing it right meant saving someone, he didn't enjoy it. He couldn't stop —he thought—because there would always be accidents, and he would never find someone to take over as fixer. Anyone trying would have to be capable of seeing the future, like he did, and that kind of person was hard to find.

Still, he did it. He's never been happier.

His girlfriend, Maggie Trent of the FBI, has not retired. Her task force just shut down the most dangerous domestic terrorist cell in the country, and she's up for an award, and a big promotion.

Everything's going their way now, and the future looks even brighter.

Unfortunately, that future is about to blow up in their faces…literally. And somehow, Corrigan Bain, fixer, the man who can see the future, is taken completely by surprise.

***Fixer Redux*** is the long-awaited sequel to ***Fixer***. Catch up with Corrigan, as he tries to understand a future that no longer makes sense.

## FANTASY
### *The Immortal Novel Series*

## Immortal

*"I don't know how old I am. My earliest memory is something along the lines of fire good, ice bad, so I think I predate written history, but I don't know by how much. I like to brag that I've been there from the beginning, and while this may very well be true, I generally just say it to pick up girls."*

Surviving sixty thousand years takes cunning and more than a little luck. But in the twenty-first century, Adam confronts new dangers—someone has found out what he is, a demon is after him, and he has run out of places to hide. Worst of all, he has had entirely too much to drink.

Immortal is a first person confessional penned by a man who is immortal, but not invincible. In an artful blending of sci-fi, adventure, fantasy, and humor, IMMORTAL introduces us to a world with vampires, demons and other "magical" creatures, yet a world without actual magic.

At the center of the book is Adam.

Adam is a sixty thousand year old man. (Approximately.) He doesn't age or get sick, but is otherwise entirely capable of being killed. His survival has hinged on an innate ability to adapt, his wits, and a fairly large dollop of luck. He makes for an excellent guide through history ... when he's sober.

Immortal is a contemporary fantasy for non-fantasy readers and fantasy enthusiasts alike.

∽

## Hellenic Immortal

*"Very occasionally, I will pop up in the historical record. Most of the time I'm not at all easy to spot, because most of the time I'm just a guy who does a thing and then disappears again into the background behind someone-or-other who's busy doing something much more important. But there are a couple of rare occasions when I get a starring role."*

An oracle has predicted the sojourner's end, which is a problem for Adam insofar as he has never encountered an oracular prediction that didn't come true ... and he is the sojourner. To survive, he's going to have to figure out what a beautiful ex-government analyst, an eco-terrorist, a rogue FBI agent, and the world's oldest religious cult all want with him, and fast.

And all he wanted when he came to Vegas was to forget about a girl. And maybe have a drink or two.

The second book in the Immortal series, Hellenic Immortal follows the continuing adventures of Adam, a sixty-thousand-year-old man with a wry sense of humor, a flair for storytelling, and a knack for staying alive. Hellenic Immortal is a clever blend of history, mythology, sci-fi, fantasy, adventure, mystery and romance. A little something, in other words, for every reader.

∾

### Immortal at the Edge of the World

*"What I was currently doing with my time and money ... didn't really deserve anyone else's attention. If I was feeling romantic about it, I'd call it a quest, but all I was really doing was trying to answer a question I'd been ignoring for a thousand years."*

In his very long life, Adam had encountered only one person who appeared to share his longevity: the mysterious red-haired woman. She appeared throughout history, usually from a distance, nearly always vanishing before he could speak to her.

In his last encounter, she actually did vanish—into thin air, right in front of him. The question was how did she do it? To answer, Adam will have to complete a quest he gave up on a thousand years earlier, for an object that may no longer exist.

If he can find it, he might be able to do what the red-haired woman did, and if he can do that, maybe he can find her again and ask her who she is ... and why she seems to hate him.

But Adam isn't the only one who wants the red-haired woman. There are other forces at work, and after a warning from one of the few men he trusts, Adam realizes how much danger everyone is in. To save his friends and finish his quest he may be forced to bankrupt himself, call in every favor he can, and ultimately trade the one thing he'd never been able to give up before: his life.

∼

## Immortal and the island of Impossible Things

*"I thought I'd miss the world."*

Adam is on vacation in an island paradise, with nothing to do and plenty of time to do nothing.

It's exactly what he needed: beautiful weather, beautiful girlfriend, plenty of books to read, and alcohol to drink. Most importantly, either nobody on the island knows who he is, or, nobody cares.

*"This probably sounds boring, and maybe it is. It's possible I have no compass to help determine boring, or maybe I have a different threshold than most people. From my perspective, though, the vast majority of human history has been boring, by which I mean nothing happened, and sure, that can be dull. On the other hand, nothing happening includes nobody trying to kill anybody, and specifically, nobody trying to kill me. That's the kind of boring a guy can get behind."*

Nothing last forever, though, and that includes the opportunity to *do* nothing. One day, unwelcome visitors arrive in secret, with impossible knowledge of impossible events, and then the impossible things arrive: a new species.

It's *all* impossible, especially to the immortal man who thought he'd seen all there was to see in the world. Now, Adam is going to have to figure out what's happening and make things right before he and everyone he loves ends up dead in the hot sun of this island paradise.

∼

## Immortal From Hell

### Not all of Adam's stories have happy endings

*"Paris is romantic and quests are cool. But the threat of a global pandemic kind of*

*sours the whole thing. The good news was, if all life on Earth were felled by a plague, it looked like this one could take me out too. It'd be pretty lonely otherwise."*

--Adam the immortal

When Adam decides to leave the safety of the island, it's for a good reason: Eve, the only other immortal on the planet, appears to be dying, and nobody seems to understand why. But when Adam—with his extremely capable girlfriend Mirella—tries to retrace Eve's steps, he discovers a world that's a whole lot deadlier than he remembered.

Adam is supposed to be dead. He went through a lot of trouble to fake that death, but now that he's back it's clear someone remains unconvinced. That wouldn't be so terrible, except that whoever it is, they have a great deal of influence, and an abiding interest in ensuring that his death sticks this time around.

Adam and Mirella will have to figure out how to travel halfway across the world in secret, with almost no resources or friends. The good news is, Adam solved the travel problem a thousand years earlier. The bad news is, one of his oldest assumptions will turn out to be untrue.

*Immortal From Hell* is the darkest entry in the Immortal series.

∾

### *Immortal: Last Call*

*"I'm something like sixty-thousand years old, and I've probably thought more about my own death than any living being has thought about any subject, ever. I used to be unduly preoccupied with what might constitute a "good death", although interestingly, this has always been an after-the-fact analysis. What I mean is, following a near-death experience, I'll generally perform a quiet review of the circumstances and judge whether that death would have been objectively good, by whatever metric one uses for that kind of thing. I'm not nearly that self-reflective while in the midst of said near-death experience. Facing death, the predominant thought is always* not like this."

A disease threatening the lives of everyone—human and non-human—has been loosed upon the world, by an arch-enemy Adam didn't even know he had.

That's just the first of his problems. Adam's also in jail, facing multiple counts of murder, at least a few of which are accurate. He may never see the inside of a courtroom, because there remains a bounty on his head—put there by the aforementioned arch-enemy—that someone is bound to try to collect while he's stuck behind bars.

Meanwhile, Adam's sitting on some tantalizing evidence that there might be a cure, but to find it, he's going to have to get out of jail, get out of the country, and track down the man responsible. He can't do any of that alone, but he also can't rely on any of his non-human friends for help, not when they're all getting sick.

What he needs is a particularly gifted human, who can do things no other human is capable of. He knows one such person. He calls himself a fixer, and he's Adam's—and possibly the world's—last hope. That's provided he believes any of it.

*Immortal: Last Call* is the sixth book in the *Immortal Novel Series*, and also the end of a long journey for one immortal man.

∼

### *Immortal Stories*

∼

### Eve

*"...if your next question is, what could that possibly make me, if I'm not an angel or a god? The answer is the same as what I said before: many have considered me a god, and probably a few have thought of me as an angel. I'm neither, if those positions are defined by any kind of supernormal magical power. True magic of that kind doesn't exist, but I can do things that may appear magic to someone slightly more tethered to their mortality. I'm a woman, and that's all. What may make me different from the next woman is that it's possible I'm the very first one..."*

For most of humankind, the woman calling herself Eve has been nothing more than a shock of red hair glimpsed out of the corner of the eye, in a crowd, or from a great distance. She's been worshipped, feared, and hunted, but perhaps never understood. Now, she's trying to reconnect with the world, and finding that more challenging than anticipated.

Can the oldest human on Earth rediscover her own humanity? Or will she decide the world isn't worth it?

∾

## *The Immortal Chronicles*

∾

### Immortal at Sea (volume 1)

Adam's adventures on the high seas have taken him from the Mediterranean to the Barbary Coast, and if there's one thing he learned, it's that maybe the sea is trying to tell him to stay on dry land.

∾

### Hard-Boiled Immortal (volume 2)

The year was 1942, there was a war on, and Adam was having a lot of trouble avoiding the attention of some important people. The kind of people with guns, and ways to make a fella disappear. He was caught somewhere between the mob and the government, and the only way out involved a red-haired dame he was pretty sure he couldn't trust.

∾

### Immortal and the Madman (volume 3)

On a nice quiet trip to the English countryside to cope with the likelihood that he has gone a little insane, Adam meets a man who definitely has. The madman's name is John Corrigan, and he is convinced he's going to die soon.

He could be right. Because there's trouble coming, and unless Adam can get his own head together in time, they may die together.

~

### Yuletide Immortal (volume 4)

When he's in a funk, Adam the immortal man mostly just wants a place to drink and the occasional drinking buddy. When that buddy turns out to be Santa Claus, Adam is forced to face one of the biggest challenges of extremely long life: Christmas cheer. Will Santa break him out of his bad mood? Or will he be responsible for depressing the most positive man on the planet?

~

### Regency Immortal (volume 5)

Adam has accidentally stumbled upon an important period in history: Vienna in 1814. Mostly, he'd just like to continue to enjoy the local pubs, but that becomes impossible when he meets Anna, an intriguing woman with an unreasonable number of secrets and sharp objects.

Anna is hunting down a man who isn't exactly a man, and if Adam doesn't help her, all of Europe will suffer. If Adam *does* help, the cost may be his own life. It's not a fantastic set of options. Also, he's probably fallen in love with her, which just complicates everything.

CPSIA information can be obtained
at www.ICGtesting.com
Printed in the USA
LVHW081336261021
701597LV00014B/443